Science Fiction and Narrative Form

Science Fiction and Narrative Form

David Roberts, Andrew Milner and Peter Murphy

BLOOMSBURY ACADEMIC
LONDON • NEW YORK • OXFORD • NEW DELHI • SYDNEY

BLOOMSBURY ACADEMIC
Bloomsbury Publishing Plc
50 Bedford Square, London, WC1B 3DP, UK
1385 Broadway, New York, NY 10018, USA
29 Earlsfort Terrace, Dublin 2, Ireland

BLOOMSBURY, BLOOMSBURY ACADEMIC and the Diana logo are
trademarks of Bloomsbury Publishing Plc

First published in Great Britain 2023
Paperback edition published 2024

Copyright © David Roberts, Andrew Milner and Peter Murphy, 2023

David Roberts, Andrew Milner and Peter Murphy have asserted their rights under the
Copyright, Designs and Patents Act, 1988, to be identified as Authors of this work.

Cover design: Rebecca Heselton
Cover image: Spiral stairs inside Arc de Triomphe in Paris France
© Tatiana Popova/ shutterstock

All rights reserved. No part of this publication may be reproduced or transmitted in
any form or by any means, electronic or mechanical, including photocopying,
recording, or any information storage or retrieval system, without prior
permission in writing from the publishers.

Bloomsbury Publishing Plc does not have any control over, or responsibility for, any
third-party websites referred to or in this book. All internet addresses given in this
book were correct at the time of going to press. The author and publisher regret any
inconvenience caused if addresses have changed or sites have ceased to exist, but can
accept no responsibility for any such changes.

A catalogue record for this book is available from the British Library.

Library of Congress Cataloging-in-Publication Data
Names: Milner, Andrew, author. | Murphy, Peter, 1956– author. |
Roberts, David, 1937– author.
Title: Science fiction and narrative form / Andrew Milner, Peter Murphy and David Roberts.
Description: London ; New York : Bloomsbury Academic, 2023. |
Includes bibliographical references and index.
Identifiers: LCCN 2022041428 | ISBN 9781350350748 (hardback) |
ISBN 9781350350786 (paperback) | ISBN 9781350350755 (pdf) |
ISBN 9781350350762 (epub)
Subjects: LCSH: Science fiction–History and criticism. | LCGFT: Literary criticism.
Classification: LCC PN3433.5 .M56 2023 |
DDC 809.3/8762–dc23/eng/20220829
LC record available at https://lccn.loc.gov/2022041428

ISBN: HB: 978-1-3503-5074-8
PB: 978-1-3503-5078-6
ePDF: 978-1-3503-5075-5
eBook: 978-1-3503-5076-2

Typeset by Newgen KnowledgeWorks Pvt. Ltd., Chennai, India

To find out more about our authors and books visit www.bloomsbury.com
and sign up for our newsletters.

Contents

Notes on Authors   vi

Introduction, *David Roberts*   1

Part 1   From the Epic to Science Fiction, *David Roberts*

1. From epic to novel   13
2. From the novel to science fiction   25
3. A theory of science fiction   41
4. The God in the machine   59

Part 2   Science Fiction and the Historical Novel, *Andrew Milner*

5. Lukács, the historical novel and science fiction   85
6. Climate fiction as the future historical novel   101

Part 3   Epic Science Fiction, *Peter Murphy*

7. The hidden God   123
8. Galaxia   161

Part 4   World Science Fiction, *Andrew Milner*

9. History or apocalypse?   193

Notes   207
References   211
Index   225

Authors

David Roberts is Emeritus Professor in the School of Languages and Literatures at Monash University, Australia. He is the author of *History of the Present: The Contemporary and its Culture*, *Art and Enlightenment: Aesthetic Theory after Adorno* and *The Total Work of Art in European Modernism*, the co-author of *Dialectic of Romanticism: A Critique of Modernism*; the editor of *Reconstructing Theory: Gadamer, Habermas, Luhmann*; and the co-editor of *Comic Relations: Studies in the Comic, Satire and Parody*.

Andrew Milner is Professor Emeritus of English and Comparative Literature at Monash University. He has also held visiting appointments at Warwick University, the University of Liverpool and the Freie Universität Berlin. He is co-author of *Ethical Futures and Global Science Fiction*, *Science Fiction and Climate Change: A Sociological Approach* and *Contemporary Cultural Theory: An Introduction*; the author of *Again, Dangerous Visions: Essays in Cultural Materialism*; *John Milton and the English Revolution*; *Locating Science Fiction*; *Literature, Culture and Society*; and *Class* among other works; and editor of *Postwar British Critical Thought* and *Tenses of Imagination: Raymond Williams on Science Fiction, Utopia and Dystopia*.

Peter Murphy is Adjunct Professor of Humanities and Social Sciences at La Trobe University in Melbourne and Adjunct Professor in The Cairns Institute at James Cook University where he was previously Professor of Arts and Society. He is the author of *The Political Economy of Prosperity*, *Limited Government*, *Auto-Industrialism*, *Universities and Innovation Economies*, *The Collective Imagination* and *Civic Justice: From Greek Antiquity to the Modern World* as well as the co-author of *Dialectic of Romanticism* and the trilogy *Creativity and the Global Knowledge Economy*, *Global Creation* and *Imagination*.

Introduction

David Roberts

The *aim* of the book is to locate science fiction among the great narrative forms. The philosophy of literary forms distinguishes between the epic and the novel. The distinction was first made systematically by G. W. F. Hegel (1770–1831), at a time when the novel had already become the dominant narrative form in modernity, but then elaborated by the Hungarian philosopher and literary critic Georg Lukács (1885–1971), who viewed the novel critically despite its ascendency. The novel conventionally focused on 'problematic' individuals alienated from society and nature. The obverse of this alienation was the novel's perception of society and life as fragmented and disjointed. Lukács hoped for a less alienated, more constructive literature, better able to conceive of society as complete, integrated and well-rounded. He imagined two ways in which this might be possible, through the epic story and through the historical novel, both of which are comparable with the classical epic form, albeit in different ways.

Science Fiction and Narrative Form returns to Lukács's criticism of the conventional psychologistic modern novel. The book argues that science fiction steps beyond the limits of the orthodox novel in three ways. First, science fiction is able to re-conceive the problems of the individual and society in ontological and theological terms, that is, in terms of values and the perennial problems of meaning posed in historically different fashion by the great narrative forms. Second, science fiction is able to represent future historical grand narratives that tie human characters and their existential decisions to social destinies. Third, science fiction is comfortable with the structures and assumptions of epic forms of writing and narration, which allow scope for authors to narrate and depict comprehensive world pictures rather than narratives of alienation and fragmentation.

The premise of the present book is simple: like the epic and the novel, science fiction is a literary form. By that we mean a *historical narrative form*, which is at the same time a *narrative form of history* – history understood, as in French or German, in the double meaning of story and history.[1] The *subject* of the present book is an investigation of the specificities and the possibilities of science fiction as a generic form through comparison with the novel (Part 1), the historical novel (Part 2) and the epic dimension of narrative (Part 3).

Our guide in this investigation will be Lukács, a key figure in the early development of the sociology of literature. He completed his PhD in Philosophy at the Royal Hungarian University of Budapest in 1909 and then enrolled at the University of Berlin during 1909 and 1910, where he attended lectures by Georg Simmel (1858–1918), one of the leading thinkers in German classical sociology. In 1913 Lukács moved to Heidelberg, where he joined the circle around Max Weber (1864–1920), perhaps the single most important figure in the development of German sociology. At the outbreak of the First World War in August 1914, both Simmel and Weber became enthusiastically nationalist supporters of the German war effort, just as Weber's French counterpart, Émile Durkheim (1858–1917), would enthusiastically support the French war effort. By 1914, both Germany and France were already modern nation states, in which nationalism played a central role in the dominant culture. But the young Lukács was Hungarian rather than German, the citizen of a multi-ethnic dynastic monarchy, the territories of which comprised not only present-day Austria and Hungary but also extensive parts of Poland, Romania and northern Italy, as well as the whole of the present-day Czech Republic, Slovakia, Slovenia, Croatia and Bosnia-Herzegovina.

Lukács seems to have been completely unaffected by nationalist sentiments and viewed the war in what he would later describe as a mood of permanent despair. In this very fraught context, still in Heidelberg, he wrote *Die Theorie des Romans*, or *The Theory of the Novel*, begun in 1914 and completed in 1916, when it was first published in the *Zeitschrift fur Aesthetik und Allgemeine Kunstwissenschaft*, and finally published in book form in 1920. Following Hegel, Lukács saw the novel as a distinctly bourgeois epic, a degraded version of its classical predecessor, that degradation occasioned by the shift from 'integrated' to 'problematic' civilizations. Lukács defined this approach as 'historico-philosophical', but we might now understand it more succinctly as simply 'sociological'. *Science Fiction and Narrative Form* is thus inspired by and in a sense a sequel to *The Theory of the Novel*.

The Theory of the Novel establishes the concept of form integral to our approach and sets the parameters for the investigation of the relationship between science fiction and the novel (Part 1), based on Lukács's comparison between the epic and the novel as the key to determining the generic specificities and possibilities of the novel form. For Lukács, the novel is the genre of a godforsaken world, a world suspended between the gods of the past and gods to come. It is the antithesis of the epic as the form of organic communal life, in which meaning is immanent (a god guides the path of the epic hero). From Achilles to Beowulf, from Hector to Siegfried, the hero is one with his (tragic) destiny because he is the representative of his tribe, his people. Lukács can therefore define the epic form as a complete organic expression of the extensive totality of life. The protagonists of the novel by contrast no longer inhabit an epic, heroic world, because the novel is the form of the prose of society as opposed to the poetry of community. Its hero is the 'problematic individual', confronted by a reality in which he is tasked with discovering the meaning of his life experience. The corollary of this emancipation from the closed organic circle of meaning is the entry of time as a reflection of the growing historical consciousness of change and hence of the growing self-consciousness of a genre, for which time is of the essence, a genre situated between the horizons of the past and the future.

Lukács's typology of the novel reflects this intermediary status of the form. Cervantes's *Don Quixote* presents us with an epic hero cast adrift in a disenchanted world, seeking in vain to resuscitate the vanished chivalric genres of the past. The exemplary journey of Goethe's *Wilhelm Meister* from enchanted illusion to disenchanted manhood is filled with references to 'sentimental' reworkings of older forms in Shakespeare's *Hamlet* and Ariosto's Renaissance epics as keys to deciphering the hero's symbolic progress. Flaubert's *Sentimental Education* represents the moment of exhaustion of the novel form, manifested in the melancholic awareness of time passing. Lukács's analysis of Flaubert directly anticipates Marcel Proust's great subjective narrative of the quest for lost time, but equally the great novels of Lukács's other contemporaries, Robert Musil, James Joyce and Thomas Mann. In the latter's *The Magic Mountain* (*Der Zauberberg*) (1924) Lukács actually appears in the character of Naphta, the Jewish Jesuit Eastern European enemy of Western European enlightenment.

Thus when *The Theory of the Novel* appeared in book form in 1920, it was indeed prophetic of the crisis of the novel, which both anticipated and expressed the crisis of the age, precipitated by the First World War. The significance of Lukács's 'historico-philosophical essay on the forms of great epic literature' was immediately recognized. Lukács's conjunction of historical form and form of history provided the catalyst for Walter Benjamin's reading of the German Trauerspiel and for Theodor Adorno's enormously influential philosophy of the crisis of modern music. One creative writer – Elias Canetti – responded in direct fashion to the whole utopian-redemptive thrust of *The Theory of the Novel*. The three parts of his novel *Auto da Fé* replay in grotesque manner Lukács's typology of soul and world in order to depict in the suicide of the hero the terminal crisis of the society of problematic individuals (Chapter 2). Just as for Canetti the time of the novel has run out, so the novels of Proust, Joyce, Musil and Thomas Mann are all novels of the times and of time, in which time is suspended at and as the limit of the form. Beyond the individual lies for Canetti the crowd, for Lukács the proletariat, in the age of the mobilized masses of the World War, marching to the beat of the revolutionary-totalitarian drum (cf. the end of Alfred Döblin's *Berlin Alexanderplatz*, 1929). However, beyond the novel lay not Lukács's dream of a new collective epic form but something quite other: science fiction is not the successor or inheritor of the novel, as the novel was of the epic but rather a companion form, both close and distant from the novel since the beginning of the nineteenth century. It is the other narrative form of the possibilization of the world, driven by technological, scientific and industrial advances, as opposed to the historical sense of social change in the novel (Chapter 4). Since the First World War at the latest, however, it has increasingly come to rival and even displace the dominance of the novel, posing the question of the end of the novel (Chapter 2). Thus a hundred years after Lukács, the Russian writer Vladimir Sorokin argues that classical realistic prose can no longer come to terms with a world that is changing so unpredictably: 'That is why I prefer complicated optics. In order to see what is real, you need two telescopes. … One from the past and another from the future' (Alter 2022). And this is why the complicated optics of science fiction have become more and more relevant to writers dissatisfied with the narrative form of the novel.

The form itself is the key to a theory of science fiction (Chapter 3). Lukács understands the great literary forms as the resolution of a fundamental dissonance of existence. This resolution – the a priori of the forms – is constituted through the relationship between answer and question. The answer always precedes the question in the sense that the form, whether in the epic or novel, is the answer. *The answer given by the successive forms progressively serves, however, to illuminate the question.* This dialectic of answer and question becomes inescapable with the novel, since its presupposition is the split between self and world and its theme the search of the novel hero for meaning. With Lukács we can formulate the difference between the epic and the novel in the following fashion: the *epic form* is the solution to the problem of meaning that holds the question latent. The answer precedes the question. The *novel form* by contrast foregrounds the problem of meaning. Hence the answer given in the novel does not solve the question. Rather, in confirming the question, it makes the question the answer. In the light of this dialectic of question and answer, *science fiction* appears as the productive but also paradoxical fusion of the epic and novel forms: now the form – as in the epic – (pre)determines the problem of meaning, but the question – as in the novel – transcends the answer and makes the answer into the question.

A prioris are historical. Lukács's starting point is the epic form, in which meaning is immanent, such that the question of meaning remains latent. The a priori of the novel form by contrast is the question of meaning. The novel can only resolve this question through the spirit of irony in response to a social reality that no longer offers self-evident meaningful goals to individuals. And science fiction? As opposed to the open question of the novel, its form is closed. This formal closure is the a priori of the science fiction form, dictated by the fact that the history it narrates is *future history*, that is, a form of narrative history predicated on invention and imagination.

Apart from this fundamental difference in their respective relationship to historical time, in what other sense can we say that science fiction lies beyond the novel? Besides its *formal* temporal transcendence of the novel form, science fiction is also defined by a *substantive* difference, which makes it coexistent with the novel and at the same time defines *ex negativo* the limits of the novel. Where the novel deals with individual biographies, the protagonists of science fiction find their function as representatives of larger destinies. Their narrative predestination is expressed in terms of future history but is carried by a dynamic belonging to the present but exterior to the novel: the development of humanity's collective powers over nature through science, technology and industrial production – developments that not only signal a coming transcendence of the historical form of the novel but more fundamentally threaten the survival of the human values, including individual human being, that give meaning to science fiction itself (Chapter 4).

The closure of science fiction is evident in the formal necessity that future histories be narrated in the past tense and by and large preserve despite all cognitive estrangement the conventions of realistic narrative. Closure is science fiction's method of addressing contradictions and moral dilemmas inherent in the present direction of world history. That is, the closure of the form – the answer given by the future history – has the function of laying bare the question through the answer. Thus Stanislaw Lem's *Solaris* (Chapter 4) reminds us in exemplary fashion that futuristic technoscience functions as metaphor for old problems in new guises, problems that now concern the rival claims of theoretical world models and the totalizing world pictures we have inherited. Istvan Csicsery-Ronay makes the useful distinction between two kinds of future history. The first relates the personal histories of a group at a critical point in mega-history (whether on our planet, the planets or galaxies). In the second, humans as a species comprise a single grand collective actor (Csicsery-Ronay 2008: 82). This distinction defines the division of labour between Parts 2 and 3, as long as we bear in mind that it scarcely holds in relation to the actual demands of narration.

In Part 2 – 'Science Fiction and the Historical Novel' – climate fiction (Chapter 6) belongs to micro-mythical rather than macro-mythical future history. The more or less imminent ecological and apocalyptic crisis of planet Earth is refracted through the feelings and fears of individual groups. Here apocalypse denotes the terminus which motivates and enables the form. Part 3 – 'Epic Science Fiction' – by contrast engages with Isaac Asimov's meta-historical mega-history of the human species as the collective actor in a universe that has been progressively colonized as empires rise and fall. The galactic dimensions of space and time offer the stage on which the various possibilities of meta-historical interpretation can be rehearsed, from utopian social experiment to the co-evolution of rival religious and social-historical formations, as they grasp the poisoned chalice of technology's powers of creation and destruction, over which hover unknown forces, hidden hands and anticipations of gods revealed or still hidden.

Lukács provides the point of departure for Part 2. The disappointment of his revolutionary expectation of a new living totality gave way in the 1930s to the resigned return to the aesthetic totality of the historical novel. He turned to the historical novel because it captured in its highest exemplars the immanent meaning of historical progress. It made the past of the historical novel future oriented in its depiction of the clash of old and new social formations and their values, for which Lukács's model was Walter Scott. In Scott, the middling or mediocre hero serves as the mediating instance between the historical actors above and the popular masses below, brought into fruitful contact under the impact of historical crisis. Scott's prototypical historical novel is thus epic in form in that it concerns history as mass experience understood against the backdrop of the French Revolution. But how does Lukács's classic model bear up today? Perry Anderson argues that Benjamin's 'catastrophic vision' of historical progress is more relevant to the contemporary historical novel than Lukács's 'progressive' diagnosis of the contemporary loss of a sense of history (Chapter 5). By contrast, Fredric Jameson proposes a re-reading of Lukács, which, following Darko Suvin, defines science fiction's future histories as essentially utopian. Andrew Milner argues, however, that science fiction cannot be defined by reference to cognate narrative forms such as utopia, dystopia or fantasy. The decisive criteria for science fiction is to be sought in its origins in the Industrial Revolution around 1800 as the practical manifestation of the impact of science and technology and now of techno-science in all its forms. This dynamic unleashed by our powers over nature makes science fiction's future history, Kim Stanley Robinson argues, not of our time yet vitally important for us. Or, to rephrase Robinson, science fiction as form is vitally important to us because it is not of our time and thus can make visible the hidden or denied consequences of our time.

Cli-fi's future histories (Chapter 6), which collectively function to reinforce our awareness of crisis, may be classified according to their proximity to the present. The imminent prospect and reality of climate collapse conveys the urgency of looming apocalyptic dangers. Longer-term future history uses ecological catastrophe, whether the result of nuclear war or climate collapse, to present and make present a post-apocalyptic future, in which existing conflicts and contradictions are replayed by means of cognitively estranged allegories as settings for a variety of scenarios. It can be to show a new emerging utopian order as in Margaret Atwood's *MaddAddam* trilogy or Frank Schätzing's *The Swarm* (*Der Schwarm*), where the planet is rescued from human folly by the self-conscious ocean. Or it can be to show the ecologically dead landscapes of Philip K. Dick's *Do Androids Dream of Electric Sheep?* or Cormac McCarthy's *The Road*. Long-range perspectives are the province of the 'ultimate' exponent of future history, Robinson himself, whose fictions expand from the near future, through *New York 2140*, across the centuries to the thirtieth century. In *New York 2140*, a series of individual lives provides the multifaceted prism through which the problems and critical challenges of the half-submerged city of New York become the catalyst for a new democratic alliance against the selfish blindness of capitalism. In *2312* the re-greening of a devastated Earth entails a future time frame of thousands of years in which to restore the planet's biosphere. The epic scope of Robinson's future history forms the bridge between Parts 2 and 3.

The focus of Part 3 is science fiction and the epic. Peter Murphy understands the micro- and macro-myths of future history as the two poles of science fiction's epic spirit. In this perspective individuals appear as particles swept up in the long waves and deep morphologies of time and space, matter and energy. Such epic histories are long, encyclopaedic and episodic in their narratives of the life and death of planets, the rise and fall of empires and civilizations, in which individual actors find themselves caught up in events that have a life and logic of their own. This relativization of the protagonists, human and post-human, demands a change in readers's perceptions and the recognition that in epic history the real actor is history itself. Murphy underlines the continuity of epic science fiction with Lukács's Hegelian understanding of the objectivity of the epic's extensive totality, which aims to present a world in its entirety. This entirety is now, however, not that of the circumscribed organic community but rather one in which the metabolism of man and nature is played out on the grandest imaginable scale.

In epic future histories of this kind, all the episodes relating to the fortunes of empires, planetary states and federations convey the sense of high-risk ventures and adventures, destinies and quests against the sublime backdrop of galactic vastness. Where the old epic already possessed the answer to the unity of society in its organic form, epic future history must pose the question of how the parts of this meta-society can relate to the whole. Murphy looks for the answer in the idea of homeostasis as the informing principle of Asimov's cyclic cosmos. If Galaxia (Chapter 8) is a Gaian 'self-supporting organism', the life cycle of the civilizations within it follows Toynbee's diagnosis of the loss of dynamic harmony as the cause of disintegration. Asimov's growing loss of confidence in the future of his successive Foundations means that nothing is finally resolved across the 500 years of narration. The structural laws of epic world-building combine Csicsery-Ronay's micro- and macro-histories, in which distance and scale are mediated by small fraternities of actors as bearers of the action and as the objects of the interplay of necessity and destiny. Behind everything lurks the 'hidden god of epic irony' with all the unintended consequences of the cunning of reason. Epic irony in this sense is the hidden god of a fiction of ideas, whose vehicle is meta-historical narrative.

Golan Trevize, a member of the First Foundation's ruling Council, sets off in 22,000 CE in *Foundation's Edge* to search for the abandoned planet Earth in a vain quest for origins. He finds instead the planet Gaia, an experimental model intended as a solution to imperial decline and disintegration. Gaia's collective consciousness contains all its parts – a new version of Leibniz's monadology, we might say, but one which does not account for the quantum leaps of imagination and creativity. Is Galaxia to be the outcome of intentional consciousness that will save the Foundation or will it follow Hegel's 'hidden, ever-operative necessity'? Can a Gaian self-organizing whole be described in terms of consciousness or necessity? Or does epic homeostasis call for a different organizing principle? These questions lead Murphy to review the models of self-organization proposed by the Asimov's characters, such as Seldon's psychohistory or Pel's kinetic theory of gases. He argues that Asimov is setting up a fundamental tension between human goals and the resistance of reality, which can be understood more productively as the conflict between intentional and adaptive behaviours, purposes and patterns. Meaning emerges out of this epic dialectic of purposes and patterns which can be tracked across the circulation and exchange of goods and ideas, migration and colonization that make up the stuff of world history. For Murphy this awareness of the cyclic nature of empires and civilizations is the true hidden god of Asimov's future history. The illusions, failures and self-deceptions of the best-laid political plans permeate the *Foundation* series. They are the incidents and accidents of the meta-social and the meta-historical patterns disengaged from the flux of history by Gibbon, Spengler, Toynbee and Sorokin, as well as their common ancestor Vico.

In Part 4, Andrew Milner, looking back at Lukács's *The Theory of the Novel*, reaffirms the fundamental distinction between science fiction and the novel. If science fiction and the novel are the two genres that best reflect the forces of global modernization, this reflection involves a clear division of labour. Where the novel typically explores the clash of old and new values under the impact of globalization, science fiction typically explores the threats and consequences of the new world that industrialization and technology have brought into being. These are questions that transcend national borders and individual experience, geopolitical constellations and power struggles and make science fiction a world genre in a double sense. First, as indicated, it is a global genre. Second, it addresses global issues: pandemics, climate change, nuclear war and artificial intelligence are Milner's four points of reference in his discussion of representative examples of science fiction's future histories from East and West. The apocalyptic scenarios he examines spring above all from a sense of a common fate and a common home and pose the question, which concerns humanity as a whole as the ultimate addressee of science fiction: Is our future to be the ongoing history of challenge and response, crisis and change or will it be apocalyptic?

To sum up, our indebtedness to Lukács lies above all in his concept of form for, according to Lukács, it is the function of form to be the mirrored meaning of its world. This correspondence of epic form and world resides in the potential of the great epic forms – for Lukács the classic and Christian epic and the epic novel – to give shape to a totality, to give shape, that is, to a world. Thus, the epic is the narrative form of the world of the warrior society, whether tribal or feudal; the novel is the narrative form of the world of modern society as opposed to community; and science fiction is the narrative form of the world itself, planet Earth and its global society, including its reach into far distant space. If science fiction stands as the other – and in some respects the successor – of the novel, it is because its world is not pregiven – as in the Homeric epic – or a world to be given meaning – as in the novel – but a possible future world and as such (of narrative necessity) an epic totality, the given imagined totality of an alternative reality. This explicit claim to totality defines the new epic form of science fiction and is the corollary of its capacity to tackle questions that largely lie beyond the competence of the novel. Science fiction thus stands in a relationship of correspondence and competition with the epic and the novel. It too wants to depict epic struggles for power and resources and to relate the rise and fall of empires. It too wants to wrestle with meaning, but not in the medium of individual learning experiences of love, loss, wisdom and resignation to the prose of life, but in terms of the most basic and all-embracing of questions: What is human being? Above all, science fiction addresses the questions that only a world literature as total form can address, the future and fate of humanity. Our book accordingly proposes a theory of science fiction as the genre that has come to stand beside the novel and, at the latest since the 1960s, has progressively subverted the modernist distinction between high and popular literature, in the light of a reality that is daily becoming more and more science-fictional in its own right. So, our work has the aim of opening up a new perspective on science fiction refracted through Lukács's theory of epic form.

Our Odyssey from Homeric epic poems to the novel and from the novel and historical novel to science fiction also has the aim of opening up the space and distance in which to discern more clearly the continuities and discontinuities of the great narrative forms each of which seeks to resolve a fundamental dissonance of their time. Our investigation aims to situate science fiction within the context of the three great forms of historical imagination: mythical history, the historical present, future history. The epic, the novel and science fiction thus represent the three temporal references by means of which the present seeks to understand itself: the past in the epic, the historical present in the novel and the future in science fiction. It is only in this larger perspective that we can understand the full meaning of these great historical forms of narration, which present – in the passage from the past to the future – the evolution of the unity of question and answer at the heart of the idea of form.

Part 1

From the Epic to Science Fiction

David Roberts

1

From epic to novel

From answer to question

The Theory of the Novel has as its subtitle 'A historico-philosophical essay on the forms of great epic literature'. The subtitle provides us with Lukács's three key terms: 'historico-philosophical essay' and 'great epic literature' are linked together through the concept of *form*, for it is in and through the form that the philosophical significance of the history of great epic literature finds its objectivation. And it is through the concept of form, which remains his most important contribution to aesthetics and to the sociology of literature, that we can grasp the central idea of the young Lukács's thinking on art and society that finds such pregnant formulation in *The Theory of the Novel*. Form is his master concept. It stands for totality, essence and meaning, because totality is always present, even in its absence. And this presence and absence is the index of the world clock, that is, of the historical-philosophical significance of the epic and the novel, respectively.

Lukács's distinction between the epic and the novel is not simply a distinction between two literary genres, the one in verse, the other in prose, the one poetic, the other prosaic. Of equal importance is Schiller's distinction between naïve and sentimental poetry, a distinction, which like the more familiar distinction between nature and culture can only be made retrospectively as the recognition of what has been lost. Loss, however, as Hegel insisted, is the condition of understanding. It is not just that Homer did not know that he was naïve. He could not know his significance in the bigger historical picture. It is we, the latecomers, who lend our historical consciousness to the past, we who give philosophical significance to European history since the Greeks, including the history of the great epic forms.

The precondition for grasping the essence of the epic in its paradigmatic expression in Homer is that it comes from a world that was already irreversibly distant for Greek philosophy. Lukács's philosophical theory of the novel is likewise predicated on the completion of the *essential* history of the novel. It concludes with the consciousness of standing on the threshold of a new age, beyond the epoch of the novel:

> Dostoevsky did not write novels … He belongs to the new world. Only formal analysis of his works can show whether he is already the Homer or the Dante of that world or whether he merely supplies the songs which, together with the songs of other forerunners, later artists will one day weave into a greater unity; whether he is merely a beginning or already a completion. (1971a: 152)

Here Lukács parts company with Hegel and his understanding of the essential truth of the novel as the unsurpassable expression of our arrival in the prose of bourgeois society. Like Hegel's philosophical and Romantic contemporaries, who anticipated a new total work of art to come that would rival ancient Greek tragedy (Roberts 2011: 38–50), Lukács, for all that he recognized the vanity of the attempts to breathe new life into the classical form of tragedy from Schiller to his contemporary Paul Ernst, now envisages under the shock of the First World War the coming redemption from the 'age of absolute sinfulness' in a new epic (Lukács 1971a: 153).

Such a historical-philosophical redemption will not be the work of the new epic form itself, since the possibility of a renewed epic totality rests on a future congruence of inner and outer worlds, of the essential self and a corresponding social world. That is, in Hegelian terms, the new higher identity of subject and substance accomplished in his philosophy. As we know, Lukács found this identical subject-object a decade later, the other side of the watershed of the Great War, in the proletariat. Does this make *The Theory of the Novel* the theoretical anticipation of the coming living form of the socialist revolution that will bring an end to alienation? Or did Lukács blindly transfer his longing for a new epic form (a new redemptive aesthetic totality) to the imaginary object of his own redemption from the age of absolute sinfulness? Looking back in 1962 on this work of his youth, which had been intended as an introduction to a book on Dostoevsky, Lukács condemns it as a 'purely utopian' exercise in abstract synthesis.

What Lukács dismisses as the method of abstract synthesis is of course Hegelian in spirit, as he acknowledges. But Hegelian in an unexpected fashion; although he accepts 'the notion that development from the historical-philosophical viewpoint leads to a kind of abolition of those aesthetic principles which had determined development up to that point', he does not accept the result. 'In Hegel himself, however, only art is rendered problematic as a result of this, the "world prose", as he aesthetically defines this condition, is one in which the spirit has attained itself both in thought and in social and state praxis.' This is precisely what Lukács rejects in *The Theory of the Novel*. Lukács reverses Hegel's argument that art becomes problematic once reality itself becomes unproblematic. On the contrary, art has become problematic because the world itself is out of joint. 'This is why the "prose" of life is here only a symptom ... of the fact that reality no longer constitutes a favourable soil for art.' Lukács insists against Hegel on the necessary 'mirror-image' congruence between society and its art. Such congruence is both the most general and the most concise definition of Lukács's socio-aesthetic concept of form. It is why 'the central problem of the novel is the fact that art has to write off the closed and total forms, which stem from a rounded totality of being – that art has nothing more to do with any world of forms that is immanently complete in itself. And this is not for artistic but for historico-philosophical reasons' (17). Moreover, *The Theory of the Novel* is not just a historical document but itself a philosophical-historical document, whose significance has not been exhausted, either in relation to the history of the novel (see Chapter 2) or in terms of the concept of form as the key to a theory of science fiction (see Chapter 3), even though such a theory offers a very different continuation to Lukács's vision of a new epic superseding the novel. But before we can explore the passage from the novel to science fiction as the new form of epic totality, it is necessary to reconstruct Lukács's reading of the passage from the epic to the novel.

The rounded totality of being that comes to unproblematic expression in the epic is evoked by Lukács neither nostalgically nor for its own sake. The epic functions throughout as the foil against which the problematic nature of the novel, as testimony to the inescapable condition of modern bourgeois, capitalist society becomes fully evident. Nevertheless, the overarching concept of form provides the key to comparison because it is *always the answer to a question*. More exactly: form is defined by the interplay of question and answer. Thus in the epic:

> Being and destiny, adventure and accomplishment, life and essence are then identical concepts. For the question which engenders the formal answers of the epic is: how can life become essence? And if no one has ever equalled Homer, nor even approached him ... it is because he found the answer before the progress of the human mind through history had allowed the question to be asked. (30)

Where *meaning* can be grasped and taken in at a glance, the world is homogeneous; the congruence between self and world exists prior to the consciousness of question and answer. This priority of the totality of life is the a priori of the epic form that contains all questions and answers: 'the Greeks travelled in history itself through all the stages that correspond *a priori* to the great forms' to unfold in their cultural development a philosophy of history. These stages correspond to the paradigmatic forms of world literature: epic, tragedy, philosophy:

> The world of the epic answers the question: how can life become essential? But the answer ripened into a question only when the substance had retreated to a far horizon. Only when tragedy had supplied the creative answer to the question: how can essence come alive? did men become aware that life as it was … had lost the immanence of the essence. (35)

And it was left to philosophy to bring to light the problematic basis of tragedy.

For the moderns, Hegel's philosophy stands as the conclusion of the path from answer to question, the path from art to enlightenment, from the 'naïve' epic world of *Beowulf* or *Chanson de Roland* to the 'sentimental' epic of Dante, in which aesthetics and metaphysics are still one; beyond this last medieval synthesis lies the path from the medieval chivalric romances to the transformation of their world of adventures into the founding form of the novel in Cervantes, the contemporary of Shakespeare's historical tragedies. If Hegel's philosophy of art represents a conclusion to the cultural quarrel of the Ancients and the Moderns, German Romanticism was at the same time its new critical continuation (Roberts 1991: 223). Lukács's romantic anti-capitalism and sympathies for the nineteenth century's 'romanticism of disillusionment' is underpinned by his identification with the Romantics' longing for a new organic totality, a new total work of art that will overcome the soulless condition of modern culture.

Lukács is under no illusion, however, that salvation lies in a resurrection of the Greek spirit. We can no longer live within their closed circle of meaning: 'we cannot breathe in a closed world. We have invented the productivity of the spirit' (Lukács 1971a: 33). Such a resurrection could be no more than a vain and artificial attempt to reunify aesthetics and metaphysics, a vain refusal to recognize that art is now but one social sphere among many and that its existence is predicated on the consciousness of its own fragmentary truth. Indeed, this recognition is modern art's a priori. It must create its own forms out of its own inadequacy. And here it is the task of the novel to show the impossibility of the goal and the nullity of its means: that is, to carry 'the fragmentary nature of the world's structure into the world of forms' (39). Where the pregiven totality of the world gave the rounded totality of the epic, the novel can aspire only to a 'created totality' as the measure of a world no longer made to our measure.

Let me stress again that form for Lukács always involves question and answer. The answer precedes the question in the epic. To say that the question precedes the answer in the novel is simply another way of saying that the form of the novel is not given and can only be posited. That the novel form, as opposed to the pregiven form of the epic, is *posited* goes to the heart of Lukács's philosophy of the history of forms. The fall of the epic and the rise of the novel signal a historical-philosophical caesura, quite distinct from the succession of the great literary genres, epic, tragedy and philosophy in Greece. There the sundial of the mind ensured the necessary coincidence of history and philosophy of history, just as this coincidence affirmed the a priori origin or home of each of these genres. And so to say that the novel form is posited is to say that 'the ultimate basis of artistic creation has become homeless' (41). The a priori of the form has lost its home, forcing the form-giving subject to find his origin and home in subjectivity. The novel is the historical-philosophical form of this transcendental homelessness, which dictates the dialectic of self and world, subject and object. Meaning in modern art can be 'deciphered and decided from the totalities of various periods but not discovered in those totalities themselves' (41).

Modern tragedy escapes the historical fate of the epic because it gives form to 'the intensive totality of essence', concentrated in the solitary tragic hero. It is able to preserve its closed totality by virtue of the power of its form, that is, by virtue of the essence that is born of form, independent of the given content of what actually exists. The epic's 'extensive totality of life' by contrast cannot transcend its ultimate principle, the world as it is: 'it can never, while remaining epic, transcend the breadth and depth, the rounded, sensuous, richly ordered nature of life as historically given' (46). The epic contains within its form the immanence and transcendence of meaning, tragedy demands transcendent meaning in order to separate and raise itself above life. Where the empirical subject and empirical world of the epic are one, the tragic hero embodies the intelligible subject, which takes upon itself loneliness and death as the transcendent affirmation of its essential relationship to destiny. That is why tragedy has been able to maintain its essential nature across the great historical-philosophical divide, which determined the demise of the epic. This historical fate is written into the birth of the novel from the spirit of the epic in *Don Quixote*, the starting point for Lukács's typology of the dialectic of self and world in the novel.

Tragedy's essence lies in the tragic hero's relationship to destiny. The novel's (negative) essence lies in the conscious and autonomous personality of the author. 'What is given form here is not the totality of life but the artist's relationship with that totality' (52). This dialectic of subjectivity and objectivity in the novel, between the 'positing subject' and his subject matter, the object singled out, can attain the grandeur of the epic's extensive totality of life only in the rarest of cases, where the author is capable of stepping back from self-conscious sovereignty to become a 'purely receptive organ of the world' – as in the cosmic humour of Cervantes or in the reconciliation of self and world in Goethe's *Wilhelm Meister.*

Lukács sums up his argument through a further comparison between the epic and the novel. Again it needs to be stressed that the epic functions not just as the original 'natural' form of the narrative of heroes and great deeds but as the means to distinguish the essential constitutive and historical-philosophical specificity of the new form of the novel, which emerges once the given, unquestioned a priori of the epic has disappeared: 'When the structures made by man are really adequate to man, they are his necessary and native home; and he does not know the nostalgia that posits and experiences nature as the object of its own seeking and finding.' Lukács may employ the Schillerian distinction between 'unconscious' and conscious creation, between the art that is nature and the art that seeks nature, the crucial distinction for him, however, is that between the 'given totality and totality as an aim' (7). Totality denotes the historical social formations and their respective systems of values and meaning, which gives rise to different literary forms. The given totality of the epic reflects man's 'necessary and native home', where, in Lukács's terminology, first and second nature, the natural and the social world, are still one.

For all Lukács's deployment of the familiar antithesis between the naïve and the sentimental, his 'romantic anti-capitalism', as he later described his stance at the time of writing *The Theory of the Novel*, in no way involved or condoned the romantic turn to nature as protest against modernity's urban 'society of strangers'. His understanding of the novel as the *negative mirror-image* of the epic rests on the continuing but now negative identity of first and second nature. Once the original communal tie between nature and the social world has been broken, first nature stands as much in opposition to the human being as the second nature of society. Nature and society are the two faces of the alienation brought about by the structures made by man: 'The first nature, nature as a set of laws for pure cognition, nature as the bringer of comfort to pure feeling, is nothing other than the historico-philosophical objectivation of man's alienation from his own constructs' (64). Second nature is the social world of convention, 'a world which is present everywhere in a multiplicity of forms too complex for understanding' (62). Neither nature nor society offers a home to the soul confronted by alien, incomprehensible powers. The 'laws' which govern nature and society hold us in thrall, whether it be to the sublime logic of science's immutable laws of nature beyond the reach of man or to the laws of social being and becoming (Max Weber's 'iron cage'). These laws stand as the embodiment of 'recognized but senseless necessities', whose real substance remains unknowable and incomprehensible and defy the individual's search for meaningful social goals.

This 'transcendental homelessness' is the origin and home of the novel. And yet the epic and the novel are both great epic forms because they relate to the overarching concept of form through the concept of totality. We thus arrive at Lukács's definition of the novel as the epic of an age, 'in which the extensive totality of life is no longer directly given, in which the immanence of meaning in life has become a problem, yet which still thinks in terms of totality' (56). To think in terms of totality applies as much to the age, however, as to its representative form. Indeed, the novel must figure the truth of the age if it is to be true to its form. This truth, this form accordingly, cannot be other than paradoxical since it circles ceaselessly around its absent centre, the absent totality. 'The epic gives form to a totality of life that is rounded from within; the novel seeks, by giving form, to uncover and construct the concealed totality of life' (60). The sovereign form-positing subject and form-giving intention of the novel are the index of the gulf that has opened up between self and world, which the form can no longer bridge but only register. The paradox of the novel's form is this: if, for Lukács, every form is 'the resolution of a fundamental dissonance of existence' (62), then 'the immanence of meaning required by the form is attained [in the novel] precisely when the author goes all the way, ruthlessly, towards exposing its absence' (72). Whether Lukács speaks of totality, immanence of meaning or form, they all serve as the mirror, in and through which the difference between the epic and the novel comes to consciousness, that is, to self-consciousness in the novel. The affirmation of dissonance is for the novel the *form itself*, the form that sees through its own abstraction. The only escape from the self-reflection of a self-positing form is, as Lukács insists, to affirm the 'normative incompleteness', the problematic nature of the novel as the source of its legitimacy. If this makes the novel the authentic child of its age, it is because it expresses 'the true condition of a contemporary spirit'. This is why the popular novel of entertainment, which combines in its 'semblance of truth' all the novel's outward features with all its inessential formal characteristics, can be no more than its shadow and caricature.

The vicious circle of self-positing subjectivity can only be overcome from within through irony, by which Lukács means irony as understood by the first theorists of the novel, the early German Romantics: the self-cancelling of subjectivity implicit in its self-recognition and self-reflexion. It applies *aesthetically* to the form and *ethically* to the content of the novel: aesthetically, irony points beyond the necessary limitations of both subject and object, self and world to the absent/present possibility of their reconciliation; *ethically*, irony serves as 'the self-correction of the world's fragility' (75). The second-order form of the novel thus corresponds to the second nature of society. The novelist is called upon to construct a relationship to the concealed totality of life, which is not given but posited, conceptual not organic and hence condemned to the endless round of ironic self-recognition and self-abolition.

If the novel can thereby attain to a kind of reconciliation between self and world, it can never attain closure and completion, just as the protagonist's search for meaning cannot transform its object, the world itself. In seeking to find an inner balance between quest and goal, becoming and being, the novelist is obliged to turn to the outer form of biography to contain the 'discrete, unlimited nature of the material of the novel' within the organic limits of a life. The hero's outer experiences are given meaning by their relevance to the inner process towards finding the meaning of life in a growing self-recognition, which in turn gives unifying shape and focus to the flux of persons and events surrounding the hero, whether in relation to the whole of life or more usually to one essential stage of development. This raises the individual qua individual as the medium of the form to a status that is both uniquely significant *and* merely instrumental: 'his central position in the work means only that he is particularly well-suited to reveal a certain problematic of life' (83). In other words, the novel's form represents the answer to the reciprocity of contingent world and problematic individual.

Past Gods and Gods to come

We have now reached the point at which the structure and meaning of Lukács's constructive categories and hence of Lukács's *own* a priori can be grasped. Form conceived as totality is *theological*: whether we take totality as a metaphor for God or God as a metaphor for totality is *formally* indifferent because form alone is the historical-philosophical index of Lukács's theoretical structure and its anticipated completion. Paradise lost and paradise regained stand as both metaphor and truth of Lukács's own search for meaning.

The 'paradise forever lost, sought and never found' is 'the deepest melancholy of every great and genuine novel', says Lukács:

> And the hard-won compromise, the unstable balance of mutually cancelling reflexions – the second naivety, which is the novelist's objectivity – is only a formal substitute for the first: it makes form-giving possible and it rounds off the form, but the very manner in which it does so points eloquently at the sacrifice that has had to be made, at the paradise forever lost, sought and never found. This vain search and then resignation with which it is abandoned make the circle that completes the form. (85)

The normative incompletion of the novel expresses the resigned insight of maturity, which has lost the absolute self-confidence of youth but cannot find the way or the goal in the outside world. 'The heroes of youth are guided by the gods.' Hence the deep certainty of the epic hero for a god always plots his path and walks ahead of him (86), whereas the novel is 'the epic of a world that has been abandoned by God.' This is the most concise, the most pregnant definition of a world that is recalcitrant to meaning and yet is nothing in itself, cut off from meaning. This theological recognition serves to define the *essential*, more exactly, the *in/essential* nature of the novel in that it defines

> the productive limits of the possibility of the novel – limits which are drawn from within – and, at the same time, ... the historico-philosophical moment at which great novels become possible, at which they grow into a symbol of the essential thing that needs to be said. (88)

When I say that Lukács's *The Theory of the Novel* is theological, I mean of course a second-order theology, in which totality and God are indifferent metaphors for the presence or absence of meaning, which is either *total or nothing*. The rounded form of the Homeric epic is the benchmark; it alone encompasses immanent and transcendent meaning, against which the Christian epic – but also tragedy ancient and modern – and the novel are measured. Tragedy knows neither gods nor demons 'for the outside world is only the occasion for the soul to find itself, for the hero to become a hero, in itself and for itself'. It is the form, in which 'the soul transforms every happening into destiny' (87). Thus it is only when drama becomes non-tragic that gods and demons appear on stage. Like Nietzsche, Lukács has in mind Euripides' introduction of the plot device of the god in the machine, the *deus ex machina*, who intervenes at the last moment to resolve all conflicts and bring the drama to an end.

The Christian epic also knows only transcendent meaning. The dual structure of Dante's universe cancels the hierarchical break between the fallen world and redemption by offering 'the coincidence of life and meaning in a present, actually experienced transcendence' (68). The architecture of Dante's poem reorders the organic totality of the epic into a hierarchical system, in which all the figures are already individuals but where the hero's journey to transcendent truth serves to represent 'the symbolic unity of human destiny in general', beyond the destiny of the communal group in the epic. In Lukács's system of genres, Dante's Christian epic combines and synthesizes the presuppositions of the epic and the novel.

Lukács's theology is not purely formal, however, not simply Lukács's own 'god in the machine', his master key to all the narrative plot devices that inform 'the forms of great epic literature'. For forms cannot be understood apart from their relationship to the civilization of the time. On this depends the philosophy of the history of forms. Not only does the world clock tell us whether a civilization is integral or problematic, it also allows us to divine, as indicated, both the productive possibilities and limits of the novel. And this is precisely the intention of part II of *The Theory of the Novel*. Lukács's typology of the novel sets out to *formally* define and *historically* delimit the productive possibilities of the genre. And in that sense *exhaust* its historical possibilities as they unfolded between Cervantes and Flaubert, whose novels, it should be added, still represent the terminus for Lukács twenty years later in *The Historical Novel* (1936).

What remains implicit until the very end of *The Theory of the Novel* is the theological interest and intention of the concluding historical-philosophical question: what lies beyond the novel, beyond our godforsaken age? Lukács's philosophy of history is ultimately theological beyond all its theological metaphors. Redemption is an absolute category, whether in its Christian other-worldly or its Romantic this-worldly longing. Both employ the same schema of paradise lost/paradise regained, community lost/community regained, destiny lost/destiny regained, in which the epic functions, as did Greek tragedy for the German Romantics, for Wagner and Nietzsche, as the once and future total work of art, as the redemptive artwork of the future. The First World War is the precipitating moment, which fused Lukács's romantic anti-capitalism and revolutionary romanticism into the leap of faith, leaving *The Theory of the Novel* an essay in/complete in itself rather than the introduction to the intended study of Dostoevsky. Had Lukács read Dostoevsky more carefully, he might have pondered more deeply the latter's assertion that tragedy 'knows no real difference between god and demon':

> But there is an essential aspiration of the soul which is concerned only with the essential, no matter where it comes from or where it leads; there is a nostalgia of the soul when the longing for home is so violent that the soul must, with blind impetuousness, take the first path that seems to lead there; and so powerful is

this yearning that it can always pursue its road to the end. For such a soul, every road leads to the essence – leads home – for to this soul its selfhood *is* its home. That is why tragedy knows no real difference between god and demon. (87)

Lukács's *The Theory of the Novel* is the product of this nostalgia of the soul and of its longing for home, driven by the spirit of tragedy to make of every happening a destiny. And just as tragedy stands outside *time* so conversely the novel draws its essence from time. It is time, Bergson's *durée*, that makes the novel the historical-philosophical genre that lives from its present/absent *telos*: the longing of the novel form *itself* to leave behind the world of alienated subjectivity, to become epic once again. That is why irony is the only objectivity that the novel form can know: the negative mysticism of times without god allows no more than the glimpse of 'the ultimate, true substance, the present, non-existent god' (90). The freedom of the novel form lies, like the freedom of irony, in the soul's glimpse of essence within the philosophical-historical confines of the times. The 'most specific essence of freedom – the constructive relation to redemption – remains inexpressible; everything that can be expressed and given form bears witness to this double servitude' (91). Part I ends with Lukács's declaration of suspended faith in the answering 'double vision' of irony:

> For the novel, irony consists in this freedom of the writer in his relationship to God, the transcendental condition of the objectivity of form-giving. Irony, with intuitive double vision, can see where God is to be found in a world abandoned by God; irony sees the lost, utopian home of the idea that has become its ideal, and yet at the same time it understands the ideal is subjectively and psychologically conditioned, because that is its only possible form of existence; … Therefore, when it [irony] speaks of the adventures of errant souls in an inessential, empty reality, it intuitively speaks of past gods and gods to come. (92)

Past gods and gods to come: this is Lukács's formula for the historical-philosophical truth but also the historical limits of the novel.

Part II of *The Theory of the Novel* maps out the three possibilities, defined by the incommensurability of soul and world, open to the novel in the historical space between Cervantes and Flaubert: the soul is either narrower, as in *Don Quixote*, or wider than the external world, as in *Sentimental Education*. 'Wilhelm Meister stands aesthetically and historico-philosophically between these two types of novel. Its theme is the reconciliation of the problematic individual, guided by his lived experience of the idea, with concrete social reality' (132). These three types exhaust the possibilities of the novel both from within and from without. On the one side *Don Quixote* spells out the verdict of history on the epic form of the medieval chivalric romances, whose degeneration into mere entertainment was the condition of the emergence of the novel. On the other side *Sentimental Education* epitomizes the finitude of the novel in a double sense: 'Only in the novel, whose very matter is seeking and failing to find the essence is time posited together with the form.' The alienation of self and world signifies in Flaubert the separation of meaning from life, of the essential from the temporal: 'We might almost say that the entire inner action of the novel is nothing but a struggle against the power of time' (122). And yet this struggle is not in vain. From it comes 'the sublime epic poetry of the novel': the victories of time given by memory and hope. If memory and hope give life experience its essential quality, they represent at the same time the novel's interiorization of the memory of lost gods and the hope of gods to come. Lukács's longing for 'a new form of artistic creation, the form of the renewed epic' (124) lies, like its object Dostoevsky, outside and beyond *The Theory of the Novel*.

2

From the novel to science fiction

Back to the metaphysical future

When *The Theory of the Novel* appeared in book form in 1920, Lukács had already left the world of the problematic individual behind for the new epic of collectivism by joining the Communist Party. This will to the transcendence of individualism finds a direct echo in Elias Canetti's novel *Auto-da-Fé*, where the post-war sense of an ending becomes one with the end of the novel as the genre of the modern age and modern subjectivity. Canetti's vision of the return of the isolated individual to the crowd poses the question of the human and the post-human, of sexuality and eros that found a direct continuation over sixty years later in Michel Houellebecq's *Atomised*. *Atomised* ends with a meditation on the modern age, the time of the subject and of the novel, which recapitulates the crisis of civilization from Aldous Huxley's *Brave New World* and Canetti's *Auto-da-Fé* at the beginning of the 1930s through to the 1990s from the safe haven of a post-human, post-historical *future present* that belongs to the brave new world of science fiction.

Canetti's world of 'Blendung' (blindness) is the monadic universe of the modern city in which love, contact and communication have fallen victim to the radical isolation of the individual. *Auto-da Fé* (*Die Blendung*) is divided into three parts. Part one, 'Head without World', describes the world of Peter Kien, at forty the greatest Chinese scholar of the age, possessor of the most important private library in the city (Vienna). Ensconced behind the windowless walls of his thickly carpeted library Kien has succeeded in isolating himself from all contact with the world. Kien, however, is overcome by the sudden impulse to marry his housekeeper Therese when he discovers her reading a book with her gloves on. But the entry of a woman into his library is the beginning of the end for Kien – it is the invasion of the body, of life, of *greed*. Therese, whose one thought is her husband's supposed fortune, soon tires of him and throws him on the street and into the mindless world of part two. 'Headless World' is the criminal underworld of the city; the cripples, hunchbacks, prostitutes, beggars and outcasts, the dirt of the teeming city. It is the grotesque counterpart to the spotless order of Kien's library-paradise but also its mirror, for each of the figures, like Kien and Therese, lives in his private world of compulsive fantasy. Kien's new companion is the ape-like hunchbacked dwarf, the Jew Fischerle, a fanatical chess player whose devotion to his 'specialization' parallels that of the scholar Kien to his books. Peter Kien finally falls into the hands of the ex-policeman and house-porter Benedikt Pfaff, who has become Therese's accomplice. And this brings us to the third part 'World in the Head' – Kien is locked up in the porter's lodge while Pfaff and Therese occupy Kien's library on the top floor – and it is here in the porter's cell-cage that the psychiatrist George Kien discovers his brother Peter crouching on the floor amid scraps of food in the dark. The presence of George soon restores Peter to his 'old self', Therese and Pfaff are banished, the library restored to its former state and its master reinstated. George can hurry back to his 800 patients in Paris, eagerly awaiting their beloved master. Once more alone, restored to the order and security of his books, Peter sets fire to his library and dies laughing in the flames.

Peter Kien's suicide is the judgement on the head which tries to deny the world, on the dream of total isolation and autonomy of the individual. His fate becomes symbolic of the dangers threatening the individual in modern society cut off from his fellow men by suspicion and fear. In fact, Kien in his library, the head without world, is only the most extreme example of the blindness of the individual and of a society in which communication and love are no longer possible. Canetti defines the total and untenable negativity of this world in terms of the individual's longing for salvation as reflected in the 'private myth' of each figure – a longing which can only be understood in the light of George's theory of the crowd, presented by him with all the fervour and enthusiasm of a millennial vision:

> 'Mankind' has existed as a mass for long before it was conceived of and watered down into an idea ... We know nothing of it; we live still, supposedly as individuals. Sometimes the masses pour over us, one single flood, one ocean, in which each drop is alive, and each drop wants the same thing. But it soon scatters again, and leaves us once more to be ourselves, poor solitary devils. (Canetti 1963: 461)

For George the urge within the individual to become 'a higher animal species, the crowd' is the motive force of history (461). The discovery overwhelms him with all the force of a redemptive revelation. The world of civilization, the world of hopelessly isolated individuals, fearful and egoistic, will be submerged, consumed by the irresistibly spreading conflagration, by the deluge – 'a single raging ocean' – that will bring history to an end, cancel individuation and the division of sexes in the return to unity in the crowd. The end is the return to the beginning, for the crowd is the source and goal of human history, the oldest animal and the future of the earth. It is, as it were, the ultimate force of *gravity*, the one universal field of force of the *world*, which the *head* denies in vain. The private myths that haunt individuals (the world in the head) are the unconscious expression of the attraction of the crowd. The novel ends with the breakthrough of suicidal irrationality in the sphere of the purely rational – the library, as the head of a civilization that can only be reunited with the world in self-destruction.

The importance of Aldous Huxley for Michel Houellebecq has long been recognized. *Atomised* (Houellebecq 2001) and *The Possibility of an Island* (Houellebecq 2006) both engage with Huxley's utopian fictions. What has not been recognized is the informing presence in *Atomised* of Canetti's *Auto da Fé*. It provides Houellebecq with the model and template for his critique of and utopian alternative to Huxley's *Brave New World* (Huxley 1932). Houellebecq works not only with the civilizational critique of Canetti's novel but also with Canetti's structuring contrast between two antithetical brothers, Peter and George Kien. Canetti's novel is exactly contemporary with Huxley's *Brave New World*. Written in 1931/2, *Auto da Fé* was published in Vienna in 1935. *Brave New World* was written in 1931 and published in 1932. It is worth mentioning that Ernst Jünger's utopia of a military state, *Der Arbeiter* (Jünger 1932) was also published in 1932. Three very striking anticipations of a post-human world arising from the ruins of European civilization.

Atomised (*Les particules elementaires*, Houellebecq 1998a) established Houellebecq's reputation as a provocative and disturbing writer. Together with *Submission* (Houellebecq 2015) it remains his best-known and most challenging work, a savage satire of our contemporary sex-and-shopping society. At the same time it is also a speculative science fiction that sets the social satire, unfolded through the life story of the brothers Michel and Bruno, in the historical retrospective of the suicide of Western civilization and the end of humanity. Houellebecq's narrative stance is that of the backward-looking prophet, who presents a future past imbued with the stamp of historical necessity. *Atomised* thus works on two levels: the narrative frame constituted by the Prologue and the Epilogue, which give the interpretative key to the story of two brothers. Their story in turn illustrates the dead end of the West's atomized society of individuals, which provides the premise and precondition of the 'brave new world' destined to replace humanity as we know it. As befits a speculative fiction, *Atomised* works with the categories of utopia and dystopia. If the lives of the brothers mirror in concentrated fashion Houellebecq's vision of the negativities of contemporary society, the utopian other of this dystopia lies beyond humanity and history.

The link between the two levels of the novel is given by the figure of Michel who realizes in wholly self-conscious fashion the necessity of leaving the world of individuals and individuality behind. Like the Buddha, Michel pierces the veil of illusion at the heart of ego-centred individualism and transcends the realm of desire and death. Michel's liberation from the self-deceiving blindness of the will to life and power springs from compassion, but it is informed by science, more exactly by the 'new paradigm' that will displace the materialism of modern science, and lead to a new era in world history (Houellebecq 2001: 5). This new era signifies a metaphysical revolution, that is, a radical, global transformation in the values to which the majority subscribe, comparable to the replacement of the pagan gods of antiquity by Christianity and the displacement of Christianity by the rise of modern science. 'When Christianity appeared, the Roman Empire was at the height of its powers: supremely organised, it dominated the known world. Its technical and military prowess had no rival; nonetheless, it had no chance. When modern science appeared, medieval Christianity was a complete, comprehensive system which explained man and the universe' (9). And yet this did not prevent its downfall. The parallels to Auguste Comte's 'Law of the Three States' of intellectual development from the theological to the metaphysical to the positive or scientific is clearly intended but with a twist that reflects Comte's late thinking on social cohesion. Houellebecq's third metaphysical revolution, of which Michel is the precursor, is presented both as the negative completion and as the utopian supersession of the era of modern Western science. On the one hand, the narrator states that metaphysical mutations tend to move inexorably to their logical conclusion. What could be more conclusive than the suicide of the individual and the self-extinction of humanity, of which we read in the epilogue? On the other hand, the logic of scientific materialism, which ends in suicidal self-cancellation, opens the way to the new era in world history that is in fact beyond history, change and time – a pure post-human utopia, which, it is suggested, reunites beginning and end, the theological and the scientific, and completes the circle of history.

The references to the Buddha certainly suggest that the enlightenment that Michel seeks is as much religious as scientific. If Buddhist enlightenment breaks the blind power of *karma*, the endless cycle of desire and suffering, Michel's 'true significance', which rests scientifically on his elimination of the genetic mutations inherent in sexual reproduction, amounts theologically to the undoing of *original sin*, through which death, suffering and evil entered the world. Houellebecq argues that it is precisely the logic of scientific materialism that has laid bare death as the sole surviving deity in a cold and meaningless world by destroying the promise of Christian grace and redemption. It is this 'universe of death' (356) that drives Michel open-eyed to suicide and Bruno blindly to madness. The brothers' abdication of the ego and of individualism announces the 'last years of Western civilisation' and prefigures the self-extinction of humanity.

The half-brothers, who have a mother in common, are constructed as polar opposites in the image of their respective fathers. Michel's father, Marc Djerzinski, is a Polish Jewish outsider and loner, who 'spoke to no one, befriended no one' and disappears mysteriously in Tibet while on a film assignment. Bruno's father is a plastic surgeon, whose profession is to cheat and deny the aging process and whose sole interests are money and girls. Conceived as opposites, we can think of the brothers as the separated halves of a complete human being or conversely as the two extremes of the failure to achieve individuation: Michel is the *head without body*, Bruno the *body without head*. Michel's utopia is reproduction without sex, Bruno's utopia is sex without reproduction. Each has been abandoned by their common mother and brought up by grandmothers. This failure of parenting and with it the possibility of love of self and others – the 'lost kingdom' of part one of the novel – is for Houellebecq a symptom of the fatal cult of the self that has created a society in which selfless love has become impossible. The generation of grandparents is the last link to such altruism: 'Historically, such human beings have existed. Human beings who have worked – worked hard – all their lives with no other motive than their love and devotion; [...] In general, such human beings are invariably women' (106).

The lives of Michel and Bruno are defined by their opposed attempts to escape from the unbearable burden of selfhood. Bruno's lifelong quest for sexual gratification seems finally to be satisfied through his meeting with Christiane. And yet, despite 'the nights when they were one, each remained trapped in individual consciousness and separate flesh' (240). Even the ultimate expression of the drive to be liberated from the self and self-consciousness in Dionysian orgy is shipwrecked on the ultimate logic of individual existence: death. As a child Bruno could not comprehend death. As an adult, in the grip of a midlife crisis, 'death was still a long way off': 'Bruno had never seriously thought about death and he was beginning to wonder if he ever would. He wanted to live to the end, ... With his last breath, he would still plead for a postponement' (142).

Bruno, it is clear, remains imprisoned in the endless cycle of desire, whose vain goal is self-oblivion. His one passing moment of enlightenment (one of the 'strange moments 'of part two) occurs with appropriate irony when, in his perpetual pursuit of sexual satisfaction, he visits the 'Lieu de Changement', a holiday camp, which is a product of 1968, dedicated to creating an 'authentic utopia'. There he suddenly recalls a moment of escape at school between the History and Physics lessons. In this brief interregnum outside of time and space, he had experienced peace and joy. Now, in the holiday camp, he realizes that for the moment he had 'stopped wishing, he had stopped wanting, he was nowhere; slowly, by degrees his spirit soared to a state of nothingness, the sheer joy that comes of not being part of the world. For the first time since he was 13, Bruno was happy' (154). This 'authentic utopia', this 'strange moment' of Nirvana remains nothing but an interlude, however, alien to his 'separate flesh', consumed by sexual desire.

The year is 1998 (the year in which *Atomised* was published), Bruno is forty-two (the same age as his author), Michel is forty. This year is the turning point for both brothers and the vantage point from which the interweaving of past and present is narrated. Bruno meets and loses Christiane, who commits suicide after her diagnosis of incurable cancer. Michel meets his childhood love Annabelle again and loses her also to cancer and suicide. At forty, Michel can see no reason for going on with life. He takes a leave of absence from his research position in molecular biology. 'For years, Michel had lived a purely intellectual existence' (138). He has withdrawn from the human world that has given him nothing but a 'series of disappointments, bitterness, and pain' to find 'a happiness both serene and intense' in the study of mathematics (77). The corollary of his retreat from the world is his hatred of nature. Already as a child, the television series 'The Animal Kingdom' had left him with 'the unshakeable conviction ... that, taken as a whole, nature was not only savage, it was a repulsive cesspit' (38). His inability to respond to Annabelle's love brings him to realize that he is cut off from life and emotions: 'Others would experience happiness and despair, but such things would be unknown to him, they would not touch him.' 'He felt separated from the world by a vacuum moulded to his body like a shell, a protective armour' (99–100). At fourteen Bruno also comes to know a comparable sense of alienation, the 'unearthly' feeling that he recognizes when he reads *The Trial*: 'Kafka's slow-motion world ... riddled with shame, where people passed each other in an unearthly void in which no human contact seemed possible, precisely mirrored his own world' (70).

Brave new worlds

Houellebecq ties the crisis of Western civilization to the whole movement of social and sexual emancipation epitomized by 1968: the triumph of the ideals of the entertainment industry in the 1960s: 'individual freedom, the supremacy of youth over age and the destruction of Judaeo-Christian values' (62), followed by divorce by consent and legalized abortion in the 1970s. The availability of the contraceptive pill fuels the sexual revolution that goes with the rise of individualism and the destruction of the family, 'the last unit separating the individual from the market' (136). By the summer of 1976 it was already apparent to Bruno that everything would end badly in frustrated desire and physical violence, 'the supreme manifestation of this focus on the individual' (184). Houellebecq finds confirmation of his radical rejection of the ideology and practice of emancipation in the writings of the French sociologist Michel Clouscard (1928–2009), a Marxist close to the Communist Party. In *Néofascisme et idéologie du désir* (Clouscard [1973] 2008) Clouscard denounced May 1968 as a liberal counter-revolution against the interests of the working classes, the counter-revolution of capitalist consumption against the producers. This libertarian-liberal 'revolution' was carried by the creation of a market place of desires, whose effect was to devalue the Protestant work ethic and its reality principle and replace it by the pleasure principle of permissive consumption. What Houellebecq calls the sex-and-shopping society, in which human relations are reduced to market relations of winners and losers, was already the theme of his first novel, *Extension de la domaine de lutte* (Houellebecq 1994), translated under the title *Whatever* (Houellebecq 1998b).

Clouscard coined the labels 'bourgeois bohemians' (bobos) and 'libertarian liberals' (lili) for the vanguard of the New Age and the New Left and its Youth Culture, who would become the denizens of the 'bohemian city' and its hi-tech clusters. The bourgeois bohemian is defined by leftism in politics and social and cultural values and rightism economically, a combination that was the key to the elitist discourse of liberation that Clouscard sees as originating in Jean-Paul Sartre and Simone Beauvoir, a discourse that, lacking as it did a critique of the existing capitalist relations of production, cemented from 1968 on the split between the 'progressive' bourgeois intelligentsia and the working classes. Emancipation remained an illusion, masking the extension of the market to the sphere of desire, the sphere of intimate relations, underpinned and augmented by the inescapable power of advertising and its aestheticization of identities and commodities. 'Creativity' now promised a seamless integration of work and leisure, individualism and consumption, governed and staged by a 'capitalism of seduction' that has dissolved the difference between reality and the phantasmal.

Bruno's compulsive pursuit of pleasure makes him representative of the age and its self-destructive illusions, Michel's pursuit of knowledge by contrast makes him the precursor of the coming metaphysical mutation. The meeting of the two brothers is placed at the centre of the novel. The subject of their conversation is utopia and dystopia: what is the other of the contemporary market place of vanities? Bruno, fresh from his encounter with Christiane at the Lieu de Changement, hails Aldous Huxley's *Brave New World* as having already anticipated with 'unlimited copulation' in 1932 what we are still trying to create. In Huxley's social world, tragedy and extremes of emotion have disappeared. 'Sexual liberation has come to stay – everything favours instant gratification.' 'Everyone says *Brave New World* is supposed to be a totalitarian nightmare, a vicious indictment of society, but that's hypocritical bullshit. *Brave New World* is our idea of heaven: genetic manipulation, sexual liberation, the war against age, the leisure society' (187). 'Huxley was the first writer to realise that biology would take over from physics as the driving force of society – long before the SF crowd' (188). Michel reminds his brother that Huxley also became a major influence on hippy culture, both through his espousal of psychedelic drugs and through his rewriting of *Brave New World* in his final book, *Island* (Huxley 1962). For Michel, Huxley remains trapped like Bruno in the metaphysical revolution that gave rise to materialism and modern science. And here we have come to the point where the relevance of Canetti for Houellebecq becomes apparent: Huxley failed to grasp, says Michel, that individualism is not only, like rationalism, the product of modern science, it is also the enemy of rationalism's optimism: 'Huxley's mistake was in not being able to predict the power struggle between rationalism and individualism – he crucially underestimated the power of the individual faced with his own death.' 'Sexual rivalry – genes competing over time – is meaningless in a society in which the link between sex and procreation has been broken. But Huxley forgets about individualism. He doesn't seem to understand that lust and greed still exist – not as pleasure principles, but as forms of egotism' (191).

Michel's critique is sharpened by his acute awareness of the blind Darwinian struggle for life in the animal kingdom, magnified in the senseless suffering and destruction caused by wars and revolutions, endlessly renewed by the 'repulsive egotism' and 'violent tendencies' of males, echoed in Bruno's typically masculine view of life as a 'battle zone, teeming and bestial' (246). In the age of scientific materialism death has become the ultimate truth of the individual, cast loose from social constraints, family and religion. Death is the rock on which the brave new worlds of utopia come to grief. The brute fact of mortality, which for Michel, as for Canetti, is the root cause of cruelty and egotism, dooms any attempt to reunite science and religion (192). And just as death stands in the way of the fusion of science and religion, so conversely the inextricable fusion of sex and death defines and determines the dystopian human world of division. Bruno and Huxley belong to the old order. Michel is the bearer of the new paradigm, of the new Law that will bring about the ultimate metaphysical revolution of a world beyond division. As the Prologue announces,

> Now that the light which surrounds our bodies is palpable
>
> Now that we have come at last to our destination
>
> Leaving behind a world of division,
>
> The way of thinking which divided us,
>
> Immersed in a serene, fertile delight
>
> Of a new Law
>
> Now,
>
> For the first time,
>
> We can retrace the end of the old order. (7)

The vanishing point of *Atomised* is the self-extinction of individuality that lies the other side of the suicides of Christiane and Annabelle, Michel's and Bruno's respective girlfriends. The abdication of the self, which is one with the abolition of sex and death, time, change and imperfection will reconcile science and religion, biology and Buddhism in the new Law that undoes the Fall, the original sin of sexual division.

Houellebecq's 'utopian' corrective to Huxley is already envisaged as we have seen in Canetti. *Auto da Fé* refers to the suicide (the sacrificial act of faith) of the central figure, the scholar Peter Kien. The French title *La tour de Babel* (Canetti 1949) refers to the impossibility of communication between the novel's figures, who are all enclosed in the monomaniacal obsessions of their private languages. The original German title *Die Blendung* refers to the self-deception of the figures, blinded by their egotism to the mass, the crowd within. Canetti presents the individual as a fragment of the crowd – a poor solitary devil, a mere drop that unconsciously longs to be reunited with the ocean. This motif is recalled in the disappearance of Michel at the end of *Atomised*: 'We now believe that Michel Djerzinski went into the sea' (365). Not only do *Atomised* and *Auto da Fé* share the same vanishing point – the suicide of the monadic individual, herald of the suicide of Western civilization – *Atomised* takes over, as we have seen, the structuring contrast between two brothers, who are opposites in every respect. The main protagonist in both novels is the utterly asocial man of learning, who is incapable of human contact.

Peter Kien is the leading sinologist of his time, who has devoted his whole life to scholarship in his windowless library (cf. Leibniz's windowless monads) – the library-heaven to which he alone possesses the keys. Already as a child, Michel 'feeds on knowledge' (34). His refuge is the laboratory, where he is safely isolated from the demands and confusions of the world outside. Both, moreover, are absolutely rigid personalities. Peter the rock prides himself on his unchanging character; Michel, who has not changed since adolescence, 'firmly believed in the concept of personal identity, some immutable core which defined him' (75). Each identifies with the force of logical argument. For Peter the scholar, knowledge and truth are identical terms: 'You draw closer to the truth by shutting yourself off from mankind' (Canetti 1963: 18). For Michel the scientist, there is no place for Christian notions of grace and redemption or for humanist notions of freedom and compassion. 'His worldview had grown pitiless and mechanical. Once the parameters for interaction were defined ... actions took place in an empty, spiritless space; each inexorably determined' (Houellebecq 2001: 104).

Peter Kien escapes from the living present into the past, the realm of all that had once been alive and is now safely dead and hence no longer subject to change. Michel escapes into a vision of a pure, unchanging post-human world to come. Both men are profoundly alienated from the natural world, from the animal kingdom's endless cycle of lust and greed, the realm of sexual division. Thus Peter dreams of a world without women – 'Adam forgets, and of One, Two are made. What misery for all time!' (Canetti 1963: 499). Michel looks forward to a world without men – 'A society of women would be immeasurably superior, tracing a slow, unwavering progression ... towards a general happiness' (Houellebecq 2001:196). The greatest insult that Peter can hurl at his brother George is to say: 'The truth is you're a woman. You live for sensations. Let yourself go then, chase from one novelty to the next! I stand firm' (Canetti 1963: 490). Peter, the man of unchanging character, has nothing but scorn for his actor brother, the mimetic personality who switches from impersonation to impersonation, surrounded by the admiring audience of his patients in the mental asylum of which he is the director. 'George had started as a gynaecologist. His youth and good looks brought patients in crowds. ... He took what fell into his lap and had difficulty in keeping up with his conquests. Surrounded and spoilt by innumerable women, all ready to serve him, he lived like Prince Gautama before he became Buddha' (Canetti 1963: 447).

George's vocation is to lose himself in the lives of others. His immersion in the mental worlds of his mad patients opens his eyes to the irrepressible power of the crowd, the mass in supposed individuals: 'For one discovery alone George flattered himself and it was precisely this: the effects of the mass on history in general and on the life of individuals; its influence on certain changes in the human mind. ... Countless people go mad because the mass in them is particularly strongly developed and can get no satisfaction' (Canetti 1963: 462). George has nothing but contempt for his colleagues:

> Of that far deeper and most special motive force of history, the desire of men to rise into a higher type of animal, into the mass, and to lose themselves in it so completely as to forget that one man ever existed, they had no idea. For they were educated men, and education is in itself a *cordon sanitaire* for the individual against the mass in his own soul. (461)

As George's predecessor as director of the asylum puts it, madness is a punishment for egotism. Egotism manifests itself above all in the form of megalomaniac fantasies of power and increase – of money, food, women, books and so on that inflate the ego (the crowd in the head). For Michel, egotism expresses the logic of our consumer society, 'where desire is marshalled and organised and blown up out of all proportion. For society to function, for competition to continue, people have to have more and more until it fills their lives and finally devours them' (Houellebecq 2001: 192). The ultimate logic of these fantasies of increase appears in *Atomised* as in *Auto da Fé* as fantasies of crowds and power. Thus David di Meola in *Atomised* begins to identify with Napoleon in his fantasies of domination: 'He admired this man who had rained fire and blood upon Europe and killed hundreds of thousands of people without even a fig-leaf of ideology or political conviction. Unlike Hitler, unlike Stalin, the only thing Napoleon believed in was himself' (250). In sum, the society of warring egos, as *Atomised* states in the prologue, is a society lacking 'love, tenderness and human fellowship' (3).

George Kien acts out the roles of Gautama and Buddha successively. Bruno and Michel personify this antithesis between blindness and enlightenment. As we have seen, despite his strange moment of illumination, Bruno remains on the level of Gautama in his quest for pleasure, in his desire to lose himself in a world of bodies, until, confronted by the shock of Christiane's cancer, paralysis and suicide, he takes flight from the 'universe of death' and seeks refuge in a mental asylum, where his sexual cravings are numbed and extinguished by a regime of lithium. Michel follows the path of the Buddha. While he waits at the hospital for Annabelle's death, his last link to human feeling, he reads a book of Buddhist meditation (340ff.). His sense of separation from human beings and compassion for their suffering drive his scientific quest for an alternative to the world of sexual division.

Crowds, cancer, clones

Canetti and Houellebecq both radically question the society of individuals, the illusion of individuals as separate entities, as discrete objects in space, illusions protected by the self-deceptions of common sense. Thus, in his last reflections, Michel muses on our separation in space.

> Uneducated man ... is terrified by the idea of space; he imagines it to be vast, dark and yawning. He imagines beings in the elementary form of spheres, isolated in space, curled up in space, crushed by the eternal weight of three dimensions. Terrified of the idea of space, human beings turn in on themselves; they feel cold, they feel afraid. At best, they move in space and greet each other sadly when they meet. But this space is within them, it is nothing but their mental creation. ... In this space of which they are so afraid human beings learn how to live and to die; in their mental space, separation, distance and suffering are born. ... Love binds, and it binds forever. ... Separation is another word for evil; it is also another word for deceit. All that exists is a magnificent interweaving, vast and reciprocal. (362)

Michel's words directly echo the premise of Canetti's study *Crowds and Power*, the unconscious longing of the individual to escape from isolation: 'Man petrifies and darkens in the distances he has created. He drags at the burden of them, but cannot move. He forgets that it is self-inflicted, and longs for liberation. But how, alone, can he free himself? ... Only together can men free themselves from their burdens of distance; and, this, precisely is what happens in a crowd' (Canetti 1973: 19).

The dual reference in *Atomised* to the 'elementary particles' of social theory and of physics allows Houellebecq to reformulate Canetti's structuring opposition of the individual and the crowd in terms of the alternation of particle and wave in quantum mechanics. Michel asks himself:

> Was it possible to think of Bruno as an individual? The decay of his organs was particular to him, and he would suffer his decline and death as an individual. On the other hand, his hedonistic worldview and the forces that shaped his

consciousness and his desires were common to an entire generation. Just as determining the apparatus for an experiment made it possible to assign a specific behaviour to an atomic system – now particle, now wave – so Bruno could be seen as an individual or as passively caught up in the sweep of history. (212)

We find the same dual reference to atomized society and to atomic system in Michel's endorsement of Comte's insistence on 'the reality of social structures as opposed to the fiction of individual existence' (358) – an opposition that Michel compares to the replacement of an ontology of objects with an ontology of states: 'In the ontology of states, the particles are indiscernible, and can be limited to an observable number. The only entities that can be named in such an ontology are wave functions, and, using them, state vectors – from which arose the analogous concept of redefining fraternity, sympathy and love' (358).

Michel's radical re-vision of molecular biology after he leaves his first position in elementary particle research is due to his familiarity with quantum mechanics: 'Biologists acted as though molecules were separate and distinct entities' (19). Max Planck's groundbreaking paper of 14 December 1900 will be matched by Michel's groundbreaking reflections in the last months of 1999 in Ireland on 'the very edge of the of the Western world' (352). Frédéric Hubczejak would write many years later:

> One of the marks of [Michel] Djerzinski's genius was his ability to go beyond his first intuition that sexual reproduction necessarily included harmful mutations. For millions of years, human societies had instinctively made the incontrovertible link between sex and death ... Djerzinski, however, realised that it was necessary to look beyond sexual reproduction to study the general topological conditions of cell division. (194)

Houellebecq's analogy between social system and atomic system extends to the self-destructive mutation of Western civilization that paves the way for the emergence of a new species 'beyond individuality'. The disorderly and destructive growth of cancerous cells not only exemplifies the harmful mutations inherent in sexual reproduction, but cancer becomes the metaphor of the destructive turn of Western civilization. Thus, although Francesco di Meola, the father of David and one of the prophets and entrepreneurs of California's New Age, which called 'for the sweeping away of Western civilisation in its entirety' (94), is still a handsome man, 'his cells had begun to reproduce in haphazard fashion'. The diagnosis is terminal: 'The cancer was inoperable and he would continue inexorably to develop metastases' (95). In turn, Michel's work on the general conditions of mutation is juxtaposed with Annabelle's cancer of the uterus that forces the abortion of her and Michel's child and the removal of her sexual organs – a termination that foreshadows Michel's asexual utopia. The logical conclusion of Michel's reflections on the edge of the Western world is his own suicide. It is his conscious exit from humanity's 'universe of death' (356). He, the enlightened one, has crossed to the other side: 'He saw space as a thin line separating two spheres. In the first sphere there was being, then space, and in the second was non-being and the destruction of the individual. Calmly, without a moment's hesitation, he turned and walked towards the second sphere' (282).

The crowd for Canetti is not simply masses of people in one place. It signifies a change of state: to become one with the crowd means liberation from the burden of existence as an individual. As Houellebecq makes clear, the double aspect of the individual as a unique person and as exemplar of a social-historical collectivity calls for a new metaphysics, an ontology of states, which replaces the familiar atomic, billiard ball model of discreet entities with that of wave functions. What *cancer* and *clones*, the DNA of dystopia and utopia, respectively, have in common is the change of state which replaces the unique with the identical. Comparable to Canetti's concept of the open crowd – 'the urge to grow is the first and supreme attribute of the crowd' (Canetti 1973: 16) – cancer unleashes a dynamic of uncontrolled cellular growth that feeds on healthy cells, evading in the process the naturally programmed death of cells. Cancer becomes the appropriate metaphor of the society of self-interest: just as cancer seeks immortality on the cellular level at the expense of the organism, so the egotism of individualism triumphs at the expense of the social organism. As the end product of genetic breakdown, cancer is the antithesis of the elimination of genetic dysfunction through the asexual reproduction of genetically identical individuals (whether cells or organisms) in cloning.

Crowds, cancer and clones share the common drive to negate differentiation and hence escape the death of the individual, cells, organisms. Each presents a version of immortality at the price of individuation. Neither Canetti nor Houellebecq (nor Huxley) is interested, however, in simply reducing humanity and human history to biology, whether genesis with Canetti or genetics with Houellebecq. Biology serves as a metaphor for our fallen state: on the one hand, the original sin of Adam that brought death, sexual division, evil and suffering into the world, on the other, the sin of egotism, whose consequences have only become fully apparent in the emancipation of the modern individual from all traditional social bonds and restraints. Between the cancer that consumes the isolated individual and the universal sympathy that binds the human clones together in a 'magnificent interweaving, vast and reciprocal' (Houellebecq

2001: 362) is an empty space, the space of the absence of truly human being (that Canetti came to conceive as an endless capacity for self-transformation and Houellebecq laments as the lost kingdom of selfless love).

Insofar as we can speak of Canetti and Houellebecq's brave new worlds, the other of the suicide of Western civilization they envisage serves to reinforce the impact of their savage depictions of the modern world of competing individuals. But to the extent that their realism exceeds the satiric intention the distinction between utopia and dystopia loses its purchase and the utopian vanishing point begins to look more and more dystopian, leaving the reader with the question – what is it to be truly human? What would a society be like that was built around 'love, tenderness, and human fellowship' (Houellebecq 2001: 3)?

Epilogue: The end of the novel

The title of the English translation of Canetti's novel, approved by the author, highlights the direct connection between *Auto-da-Fe* and Cervantes's *Don Quixote*. Not only do the wanderings of Kien and Fischerle through the 'headless world' recall those of Cervantes's knight and squire, there is also a reciprocal relationship between the beginning and the end of the two novels. *Don Quixote* starts with the 'inquisition' in the hero's library by the secular and religious authorities, the village priest and barber, and 'punishment by fire' of the books that have unhinged the mind of the noble knight. The novel as genre is born from this 'massacre of the innocents' and it dies, Canetti argues, in the fire that consumes Kien and his library. The time of the novel and the time of its 'mad subject' have run out. This is precisely the theme of the Epilogue to *Atomised*.

The novel's epilogue, the narrator tells us, belongs to 'History' as opposed to the 'fictional reconstruction' of the lives of the brothers Bruno and Michel. The fictional reconstruction thus functions as the *novel*, which is revealed in retrospect as a historical fiction, narrated some eighty years after Michel's suicide in 1999 and framed by the prologue and epilogue of Houellebecq's *science fiction*. The nearly seventy years that separate *Atomised* from *Auto-da-Fe* allows Houellebecq to present his novel of the end of the novel as a citation from the past, separated from the now of History by a 'fracture' in time. Just as the metaphysical revolutions of the past had separated the time of Christianity from that of paganism, the 'ancient literature of a Christian age' from the age of materialism, so now the fracture enables us to 'listen to this story of materialism and its time as an antique story of men'. Beyond the threshold and horizon of their 'universe of death' lies a new paradigm, a new religion that arises from the selfless eros of fraternity. It has given us a restored 'sense of community, of permanence and of the sacred', which will make possible the reconciliation of humanity through the establishment of 'public opinion on a planetary scale' and of a future world government. The condition of this fraternal religion is the creation of a 'new, intelligent species, made by man "in his own likeness"' (376–8).

If this is the last word of 'History', it is not the last word of Houellebecq's meditation on being and time:

> History exists, it is elemental, it dominates, its rule is inexorable. But outside the strict confines of history, the ultimate ambition of this book is to salute the brave and unfortunate species which created us. This vile, unhappy race, barely different from the apes, had such noble aspirations. Tortured, contradictory, individualistic, quarrelsome, it was capable of extraordinary violence, but nevertheless never quite abandoned a belief in love. This species which, for the first time in history, was able to envisage the possibility of its passing and which, some years later, proved capable of bringing it about. As the last members of the species are extinguished, we think it just to render this last tribute to humanity, a homage which itself will one day disappear, buried beneath the sands of time. It is necessary that this tribute be made, if only once. This book is dedicated to mankind. (379)

Houellebecq ends not with the answer but with the question of his prologue: what would a society be like that was built around 'love, tenderness, and human fellowship' (3)? The question belongs to the world of the novel but it finds its compelling expression in a novel that has become science fiction, Kazuo Ishiguro's *Never Let Me Go*.

3

A theory of science fiction

The a priori of the form

Read in the light of *The Theory of the Novel* Houellebecq proposes a radical alternative to Lukács's anticipation of a new epic form that will take the place of the novel just as the novel had displaced the medieval romances. Like Canetti's *Auto da Fé*, *Atomised* is a novel of the end of the novel, synonymous with the end of the age of individualism. Houellebecq presents the new form of science fiction as completing, cancelling and transcending the search for meaning in the novel. It completes the search for meaning by leading us out of the wasteland, the world of suffering humanity, into the new totality, the promised land of clones. Their pre-established harmony cancels the travails of isolated existence as an individual, thereby transcending the very raison d'être of the novel. Houellebecq's framing narrative formally demonstrates the a priori of the new form that is deemed capable of completing, cancelling and transcending the old form. In this sense he confirms Lukács's diagnosis eighty years earlier of the limits of the novel. But he also confirms Lukács's strictures on the dangers of abstraction, which threaten all the constructed totalities of the moderns. Lukács is careful not to let hope outstrip reality. If ever the new world, in which man exists as man, not as social being or isolated individual, comes into being, then 'the form of the renewed epic' will have found, like the old epic, its constitutive a priori: 'It would be a world to which our divided reality would be a mere backdrop':

> But art can never be the agent of such a transformation: the great epic is a form bound to the historical moment, and any attempt to depict the utopian as existent can only end in destroying the form, not in creating reality. (Lukács 1971a: 152)

By 'utopian' Lukács means an abstract, merely posited reality. This is not to deny that the novel is itself a posited form, that the only totality the novel knows is aesthetic and that its truth lies in laying bare by bearing witness to the divided and fragmented nature of its subject matter: the problematic individual in a contingent world. Nevertheless, Lukács gives us the means to follow Houellebecq and to *construct* the new form of science fiction and in the process trace the passage from one narrative form to another, from the novel to science fiction.

How does the form of science fiction relate to the forms of the epic and the novel? What form does totality – and with it the immanence of meaning – take in science fiction? As opposed to the epic, the a priori of science fiction's form is not given but posited. As opposed to the novel, the posited form of science fiction presupposes a given, not an absent totality. Science fiction is thus formally similar to the epic and formally dissimilar to the novel. This apparent paradox is explained by its fundamentally new relationship to reality. It is 'utopian' in Lukács's sense of abstract, non-existent. Science fiction stands in terms of meaning at the opposite pole to the epic, since the immanence of meaning resides solely in the inner consistency of its given, imagined world, not in its congruence with the given, unquestioned world as in the epic. To borrow here Hans Blumenberg's distinction between *world model* and *world picture*, empirical reality and its interpretation (Blumenberg 2021: 40–61): the identity of world model and world picture guarantees the epic's extensive totality and its immanence and transcendence of meaning. Such totality is denied the novel but is again claimed by science fiction, even though both share the defining and constitutive a priori of a *posited* form. Since all literary forms suppose and express a relation to reality, the difference between the posited forms of the novel and science fiction can be put in the following way: the novel presents a real possible world whereas science fiction presents a possible real world, or alternatively, the given reality of a possible world.

To come back to the 'utopian', which, says Lukács, must destroy the novel form if it is taken to its conclusion: this is precisely the path taken by science fiction. It destroys the novel form and its relation to reality in order to posit the reality of a possible world as the means to establishing a new 'abstract' relation to the world from which it springs. The interest in this new relationship to reality derives from the pluralizing and the possibilizing of the world since Giordano Bruno and Leibniz as reflections of the whole process of transition from a closed to an open universe, in which the modern scientific world models have progressively destroyed the world pictures that have always offered the comfort and closure of total meaning. It would be too simple, however, to conclude that science fiction has abandoned the novel's search for meaning. On the contrary, in destroying the 'limited' form and the 'negative' meaning of the novel, science fiction again lays claim to totality and hence to the immanence and transcendence of meaning. That is the a priori of its form, exemplified in Houellebecq's completion, cancellation and transcendence of the novel. Let us say more neutrally: by reversing the relationship between the real and the possible, science fiction both cancels and *potentiates* the a priori of the novel by extrapolating the dynamic latent within its posited form. If the paradox of the novel lies for Lukács in ruthless exposure of its abstraction, then the paradox of science fiction lies in the systematic unfolding of its abstraction, systematic because there can be nothing outside and beyond the confines of its imagined world, as opposed to the necessary incompletion of the novel's form and quest for meaning, which can only be redeemed 'by recognizing, consciously and consistently, everything that points outside and beyond the confines of the world' (Lukács 71). Science fiction's relationship to the epic and the novel is, to repeat, paradoxical. Like the epic it claims totality, like the novel it is governed by the question of meaning. Indeed, we may say that science fiction imitates the closed totality of the epic as the condition of posing the open, even infinite question of meaning, outside and beyond the confines of the novel's world. Its search for meaning is no longer the individual's quest but fundamentally the relationship between world model and world picture, science and religion.

My argument presupposes Lukács's Hegelian understanding of the progressive enlightenment of the Greek spirit from the epic to tragedy to philosophy. At the beginning stands the complete latency of the epic form, the latency that allows Lukács to observe: 'The world of the epic answers the question: how can life become essential? But the answer ripened into a question only when the substance has retreated to a far horizon' (35). The epic form is completely latent because it is *unquestionable*, the given product of communal self-expression. At the end stands philosophical *poetics* as the self-consciousness of epic and tragic forms as embodying the answer to a question. More exactly, the a priori defines form in terms of the relationship between answer and question. The answer always precedes the question in the sense that the form, whether in the epic, tragedy or novel, is the answer. *The answer given by the successive forms progressively serves, however, to illuminate the question.* This dialectic of answer and question becomes inescapable once the given form and totality of the epic is replaced by the posited form of the novel. A posited form is problematic, inescapably abstract, in Hegel's terms, once the split between subject and object, self and world means that the answer can only be individual and subjective.

We are now in position to propose a first definition of the a priori of science fiction:

The *epic form* is the solution to the problem of meaning that holds the question latent. The answer precedes the question.

The *novel form* expresses the problem of meaning and the answer confirms the question. The question is the answer.

In *science fiction* the form (pre)determines the problem of meaning but the question transcends the answer. The answer is the question.

As opposed to the one really existing world of the novel common to author and readers, science fiction has nothing outside its purely possible world. Internal self-consistency must take the place of external reference. The totality of the form is neither the given totality of the epic nor the posited totality of the novel but a totality in the original theological sense of a *thesis*, that is, something posited by a god, hence predetermined, a creation by *fiat* that lives from the faith, the credit afforded it by the reader. If novel fictions function as *as-if* constructions in relation to a reality shared by author and reader, science fictions function as *what-if* constructions in relation to hypothetical thought experiments. Where the closure of the epic form solves the question of meaning, the closure of science fiction can offer only a tautological identity of answer and question. And that is why the a priori in science fiction is the *deus ex machina* both formally and substantively.

The god in the machine who appears at the end to solve through his or her intervention the problem and resolve the question is a familiar plot device. That does not mean that it has been understood. Ironically, practice exceeds theory.

The dictionary definition gives the familiar understanding: the *deus ex machina* is 'a plot device whereby a seemingly unsolvable problem in a story is suddenly and abruptly resolved by an unexpected and unlikely occurrence' (*Merriam-Webster*). It makes a mockery of the role of Pallas Athene in Aeschylus's *Eumenides*, but it does have a greater relevance in the plays of Euripides, generally seen as the originator of the device. Thus in *Medea* the sun god Helios rescues his granddaughter Medea from the wrath of her husband Jason; in *Alcestis* the wife's willingness to sacrifice herself to save her husband's life is solved by her rescue from the clutches of Death by Heracles. In the *Thesmophoriazusae* in which Euripides is put on trial for his depiction of women by the women celebrating the festival of Thesmophoria, Aristophanes parodies the device by bringing the accused playwright on stage in the machine. Shakespeare employs the device in his late romances, *Pericles* and *Cymbeline*. In *Measure for Measure* it becomes in the figure of the Duke the commanding intelligence of the plot.

Aristotle sums up the obvious criticism of the device in his *Poetics*: 'It is obvious that the solution of plots ... should come about as a result of the plot itself, and not from a contrivance, as in *Medea*' (*Poetics* 1454 a: 33). This criticism is shared by Lukács. The Euripidean *deus ex machina* appears precisely at the point where the transcendence of meaning essential to tragedy disappears. Like Nietzsche, Lukács treats it as the *overt* symptom of the death of tragedy, of the death of the gods under the gaze of Socratic enlightenment. But what this signified is grasped only negatively by Nietzsche and Lukács. They have forgotten Horace's saving proviso in his *Ars Poetica* (lines 191–2). Poets should never resort to a 'god from the machine' to resolve their plots 'unless a difficulty worthy of the god's unravelling should happen'.

The god who appears in Euripides is the personification of the author who can no longer accept the pre-given myth and its tragic ethical dilemmas. A god is needed to rescue the protagonists from the blind decrees of mythical fate: that was precisely the divine achievement of Pallas Athene in the *Eumenides*. It was not Socratic doubt that destroyed tragedy. Euripides testifies to the death of a form that could no longer resolve, in Lukács's words, a fundamental dissonance of existence. Tragedy dies once the a priori of its form is no longer guaranteed by the transcendence of meaning, that is, when the a priori of the form can no longer preserve its latency. The appearance of the god dissolves the tragic form by revealing its hidden transcendental a priori. The *deus ex machina* is this *open secret of the closed form*, which manifests the intelligence of the plot. In the novel it appears as the irony of the absent god. In science fiction it takes the form of an intelligence that is formally omniscient (it can confound the reader but it cannot surprise itself). Its function, however, is not to deliver answers but to pose by means of the posited form questions of a 'difficulty worthy of a god's unravelling': in other words, questions, which are unanswerable but nevertheless supremely meaningful. The tautological a priori of question and answer in science fiction demands the god in the machine in order to unravel this tautology and transform it into the open-ended dialectic of positing intelligence and the problem of meaning at the heart of the form.

The god in the machine thus appears in a double guise. On the one hand, on the level of plot, it is the self-reflexion of the form. By this I mean, in Lukács's formulation, that in the novel the posited form 'assumes form as the result of the abstraction seeing through itself' (Lukács 72). Carried to the limit, this self-reflection of abstraction destroyed the novel form to become a new artistic creation, one in which transcendence of the tautology of the form is given meaning by a problem that only a god can unravel.

Euripides' *deus ex machina* presupposes the death of the pagan gods, who are ironically resurrected as stage props to effect a merely conventional deliverance. The *deus ex machina* of science fiction is predicated in turn on the death of the Christian god, ironically and fatefully resurrected as the modern Prometheus: *homo deus*.

Four additional remarks:

1. Science fiction's dialectic of answer and question, form and content, is in danger of being dissolved where the *form* becomes the open licence for space operas, star wars, action, horror or fantasy, that is, it runs the risk of *trivialization* of meaning where it becomes a hybrid of genre-splicing, in which entertainment evades the question of meaning. The dialectic is also in danger of dissolving where the *content* becomes the open licence for pseudo-profundity, that is, it runs the danger of *mystification* of meaning, where it ransacks the mythologies, magic symbolism, esoteric teachings of the world in search of the requisites of meaning.
2. The closed totality of science fiction has two narrative poles. The first is the *intensive-dramatic totality*, as in the desert island, the spaceship, the space station, the laboratory etc. Its chronotope converges on the intensive unity of time, space and action (Chapter 4). The second is the *extensive-epic totality*, in which the action unfolds across the vastness of galactic space and time and typically takes the form of the series in both literature and cinema. Its chronotope is the open-ended series of adventure time (Part 3). In between lie *intensive-epic totalities*, such as climate fiction, where the urgency of ecological threats compresses the time of the action. Its chronotope retains a strong sense of relationship to the reader's present (Part 2).
3. The dis/continuity between the novel and science fiction resides in the latter taking the inherent abstraction of the novel form to its conclusion. Lukács points the way to this dis/continuity: 'In a novel, totality can be systematized only in abstract terms, which is why any system that could be established – the novel – a system being, after the final disappearance of the organic, the only possible form of a rounded totality – had to be one of abstract concepts and therefore not directly suitable for aesthetic form-giving' (Lukács 70). Dante alone accomplished the triumph of system over organic form. What, however, ensured the unique triumph of Dante's *Divine Comedy* (shared only by Milton's *Paradise Lost*)? Lukács's answer highlights the predestined affinity of the literary form and the cinematic realization of

science fiction: 'The totality of Dante's world is the totality of a visual system of conceptions' (70). Hence, we may say, the more abstract the totality the greater the potential for its visual realization, as for instance in *2001* and *Blade Runner* in relation to their literary models, and conversely the more powerful the literary 'aesthetic form-giving' the less compelling the film version, as for instance with *Never Let Me Go* or *Atomised*. Not to speak of the film versions of *Don Quixote*, *Wilhelm Meister* or *Sentimental Education*.
4. Lukács introduces the question of time in the novel in relation to Flaubert. Time only acquires for Lukács its historical dimension as distinct from the biographical experience of lived time in the historical novel. The historical novel as conceived by Lukács in the 1930s stands completely outside the theoretical scheme of *The Theory of the Novel*. Its totality is of a new kind, informed by a Hegelian-Marxian philosophy of history, which is to give both meaning and form to humanity's struggle for emancipation. Its hero is collective rather than individual. It thus stands between the novel and science fiction and acts as the bridge to the new epic sense of history as future history, explored in Parts 2 and 3.

The historical-philosophical conditions of the form

In driving the transcendental homelessness of the problematic individual to the point at which the isolation of the individual and the atomization of society reach their extremity, Canetti announces and Houellebecq pronounces the transformation of the novel into a new post- or transhuman totality. Science fiction asks: what becomes of human nature and human being the other side of the self-destructive world of problematic individuals? Will it be Houellebecq's transhumanism or a symbiosis of man and machine? Will it be the total isolation that destroys human being in a totalitarianism system of power (Hannah Arendt), or will it be the no less total power of the all-caring welfare state that reduces citizens to dependent children and promises 'immortality' through the farming of 'sub-humans'? Or will it lead to other possibilities of the transhuman that subsume the human into a greater organic or alternatively artificial life form? These perennial themes of science fiction stand at the opposite pole to Lukács's anticipation of the redemption of the individual in a new transparent communal totality. This polarity reflects the ongoing dialectic of European modernity between romantic *organicism* and enlightenment *artifice*. The one *seeks* deliverance in the passage from the novel to a renewed epic, the other *poses* the question of deliverance in the passage from the novel to science fiction. Since science fiction is a *posited* form, it can neither transcend nor supersede the novel. We can think of it rather as the *abstraction* of the novel that liberates the form from the constraints of reality and elevates it to the a priori of the mega-imaginary of science fiction, which offers the imaginative space to address all the potencies and possibilities of technoscience that lie outside and beyond the scope and interest of the novel. It is not simply a matter, however, of a generic division of labour. The question of the human remains fundamental, but it appears in its most essential and exemplary, that is, abstract form.

The abstract nature of science fiction thus stands as the antithesis to Lukács's dream of the new closed and concrete totality of the epic that will undo the split between self and world, being and destiny, life and essence. Lukács's dream of the redemptive new is still the old dream of paradise lost and paradise regained, whose direct antecedent is to be found in the German Romantics' promotion of the art work to the true and eternal organon of philosophy. In his *System of Transcendental Idealism* (1800) Friedrich Schelling declares:

> Art is paramount to the philosopher, precisely because it opens to him, as it were, the holy of holies, where burns in eternal and original unity, as if in a single flame, that which in nature and history is rent asunder, and in art and action, no less than in thought, must forever fly apart. The view of nature which the philosopher frames artificially, is for art the original one. (Schelling 1978: 231)

Art accordingly holds the promise of a new synthesis of the ancients and the moderns, of the Greeks' mythology of nature and Christianity's mythology of history. This 'new mythology' will complete and consummate the modern age in a poem of unity, the epic of a new Homer (*Philosophy of Art*, 1801–5). When and how this once and future epic will come to be is the question Schelling bequeaths to Lukács:

> But how a new mythology (which cannot be the intention of an individual poet but only of a new generation that represents things as it were a single poet) can itself arise, is a problem for whose solution we must look to the future destiny of the world and the further course of history alone. (Schelling 33)

Dostoevsky could only be an interim solution to the problem that only a 'new generation that represents things as if it were a single poet' can realize. And this single poet Lukács found, as we know, in the identity of subject and object embodied in the proletariat: 'the living body of the total system' of Hegel's philosophy, as Lukács hailed it in *History and Class Consciousness* (Lukács 1971b: 147), and thus the ultimate organon of philosophy.

There is, however, another new mythology of the Romantic Age of Revolution. Its founding text is Mary Shelley's *Frankenstein or the Modern Prometheus* (1818). It introduces a new problematic, completely distinct from the problematic of the novel. This new mythology, the antithesis of Romantic organicism (for all that *Frankenstein* expresses a romantic critique of Promethean science), knows no *telos* beyond that of ultimate questions, since like the novel it knows no home. All answers, all syntheses are at best provisional because its dialectic springs from the dynamic unleashed by the exponential expansion of man's Promethean powers, which forces us to recognize a new relationship between technology and nature, mind and matter.

The story of Frankenstein, writes Percy Bysshe Shelley in his preface to the first edition of 1818, does not depend for interest on the weaving of supernatural terrors, on spectres or enchantments. Its merit lies quite elsewhere. Its fantasy is justified by 'the novelty of the situation which it develops'. However physically impossible, this novelty 'affords a point of view to the imagination for the delineating of human passions more comprehensive and commanding than any which the ordering relations of existing events can yield' (Shelley 2003: 11). We have here *in nuce* the definition of a new narrative genre, whose constituting a priori is the novelty, the *novum* impossible in relation to the physical world but thereby offering a new, more comprehensive and commanding perspective on human passions. It is Mary Shelley, however, who creates and gives life to the new genre with a single sentence. It expresses the essence of the novelty of the new genre: 'The world was to me a secret which I desired to divine' (Shelley 2003: 39).

'To divine': science fiction is the art of *divination* in all the meanings of the term: to foresee, to foretell, to predict, to prophesy, to be inspired like a god, to discover and perceive intuitively hidden knowledge. In short, to possess divine imaginative powers capable of anticipating the future and intended to guide, forearm and forestall by means of warnings. But this does not make science fiction simply old mythology. Its new mythology is the divinization of man, *homo deus*, who seeks omnipotence through the divining of the secrets of nature. But as Mary Shelley's tale makes clear, the modern Prometheus, Prometheus unbound, is still bound to the rock, he must still divine the meaning of his usurpation of divine powers. Although we are right to read Frankenstein's creation of a monster made in his image as the image of the sorcerer's apprentice who unleashes forces beyond his control, the runaway forces no longer of magic but of technoscience,

Mary Shelley turns to the old mythology to give meaning to the new mythology of man's second Fall, as the epigraph from Milton's *Paradise Lost* indicates (see the analysis of *Frankenstein* in Chapter 4).

The Fall of Adam marks the point of no return, the event horizon that separates us from the original paradisal oneness of Creation, the act of division that set history into motion. The second Fall of man is man's assumption of Promethean powers that finds its event horizon in the Atom Bomb, reinforced by the looming threat of irreversible climate change. The second Fall, as the rejection of the Christian promise of redemption, of paradise regained, is for Dostoevsky the key to the future history of the world (see Chapter 4): the usurpation of all earthly power in the name of the promise of the redemption of suffering mankind. Christianity is remade as scientific Socialism to become 'Christianity without tears' in Huxley's *Brave New World* and totalitarian terror in the Soviet Union and China. The nineteenth-century utopias of scientific progress become the dystopias of the twentieth century. Beyond lies Philip K. Dick's 'World War Terminus' that divides us from what he calls 'pre-colonial' science fiction: 'Stories written before space travel but about space travel' (Dick 1968: 94). 'World War Terminus', the metaphor for the World Wars and the A-bomb as the event horizon of much science fiction from *1984*, *The Lord of the Flies*, *Do Androids Dream* to *The Road*, thus defines science fiction as simultaneously pre- and post-'colonial' (colonization of the planets), pre- and post-apocalyptic acts of divination.

Frankenstein already delivers the model of divination as the unfolding of *predestination*. What predestination – the a priori of the closed form of science fiction – unfolds is the unanswerable question of Adam, the unanswered question of Frankenstein's creature: the question of human nature, the question, that is, of *the inseparable separation of human/nature*. The consequences of this separation constitute an endless question for science fiction. *Frankenstein* thus offers the theoretical and theological model of man's second Fall, of the new mythology of the Enlightenment, in the form of a popular myth. Ironically, the enduring question of *Frankenstein* is largely ignored in the popular myth, which reproduces Frankenstein's blindness towards the monster as Other, suspending the whole question of self-recognition in the Other.

It must be stressed that this new mythology is neither identical nor reducible to Adorno's dialectic of enlightenment. Even though Western and Eastern Marxism parted ways after Lukács's *Theory of the Novel*, Adorno's fragmentary *Dialectic of Enlightenment* stands as the shadow and negative mirror of *History and Class Consciousness*. They make up the two sides of the one idea of totality. Adorno's deconstructive dialectic is as closed as Lukács's constructive dialectical method, which claims to grasp 'reality concretely as historical process'. Lukács seeks a new synthesis of man and nature beyond the capitalist reification of first and second nature, in which 'men constantly destroy "natural", irrational bonds and create in their "made" reality a second nature which evolves with the same necessity as was the case with irrational forces of nature' (Lukács 1971b: 187, 128). Adorno reduces the dialectic of man and nature to an enlightenment that has already always reverted to myth, to the blindness of fate as the one inescapable logic of power. Science fiction, even at its darkest, most dystopian and apocalyptic, *refuses closure*. Its a priori is predicated on the interplay of closed form and open problem.

Nevertheless, science fiction is *still* a mythology because it is the historical-philosophical form born of the *death of God*. The hidden God of the novel has exited the stage to leave man as the new god, the Prometheus who has stolen the fire from heaven. Mary Shelley's dramatization of the challenge of human powers to divine creation frames the dialectic of science and fiction inherent in the form, that is, the open-ended dialectic between knowledge and meaning, world model and world picture. Science fiction is thus by virtue of its constitutive division also of necessity theological. There has to be a god in the machine.

Behind the mutual critique of romantic organicism and enlightenment artifice in modernity stands the question of technology. For Lukács or Adorno on the left or Spengler or Heidegger on the right it is the instrument of the reification that brought about the end of traditional, organic and concrete production and subjected man to the alien 'laws' of first and second nature. For Lukács these 'laws' represent the process of rationalization that has *formalized* the partial, differentiated spheres of modern capitalist society into autonomous and self-validating systems, which can no longer grasp their material and social base. Reification accordingly amounts to a process of *abstraction* that has separated *form from content*, knowledge from meaning.

Does this critique invalidate the abstract form of science fiction? Not if we understand form without content – epitomized for Marx in the relation money has to itself as interest-bearing capital (Lukács 1971b: 94) – to mean the relation that form has to itself. *Form without content* is a *form without latency*, a wholly posited form. And just as money qua credit operates as enabling fiction, so too we can think of science fiction as an enabling fiction, which simultaneously opens a space for the production of imaginary possibilities and limits it by giving it form, a form that we can think of as an allegory of humanity's unknown destiny. Since the Atom Bomb, at the latest, the cognitive primacy of reality, governing the novel, is challenged by the cognitive potential of science fiction as the representative genre of technological civilization's promises and its terrors. Nevertheless, the new technological imaginary cannot escape the old ethical and philosophical problems of meaning, which defined and informed the great literary genres of the epic, tragedy and the novel. That science fiction's answers to the question of meaning can only be hypothetical, experimental makes it clear that there is and can be *no god* in the machine. *A form without latency is a form that has itself become the god in the machine.*

Excursus on art, technology and modern creativity

Lukács's whole sociological theory of literary forms is predicated on the difference between the ancient organic world of community and the artificial, man-made world of modern society and its consequences for art. Blumenberg's theory of art and technology rests in similar fashion on the difference between the ancients' and the moderns' conception of nature. In asking how the ancient conception of art and nature was transformed since the Renaissance, Blumenberg is seeking to understand the emergence of the formative power that prompted the radically new self-understanding of the moderns.

> For almost two thousand years, it seemed as if the conclusive and final answer to the question, 'What can the human being, using his power and skill, do in the world and with the world?' had been given by Aristotle when he proposed that 'art' was the imitation of nature, thereby defining the concept with which the Greeks encompassed all the actual operative abilities of man within reality – the concept of *techne*. With this expression, the Greeks indicated more than we today call technology: it gave them an inclusive concept for man's capacity to produce works and form shapes, a concept comprising the 'artistic' and the 'artificial' (which we so sharply distinguish between today) … 'in general', then, according to Aristotle, 'human skill [*techne*] either completes what nature is incapable of completing or imitates nature'. (Blumenberg 2021: 316)

Only against this enduring tradition of the identity of being and nature can we understand the radicality of the modern revolt that broke the nexus between art and technology and nature, separated art from technology and set both in opposition to nature, an opposition, which reduced nature to the object of the absolute claim of technical and artistic works. The formula 'art imitates nature' – art understood as *techne* – held sway as long as nature signified the sum of all possibilities, as long as the implications of the biblical *creatio ex nihilo* remained latent within the correspondence of being and nature, as long, that is, as there was and could be only the world created by God. Once, however, God's omnipotence is conceived as infinite then the complete and closed cosmos could no longer exclude the possibility of unrealized being, the space of possibility that would eventually become the space of 'humanity's inquiry into its own potential' (Blumenberg 344), the space not of divine but of originary human creativity.

Blumenberg's argument in his 1957 essay '"Imitation of Nature." On the Prehistory of Modern Creativity' (Blumenberg 316–57) can only be fully understood when we see it as an answer to Martin Heidegger's 1954 essay 'The Question concerning Technology'. In this essay Heidegger sets out to determine the essence of technology, since it 'is by no means technological' (Heidegger 1993: 311). It concerns rather the revealing of beings and this power of revealing provides in turn the key to the essential relationship between technology and art, recognized by the Greeks. Heidegger distinguishes between two opposed ways of revealing: the ancient as a poietic *bringing-forth* and the modern as a technological *challenging-forth*. For Heidegger the essence of *techne* concerns revealing. It is 'as revealing, and not manufacturing, that *techne* is a bringing-forth' (Heidegger 319).

Modern technology has thus decisively altered the relationship between art and technology. Art is now, says Heidegger, 'on the one hand, akin to the essence of technology, and, on the other, fundamentally different from it' (340). The kinship and difference between art and technology is summed up by the paradox inherent in the essence of modern technology: enframing entails challenging-forth, which is still a way of revealing but one that now conceals and holds in reserve the other saving way of revealing, poetic bringing-forth. Precisely this fraught relationship destines *art* according to Heidegger, as the realm where the 'essential reflection upon technology and decisive confrontation with it must happen' (340). In other words, art is called to reveal and confront the essence of technology, which is nothing technological in itself.

Against Heidegger, I want to argue (side by side with Blumenberg and Ernst Cassirer) that the essence of modern technology and art resides in the essential kinship of their way of revealing, and that the revealing, which Heidegger terms 'challenging-forth', needs to be rethought not only in relation to technology but also in relation to modern art.

Cassirer's answer to the accusation – namely that the potential of technology has resulted in our alienation from nature and from human nature, that is, not in liberation but enslavement – is to reverse perspectives: 'As a mere creature of nature, a physical-organic being, man is not the creator of art – on the contrary art proves to be the creator of humanity, which first enabled and constituted the specific "way" of being human' (Cassirer 2004: 18). If with Schiller we think of art as a 'second creator' of humanity, then with Cassirer we must think of technology in the same fashion, not only in respect of material culture but equally in respect of the self-reflection and self-knowledge to which technology gives rise. Each new aspect of the world revealed by the use of tools opens up a new aspect of our inner world. Cassirer's argument in his 1930 essay 'Technik und Form' is not premised on the distinction between ancient and modern technology. On the contrary, the very first use of tools set in train an ongoing process of revealing as unconcealment, that is, the uncovering of what is present but hitherto concealed in the world. The nature waiting to be shaped and given form by technology is thereby revealed as essentially incomplete. From the beginning technological 'discovery' signifies the experimental path of transformation mediated by the essential plasticity of nature. The spirit of technology therefore resides for Cassirer in its capacity to reveal the latent in nature, waiting to be actualized. This spirit requires an attitude capable of withdrawing from a given reality in order to posit the possible. Cassirer terms this 'possibilization' of the world 'the greatest and the most remarkable achievement of technology' (Cassirer 2004: 24). He compares the technician with Leibniz's demiurge, who creates neither the essence nor the potentialities of objects but chooses rather the most perfect of the available possibilities, the best of all possible worlds, constrained by the limits imposed by the general laws of nature.

Cassirer raises the question of the similarities and differences between technology and art only at the end of his essay. The similarities flow from his understanding of technology:

> Technical creation never ties itself … to the given aspect of things, but stands under the law of a pure anticipation, a prospective view, which anticipates the future and brings about a new future. … With the insight into this state of affairs the actual centre of gravity of the world of technical 'form' moves further and further from the purely theoretical sphere into the sphere of art and of artistic creation. (Cassirer 2004: 24–5)

This insight remains no more than a suggestion, cut off by Cassirer's rather conventional insistence on the differences between artistic and technological objectivation. More helpful here is Cassirer's reference to the Leibnizian demiurge, since it points to a direct historical link between the spirit of modern technology and the spirit of modern literature. The Leibnizian concept of possible worlds played a key role in the first half of the eighteenth century in rethinking the classical doctrine of art as the 'imitation of nature'.

In his reconstruction of 'the prehistory of creative man' Blumenberg takes as his starting point the connection between the creative poet and possible worlds. With the recognition of human creativity in the early eighteenth century, hitherto concealed by the doctrine of imitation, the work of art and the work of technology become ontologically original. And what this signifies according to Blumenberg is nothing less than *the displacement of nature by art and technology*. The modern spirit is in this sense '*after nature*': the spirit of creation takes the place of the *imitation of nature,* technology emancipates itself from the model of *physis* to become the evolutionary supplement of nature. The height of this quasi-deification of man's creative powers is reached with the concept of the artist as genius, who in Kant's formulation does not take but gives rules to nature. Fittingly, Blumenberg refers here to Oskar Walzel's 1932 study of the symbol of Prometheus from Shaftesbury to Goethe. The attempts to explain and come to terms with the idea of original creation by expanding the old, mimetic conception of art are particularly instructive, as the following quote from Johann Jakob Breitinger's (1701–1776) *Critische Dichtkunst* (Critical Poetics) of 1740 on the 'aesthetic' application of Leibniz's doctrine of possible worlds makes clear:

> The poet finds himself in the position of God before the creation of the world, facing the entire infinitude of possible worlds, out of which he may choose; therefore, poetry is an imitation of creation and nature not only in their reality but also in their possibility. (Blumenberg 353)

The imitation of nature has mutated into the imitation of creation. In a similar vein, Breitinger's fellow Swiss Johann Jakob Bodmer (1698–1783) in his 'Critical Treatise on the Wonderful in Poetry' (*Abhandlung von dem Wunderbaren in der Poesie*, 1740) takes Milton's *Paradise Lost* (1667, 1674), which he had translated in 1732, as the example for his argument that it is 'always preferable that the material to be imitated come from the possible rather than the present world'. *Paradise Lost*, the epic poem meant to encompass all space and time, and Leibniz's *Theodicy* (1710), both set out to justify the ways of God to man. Both appealed to the best of all possible worlds that is able to combine 'the goodness of God, the freedom of man and the origin of evil' (Leibniz's subtitle). In the process poet and philosopher also *authorized* the imaginative rights of literature by replacing the classical imitation of nature with the modern 'imitation of creation'.

'The poet finds himself in the position of God before the creation of the world, facing the entire infinitude of infinite worlds, out of which he may choose': Breitinger's appeal *to creatio ex nihilo* already delivers the modern idea of creation, which by the end of the eighteenth century had bifurcated into two new narrative forms of worlds – the present and the possible – made in man's image, the novel and science fiction (against a background of utopian writings since the Renaissance). It is not by chance that *Frankenstein* reworks Milton's *Paradise Lost*. And if for Blumenberg art no longer points to the exemplary being of nature as its model and has become itself 'this exemplary being for the possibilities of humanity' (Blumenberg 356), there remains a fundamental historical-philosophical difference between the novel as the theodicy of the hidden God and science fiction as the theodicy of the death of God. Science fiction will only fully enter into its kingdom after the Atom Bomb, after humanity was forced to face the consequences of its originary creativity, which has exploded any last vestige of the bounded cosmos of nature and made art and technology the twin expressions of a new *techne* in the name not of nature's or God's but of man's powers.

But in order to understand how the modern separation of art and technology paved the way to a new alliance, even symbiosis of the two in a new *techne*, we must first explore the modern relation of technology to nature. In Blumenberg's anthropology, as with Cassirer and above all Arnold Gehlen, man is a deficient being, who has always been a toolmaker because he must live with what he has not made. What distinguishes modern from traditional technology, says Blumenberg, is 'the conscious and deliberate implementation of a necessity rooted in human nature' (Blumenberg 362). This conscious will is both effect and cause of technology's separation from nature: technology is no longer defined in relation to nature as its model, on the contrary technology defines nature as the raw material of an endless process of transformation in the service of human power. The first nature of the Greek cosmos has become the 'second nature' of a world of machines that function 'out of themselves' (Blumenberg 314). Such machines, such 'automata', testify to the autonomous dynamic of technology and establish technology and art as separate and distinct spheres of invention in the modern period. Ironically, it was this self-validating autonomy of technology and art, which long concealed the underlying unity of their respective expression of man's ability to create works: man's 'second creation' that can only be understood out of itself and yet remains dependent on the first creation.

Modern technology has thus fundamentally changed the equation between world model and world picture. Science's total model of nature combined with the infinite project of technological transformation have progressively devalued and displaced the capacity of world pictures to give anything but partial meaning to a world in motion. The plurality of partial meanings is of course fatal to the totalizing function of world pictures, whether religious or philosophical. All that is left, Lukács and Blumenberg agree, is art's aesthetic totality as a surrogate world picture that is called upon to give meaning to a social world that exceeds limited human capacity (the novel) or to make sense of the infinite project of technology beyond human understanding (science fiction).

The history of science fiction may be divided into two main phases, the first from 1800 to 1945 with the First World War as the first critical watershed and 1945 as the second major watershed, introducing the second phase of science fiction. The first watershed phase is the period of classic or high modernism, distinguished by the autonomy of art and science, corresponding to the cultural polarity of romanticism and enlightenment. The second period since the Second World War is characterized by the progressive dissolution of the autonomy of the arts and sciences and the merging of science and technology into technoscience. To which corresponds in turn the ongoing aesthetization and scientization of the life world (Roberts 2021: 15–26). These two phases trace the path of science fiction from the margins of high literature to a recognized genre in its own right, whose origin in popular culture has come now to epitomize the progressive merging of mass and elite culture. Few would dispute these trends, but when it comes to aesthetic evaluation it is all too easy to reduce this merging to a cultural sociology of the market. In order to go beyond the sociology of the market on the one hand and its cultural critique in Western Marxism or in Heidegger on the other, we need to go back to Blumenberg's defence of the essential kinship of modern art and technology's way of revealing. Against Heidegger's critique of modern technology, under which he subsumes modern art, Blumenberg legitimizes the modern age in the name of the powers of its second creation.

So rather than dividing the arts and sciences into two separate cultures, we should be more attentive to what Alistair Crombie terms the interpenetration of the two since the Renaissance:

> Scientists and artists alike were creating possible worlds that would in some way explain the real world of experience. They were both in different ways creating theoretical models, and it is through the model in its various forms that the interpenetration of art and science can be seen at its most telling. ... The invasion of science by art through the method of hypothetical modelling went very deep during the seventeenth century. (Crombie 1986: 63)

Perhaps the best example of this new techne is to be found in the complete break with the entire tradition of the mimetic relation to the world out there.

The imitation of nature has been replaced by simulation in digital creation and it celebrates its original creativity not only in scientific modelling but also in the special effects of science fiction films.

Crombie's 'theoretical models' encompass the arts and sciences. The 'model', however, is too general to account for the generic differences between literary genres, in our case between the novel and science fiction and the related question of aesthetic evaluation. Here the *abstraction* of the science fiction form is decisive. Science fiction is not only a theoretical model, it poses at the same time the question of the meaning of its hypothetical experiment. (It is not chance that the reversal of roles between the subject and the object of the experiment has been a recurrent trope of science fiction since *Frankenstein*.) In this sense science fiction is a second-order theoretical reflection on the world models of modern science. This makes the self-validation of the form theo-logical rather than aesthetic. As opposed to the irony of the novel, the spirit of science fiction, however playful it may be, is allegorical and didactic. Like the arts of the old *techne* it too seeks to instruct and entertain. No longer by *poiesis*, however, but by *thesis*: the creation of possible worlds, which probe the productive limits of its form, the limit along which the dialectic of world models and world pictures, science and fiction plays out. Meghan O'Gieblyn sums up science fiction's double roots in science and theology:

> To discover truth, it is necessary to work within the metaphors of our time, which are for the most part technological. Today artificial intelligence and information technologies have absorbed many of the questions that were once taken up by theologians and philosophers: the mind's relationship to the body, the question of free will, the possibility of immortality. (O'Gieblyn 2021: 12)

Technology now provides the metaphors for the perennial problems of human nature and humanity's destiny. The subtitle of O'Gieblyn's *God, Human, Animal, Machine*, 'Technology, Metaphor and the Search for Meaning', aptly captures the ultimate meaning of science fiction's god in the machine.

4

The God in the machine

Human nature: Original sin

Shipwreck has been a staple of storytelling since *The Odyssey*. It is an indispensable narrative device to give a sudden fateful twist to the wheel of fortune. In English law fateful accidents of this kind are deemed natural hazards outside of human control, for which no one may be held responsible, and are classed under the category 'acts of God'. Unless of course we *are* in the presence of an act of God. In which case we are dealing with a clear case of divine logic: in a universe governed by God, there can be no chance events. And in a universe governed by its author, there can be no chance events either. When the two logics coincide, as in Daniel Defoe's *Robinson Crusoe* (1719), Providence is the name given to the divine interventions that govern the life of the castaway at the same time as they authorize the twists and turns of the plot. Defoe himself appeals to the authorial alibi, patented by Cervantes, in order to present himself as no more than the intermediary, editor or translator, of a true story.

> The author believes the thing to be a just story of fact; neither is there any appearance of fiction in it. And however thinks, because all such things are disputed, that the improvement of it, as well as the diversion, as is the instruction of the reader, will be the same. (Defoe 1994: 7)

Or shall we say: the improvement will be the same, whether divine or authorial in origin, since coincidence is never by chance?

Anniversaries serve to underline the role of coincidence. Crusoe boards the ship, destined to be wrecked, 'in an evil hour', eight years to the day 'that I went from my father and mother in Hull, in order to act the rebel to their authority and the fool to my own interest' (44). That day, the 30th September, the day of his *original sin* (191), is his birthday. And if all the fateful events of his life belong to this day (133), it is because original sin signifies the coincidence of fall and deliverance. And so it is on this day in 1659 that Crusoe is shipwrecked. His survival seems to him a 'dreadful deliverance' (50): 'I had great reason to consider it as a determination of Heaven, that in this desolate place and in this desolate manner I should end my life' (65). But then reason begs him reflect that he alone was saved. 'Why were you singled out?' Was he not 'miraculously' saved from death and 'wonderfully' sent a ship close enough to shore that he might be supplied with all that was needed to sustain life, from carpenter's tools to seed? And when this spoilt seed that he had thrown away grows, Crusoe begins to realize that his 'chance' progress from hunter-gatherer to cultivator 'was really the work of Providence as to me' (81). It needs a further act of God, however, beyond rescue and the provision of necessities to life, beyond the terrors of an earthquake, before he is ready to understand how 'thoughtless of a God, or a Providence' he had been, to understand that a life directed solely to self-preservation signals no more than living 'like a brute from the principles of nature'. The further act required is a violent fever, from which arises the dreadful figure of the voice of conscience and belated repentance (89–90).

Seized by terror at the invisible and secret Power, which directs all things, he is brought to ask: 'What is this earth and sea ... whence is it produced, and what am I, and all the other creatures, wild and tame, human and brutal, whence are we?' (93) Why has he been reduced to the miserable circumstance of shipwreck and isolation: '*Why has God done this to me? What have I done to be so used?*' (94). His questions call forth the answer given by the 'chance' discovery of a Bible in his search for tobacco as a remedy against fever in one of the chests saved from the wreck. The answer given him transforms the desert island from his prison into the place and condition of his deliverance from his original sin (98).

As one of the elect, who has been singled out, Crusoe is now ready to enter into his *earthly* kingdom and take possession of the island. 'I was king and lord of all this country indefeasibly and had a right of possession; and if I could convey it, I might have it in inheritance, as completely as any lord of the manor in England' (101). He is checked in the enjoyment of his possession by the realization that his sovereignty is purely potential without access to the trading of products. His solitary state has banished exchange value, leaving only use value, just as the division of labour integral to capitalist accumulation is replaced by Crusoe's laborious mastery of all the trades needed to secure life, from baker to basket maker, from carpenter to butcher, from hunter to farmer, from builder to bullet maker. Thus, untempted by vice or greed, Crusoe achieves a resourceful but simple untroubled existence, whose purity is preserved by his total isolation. No wonder Rousseau made it the sole reading of his young pupil Emile.

With this untroubled existence, in which spiritual deliverance is blessed by mastery over nature, the novel's essential theme is already completed at the point, halfway through the novel, when Crusoe discovers a footprint in the sand. From this point the outer world, in the form of fear and anxiety, breaks into the hermetic closure of the desert island, which has been the condition of the experiment whereby Crusoe is transformed from the object to the subject of Providence. And so heavenly providence hands back the baton to worldly interests: Crusoe's twenty-eight years as a castaway are indeed not without interest, for all the while his capital, his plantation in Brazil, worked by slaves, has been accumulating profit, awaiting redemption in Lisbon. Moreover, he does finally convey his island, whose riches can now be exploited through its colonists.

Should we regard *Robinson Crusoe* as the first novel and its hero as epitomizing one of the modern myths of individualism, as Ian Watt argues? Or should we treat this work of Providence as a text truly intended to instruct, that is, as an allegory of Calvinist-Puritan election that employs the tale of 'the wonders of this man's life', exceeding all that can be found extant, in order to instruct and entertain? The one does not exclude the other but neither captures the essence of Defoe's invention: the solitary castaway on a desert island, made fruitful by the abstraction of the form, that is, by the complete exclusion of the external world, other than in the rescued tools and Bible as the necessary initial materials of the experiment to humanize nature and spiritualize man. In this metabolism with nature we are a long way from the novel of the problematic individual and its dialectic of self and world, to which the letter novels of Samuel Richardson have a far better claim. Instead, we encounter *the wholly self-created and wholly self-enclosed world* of Defoe's fiction, figured in that of his hero – self-created because it is totally abstracted from the external world to form a totality of meaning. It is this absolute abstraction, which makes *Robinson Crusoe* a prototype of science fiction rather than of the novel (as the numerous SF adaptations and borrowings show). Only such abstraction makes it possible to pose the question of human nature so purely and absolutely, even if Crusoe does go so far as to question the sovereignty of Providence and the arbitrary disposition of things: the forbidden Promethean question that Frankenstein's creature will pose and that Crusoe answers, 'as we are all clay in the hands of the Potter, no vessel could say to Him, "Why hast thou formed me thus?"' (206).

The secret intelligence which governs the fate and fortune of Robinson Crusoe reveals the a priori of the form in singular purity as the logic of a thesis, a theological positing. In *Robinson Crusoe* the author still speaks with His Master's

Voice, simultaneously concealing and revealing the hidden God of the form. It is not the hidden God of Pascal and the Jansenists, not the hidden God of the novel but of the closed form as the type and prototype of science fiction. The presiding spirit of science fiction is not irony or negative mysticism but it is no less theological. It is the spirit of *predestination*, the question directed not to the individual but to human nature and destiny, cast adrift from Providence in a world of human creation.

Crusoe's individualism is not singular. The castaway's mythical status is tied to its representation of a new social type, Puritan economic individualism and the equation of this-worldly debit and credit with the divine balance of evil and good (68). Defoe's thesis invited not only endless imitations but also anti-theses. In *Friday or the Other Island* (Tournier 1969) Michel Tournier has quite another destination for his castaway in mind in his total critique of Puritan and capitalist values. And William Golding's inversion of one of the most popular nineteenth century Robinsonades, R. M. Ballantyne's *Coral Island* (1857), likewise uses the closed desert island form to pose the fundamental question of human nature in the form of a didactic experiment.

As Tournier's title, *Friday or the Other Island* tells us, his intention is a complete reversal of *Robinson Crusoe*. At stake is the taking back and undoing of the Christian myth of Eden and the Fall. The setting is the Other Island, which the new Robinson calls Speranza, but which is slow to reveal its otherness because the castaway is determined to assert, like his predecessor, civilizational order over his new domain and claim authority over the land and all its creatures. He ceremoniously proclaims himself governor and sets about creating an elaborate system of laws and punishments. Nature, however, is not so easily tamed and he is led into a process of inversion when he enters his telluric phase. With his descent into a cave he returns to the womb of the island mother to begin his rebirth as he ascends, first into vegetable life and then sexual life through union with the earth, engendering mandragoras. The process of rebirth is temporarily halted when he rescues a native from death by his fellows. He calls him Friday, because as a half breed he is neither human nor object, and treats him like Defoe's Robinson as his slave. But all this reassertion of colonial difference is blown away when Friday accidentally sparks the explosion of the store of gunpowder, destroying the whole edifice of order laboriously constructed by his master. Liberated in this fashion from the inherited forms of civilization, Robinson is open to deliverance by pagan nature rather than by Christian Providence. Through his new relationship with his 'brother' Friday, Robinson comes to feel his kinship with the island. The master had become the pupil and the slave has become the guide to Robinson's solar rebirth. And so when a rescuing ship appears, Robinson chooses to remain on the island while Friday, awoken to his civilizational other, secretly escapes. Robinson's loss of his brother and teacher is compensated, however, by a cabin boy who has fled the ship. Robinson names him Thursday and initiates him in turn into his sun worship.

Tournier's novel is a novel of initiation, in which the island serves as the laboratory for the alchemical process of recovery through transmutation of the *materia prima*, the solar gold, to which the red hair of Robinson and Friday bear witness, from its civilizational corruption. For Tournier it is not a question of the alchemical process of the spiritualization of human nature but of man's *renaturalization*. Tournier's counter-process is an allegory of re-creation which undoes the original sin of the Fall, the division of the sexes (cf. Canetti) and our alienation from nature. Robinson's rebirth cancels the first birth of Adam. We return to a world of pagan *physis*, with its harmony of micro- and macro-cosm, in which technology is no longer exploitative or lethal but purely aesthetic. The Aeolian harp constructed by Friday is symbolic of the celebration of the reconciliation of man and nature and the reinstauration of human nature. The Nietzschean inspiration for Tournier's Dionysian revaluation of all values is evident:

> Singing and dancing the individual expresses himself as member of a higher communion: he has forgotten how to walk and talk, and is about to fly dancing into the heavens. ... Man is no longer an artist, he has become a work of art: the artistic power of the whole of nature reveals itself to the supreme gratification of the Primal Oneness. (Nietzsche 1993: 17)

The naval officer in *Lord of the Flies* (1954), who intervenes at the last moment to save Ralph from the pursuing hunters, functions as the *deus ex machina*, who undoes – for the moment – the 'act of God', the plane crash, which originally precipitated the action. He rescues the schoolboys, who have been left marooned on a desert island in the Pacific, when, fleeing the atomic war that has left a civilization in ruins (Golding 1962: 59), the plane evacuating them crashed. He is thus a last representative of an ordered world, whose arrival calls a halt to the fatal demonstration, under the experimental conditions of isolation, of 'the darkness of man's heart' (192).

What had at first seemed to the boys like a real life adventure 'like in a book' (34), *Coral Island* to be exact, soon turns from a 'boys own' story into the boys' 'own adventure', which splits them into two opposing camps: the defenders and enemies of civilization, led by Ralph and Jack, respectively (the protagonists and pals of *Coral Island*). The rallying cry of the defenders is the beacon fire needed to alert passing ships and deliver them from the island. The rallying cry of the enemies is the hunt for food, releasing the 'throb and stamp of a single organism' delivered up to their 'liberation into savagery' (164). The defenders unite behind Ralph's conch shell as the symbol of democratic procedure and Piggy's spectacles as the instrument of fire-making. The enemies are united by their red, white and black masks, their symbol the hunting knife of Jack the leader. These are the two opposed answers to their inner fears and terrors, which are projected onto the figure of the Beast, the mythical figure of the hunters hunted, adumbrated in the scene, where Jack and his band flee from the wildfire, over which they have lost control and which claims the first victim, one of the little ones. The bloodlust of the hunters – 'Kill the pig. Cut her throat. Spill the blood' (66) – is one with the terror that can only be propitiated by sacrifice.

Simon is the only one among the boys, who tries to confront their collective fears. He sets out to search for the ghost the little ones have seen in the jungle. There he finds a grinning sow's head on a stick, left as a gift to the Beast by Jack. The Lord of the Flies addresses Simon: 'Fancy thinking the Beast was something you could hunt and kill.' 'You knew didn't you? I'm part of you?' (137). Simon, who alone senses 'mankind's essential illness' (85), is killed in the darkness when he returns to enlighten the others. At the end as he mourns the death of his true, wise friend Piggy, Ralph weeps 'for the end of innocence' and 'the darkness of man's heart'.

Human nature: The original sin of the modern Prometheus

The epigraph to *Frankenstein or the Modern Prometheus* (Shelley 2003) comes from *Paradise Lost*:

> Did I request thee, Maker, from my clay
> To mould me man? Did I solicit thee
> From darkness to promote me?

The centrality of this question to Frankenstein and his creature is obvious. Its significance for Mary Shelley only fully appears, however, when we read Milton's question in the light of a second quotation from Milton from his *Aeropagitica*:

> Good and evil we know in the field of this world grow together almost inseparably… It was from out of the rind of one apple tasted, that the knowledge of good and evil, as two twins cleaving together, leaped forth into the world. (Milton 1918: 19)

Frankenstein and his creature are these two twins cleaving together. His creature has also read *Paradise Lost* – a moment of identification that is lost on Frankenstein. Each is the other's shadow, for they are indeed inseparable – the conjoined offspring of the knowledge of good and evil. The original sin of Frankenstein is his fateful denial of his creature, his blind insistence on the separability of good and evil. He cannot grasp the evil in his intended good – 'A new species would bless me as its creator and source' – nor correspondingly the good in the evil he has made. This for Mary Shelley is the *predestined* truth of the modern Prometheus, the maker of a creature in his own image that he does not recognize. The a priori of the tale resides in this *identity of opposites* brought about by the failure of self-recognition. (For all the 'self-evident' difference between master and slave, Crusoe nevertheless recognizes the innate goodness of Friday.) This is the secret spring, which releases the 'machinery of a story' (7), as Mary Shelley called it in her 1831 introduction to the standard edition of her work.

The machinery of the story is set into motion when the original harmony of Frankenstein's upbringing, overseen by the guardian angel of his mother and the saintly soul of Elizabeth, his wife-to-be, 'the living spirit of love', and his bosom friend Clerval, the clear-sighted moralist, is broken by his thirst for knowledge, which predestines him to destroy the 'spirit of love' and the 'moral relation of things' in his quest to divine the hidden laws of nature. The identity of opposites governs the fatal logic of Frankenstein's quest: 'To examine the cause of life, we must first have recourse to death' (52). Frankenstein's moment of revelation comes as he ponders the transformation of the blooming cheek of life into the corruption of death in the gloom of the charnel house: 'from the midst of this darkness a sudden light broke in upon me – a light so brilliant and wondrous' that it will enable him to animate lifeless matter. Success is not crowned by triumph, however. The beauty of the dream gives way to breathless horror and disgust. What he now dreams foretells the horrors to come – Elizabeth in the bloom of health dies from his kiss, leaving in his arms the body of his dead mother. He wakes to see the monster – this 'demoniacal corpse given life' – watching over him.

The murder of his brother William drives Frankenstein into the mountains, where in the stormy night he sees the monster illuminated by a flash of lightening and recognizes for the space of an instant 'my own vampire, my own spirit let loose from the grave' (78) – a recognition that is just as instantly denied. When he returns to the mountains in search of a 'sublime ecstasy' that could lift him out of the darkness into the light, he is again confronted by the monster, by the question of his creature: 'you, my creator, detest and spurn me, thy creature … You purport to kill me? How dare you sport thus with life?' (102) 'Remember, that I am thy creature; I ought to be thy Adam, but I am rather the fallen angel' (106). If Adam was offered redemption from original sin, it is now the creator who is guilty of the original sin of seeking to rival God, thus becoming himself the fallen angel, the very image of his nameless, unbaptized creature. In the icy wastes of the Alps, to which the monster has fled from the inhumanity and barbarity of man, Frankenstein can find no self-redemptive answer to his creature's suffering, the creature to whom he is bound by ties only dissoluble by their mutual annihilation.

Just as the monster appears as Frankenstein's shadow so Rick Deckard in *Do Androids Dream of Electric Sheep?* (Dick 2009) perceives Mercer in his own shadow. But where the monster represents Frankenstein's demoniacal self, Mercer represents Deckard's better self. The comparison is relevant because both narratives explore the deadly logic of the denial of the 'almost inseparable' identity of opposites between creator and creature, the organic and the artificial – the denial on which *human* identity is based in Frankenstein's and Philip K. Dick's worlds. Indeed, it is Deckard's function to police this divide. He lives from retiring 'organic androids'. His fellow bounty hunter, Phil Resch, sums up their role: we are the barrier 'between Nexus-6 [the most advanced android manufactured by Rosen Association] and mankind, a barrier which keeps the two distinct' (Dick 88). The only reliable *scientific* means of distinguishing between the two is the Voigt-Kampff Empathy Test, which the bounty hunters are legally required to administer to suspects. And since it is so difficult to be sure otherwise, Phil Resch insists on taking the test himself to prove to Deckard that his suspicions towards him are false. These suspicions are justified in that the test reveals a defect in his empathetic, role-taking ability (87), precisely the defect, which makes it possible for Resch to be such a ruthless guardian of the barrier which separates humans and androids. Deckard instinctively feels that he is right to sense a difference between Resch and himself. 'Empathy towards an artificial construct? he asked himself.' 'I wonder, he wondered, if any human had ever felt this way before about an android?' (88).

Dick does not make the answer easy, for it is also precisely the absence of empathy in the androids that determines Deckard to complete his mission and retire six of the eight androids who are on the run. Dick doubles down on the negative identity of creator and creature, hunter and hunted in *Frankenstein*. In the dead world of post-apocalyptic San Francisco humans are as lifeless as their surroundings. The androids are the mirror of the dead world of post-apocalyptic

San Francisco, itself the mirror of the pre-apocalyptic world of 1960s America. Life is bearable only as simulation – the simulated difference between the organic and the artificial, sustained solely by the mood organ and the empathy box. The 'artificial brain stimulation' organ is designed to blot out 'the absence of life', the all-enveloping world-silence of God (12), which manifests itself in the endless accumulation of rubbish – 'kipple' in Dick's memorable term. The empathy box unites its communicants in identification with the solitary figure of Mercer in his endless ascent from the Tomb World. Mercerism is the religion of the world-silence, of the God of entropy and death, whose agent is Deckard. He reflects that he is part of 'the form-destroying process of entropy', who unmakes the androids created by the Rosen Association (60). Death, Mercer tells him, is the ultimate shadow and defeat of creation, the curse the feeds on life. All Mercer can offer is empathy, compassion, that is, the possibility of identification with others across the great divide of in/human nature.

Dick's humans not only live in a world of simulation, they create simulacra of themselves. Joshua Foa Dienstag sees these living simulacra, the android replicants of *Blade Runner*, as film itself come to life in the uncanny experience of original and copy sharing the same 'representational' space (Dienstag 2019: 3). More fundamentally, these living simulacra bring us back to the invisible difference (made 'visible' in the film) between original and copy, creator and created that only empathy, identification and recognition can cross (Dienstag 2019: 51).

There are two invisible boundaries in Ishiguro's *Never Let Me Go* (Ishiguro 2005). The one is that between the clones and the 'normals', the distinction that the reader perceives through the perspective of the narrator Kathy, as she looks back at her formative experiences of friendship and love at the experimental institution called Hailsham, with all the features of an English private co-ed boarding school in its parklike grounds. There is no electric fence separating it from the world outside but the children know that they are different, they are more or less clearly aware that they will grow up to be carers and donors for the National Health System. This boundary between the students and the normal is pregiven just as their lives are predestined. How much should the students be told is the question dividing their guardians, should they be prepared or should they be sheltered? And so it is from what they hear from the guardians that the students seek the meaning of their future roles at the same time as they struggle to understand their own confused feelings and relationships as adolescents. Like the students, Ishiguro's readers are faced by the task of coming to understand what they have learnt, the reality of the student's roles as carers and donors. That is, the reader must experience what it means to live in a world of predestination, a world in which not only the institutional guardians and the normal are simply other but where the 'high ups', the authorities are completely beyond reach. It is a world in which God is dead and death is now God, a world in which everything is permitted to lengthen life for the normal, including the production of clones for organ-harvesting. In short, we are inside the closed form of a dystopian science fiction, in which everything partakes of a predestined experiment, which invites the reader to imagine and enter an alternative reality (that is not actually alternative in some parts of the world), in which the guardians of the UK's benevolent health system have seen the way to curing 'so many previously incurable conditions' (257) by means of the systematic farming of human organs. All the more poignant the vain hope that carers cling to, that under exceptional circumstances, in which they can prove their 'human' worthiness, they might be granted a 'deferral', a reprieve of a few years, before they 'complete'. But as Kathy and her school friend Tommy, now a donor, finally learn, they and their institution, Hailsham, were part of a failed experiment in treating students more humanely. So Kathy and Tommy are left only with their memories, with their time together at Hailsham, the memories which never let them go in a system that never lets them go.

The second invisible boundary is that between science fiction and the novel. In inviting us to read *Never Let Me Go* from the other side of the electric fence, that is, from the safety of the experimenter, Ishiguro is using the closed form of predestination to ask the same question of us. What sense can we make of life, of friendship and love in the face of our inescapable mortality, against which we can no more rebel or rage than the students, who have mutely accepted the purpose and 'completion' of their lives? And so just as in *Atomised*, the invisible boundary between science fiction and the novel focuses the question, not on Ishiguro's down payment on immortality, funded by the clones, nor on the prospect of 'immortality' as clones, but on Houellebecq's question, whether 'love, tenderness and human fellowship' is still possible – the question, which Houellebecq poses through what he says and Ishiguro by what he leaves unsaid.

Human nature. The knowledge of good and evil

If *Frankenstein* and its avatars leave us with that creature's unanswered question to the Creator, Dostoevsky's Grand Inquisitor in *The Brothers Karamazov* (1879) will answer the question when he orders the arrest of Christ, who has returned to sixteenth-century Seville. With his gentle smile of infinite compassion, he is recognized by everyone. The Grand Inquisitor justifies the necessity of arresting and burning Christ at the stake in his interrogation of the prisoner. In the face of Christ's silence both question and answer are left to the Inquisitor and this is as it must be, because he speaks in Christ's name, in the name of Christ's delegation of full powers to the Church of Rome. You promised to make men free but it is we, the Church, who have solved the problem of freedom. We have abolished it 'in order to make men happy'. For the burden of freedom is unbearable. There will never be enough freedom and bread for everyone. Man is weak, he wants earthly bread, he wants to be enslaved, he wants someone to worship. You offered man 'free choice in the knowledge of good and evil'. But men do not want your terrible gift of freedom, they want our mystery, our miracle, our authority, because 'freedom, a free mind and science' confront them with such insoluble mysteries that they long to be enslaved. It is we, the Church, who have taken upon ourselves the curse of the knowledge of good and evil. Ours is the true compassion, the true love for mankind. If you had not rejected the three temptations in the wilderness you could have united humanity in the universal peace of a world state, 'a common, harmonious, and incontestable ant-hill'. The Devil's three temptations, the Grand Inquisitor continues, sum up 'all the insoluble historical contradictions of human nature all the world over'. Together they express 'the whole future history of the world and mankind'.

'The whole future history of the world and of mankind' is Dostoevsky's vision of the coming enslavement of all by socialism, mankind's would-be saviour. The Grand Inquisitor provides the dystopian blueprint for a future totalitarian state, in which in the name of God everything is permitted. Dostoevsky's dystopia is the truth of the nineteenth-century utopias of harmonious anthills, in which all the insoluble historical contradictions of human nature – freedom and obedience, good and evil, compassion and power – are resolved through universal peace and plenty. Dystopia is the truth of utopia, in that both are closed forms that raise the claim to total meaning and turn the dialectic of question and answer into a catechism. Dystopia replaces the questions, which utopia aims to answer, by answers that *extinguish* all questions: in practical terms, the elimination of all those who ask forbidden questions.

Dostoevsky's blueprint starts and ends with the Guardians, who in the name of the redemptive doctrine of Christianity speak of its secular equivalent, socialism. The Guardians preach liberation from sin and suffering. Behind the mask of the founders, however, they practise the total *revaluation of all values*; the ultimate logic of the death of God is Death as God. For 'God is Power', as

Winston Smith learns, and power can only be absolute when all heretics have been destroyed – a task, of course, that can never be completed, for what would orthodoxy do without heresy? From Dostoevsky to Huxley's *Brave New World* the caste system of society (already integral to Plato's *Republic*) undergoes elaboration, to be then systematized into a sociology of industrial-technological civilization in Koestler and Orwell. *Brave New World* in the wake of the First World War signals the moment of the coincidence of utopia and dystopia and reveals the only possible utopia to be the possibility of exiting the closed form – the prison door that the Grand Inquisitor opens to allow Christ to disappear into the night. The door that only individuals can go through, that opens to a promise of happiness, to an escape into the dream of human nature. This utopian other exists only as the vanishing point of *Brave New World* (1931), Koestler's *Darkness at Noon* (1940) and Orwell's *Nineteen Eighty-Four* (1949). They stand as paradigms of the dystopias of the twentieth century and beyond, at the intersection of utopia and dystopia on the one hand and of the novel and science fiction on the other. But all are true to the demands of the form: the unfolding of the ultimate logic of the crushing of human freedom in the name of happiness. This logic unfolds through the catechism of question and answer. As Rubashev observes in *Darkness at Noon*, the speeches and articles of No.1 'had, even in their style, the character of an infallible catechism; they were divided into question and answer with a marvellous consistency in the gross simplification of the actual problems and facts' (Koestler 1964: 142). 'So much the worse for him who took the comedy seriously, who only saw what happened on the stage, and not the machinery behind it' (144). Winston in *Nineteen Eighty-Four* makes the same observation about Big Brother's familiar trick of asking questions only to promptly answer them.

The working of the machinery follows its own inner logic from Huxley to Koestler to Orwell. In each case the subject in question is the object of an experiment. Huxley's Savage is left to destroy himself, Rubashev is led inexorably by his interrogator to accept the answers dictated to him. For Winston, however, is reserved the ultimate truths of the Guardians – the key to the truth of all oligarchies, delivered by his tempter and torturer: 'he was the tormentor, he was the protector, he was the inquisitor, he was the friend' (Orwell 2003: 280). In the catechism of O'Brien, the representative of the Inner Party, we arrive at the *form without latency*: 'we know what we are doing' (Orwell 2003: 302). O'Brien unveils the plotting intelligence at the heart of the will to total power, the plotting intelligence that from Dostoevsky to Orwell and beyond has the task of justifying the god in the machinery of dystopia, the god who is the presiding spirit of technological civilization. As Mustapha Mond explains to the Savage in *Brave New World*, there used to be something called God before the Nine Years' War. Now, however, religious sentiment is superfluous. God exists but 'manifests himself as an absence' (chapter 17). But how could it be other in our civilization? Science, medicine, machinery and universal happiness don't mix with God. In fact, universal happiness demands more than the banishment of religion. Art and science must also disappear. Just as religion is impossible, so too is Shakespeare in a completely stable society of clones, without children, lovers, wives, parents, illness or death to trouble them. And you want to throw all this away plus *soma* and 'unrestricted copulation' in the name of liberty (chapter 16). Moreover, our caste system ensures that everyone is satisfied. Religion, art and science threaten happiness and stability. It is a high price to pay but Mustapha – the Resident World Controller for Western Europe – who has read both Shakespeare and Dostoevsky, foregoes everything that distinguished the old intelligentsia in order to serve happiness: 'Happiness is a hard master – particularly other people's happiness.' The Savage's flight back to nature, back to 'the visible presence of God' is of no avail, since nature has now become an open air zoo in which he appears as the chief exhibit of 'savagery'.

And yet the hidden God continues to make his presence felt, courtesy of Dostoevsky. Rubashov's interrogator and fellow intellectual, Ivanov, the 'son' of Ivan Karamazov, declares:

> I would like to write a Passion play in which God and the Devil dispute for the soul of Saint Rubashov. After a life of sin, he has turned to God ... Satan, on the contrary, is thin, ascetic, and a fanatical devotee of logic. ... he is cold and unmerciful to mankind, out of a kind of mathematical mercifulness. (Koestler 1964: 122)

In this Passion play Ivanov and Rubashov personify the divided soul of the *first* revolutionary generation, because, as Ivanov puts it and as Plato already knew, 'monologues in the form of a dialogue are a useful institution'. Both Ivanov and Rubashov will be liquidated by the end of *Darkness at Noon* to make room for the new intelligentsia, ignorant of religion, art and science. Nothing remains for Rubashov but to justify this historical logic and accept the necessity of his own disappearance in the name of the Party by recognizing that the 'relative immaturity' of the masses renders absolute dictatorship necessary. This is his theory of the pendulum movement of history from freedom to tyranny and back. Technical civilization outstrips the understanding of the masses. The only choices left to the dissident are either the quixotism of impotent revolt and suicide or acceptance of the logic of 'social utility' as the revolutionary's only moral criterion. 'In short, the public disavowal of one's conviction in order to remain in the Party's ranks.' As he is led to execution, one question still remains to which he would have liked an answer: 'But where was the Promised Land? Did there really exist any such goal for this wandering mankind?' (210).

Rubashov's last musings – 'The Party denied the free will of the individual – and at the same time it exacted his willing self-sacrifice' (204) – could serve as the epigraph to *Nineteen Eighty-Four*, since it sums up the ultimate purpose of O'Brien's temptation and destruction of Winston Smith: 'When finally you surrender to us, it must be of your own free will.' We make the heretic one of ourselves before we kill him (Orwell 2003: 292). This act of integration in the form of self-destruction involves three stages: learning, understanding, acceptance. Winston learns through reading the analysis of the Inner Party by its Inner Enemy, Emmanuel Goldstein. His Book of the Brotherhood, *The Theory and Practice of Oligarchical Collectivism* (Trotsky's *The Revolution Betrayed*), is given to Winston by O'Brien. Winston learns that Oceania, Eurasia and Eastasia are engaged in perpetual mobilization and warfare in order to protect their hierarchical societies and caste system from the utopia of common wealth promised before 1914 by the development of science and technology. This possibility has been usurped since the First World War by the new aristocracy of technological civilization, the Party's managerial intelligentsia (cf. Burnham's *Managerial Revolution* of 1943), which wields power through the technology of constant surveillance, a surveillance directed above all against Party members themselves, since the preservation of power depends above all on the morale of the Party, that is, on the will to the ruthless elimination of all inner-Party opposition by means of purges of 'persons who might perhaps commit a crime at some point in the future' (241).

Learning is the *first* stage of understanding the future history of the world as expounded by the Grand Inquisitor. It requires what Orwell terms *Doublethink*, that is, the mental capacity required to retain power indefinitely through the ability to reconcile contradictions (WAR IS PEACE FREEDOM IS SLAVERY IGNORANCE IS STRENGTH). It enables the Party (and the Church) to preserve the name of the cause it supposedly serves and pay lip-service to its ideology (233). 'Thus, the Party rejects and vilifies every principle for which the Socialist movement originally stood, and it chooses to do this in the name of Socialism' (244). This reconciliation of contradictions is the principle, that is, the cause and effect, of the closed form. Understanding, the *second* stage, accordingly takes place in the prison within Oceania's prison.

O'Brien reveals to the prisoner that the Book of the Brotherhood, this compendium of all heresies, has been written by a Party collective including himself. He can therefore vouch for its truth as a self-description of the system. Doublethink requires that the Inner Party be its own Inner Enemy. It is thus not enough to know *how* the Party works. The real question is *why*. Winston believes he knows the answer:

> The choice for mankind lay between freedom and happiness and that, for the great bulk of mankind, happiness was better. That the Party was the eternal guardian of the weak, a dedicated sect doing evil that good might come, sacrificing its own happiness to that of others. (301)

But he has not yet understood either the logic or the truth of Doublethink: 'The Party seeks power entirely for its own sake', since 'God is power'. We, the high priests of power, can only attain integration ourselves through the acceptance of self-destruction, that is, through recognizing that power resides in the collective, through recognizing that slavery *is* in fact freedom. The only exit from the *prison of identity* for the individual is to merge in this *third* stage with the Party, then 'he *is* the Party, then he is all-powerful and immortal' (303), at one with the intoxication of power. However, one last terrifying 'experiment' is still needed before Winston finally accepts that he only imagined that 'there is something called human nature' (308).

Post/human/nature: The body of technology

In his 'Project for a Glossary of the Twentieth Century' J. G. Ballard (1992) defined science fiction as 'the body's dream of becoming a machine'. If we ask where this dream came from, it will not lead us to the usual suspects. Mary Shelley's *Frankenstein*, the archetypal science fiction text, is animated by precisely the opposite dream of creating life from death. On the other hand, the Superman or Batman comics of the 1930s and their second life as films can be seen as trivial versions of Ballard's dream, magic parallels to the contemporaneous totalitarian desire to transform men into machines, into what Lewis Mumford called the mega-machine, composed of living parts (Mumford 1967). The fusion of man and machine in the Worker, the Stakhanovite, the Man of Iron, the Man of Steel (Stalin!) was born from the logic of total mobilization unleashed by the First World War, a logic that no longer distinguished between the battlefield and the assembly line. The body's dream of becoming a machine has another source, however, which appeared before the First World War: Marinetti's *Manifesto of Futurism* (1909). It bequeathed to the European avant-garde of the interwar years two themes that have retained their prophetic power: the will to the transcendence of art and the will to the transcendence of man and nature in the new world of technological civilization. Marinetti styles himself as the leader of a vanguard of Supermen who have conquered Space and Time and stand on 'the furthest promontory of the ages!' 'Why should we be looking back over our shoulders, if what we desire is to smash down the mysterious doors of the Impossible?' (Marinetti 2006: 14).

Marinetti's coupling of art and the machine announced a new aesthetic: the destruction of the museums and academies is to clear the ground for a new beauty, the beauty of speed: 'A racing car, the bonnet decked out with exhaust pipes like serpents with galvanic breath … a roaring motorcar, which seems to race on like machine-gun fire, is more beautiful than the Winged Victory of Samothrace' (13). In 'Extended Man and the Kingdom of the Machine' (1910) Marinetti foresees the creation of a new non-human species in the 'imminent inevitable identification of man with his motorcar', which is but the prelude to 'an incalculable number of human transformations, and we are not joking when we declare that in human flesh wings lie dormant' (86). Here Marinetti is responding to the advent of flight, which offered a new myth for the new century: the Promethean Assumption of Man into the heavens (Wohl 1994: 121). The racing car and the airplane are the heralds of a new civilization that has broken free from the shackles of the past to make speed, the conqueror of space and time, the new god. Marinetti's metallized man announced the new aesthetic of the new civilization: the prototype of collectivized and militarized human beings that appears in the mechanical ballets of the 1920s; in Karol Čapek's play *R.U.R* (Rossum's Universal Robots); in Léger's paintings; in Brecht's play, *A Man Is a Man*; in Jünger's 'organic construction' of the worker as soldier and the soldier as worker.

Film translated the Futurist rhetoric of the 'end of art' into the reality of a new popular technological medium that owed very little to the art of the past and was in the process of developing its own generic conventions. The new medium of film marked in Gianni Vattimo's words the moment of the passage from the avant-garde to the technological death of art, in the form of a theory of mass culture (Vattimo 1988: 151). *Metropolis* (1927) set the pattern for the encounter between technology and art in science fiction cinema. The world of technology is represented in *Metropolis* by the Futurist City and the Factory, presided over by the Master Builder and the Corporation at the summit of the hierarchical architecture of the science fiction city. The Robot hovers between technical wonder and magic aura, just as the film oscillates between the brave new world of technological civilization and archaistic allegory. Thus the machine appears as

Moloch, beneath the Factory are the catacombs of the workers; the longed-for Saviour is the son of the Master Builder; the Robot is burnt as a witch; and society is reborn from the Flood through the reconciliation of head and hand, scientific management and the working class. In the closing scene the cathedral once more asserts its place as the compassionate heart of the city. *Blade Runner* pays tribute to *Metropolis*: the office of the Master Builder returns in the office of the CEO of the Tyrell Corporation, which specializes in robots 'more human than human'. Now it is not the son of the Master Builder but his replicant 'niece', who assumes the role of saviour by embodying the claim to human values in a post-human world. *Metropolis* is thus a landmark in the passage from high to mass culture.

In *Prosthetic Gods* Hal Foster brings out very clearly the ambivalence present from the beginning in the avant-garde dream of the body becoming a machine. He speaks of the double logic of the prosthetic machine governing the machinic imaginary of high modernism in the first decades of the twentieth century: on the one hand, the utopias of the technological enhancement of the body, on the other hand, the dystopias of the dismembered body on the battlefields of the First World War. While the utopian left, mostly constructivist in spirit, was searching for a 'new principle of physical being, a "New Man," especially in revolutionary Russia' through the mechanization of the body (Foster 2014: 110), there was the proto-fascist desire on the right to raise self-alienation to an absolute value. The body is treated as if it were *dead*, waiting to be reassembled in the collective, in Taylor's mechanical assemblage of partial functions and partial organs, in Ernst Jünger's 'organic construction', in Mumford's mega-machine. The death wish of the threatened subject gives rise to an uncanny vitalism: as Foster says, for Marinetti and for Wyndham Lewis the old opposition between the organic and the inorganic has been overcome to produce 'an identity that is at once primordial and futuristic'. Futurism signifies in this sense a wager with reification and death. Behind all the calls for the New Man there lurks the call of the inhuman. The transcendence of man reverses into the armoured body, the soldier into the killing machine (*Robocop* and its sequels attest to the perennial attraction of this theme), the worker into slave. It is left to the 'undead', the avatar replicants of Frankenstein to pose the question of the human in the post-human.

Post/human/nature: *Deus Sive Natura*

When James Lovelock's *Gaia: A New Look at Life on Earth* was published in 1979, in which he advanced the hypothesis that the entire surface of the Earth including life formed a self-regulating entity, it was greeted with scepticism or rejection by the scientific community. The thesis added up to no more than metaphor, a fiction closer to fairy tales about a Greek goddess than to science. It took until the end of the century for the Gaia hypothesis, developed by Lovelock together with the microbiologist Lynn Margalis, to find acceptance as Gaia theory, providing the impetus to the new disciplines of Earth Science systems and Geophysiology and their research programmes. The original idea emerged from the search for ways to detect the presence of life on Mars. It led Lovelock, then working for NASA, to expand the concept of life to all systems from cells through to the biosphere capable of maintaining themselves by decreasing internal entropy. He borrowed the name Gaia from William Golding, his neighbour in the village of Bowerchalke in Wiltshire, for this superorganism composed of all life, tightly coupled with the Earth's atmosphere, oceans and surface rocks. Gaia signifies the remarkable avoidance of the second law of thermodynamics by means of its total cybernetic feedback system which seeks an optimal physical and chemical environment for life on this planet. Gaia thus stands for a self-regulating homeostatic system as an emergent property of interaction among organisms, which has enabled the evolution of life on Earth over billions of years. The first images of the Earth from space reinforced Lovelock's 'new look' at life on Earth – it was, said Margulis, symbiosis seen from space.

Lovelock and Margulis's superorganism was not just new science, however. It was also a tale about the Greek goddess of the Earth, Gea, understood as the mother of all living things. In Plato it appears as the mythic tale of Timaeus, who prefaces his account by cautioning his listeners that since we are all mortal beings we should accept his tale as probable. According to Timaeus, the Demiurge, the Divine Artificer, created order out of chaos and made the universe 'a living creature truly endowed with soul and intelligence' (Plato *Timaeus* 30b). Being a living creature, the world was created according to the likeness of an animal: 'let us suppose the world to be the very image of that whole of which all other animals both individually and in their tribes are portions. For the original of the universe contains in itself all intelligible beings, just as this world comprehends us and all the other visible creatures' (30c, d). In Plato, intelligence precedes and informs the visible copy. In Lovelock, intelligence emerges as a property of living systems, understood as the ability to answer questions correctly through a feedback process of trial and error, as in, for instance, maintenance of homeostasis. Lovelock sees human intelligence as already beginning to function as the brain and nervous system of Gaia, giving us the ability to anticipate climate change. Or, more ominously, setting up the wager between our skills in developing and processing information and our capacity to produce ever more energy and pollution. It is this wager that is at the heart of David Deutsch's deduction of a future galactic synthesis of information and energy that will ultimately lead literally to the God in the machine. Deutsch's deduction, however, is at best (for the next billion years or so) a scientific *fiction*.

But before turning from the extension of the concept of *life* in Lovelock to the extension of the concept of *intelligence* in Deutsch, let me first confront Lovelock's science with Stanislaw Lem's fiction *Solaris* (1970). Even though *Gaia* has progressed from myth via hypothesis to theory, Lem has taken Timaeus's initial proviso to heart, that as mortal men we should not attempt to demand more than probability in relation to our conjectures about the meaning of the universe, even though there seems little doubt that the planet Solaris, covered by water except for a few islands, is a 'homeostatic ocean' (Lem 1970: 18). Whether this signifies primitive oceanic life, as the biologists think, or an extraordinarily evolved structure exceeding terrestrial organic structures, as the astronomers think, was a major debate that has long been superseded by new scientific controversies concerning this 'metamorphosizing ocean', which only serve to replace one enigma by another. Some eighty years of Solaris studies, investigations and experiments have not led to a single indisputable conclusion, leaving young scholars to ask whether the real question is not in fact that of the limitations of human knowledge (23).

Of the three scientists on the space station observing Solaris, one commits suicide on the day Kelvin, sent to decide the future of the whole enterprise, arrives. The two remaining scientists, Snow and Sartorius, are both profoundly affected by their strange experiences in the form of visitors, who seem to form part of an experiment performed on them by the planet. Snow has abandoned any belief in either the protective or predictive power of science, Sartorius by contrast clings desperately to the ideal of scientific knowledge whatever the human cost. Kelvin too soon comes to realize that he is not the subject but the object of an experiment, one in which he, the psychologist, is forced to recognize that man 'has gone out to explore other worlds and other civilizations without having explored his own labyrinth of dark passages and secret chambers' (157). As Snow tells him, if we stay, we might learn something about ourselves (77). Kelvin is forced into this painful process of self-scrutiny by his visitor from Solaris, the living projection of Rheya, his partner who committed suicide ten years earlier. Is *contact* with the planet – the goal of the scientists – perhaps really a question of contact with the self? Kelvin wants to sacrifice all his scientific studies to the living presence of Rheya, 'alive inside me'. Sartorius – mocked by Snow as the Last Knight of the Holy Contact (184), the Don Quixote of service to science – remains determined 'to renounce all personal feelings in order to accomplish our mission' and 'establish an intellectual contact' (160). But whether it is the dream of emotional contact as with Kelvin or of intellectual contact, is contact even possible or meaningful? Snow's is the voice of despairing scepticism: 'We think of ourselves as the knights of the Holy Contact. This is another lie. We are only seeking Man. We have no need of other worlds. We need mirrors' (72). A viewpoint reinforced by the last dream message from the dead third scientist: 'Where there are no men, there cannot be motives accessible to men' (134). All this is summed up in a small heretical pamphlet of the Solaris outsider, Grastrom, who denies the possibility of any form of contact between mankind and non-human civilization. There can be no contact, because such knowledge is incommunicable: 'Transposed into any human language, the values and meaning involved lose all substance' (170, 172).

So we are left as readers with Gastrom's conclusion: 'Solaristics is the space age's equivalent of religion's faith disguised as science.' Lem, it seems, has led us into a hall of mirrors, in which the relation of religion to God and science's relation to nature are mutually reflecting mirrors. The space station remains cut off from the planet outside, connected only by incomprehensible data and visitations. If the space station itself functions as the mirror of the closed form, as the a priori of Lem's allegory, it is in order to show that the answers of religion and of science to 'the meaning of the destiny of man' (172) are solipsistically closed in themselves, two versions of the vain longing for Revelation and Redemption through the Other, whether we call it nature or god. Neither the old answers of humanity's world pictures nor the new answers of the scientific world models amount to more than Timaeus's probable tales. Science is as much a fiction as religion. But is this the last word of *Solaris*? Perhaps there can be no last word other than Kelvin's decision to remain on the space station in the vicinity of Solaris as the adept, the pupil of an imperfect god, a sick god, whose ambitions exceed his powers. This god, who has evolved with mankind, is a god who saves nothing and fulfils no purpose (199). And so Kelvin remains on the shore of the Ocean. 'In the hope of her return? I hoped for nothing. And yet I lived in expectation. Since she had gone, that was all that remained' (204).

Is Kelvin's religion, like Dick's Mercerism, one in which compassion alone gives meaning to the meaningless?

Post/human/nature: *Deus Ex Machina*

Faced by a universe that may well be beyond the comprehension of humans, there are two alternatives. The first, with Lem, is to bow to the mystery. The second is to continue the quest for self-transcendence of the limits of human cognition – a journey, in which theology and science, religion and technology can be seen either as rivals or fellow travellers but also – precisely in science fiction – as mutually illuminating metaphors of humanity's quest for meaning. Max Tegmark sums up the problem very clearly. Matter has two basic drives: the cosmic drive to entropy (physics) and the cosmic drive towards life (biology). If the Earth is an evolving self-organizing system and life is an emergent property of this evolution, then life may be defined as a drive to self-transcendence, which Tegmark divides into three stages: biological evolution, Life 1.0; cultural evolution, Life 2.0; technological evolution, Life 3.0. The third stage is in the realm of science fiction, because, however powerful our current technologies, life is still tied to its biological hardware. We cannot live for a million years, we cannot transform our largely lifeless cosmos into a diverse biosphere that will flourish for billions of years, enabling our universe to fully wake up: 'All this requires life to undergo a final upgrade, to Life 3.0, which can design not only its software but also its hardware. In other words, Life 3.0 is the master of its own destiny, finally fully free from its evolutionary shackles' (Tegmark 2017: 29). There is no reason to suppose, however, that this future master of its own destiny will have any place or use for humans. Under the title Life 3.0 Tegmark's subtitle poses the question of 'Being Human in the Age of Artificial Intelligence'.

What might 'being human' amount to in the age of AI? A preliminary answer takes us back to the physics/biology distinction. The Nobel Prize physicist Steven Weinberg famously observed: 'The more the universe seems comprehensible the more it seems pointless.' To which his fellow physicist Freeman Dyson responded in a seminal article that life is introducing ever more meaning into a pointless universe and concluded that before long we shall know whether Weinberg's universe or his is closer to the truth (Tegmark 314). It is highly likely, as many researchers think, that AI will surpass human intelligence within the foreseeable future with unforeseeable consequences. This confronts us with two fundamental problems, one practical, how do we control the dangers of what Tegmark calls an 'intelligence explosion', and one theoretical, how might we reconcile being human with superintelligence? In his most recent book *Novocene* (2019) James Lovelock envisages a benevolent eco-friendly artificial superintelligence as the future dominant life form on Earth. Nick Bostrom, the Director of the Future of Humanity Institute, Oxford University, by contrast warns of the enormous danger posed by a superintelligent system that would be surprisingly difficult to control because whatever benevolent goals are programmed, their translation into machine-implementable code will likely have unforeseen and unwelcome consequences (Bostrom 2014). Tegmark shares Bostrom's fears. He has been the driving force in establishing the Future of Life Institute, which has brought together such luminaries as Elon Musk and Larry Page together with AI research leaders from academics to companies such as DeepMind, Google, Facebook, Apple, IBM, Microsoft and Baidu; economists, legal scholars and philosophers; and alliances with sister organizations at Berkeley, Oxford and Cambridge Universities and Open AI, a non-profit company, funded by Elon Musk and run by Sam Altman in San Francisco. They all share a common focus on making AI not only beneficial but also safe, according to the AI Principles agreed at the Asilomar (Mexico) conference of The Future of Life Institute in 2017 (Tegmark 326–31).

Tegmark takes us through a series of plausible scenarios following the arrival of superintelligence, ranging from a totalitarian surveillance society, Promethean control over humans, to cyborgs and uploads but only as a prelude to 'The Next 10,000 Years' (chapter 5). There the twelve scenarios fall into recognizable patterns, in only three of which humans remain in control and they are all discouraging: *1984* – a surveillance state bans certain kinds of AI research; *Reversion* – AI is halted by retreat to a pre-technological society; *Enslaved God* – AI is controlled by humans and creates wealth that can be used for good or evil. In the other scenarios AI operates with partial or full control over humans in either protective or destructive fashion. Beyond these scenarios lies the next billion years and beyond that the progressive transformation of matter into mind. And this brings us to Tegmark's question: being human in a post-human world, after Life 2.0 has been superseded by Life 3.0, which has severed the biological link between humans and nature. Tegmark's answer to the question of being human after human nature is to divorce consciousness, hence meaning, from any biological substratum. Life is consciousness, because consciousness is information, that is, a form in a medium, a pattern (such as waves, memories, computations), that has properties independent of its specific physical substratum (Tegmark 300–4). So what does this entail for the next billion years? For Tegmark it means harvesting our cosmic endowment.

Let me conclude with two science-fictional answers to the meaning of the evolution of life – the God in the machine. The one answer is that of David Deutsch, a foundational theorist of quantum computation at Oxford University.

The other is that of Isaac Asimov. They share a common a priori: given sufficient time (approaching infinity) intelligence will attain the ultimate singularity, the ultimate *novum*.

The final chapter 'The Ends of the Universe' of *The Fabric of Reality* (Deutsch 1997) is prefaced by a quotation from Karl Popper: 'Although history has no meaning, we can give it meaning.' The meaning Deutsch proposes is the transcendence of the finite space time of the universe in the release of infinite energy in the universe's final moments – energy that will power the infinite computational capacity of the universal computer. This omega-point will be *omniscient, omnipresent* and *omnipotent* (Deutsch 1997: 355–6). 'The universe will in the end consist, literally, of intelligent thought-processes' (364). And since these thought processes will occur at infinite speed, the end will be endlessly suspended. This ultimate knowledge is, however, pure incommunicable self-knowledge.

Asimov's 'The Last Question' (1956) is his best-known short story and his own favourite. It follows the development of a global computer through a succession of ages, in each of which the latest version is asked the same question: how can the heat death of the universe be averted by decreasing the overall entropy of the system? This is the ultimate question and each time the answer is the same: there is as yet insufficient data for a meaningful answer. Fast forward to the unfolding death of the universe as matter, energy, space and time are extinguished and the collective intelligence of trillions of humans who have colonized the universe is still unable to answer the question. Long after their extinction the computer continues to ponder the problem and finally realizes the way to the reversal of entropy. Since there is no one left to tell, the computer decides on a demonstration: ' "LET THERE BE LIGHT!" And there was light.'

And the cosmic cycle begins again.

Part 2

Science Fiction and the Historical Novel

Andrew Milner

5

Lukács, the historical novel and science fiction

From *The Theory of the Novel* to *The Historical Novel*

Lukács's intellectual reputation hinges on the reception of three main texts, *The Theory of the Novel* (1916), *History and Class Consciousness* (1923) and *The Historical Novel* (1937). David Roberts discussed the first of these extensively in Part 1. The second is widely regarded as a foundational text for what Maurice Merleau-Ponty dubbed 'Western Marxism' (30) and also, along with Karl Mannheim's *Ideology and Utopia* (1936), for what we know as 'the sociology of knowledge'. Like Mannheim, Lukács realized that the social determination of belief postulated by the sociology of knowledge threatened to undermine the pretensions to scientific objectivity of sociology itself. But where Mannheim sought a solution to this dilemma in the role of a socially detached intelligentsia, Lukács's *History and Class Consciousness* sought it in the collective self-knowledge of the working class, Marx's proletariat. This text announced his conversion to a thoroughly Hegelianized Marxism, built around the opposition between 'totality' and 'reification'. Where the 'orthodox Marxism' of the Second and Third Internationals had theorized the relationship between culture and society in terms of a base/superstructure model, in which the economic 'base' determined the cultural 'superstructure', Lukács sought to understand both the base and the superstructure as particular moments within a contradictory totality. So, the 'revolutionary principle' in Marx, as in Hegel, was that of the dialectic, he wrote, 'the concept of totality, the subordination of every part to the whole unity of history and thought' (1971b: 27–8).

For the Lukács of *History and Class Consciousness*, this notion of totality provided the positive pole against which to develop the central, critical concept of 'reification'. Here, he expanded on the discussion of commodity fetishism in volume 1 of Marx's *Capital* (1970: 71–83), reading it in the light both of Hegel and of Max Weber's rationalization thesis, but not that of Marx's own still unpublished *Economic and Philosophical Manuscripts* (1844), to develop what was, in effect, a version of the theory of alienation (1971b: 83–110). By reification Lukács meant something very similar to what Marx had meant by commodity fetishism. But Lukács generalized the notion beyond the commodity relation, so as to insist that capitalism was itself a system of reification. Human reality is necessarily detotalized under capitalism, he argued, both by commodity fetishism and by other reified forms of consciousness, the most important of which is, in fact, science (6–7). For Lukács, reified thought would be overcome only by the proletariat's coming to consciousness of itself as the identical subject and object of history: 'From its own point of view self-knowledge coincides with knowledge of the whole so that the proletariat is at one and the same time the subject and object of its own knowledge' (20). In the early 1920s he clearly viewed the prospects for such a development as fairly imminent: the 'imputed' class consciousness (51) embodied in Marxism would be actualized in the empirical consciousness of a working class led by the revolutionary party. But, as Lukács recoiled from Nazism and, to a lesser extent, from Stalinism, this political optimism gave way to an increasing reliance on the realist novel as the principal totalizing instance in our culture. So, while Perry Anderson is mistaken to see Western Marxism as *born* from a moment of failure (quite the contrary – it was born from a moment of high revolutionary optimism), in Lukács it would eventually be characterized by a 'latent *pessimism*' (1976: 92, 88). Hence, the preoccupation with how culture as ideology functions so as to legitimate the capitalist system, and hence too the growing scepticism as to the possibilities for successful working-class opposition.

The third Lukácsian text, *The Historical Novel*, is a defence of the conventionally Stalinist, or 'Zhdanovite', notion of realism delivered in distinctly non-Stalinist terms. There is, of course, nothing necessarily Stalinist, nor even Marxist, about the concept of realism; to the contrary, it is a fairly conventional category used by both authors and critics to describe the nineteenth-century European novel. But Soviet Communist policy, as laid down by Stalin and other party functionaries, notably Andrei Zhdanov, was built around the combination of, first, a deterministic cultural sociology, representing literature as the determined superstructure of an extra-literary economic base; second, an aesthetic valorizing realism as a mode of cognition; and third, a diagnosis and denunciation of non-realistic bourgeois art forms as 'decadent'. All three themes were elaborated upon by the 1934 Soviet Writers' Congress, where the new cultural policies of 'socialist realism' and 'revolutionary romanticism' were formally announced. In his opening speech to the Congress, Zhdanov insisted that Soviet literature was 'an expression of the successes ... of our socialist system' (17). For Zhdanov, the greatness of great art consisted in its indebtedness to reality: 'Our Soviet writer', he explains, 'derives the material of his works of art ... from the life and experience of the men and women of Dnieprostroy, of Magnitostroy' (20). To achieve this 'means knowing life so as to be able to depict it truthfully', he continued, 'not simply as "objective reality", but to depict reality in its revolutionary development' (21). By contrast, 'the present state of bourgeois literature is such that it is no longer able to create great works of art ... Everything now is growing stunted – themes, talents, authors, heroes ... Characteristic of the decadence and decay of bourgeois culture are the orgies of mysticism and superstition, the passion for pornography' (19). It seems unlikely that a thinker as sophisticated as Lukács would have fully subscribed to all this. But he had good reason to play down his differences: he had fled Berlin in 1933, moving to Moscow, where *The Historical Novel* was written during the winter of 1936–7. And, as Brecht famously observed to Walter Benjamin, when asked whether he had friends in the Russian capital: 'Actually, no I haven't. Neither have the Muscovites themselves – like the dead' (Benjamin 1980: 97–8).

It is common to stress the discontinuity between *The Theory of the Novel* and *The Historical Novel*, marked by the break with Weber (and Georg Simmel) and conversion to Marx (and Lenin). So, where *The Theory of the Novel* subscribes to an essentially Romantic and tragic conception of the novel as the fallen reflection of a prior plenitude, *The Historical Novel* is both determinedly progressive and distinctly anti-Romantic. Hence, Lukács's insistence that it is 'completely wrong' to treat Scott as a Romantic (1969: 34). There are important continuities nonetheless, as signalled by Lukács's continuing commitment to the view that 'in literature what is truly social is form' (1967: 9). Quite apart from this general congruence, there is also a more specific continuity between their respective understandings of the relationship between the epic and the novel. In *The Theory of the Novel*, Lukács had defined the classical epic, which gives form to the 'extensive totality of life', against classical tragedy, which gives form to the 'intensive totality of essence'; and then the novel against the epic proper, as 'the epic of an age in which the extensive totality of life is no longer directly given ... yet which still thinks in terms of totality' (1971a: 46, 56). So, in the novel heroes become seekers after totality, individuals rather than representatives of a community (60, 66). In *The Historical Novel*, he returns to this understanding of the novel as a bourgeois epic, and once again counterposes the epic to the drama. 'In drama', Lukács writes, 'historical authenticity means the inner historical truth of the [great historical – AM] collision.' In the novel, by contrast, the aim 'is to represent a particular social reality at a particular time, with all the colour and specific atmosphere of that time ... Everything else, both collisions and ... "world-historical individuals" ..., is no more than means to this end' (1969: 177).

The Historical Novel opens with an argument that the central achievement of the early nineteenth-century historical novel, above all in Sir Walter Scott, was its capacity to represent the difference between the pre-capitalist past of 'gentile' or clan society and the capitalist present, through historically different typical characters in historically different typical situations. 'What is lacking in the so-called historical novel before Sir Walter Scott', Lukács wrote, 'is precisely the specifically historical ... derivation of the individuality of characters from the historical peculiarity of their age' (15). So, while earlier supposedly 'historical' novels had imagined characters from the past as essentially identical to people in the author's present, Scott was able to portray 'the struggles and antagonisms of history by means of characters who, in their psychology and destiny, always represent social trends and historical forces' (33). Lukács draws two important inferences from this more general proposition. The first is that the 'great figures' in these novels, for example Rob Roy, or Robin Hood in *Ivanhoe*, normally play only minor compositional roles and, conversely, that the protagonists, by contrast, are normally 'mediocre' figures. Scott, he argues, 'lets his important figures grow out of the being of the age, he never explains the age from the position of its great representatives, as do the Romantic hero-worshippers. Hence, they can never be central figures of the action' (40). The second is that 'Scott aims at portraying the totality of national life in its complex interaction between "above" and "below"'. These are national stories, then, stories of how nations are made, in which ' "below" is seen as the material basis and artistic explanation for what happens "above"' (52). And Scott 'affirms this progress', Lukács writes: 'He is a patriot, he is proud of the development of his people.' This patriotism is 'vital', Lukács continues, insofar as it establishes a 'felt relationship to the present', which brings 'the past to life as the prehistory of the present' (57). For Scott (and Lukács), historical characterization doesn't mean mere detail. Rather, 'it means that certain crises in the personal destinies of a number of human beings coincide and interweave within the determining context of an historical crisis' (42).

This difference between Scott and his predecessors is not merely a matter of individual talent, but of collective historical experience, Lukács writes, because 'the French Revolution, the revolutionary wars and the rise of Napoleon ... for the first time made history a *mass experience*, and moreover on a European scale' (20). Lukács asks why this should have happened initially in 'England' rather than France or Germany? As an aside, it's worth noting that this actually occurred in Scotland, rather than England, a distinction which escapes Lukács's notice. Not only was Scott himself Scottish, however, but so too are all nine of the Waverley novels published before *Ivanhoe* (1820), from *Waverley* in 1814 to *A Legend of Montrose* in 1819. So, Lukács sees Scott as the storyteller of the making of a British nation, but this was only true insofar as the British story can be understood as an amalgam of different stories about the making of different Scottish and English nations. Lukács's answer to his own question, nonetheless, is that 'the relative stability of English development during this stormy period, in comparison with that of the Continent, made it possible to channel this newly-awoken historical feeling artistically into a broad, objective, epic form' (31). This objectivity is further enabled by Scott's political conservatism, which sought the 'middle way' between extremes and thus distanced itself from triumphant Hanoverian Whiggery, in what Lukács, following Engels, terms a 'triumph of realism' (59). Elsewhere in Europe, Lukács argues, the historical novel remains underdeveloped until Balzac, who 'passes from the portrayal of *past history* to the portrayal of the *present as history*' (94) in *La Comédie Humaine* (1829–47) and Tolstoy's *War and Peace* (1869), which represents 'a brilliant renewal and development of Scott's classical type of historical novel' (98).

The decline of the historical novel?

After a long aside on the historical novel and historical drama, built around Hegel's contrast between a 'totality of objects' in the epic and a 'totality of movement' in the drama, Lukács turns to what he terms 'the crisis of bourgeois realism' after 1848 (202). Just as Scott's Waverley novels had marked the emergence of a new historical sensibility, so Flaubert's *Salammbô* (1862) marks its decline into 'decorative monumentalization, the devitalizing, dehumanizing and at the same time making private of history' (237). This, too, is a matter of collective experience rather than individual talent, a direct product of the bourgeois revolutions of 1848 and the consequent changes in dominant conceptions of history and progress, which led increasingly to the elimination of notions of contradiction, in short, to the transformation of revolutionary democracy into compromising liberalism (202). Lukács's editorializing against post-1848 bourgeois liberalism is the political corollary of the anti-modernist aesthetics he would develop elsewhere (1963: 17–46), here prefigured in the polemic against 'naturalism' in the historical novel. Neither seems especially pertinent to a world that has now become both post-bourgeois and post-modernist, although not thereby post-capitalist. And his predictions of the genre's decline are clearly falsified by the evidence of the continuing vitality of what his former postgraduate student, Agnes Heller, would later describe as the 'contemporary historical novel'. For Heller, the postmodern historical novel, inaugurated by Umberto Eco's *Il nome della rosa* (1980), sees history as a series of riddles to be solved, after the fashion of the detective novel, rather than as an account of teleological progress (93).

Writing in the same year as Heller, Anderson traced the 'postmodern turn' in the historical novel to Latin American magic realism. He identified the contrast between Lukács's *The Historical Novel* and Benjamin's last major work, the 'Theses on the Philosophy of History', written shortly before his suicide at Port Bou in 1940, as that between 'progress' and 'catastrophe'. Benjamin's ninth thesis, on Paul Klee's 'Angelus Novus', famously represents history as a catastrophe, a storm blowing from Paradise, which propels the angel of history 'into the future to which his back is turned, while the pile of debris before him grows skyward. This storm is what we call progress' (1973: 260). Anderson concludes that the postmodern historical novel is much closer to Benjamin's vision than to Lukács: 'The persistent backdrops to the historical fiction of the postmodern period are at the antipodes of its classical forms. Not the emergence of the nation, but the ravages of empire; not progress as emancipation, but impending or consummated catastrophe' (2011: 28). This is clearly a much bleaker account than that in Heller. As a judgement on Latin American magic realism, towards which it is primarily directed, it makes a certain sense. But is it really fair comment on Eco, whose William of Baskerville represents critical reason in the face of medieval superstition, even if reason finally fails? Or on Hilary Mantel's Thomas Cromwell trilogy, *Wolf Hall* (2009), *Bring Up the Bodies* (2012) and *The Mirror and the Light* (2020), the most commercially and critically acclaimed of all recent Anglophone historical novels, in which Cromwell represents the triumph of critical reason and upward social mobility, even if both are eventually thwarted? Anderson himself seems to believe that the collapse of the Soviet Union in 1991 has resulted in a collective loss of a sense of history. Hence, his judgement that the postmodern historical novel represents 'a desperate attempt to waken us to history, in a time when any real sense of it has gone dead' (2011: 28). But this seems a very peculiar verdict on both the history and the literature, given that the momentous events of 1989–91 were experienced by many, perhaps most, as precisely the kind of mass experience of history Lukács detected in the French Revolutionary and Napoleonic periods.

The concluding chapter to Lukács's *The Historical Novel* is devoted to the 'historical novel of democratic humanism', that is, the anti-Fascist novel exemplified by writers like Lion Feuchtwanger, Heinrich and Thomas Mann, and Romain Rolland. This is clearly in Anderson's terms progressive rather than catastrophic criticism. Hence, Lukács's own admission in the 'Preface to the English Edition' that its politics were 'too optimistic' (1969: 10). During these years when Lukács and Benjamin were writing about history writing, that is, roughly 1936–40, external history had indeed become catastrophic rather than progressive. But the Allied victory in 1945 clearly reversed this judgement. Hence, the distinctly progressive register of much US American and Soviet Russian post-war science fiction, or SF, for example Isaac Asimov's *Foundation* trilogy (1951–3) and Arkady and Boris Strugatsky's *Noon Universe* novels (1961–85). No doubt, this was less true of French and British SF, the sociopolitical subtext of which seems for the main part to be the decline of Empire rather than the Allied victory. But here, as elsewhere, history is written by the victors, that is, by the Americans and the Russians. Lukács might well have noted that his concluding chapter was not only too optimistic, at least in the short term, but also too prescriptive, insofar as its political aesthetics trumped its sociology. Stripped of its more aggressively prescriptive aspects, however, that is, rendered more properly sociological, Lukács's account came to provide Fredric Jameson with the raw materials for a powerful new reading of the relations between the historical novel and SF. It is to this that we now turn.

The historical novel and science fiction

In some accounts, SF is represented as having had a very long history. So, Darko Suvin, the doyen of academic SF studies, identifies six main instances of SF in the 'Euro-Mediterranean tradition': the Hellenic (Aeschylus, Aristophanes, Plato, Theopompus, Euhemerus, Hecataeus, Iambulus); the Hellenic-cum-Roman (Virgil, Antonius Diogenes, Lucian); the Renaissance-Baroque (More, Rabelais, Bacon, Campanella, Cyrano, Swift); the democratic revolution (Mercier, Saint-Simon, Fourier, Blake, Shelley); the fin-de-siècle (Bellamy, Morris, Verne, Wells); and the modern (from Wells, Zamyatin and Čapek through Gernsback to the present) (2016: 105). Adam Roberts's (2005) *The History of Science Fiction* takes a similarly long view, tracing the genre back, firstly, to the ancient Greek novel and, secondly, to Reformation Protestantism, the two beginnings seen as separated by an 'interlude' between AD 400 and

1600, during which fantasy prevailed over SF (32–5). I confess to some scepticism about such long histories for the very reason Roberts discounts, that '*something* happened to science in the Victorian age' (xv, 4). Something did, indeed, happen to science in the nineteenth century, not the cultural division between arts and sciences he addresses, but rather the development of new kinds of relationship between science and technology. Clearly, any culture that possesses both science and fiction can logically produce SF (which incidentally precludes the European Middle Ages). But specifically modern SF, that is, fiction concerned with science as technology, has a much shorter history: it emerges in England and France in the nineteenth century; the key texts are Mary Shelley's *Frankenstein* (1818), Jules Verne's *Voyages Extraordinaires* (1863–1905) and H. G. Wells's 'scientific romances', utopias and dystopias (1895–1939). When Suvin treats science as 'cognitive logic' (79) and Roberts as a 'philosophical outlook' (11–12) both thereby overlook the fundamental historical difference between our contemporary understandings of science and those of antiquity and early modernity, that is, that the Industrial Revolution decisively and definitively redefined science into an intensely practical activity inextricably productive of new technologies. And this is clearly how contemporary SF continues to understand science: Ursula K. Le Guin's Hainish Ekumen is made possible by the ansible produced from Shevek's General Temporal Theory; Gene Roddenberry's United Federation of Planets by the science that produced Starfleet's warp drive. Nothing even vaguely similar exists in Aristophanes or Lucian, Campanella or Cyrano.

So, how do we make sense of the emergence of this comparatively recent new genre? Jameson understands 'the new genre of SF as a form which now registers some nascent sense of the future, and does so in the space on which a sense of the past had once been inscribed', that is, the space of the historical novel (2005: 286). The connection between the genres arises, he explains, because each is 'the symptom of a mutation in our relationship to historical time' (284). He argues that the historical novel ceased to be 'functional' roughly contemporaneously with the beginnings of SF, in the simultaneous historical moment of Flaubert's *Salammbô*, in 1862, and Verne's *Cinq Semaines en ballon*, in 1863 (285). This is empirically very astute, for, just as French publishing in the earlier decades of the nineteenth century was dominated, in terms of both sales and translations, by the historical novels of Alexandre Dumas – whom Lukács systematically ignores – so the later decades would be dominated by Verne's *Voyages Extraordinaires*. We might add that Verne was a protégé of Dumas and that Verne's second SF novel, written in the same year as *Cinq Semaines en ballon*, but rejected by Hetzel as too pessimistic, was in fact the future history *Paris au XXe siècle*.

Jameson sees the emergence of SF and the decline of the historical novel into 'archaeology' as functions of an increased collective inability to understand the present as history. The new genre's sense of the future cannot therefore entail the imaginary representation of any real future, but must rather work primarily 'to defamiliarize and restructure our experience of our own *present*' (286). And it does so primarily by 'transforming our own present into the determinate past of something yet to come' (288). He concludes that 'SF thus enacts and enables a structurally unique "method" for apprehending the present as history, and this is so irrespective of the "pessimism" or "optimism" of the imaginary future world which is the pretext for that defamiliarization', citing Verne as the paradigmatic optimist and Philip K. Dick as the paradigmatic pessimist (288). Jameson's interests lay with late twentieth-century US American SF rather than nineteenth-century French, so the argument slips very quickly from Verne to Dick, and thence to the proposition, repeated throughout *Archaeologies of the Future*, that the 'deepest vocation' of both SF and utopia is to bring home 'our constitutional inability to imagine Utopia' (289). But utopia and SF are nothing like so implicated in each other as Jameson believes. The term 'utopia' was, of course, coined by Thomas More in 1516, and the epigraphic hexastichon included in the first four editions of *Utopia*, reminds us that this neologism was, in the first instance, a Greek pun in Latin between 'ou topos', meaning no place, and 'eu topos', meaning good place (18–19). Topos means place or space, as noted, rather than time. And the most important historically recent transformation in the utopian genre, clearly occasioned by European success in mapping the world, has been the relocation of plausible better and worse worlds from geographical now-space into historical future-time. So SF, whether utopian, dystopian or neither, has overwhelmingly become future history. Hence, the shift discussed by David Roberts in Part 1, from what it means to be human to what it might mean to be post-human: post-humanity is always logically ahead of us, even if located temporally in our past, as it was in Shelley's *Frankenstein*.

Science fiction and utopia

Jameson's own stress on the close interconnections between SF and utopia derives substantially from Suvin, who had argued that utopia 'is not a genre' in its own right, but rather '*the sociopolitical subgenre of science fiction*'. For Suvin,

'SF can finally be written only between the utopian and anti-utopian horizons. All imaginable intelligent life ... can be organized only more or less perfectly' (76). Persuasive though this might seem, it very obviously isn't so: as the history of literary realism attests, fictional worlds can in fact be organized very much like our own reality, neither more nor less perfectly. And this is actually also the case for SF, which might occasionally be utopian, has more often been dystopian, but is even more often neither. By virtue of this move Suvin had, however, expanded SF to accommodate not only More and Bacon, Rabelais and Campanella, Saint-Simon and Fénelon, but also Aeschylus and Aristophanes. It is a move clearly at odds with contemporary usage among most SF writers, fans and critics, but warmly endorsed by Jameson on at least five occasions (2005: xiv, 57, 393, 410, 414–15). Phillip Wegner, a former student of Jameson, is similarly supportive of the view that 'science fiction and utopia are inseparable' (xviii). And Carl Freedman, yet another Jamesonian, argues that SF 'reinvents the older genre and energizes it with the kind of concrete utopian potentiality ... available in the age when the future has ... finally come into existence' (78). In effect, Freedman, Wegner, Suvin and Jameson are each attempting a redefinition of SF aimed at retrospectively 'englobing' the genre of utopia (Suvin 2016: 76).

Jameson's own intentions were, of course, expressly political. 'What is crippling', he writes, 'is ... the universal belief ... that no other socio-economic system is conceivable, let alone practically available'. The value of the utopian form thus consists in its capacity as 'a representational meditation on radical difference, radical otherness, and ... the systematic nature of the social totality' (xii). This tells us much of what we need to know about the politics of utopia as a genre, but not necessarily about those of SF. The argument is resumed when Jameson later writes that utopia provides 'the answer to the universal ideological conviction that no alternative is possible'. It does so, he insists, 'by forcing us to think the break itself ... not by offering a more traditional picture of what things would be like after the break'. Hence, the conclusion that utopia is 'a meditation on the impossible, on the unrealizable in its own right' (232). Here, however, Jameson's argument is linked to a distinctive case for the peculiar contemporary relevance of utopia. Ever since Marx and Engels, supposedly 'scientific' socialisms have repeatedly asserted their superiority over utopianism on the grounds that they know, scientifically and theoretically, how to achieve what utopians can only imagine in fantasy. As *The Communist Manifesto* puts it, utopias are merely 'fantastic pictures of future society, painted at a time when the proletariat is still in a very undeveloped state and has but a fantastic conception of its own position' (116). But Jameson picks up on an observation of the ageing Lukács that by the 1960s this had clearly ceased to be the case (1974: 115–16). The erstwhile weaknesses of utopianism, its inability to provide an adequate account of either agency or transition, therefore 'becomes a strength', Jameson concludes, 'in a situation in which neither ... seems currently to offer candidates for solution'. In the early twenty-first century, then, and for much the same reasons as before 1848, utopia 'better expresses our relationship to a genuinely political future than any current program of action' (2005: 232). No doubt, Jameson has every right to define his position against anti-utopianism: we probably do 'need to develop an anxiety about losing the future ... analogous to Orwell's anxiety about the loss of the past' (233). It isn't at all obvious, however, that any of this has any necessary relation to SF in general, as distinct from Jameson's own preferred examples of the genre.

The first part of Jameson's *Archaeologies* closes with a moving invocation of the Mattapoisett utopians in Marge Piercy's *Woman on the Edge of Time*, who travel back in time 'to enlist the present in their struggle to exist' (233). But the juxtaposition of Orwell and Piercy serves to remind us that Jameson's anti-anti-utopianism is textual as well as contextual, that it is informed by and in turn informs a clear preference for the utopian SF of his own time and place, the American New Wave, as against other versions of SF, such as the American hard SF of the 1940s and 1950s, or early-mid twentieth-century European dystopian SF. The vantage point from which Jameson writes is clearly that of an American sixties radical adrift in postmodern late capitalism. Its inner sympathy with novelists like Piercy and Le Guin, Robinson and Dick, provides his writing with real strengths. But, to reverse Jameson's own reversal of Benjamin, the effectively utopian is also, at the same time, necessarily ideological (1981: 286). And this is as true of anti-anti-utopianism as of utopianism itself. We can conclude, then, that SF may indeed be occasionally utopian (as in Bellamy's *Looking Backward* or Iain M. Banks's 'Culture' novels); it has more often been dystopian (Karel Čapek, Huxley, Orwell, Zamyatin); but is even more often neither. Not one of the fifty-four novels Verne published in his lifetime is a utopia and the sole dystopia, *Paris au XXe siècle*, remained unpublished until 1994. Of the eight novels in Victor Gollancz's 1933 collection of *The Scientific Romances of H.G. Wells*, only *In the Days of the Comet* and *Men Like Gods* were utopias and the first, simultaneously both utopia and dystopia, was dropped from the *Seven Science Fiction Novels* collection published in the United States the following year. Wells's most successful experiment with utopia as a genre, *A Modern Utopia*, is hardly science-fictional at all. One way to represent the relationship between utopia, SF and 'fantasy', the obvious third term in these discussions, would be through a Venn diagram, showing three circles each representing a different non-realistic genre. The overlap between the circles would then mark the four logically possible hybrid forms, utopian fantasy, utopian SF, SF-fantasy and, where all three overlap, utopian SF-fantasy. Empirical examples of the first include Morris's *News from Nowhere*, of the second Banks's Culture novels, the third China Miéville's New Crobuzon trilogy, and the fourth Piercy's *Woman on the Edge of Time*. The areas of non-overlap, by contrast, would represent non-hybrid forms of utopia, SF and fantasy, examples of which include, respectively, More's *Utopia*, Verne's *De la terre à la lune* and Tolkien's *The Lord of the Rings*. The significant point here is that More and Tolkien fall outside the SF tradition, while Banks, Miéville, Piercy and Verne do not.

Here, it might prove helpful to draw on Raymond Williams's analysis of the relations between SF, utopia and fantasy, which he understood as distinct but cognate forms. There are four characteristic types of alternative reality, he argues, the paradise or hell, the positively or negatively externally altered world, the positive or negative willed transformation and the positive or negative technological transformation. SF, utopia and dystopia are each centrally concerned with the 'presentation of *otherness*', he continues, and thus depend on an element of discontinuity from 'realism'. But the discontinuity is more radical in non-utopian/non-dystopian SF, since the utopian and dystopian modes require for their political efficacy an 'implied connection' with the real: the whole point of utopia or dystopia is to acquire some positive or negative leverage on the present. By contrast, other kinds of SF and fantasy are free to enjoy greater latitude in their relations to the real. The willed transformation and the technological transformation are therefore the more characteristically utopian or dystopian modes, because transformation – how the world might be changed, whether for better or worse – will normally be more important to utopia than otherness per se.

SF can and does deploy all four modes, but in each case drawing on science. So, SF may be utopian or dystopian, and utopias and dystopias may be science-fictional, but the genres are analytically distinguishable, nonetheless, by virtue of the presence or absence of science, technology and quasi-science (the example Williams gives is time-travel) (95–8). This issue is carefully avoided by Suvin's own treatment of science as equivalent to cognition (19–22), but remains central for Williams. And rightly so, for this is what most clearly distinguishes SF, not only from the 'older and now residual modes' such as the Earthly Paradise, the Blessed Islands, the Land of Cockayne, but also from non-SF utopias (Williams: 97). Williams traces the utopian tradition from More and Bacon through to Bulwer-Lytton, Bellamy, Morris and Wells, but sees it as running aground in the early twentieth century, when it is effectively superseded by dystopia. In these chronologically subsequent dystopias – paradigmatically, Zamyatin, Huxley and Orwell – utopia 'lies at the far end of dystopia, but only a few will enter it; the few who get out from under'. Hence, Williams's conclusion that utopia and SF tend eventually to travel the path followed by 'bourgeois cultural theory' more generally, from 'universal liberation', through a phase when the 'minority' educates and regenerates the 'majority', to the 'last sour period', when 'minority culture' searches out and finds a hiding-place 'beyond both the system and the fight against the system' (107). This pessimism is offset, however, by Williams's more general insistence that SF 'is always potentially a mode of authentic shift: a crisis of exposure which produces a crisis of possibility; a reworking, in imagination, of *all* forms and conditions' (109).

But what of Jameson's further claim that SF is constitutionally incapable of imagining utopia? Kim Stanley Robinson is a distinguished SF writer, winner of two Hugo Awards for Best Novel, a would-be ecotopian and, interestingly, a former student of Jameson, who has explicitly argued to the contrary. He writes: 'All portrayed societies are stylised and hypothetical ... this notion that we cannot imagine utopia is mistaken. We can imagine utopia ... The constraints are very slack and our imaginations strong. We are quite capable of taking the present situation, and all history too, and ringing every possible physical and logical change in our ideas to make something new' (2016: 7). The problem, he adds, is not that of imagining utopia but of 'getting from here to there' (8). Hence, his diagnosis of the central weakness of his own utopian novel, *Pacific Edge*, that it cannot deal with the fact that 'there are guns under the table' (3).

That said, Jameson's notion that SF and the historical novel are closely cognate genres, insofar as, at the most fundamental of levels, both take human historicity as their central subject matter, seems a much more productive starting point than the post-Suvinian preoccupation with More, which actually directs most of *Archaeologies*. For, the typical subject matter of SF is future history, uchronia and dyschronia rather than utopia and dystopia, its precursors therefore Scott and Dumas rather than More and Francis Bacon. Hence, the ritualistic invocation of 'tomorrow' by Hugo Gernsback in his *Amazing Stories*, even of 'tomorrow and tomorrow's tomorrow' by John W. Campbell in *Astounding Science-Fiction* (Gernsback 1926: 3; Campbell 1938: 37). Hence, more interestingly, Robinson's argument that SF 'is an historical literature', in which there is always 'an explicit or implicit fictional history that connects the period depicted to our present moment'. 'The two genres are not the same', he continues, but 'more alike ... than either is like the literary mainstream'. 'They share some methods and concerns', he concludes, 'in that both must describe cultures that cannot be physically visited by the reader; thus both are concerned with alien cultures, and with estrangement. And both genres share a view of history which says that times not our own are yet vitally important to us' (1987: 54–5).

Robinson is a political optimist and an avowed humanist, but a similarly historical conception informs the work of as pessimistic a misanthrope as Michel Houellebecq. The post-human narrators of the latter's first SF novel, *Les particules élémentaires*, explain that 'Ce livre est avant tout l'histoire d'un homme, qui vécut la plus grande partie de sa vie en Europe occidentale, durant la seconde moitié du XX siècle ... les hommes de sa generation passerent en outre leur vie dans la solitude et l'amertume. (This book is principally the story of a man who lived out the greater part of his life in Western Europe, in the latter half of the twentieth century ... the men of his generation lived out their lonely, bitter lives)' (2000a: 7; 2000b: 3). The novel is, in short, a history of how post-68 France produced a culture so dire as to prompt humanity to preside over its own abolition. Houellebecq's third future history novel, *La carte et le territoire*, repeats the trope: 'L'oeuvre qui occupa les dernières années de la vie de Jed Martin peut ainsi être vue – c'est l'interprétation la plus immédiate – comme une méditation nostalgique sur la fin de l'âge industriel en Europe, et plus généralement sur le caractère périssable et transitoire de toute industrie humaine. (The work that occupied the last years of Jed Martin's life can thus be seen – and this is the first interpretation that springs to mind – as a nostalgic meditation on the end of the industrial age in Europe, and, more generally, on the perishable and transitory nature of any human industry)' (2010: 428; 2011: 291).

Precisely because SF is historical it often deploys very similar strategies to those in the historical novel. A good example of this is in its treatment of fictional 'great figures'. Where these appear in SF, they are typically marginal to the action in the way Lukács had observed in the historical novel, for example: Verne's Captain Nemo in *Vingt mille lieues sous les mers* (1869–70); Aldous Huxley's Mustapha Mond in *Brave New World* (1932); George Orwell's Big Brother and Emmanuel Goldstein in *Nineteen Eighty-Four* (1949); Asimov's Hari Seldon and the Mule in the original *Foundation* trilogy; Le Guin's King Argaven Harge XV in *The Left Hand of Darkness* (1969); J. G. Ballard's President Jerry Brown in *Hello America* (1981); William Gibson's Tessier-Ashpools in the *Neuromancer* trilogy (1984–8); Wolfgang Jeschke's Nicholas Cusanus in *Das Cusanus-Spiel* (2005); Jean-Marc Ligny's Anthony Fuller in *Aqua™* (2006); Robinson's Phil Chase in the *Science in the Capital* trilogy (2004–7); Margaret Atwood's Crake and Adam One in the

MaddAddam trilogy (2004–13); Paolo Bacigalupi's Catherine Case in *The Water Knife* (2015); Houellebecq's Mohammed Ben-Abbes in *Soumission* (2015). More importantly, most SF, though not all, is quite explicitly future history. Of course, some is set in the present or a near future almost indistinguishable from the present, many of Verne's voyages, for example, and some are set in the past, like Shelley's *Frankenstein*, but the vast majority are set well into the future. Some of the most important recent examples of future history are those congregated around what Daniel Bloom in 2007 dubbed 'cli-fi' (Merchant 2013), that is, the fiction of anthropogenic global heating. This is so for the very obvious reason that climate fiction typically projects into the future from observable current trends in climate behaviour so as either to warn or inspire. In the next chapter we will explore the historicity of recent European and North American cli-fi.

6

Climate fiction as the future historical novel

Climate fiction, progress and catastrophe

Fictions about extreme climate change are at least as old as the story of Ūta-napišti in the *Sha naqba īmuru/Epic of Gilgamesh* Tablet XI (George 2003) and the story of Noah in *Bereshith/Genesis* VI–VIII. Both tell of world-destroying floods and in both the cause is divine, or theogenic. There is no denying the power of these flood narratives nor their enduring influence over subsequent Judaeo-Christo-Islamic culture. Interestingly, there are no equivalent ice or fire narratives in any of the extant Akkadian or Hebrew sources. So, when modern SF began to take shape in Europe in the early nineteenth century, it is unsurprising that it inherited a preoccupation with the Great Flood from its parent cultures. Witness, for example, the closing scenes in Mary Shelley's *The Last Man* (1826) and both parts of Richard Jefferies's *After London* (1885). These texts – and many others besides – tell of floods that destroy or damage human civilization, but which are never strictly speaking anthropogenic. There is, however, a limit text, published only four years later than *After London*, where anthropogenically produced rising sea levels are anticipated, but nevertheless not actually realized, Verne's 1889 novel *Sans dessus dessous*.

Verne's novel is the third in the 'Baltimore Gun-Club' trilogy, following *De la terre à la lune* (1865) and *Autour de la lune* (1870). Here, the same three American characters, Impey Barbicane, J. -T. Maston and Captain Nicholl, come out of retirement, planning to use the recoil of a huge cannon, the same technology as in the earlier novels, to shift the tilt of the earth's axis, so that it becomes perpendicular to the planet's orbit. As a result, the vast coal deposits under the polar ice cap will be made available for mining. Barbicane explains to their investors: 'le but de notre nouvelle Société est l'exploitation des houillères du Pôle arctique, dont la concession nous a été faite par le gouvernement fédéral' (the object of our Club is to explore the large coal fields situated in the Arctic regions, which we have recently purchased and to which we hold a title from the [American] Federal Government) (1978: 93). Interestingly, Barbicane's pitch nicely anticipates twenty-first century concerns about peak oil: 'Il est donc certain ... que la houille, cette substance précieuse entre toutes, s'épuisera en un temps assez limité par suite d'une consommation à outrance.' (It is certain that coal is the most precious substance, and will some day, on account of the large consumption of it; fail in its supply) (94). The Gun-Club is thus planning for nothing less than intentionally induced anthropogenic climate change, in which the relocation of the poles will result in their being melted. The Gun-Club does succeed in producing a man-made tsunami and flood, but it fails in the attempt to melt the ice caps. And the explanation is reassuringly simple: Maston had made a crucial mistake in his calculations by accidentally erasing three zeros during a telephone call from the widowed Mrs Scorbitt, who has largely financed their project (204). The novel's conclusion is equally reassuring: 'les habitants du globe peuvent dormir en paix. Modifier les conditions dans lesquelles se meut la Terre, cela est au-dessus des efforts permis à l'humanité' (the inhabitants of the earth may sleep in peace. To modify the conditions in which the earth is moving is beyond the efforts of humanity) (208). But twenty-first century readers might sleep less well. For, although it's still not possible to shift the earth's axis, powerful processes are now at work that could indeed melt the ice caps and make it practicable to mine for coal or drill for oil in both the Arctic and Antarctica.

There is an interesting theoretical point to make here. In the previous chapter we noted the contrast between Lukács's progressive view of history and Benjamin's catastrophic view. These each imply different ways of reading historical texts. For Lukács, it means situating the text in its historical context; for Benjamin's fourteenth thesis, however, it means filling time 'by the presence of the now [*Jetzteit*]', that is, blasting it 'out of the continuum of history' (1973: 263). Our approach here will be mainly Lukácsian, but it is worth noting that, in the midst of the twenty-first century climate crisis, a Benjaminian remaking of *Sans dessus dessous* might prove very compelling. For Benjamin himself, this would have been the work of the 'historical materialist' critic; but today it could just as easily be that of the film or television adaptation. An obviously relevant example is Darren Aronofsky's *Noah* (2014), which retells the *Bereshith* story in ways that point directly towards the twenty-first century. In rough outline, the film follows the narrative set out in the Hebrew original, but this is elaborated upon in very original fashion. So, the wickedness of the antediluvian human society the Creator determines to punish is represented as industrialized and polluting in ways that resemble our world in our time but which no early historical society can ever have been. And the 'Watchers', the fallen angels who help Noah build his ark, and who clearly have no counterparts in any Jewish canonical text, are thoroughly science-fictional stone monsters who could have been at home in *Flash Gordon* or *Galaxy Quest*. As a result, the film has a certain timeless quality, which renders it much closer to SF than to the more traditional Hollywood biblical epic. It also makes a radically controversial intervention into contemporary theological debates over the relationship between humankind and the natural world, generally polarized between those who stress 'dominion', typically right-wing fundamentalist creationists, and those who stress 'stewardship', typically the more liberal ecotheologians. Aronofsky's Noah is an ecotheologian avant la lettre, while the argument for dominion is made by the film's chief villain, Cain's descendant Tubal-cain, here played as a kind of Renaissance cockney gangster.

Short-term future history

So, what kinds of future history has contemporary cli-fi produced to date? Some utopian cli-fi clearly deals in very short-term history, for example Dirk C. Fleck's *Maeva!* trilogy (2008–15). The trilogy comprises *Das Tahiti-Projekt* set in 2022, *MAEVA!*, or *Das Südsee-Virus*, set in 2028, and *Feuer am Fuss* set in 2035. In combination, they recount the immediate future history of a world threatened by climate collapse, but ultimately saved by the 'Equilibrist' notions propounded by Maeva, originally as president of Tahiti, later as head of the 'United Regions of the Pacific', later still of the 'United Regions of the Planet' (2011: 209). The URP develops initially as a loose ecotopian alternative to the United Nations, inspired by the success of Maeva's 'Tahiti-Projekt', but soon opens itself up to subnational regions like Alaska, South Tyrol, Dithmarschen and Alsace, as well as nation-states. Fleck has himself been the most determinedly utopian of all cli-fi writers in contemporary Germany, which is perhaps why there is so little that we might recognize as history, fictional or real, in his novels. Rather, the URP wins by force of its ideas and Maeva's personality, whether present in the flesh or as 'der Maeva-Mythos ... im Cyberspace möglich geworden' (the Maeva-Mythos ... made possible by Cyberspace) (170). Insofar as there is history, it is Tahitian and global, with Maeva herself as the trilogy's equivalent to a world historical figure. She therefore remains marginal to the action, in which the central protagonist and sometime narrator is her German lover, the cynical older journalist, Cording, a reporter for Rupert Matlock's news magazine *EMERGENCY*. One of the trilogy's more interesting subplots is the encounter between the URP and the Californian ecodictatorship ECOCA. The similarity between ECOCA and Ernest Callenbach's *Ecotopia* is no doubt intentional, as is the commentary that likens it to Kampuchea under the Khmer Rouge (246). In *Feuer am Fuss*, Cording travels to ECOCA to report on the impending show-trial of yet another 'great figure', kidnapped former president Barrack Obama, who is charged with the capital offence of having given Monsanto free reign in the United States.

A dystopian near-future counterpart to Fleck's utopianism can be observed in Antti Tuomainen's *Parantaja* (2010), a SF/crime hybrid fiction, where the crime is framed by the logics of ecoterrorism. The novel's protagonist-narrator, Tapani Lehtinen, is a poet living in a climate-ruined Helsinki, whose journalist wife, Johanna, disappears two days before Christmas, and it recounts his three-day search for her. Tapani discovers that Johanna has been investigating a serial killer who styles himself 'Parantaja (the Healer)', a killer who murders business executives and politicians he deems in some way responsible for climate change. DNA evidence suggests that Parantaja is in fact Pasi Tarkiainen, a one-time medical student who supposedly died five years previously in a flu epidemic. Tapani's computer searches discover that Johanna and Pasi had once lived together and her old friend Elina Kallio explains that she, Johanna and Pasi had all as students been radical environmental activists. The crime narrative follows Tapani in his search for Johanna and Tarkiainen, a search that eventually leads to a northbound train at the railway station. In the denouement Tapani and Police Chief Inspector Harri Jaatinen succeed in rescuing Johanna, but Tarkiainen nonetheless escapes. And in the climactic encounter between Tapani and Pasi, the poet and the killer, the latter insists that 'Mä olen Tapani hyvän puolella. Ei mulla aikoinaan ollut sen vähäisempää tavoitetta kuin maailman pelastaminen. Nyt kun maailman ei voi pelastaa, pitää huolehtia siitä, että hyvä elää ainakin yhtä pitkään kuin pahuus ja itsekkyys' (I'm on the side of good, Tapani. There was a time when I strove for nothing less than saving the world. Now that the world can't be saved, I have to make sure that good continues to live for as long as evil and selfishness) (2013a: 215; 2013b: 204). The key phrase here is 'Nyt kun maailman ei voi pelastaa' – now that the world can't be saved. This view of the planet as already inevitably and irreparably damaged is as much the stance of the novel itself as of Pasi in particular. Bereft of social hope, we are left with individual sexual love as the only outstanding positive value in *Parantaja*. As Tapani reflects, after reading an unrepentant email from Tarkiainen the following Good Friday: 'Jotakin tapahtuu kun kosketan Johanna. Jokin sydämessä liikahtaa, sanoo, että nä on hyvä. Ja näin on hyvä … Mitä tahansa tapahtuukin, minä rakastan Johanna.' (Something happens when I touch Johanna. Something in my heart stirs, something says this is right – this is good. And it is good ... Whatever happens, I will love Johanna) (2013a: 221; 2013b: 211). What will happen, we know, is that sooner rather than later the world will end.

Longer-term future history

Normally, however, dystopian climate fiction tends to work in the longer term, albeit often punctuated by some kind of catastrophic interruption, as for example in Margaret Atwood's *MaddAddam* trilogy, comprising *Oryx and Crake* (2003), *The Year of the Flood* (2009) and *MaddAddam* itself (2013). All three novels are set partly in a post-apocalyptic future, partly in flashbacks to a pre-apocalyptic hypercapitalist extension of our present. Atwood gives no dates, but they are clearly set further into the future than *Feuer am Fuss*. Here, once again, the history is global, although mainly witnessed from within the United States. The social contradictions in the pre-apocalypse are fought out between the corporations, OrganInc, HelthWyzer, and so on, and the God's Gardeners environmentalist sect. In the post-apocalypse, they run between the Painballers, vicious former criminals who had been sentenced to perform in the Painball arena, and the Crakers, peaceful, herbivorous post-humans, immune to mosquito bites, who are occasionally sexually polyandrous, but normally sexually latent, and their allies, the few remaining humans and the Pigoons, intelligent, telepathic genetically modified pigs. The fictional world historical figures are Glenn/Crake, who created the Crakers and designed the lethal 'JUVE virus' that wiped out most of humanity, and Adam One, the founder of the Gardeners. And both are much less central compositionally than their mediocre counterparts, Jimmy-the-Snowman and Zeb, or Adam Seven. The contradictions are finally resolved into a utopian outcome for the Crakers, Pigoons and surviving non-Painballer humans. As Toby explains to the Crakers, Crake had understood that 'the people in the chaos cannot learn. They cannot understand what they are doing to the sea and the sky and the plants and the animals ... Either most of them must be cleared away while there is still an earth, with trees and flowers and birds and fish and so on, or all must die when there are none of those things left' (2013: 291). So, he made the 'Great Emptiness' – the end of history – in which their community could finally flourish. This pattern of a lengthy extension of the hypercapitalist present brought to a sudden catastrophic interruption recurs elsewhere in 'posthuman' cli-fi. So, for example, in Frank Schätzing's *Der Schwarm*, the most commercially successful of German ecofictions, the planet is saved ultimately through the intervention of 'die Yrr', 'Der sich seiner selbst bewusst gewordene Ozean (the ocean become conscious of itself)' (965). Craig Russell's *Fragment* – like *MaddAddam*, an Anglophone Canadian text – ends in a similarly post-human outcome, when 'the Nation of Whales, claiming ownership of everything outside the 200 mile coastal limits', is admitted to the United Nations (212).

But cli-fi can also work on an even longer timescale, more reminiscent of Scott. This is true, for example, of Ligny's climate trilogy, which begins with *Aqua^{TM}* (2006) in a dystopian 2030, proceeds in *Exodes* (2012) through the catastrophe of 2100, and ends with *Semences* (2015) in the post-apocalyptic twenty-fourth century, where the 'fourmites', evolved ants, have supplanted the surviving humans as the dominant species. The first and most critically and commercially successful volume in the trilogy, *Aqua^{TM}*, is set at a time when drought and global warming have transformed drinking water into an extremely valuable commodity. The novel's two protagonists, both 'mediocre' characters, are Laurie Prigent, a French SaveOurSelves (SOS) activist, and Rudy Klaas, a former tulip grower, whose family were drowned by catastrophic Dutch flooding. Laurie's hacker brother, Yann, pirates a satellite picture from a GeoWatch EcoSat, which shows that there is an extensive underground water layer beneath the surface of drought-stricken Burkina Faso. But Resourcing, the big American consortium which owns the satellite, claims possession of the newly discovered water layer. Laurie is sent by SOS to transport drilling equipment to Burkina Faso and Rudy is hired as her driver. SOS and the Burkina Faso president, Fatimata Konaté, are thus pitted against GeoWatch, Resourcing's CEO, Anthony Fuller, another compositionally marginal great figure, and la Divine Légion, a US American Christian fundamentalist sect which believes that Fuller's cloned son, Tony Junior, is the new Messiah. This opposition between an alliance of European NGO activists with non-Western subaltern peoples, on the one hand, and of American corporate capitalism with American Christian fundamentalists, on the other, allows the first to be constructed as positive sites of resistance within a wider globalized dystopia. This contradiction is resolved when Rudy joins in an attack by Shawnee Indians on the ranch belonging to John Bournemouth, governor of Kansas, and a Resourcing and Divine Légion loyalist, that is, in Lukácsian terms, yet another 'great figure': 'les Shawnees vont fourrer leur butin dans le pick-up de Rudy, incendient le ranch, montent sur leurs chevaux nerveux et s'éloignent dans la grande prairie desséchée, en entonnant un très ancien chant de guerre (the Shawnees poked their booty into Rudy's pick-up, burnt the ranch, mounted their nervous horses and rode away into the vast parched prairie, singing a very ancient war song)' (2006: 719).

Set only seventy years later, *Exodes* is, by contrast, essentially a doomsday novel – its last chapter is entitled 'Exterminer, annihiler, détruire!' (2012: 503) – when human civilization is already close to collapse and humanity itself seems doomed. The elites have withdrawn into domed enclaves, one of which is nicely located at Davos in Switzerland; the planet's equatorial regions have become uninhabitable; there are immigration wars, roaming bands of cannibalistic 'Mangemorts', or Deatheaters, and incendiary 'Boutefeux', or Firebrands. Hence, the eponymous mass exodus, in which humans from all across Europe attempt to escape from conditions from which there is no escape. The novel is thus structured around doomed escape attempts by six main characters: Pradeesh Gorayan, an Indian geneticist working on life expectancy in the Davos dome; Mercedes Sanchez, a Spaniard who joins a religious cult which believes that angels will arrive by UFO to take them to the Garden of Eden; Mercedes's son Fernando Sanchez, who leaves home on his eighteenth birthday to join les Boutefeux; Paula Rossi, an Italian concerned above all for the health of her young sons, Romano and Silvio, who trades her body for food, water and transport; Mélanie Lemoine, a French woman living alone with her dog in the Forez Mountains, who uses her last days to try to save the remaining animals; and Olaf Eriksson, a Norwegian fisherman, who flees from the Lofoten Islands, which have been overwhelmed by refugees, in search of something better further south. All of these are 'mediocre' characters in Lukács's terms; the end of history has no room for world historical figures. Ultimately, the characters converge near Davos – which is attacked by Fernando's Firebrands – in an ironically dark denouement: Pradeesh suggests to Paula, Romano and Mercedes that they can still find 'l'un des derniers havres de paix existant sur cette planète (one of the last havens of peace remaining on this planet)' in 'Les îles Lofoten' (534).

The most sympathetic of the six characters is almost certainly Mélanie, whose home in the Forez Mountains is close to Ligny's own and whose escape to her fortified farm is metaphorical rather than literal and is, in any case, dedicated to the protection of the non-human. She is also the character whose close observations of the natural environment most anticipate developments between *Exodes* and *Semences*. Mélanie sees herself as living 'en harmonie avec la nature – une nature certes revêche, avare et hostile, mais qui la nourrit encore (in harmony with nature – a rogue nature it had become, greedy and hostile, but it still nourished her)' (62). When her neighbour Séverine asks to see the animals, Mélanie shows her around and eventually insists that the anthill takes pride of place over everything else. 'En fait, c'est un ville en pleine expansion, qui grossit de jour en jour (In fact, it's a city in full expansion, which gets bigger every day)', she explains (68). Séverine thinks this merely a tall story, but Mélanie is insistent that it is actually reality: 'Peut-être que, tout simplement, elles ont senti – ou la nature leur a fait comprendre – que l'ère de l'homme était passée, que leur était venu de dominer le monde (Perhaps, quite simply, they sense – or nature makes them understand – that the era of man has passed, that their turn has come to dominate the world)' (70). The full significance of this passage only becomes apparent in *Semences*, when we learn that, during the intervening two hundred years, the ants have evolved into 'les fourmites' – a linguistic and biological cross between 'les fourmis' and 'les termites' – and have become capable of near-telepathic communication, not only with each other but also with humans.

In *Semences*, the two main characters, Denn and Nao, are members of a small, primitive, cave-dwelling tribe, living in symbiotic relationship with the fourmites. The couple come across a dying man, 'Un demon des Âges Sombres (A demon from the Dark Ages)' (2015: 76) of the twentieth and twenty-first centuries when human science and technology flourished, who bequeaths them a silk scarf depicting images of what seems to be an Earthly paradise of snow-capped peaks and fertile valleys. We know from the novel's prologue that this man is Natsume and that the Greenland Inuit tribe he abandoned – also small, also primitive, also cave-dwelling, also in symbiotic relationship with fourmites, and also ignorant of the world beyond itself – was certainly not the 'dernier paradis sur Terre (last paradise on Earth)' (7). Carrying a micro-society of fourmites with them, Nao and Denn journey through the blasted landscapes of a ravaged planet, attempting to trace their way to the dead man's home. In this burning world, where temperatures are about 100°C during the day, and where the few surviving humans live underground, the tropics are now completely uninhabitable, the old temperate zones have become tropical and the poles temperate, the oceans are swollen and acidified, biodiversity has collapsed into homogeneity through mass extinction – there are no birds – and the ruins of the old cities are irradiated.

Yet, Denn and Nao also discover new life, and with it new kinds of hope, wherever they travel. They also discover each other as their relationship, initially akin to that between brother and sister, acquires an increasingly sexual character. By comparison with the sheer hopelessness of *Exodes*, *Semences* is, then, a cautiously optimistic text. But what hope it holds out is accorded either the two teenage lovers as individuals or the planet as a whole living system, that is, as Gaia: Lovelock in French translation figures prominently in Ligny's recommended readings (540). Human civilization, by contrast, has not only auto-destructed, but has also been responsible for the destruction of 95 per cent of the species on land. As a result, the fourmites rather than humanity will become the planet's dominant species. In the novel's closing pages, Nao realizes that the long-standing Accords between humans and fourmites are over: 'C'est fini. Finie la collaboration. Finie la symbiose. Finie les Accords (It's finished. The end of collaboration. The end of symbiosis. The end of the Accords)'. But why?, she asks: 'Les fourmites ne répondent pas, mais la réponse, évidente, s'étale devant ses yeux ... L'époque de la domination des humains sur la Terre est révolue, c'est désormais l'avènement des fourmites (The fourmites don't respond, but the answer is evidently spread out before her eyes ... The epoch of human domination on Earth is over, it's now the rise of the fourmites)' (408–9). Given the inevitably human subject position from which Ligny writes and his readers read, *Semences* has to be understood as ultimately an extension of the dystopian pessimism of *Exodes*: hope for human civilization exists only outside the text in its capacity as warning and its author's as harbinger.

Long-range future history

The longest cli-fi future histories, however, are among those written by Kim Stanley Robinson, the best-known of all US American cli-fi writers. The cover to his *Galileo's Dream* (2009), set in part three thousand years into the future, quotes the *Daily Mail*'s description of it as 'The ultimate in future history'. And perhaps it is. But Robinson's work takes many and various forms. He is famously both a declared socialist and a committed environmentalist, so it is unsurprising that his SF has become increasingly focused on the promise of radical social change and the threat of runaway climate change. Indeed, there is a sense in which his recent fiction can be read as a kind of extended comparative sociology of climate and social change. So, just as Weber sought to compare the implications for economic activity of different world religions, so Robinson's novels compare the implications for climate change of different political strategies for social change, some comparatively short-term, others very much longer.

Robinson's *Science in the Capital* trilogy, comprising *Forty Signs of Rain* (2004), *Fifty Degrees Below* (2005) and *Sixty Days and Counting* (2007), is set in the very near future, leading to the Phil Chase presidency, which opens up the prospect for real action to deal with climate change. Robinson's work has often been described as 'hard SF' and is justly famous for the quality of its scientific research. But here, where the subject matter appears closest to the author's deepest concerns, the reader is almost overwhelmed by the details, not only of the science, but also of the internal mechanisms of scientific policymaking. Indeed, remarkably little actually happens in the first volume, *Forty Signs of Rain*, until the spectacular flooding of Washington, DC, at its conclusion (2004: 326–56). *Fifty Degrees Below*, which deals with the stalling of the Gulf Steam, and *Sixty Days and Counting*, which recounts the opening stages of the Chase Presidency, are faster-moving, but still often overburdened with scientific and technical detail. Moreover, the whole trilogy suffers from a preoccupation with American internal politics that might not excite very much international interest. As we've already noted, Chase himself is the trilogy's world historical figure, in effect an idealized amalgam of an Al Gore who managed to get elected and a Barack Obama who managed to get things done. The trilogy's mediocre protagonist, however, is Frank Vanderwal, a Californian biomathematician and rock climber, whose initial cynicism about science policy is eventually superseded by active enthusiasm for a Chase administration.

In the trilogy's 2015 omnibus edition, *Green Earth*, its 1,632 pages are reduced by about 300 pages (2015a: xiii) and much of the political and scientific policy detail cut back. In the author's introduction, Robinson explains that he had intended to write a realist novel as if it were SF, 'describing Washington D.C. as if it were orbiting Aldebaran', but concedes that 'afterward it seemed possible that occasionally I might have gone too far' (xii). Insofar as the trilogy toys with the notion of a positive outcome from climate change, this is, of course, centred around Chase, whose election to the Presidency seems to offer the promise of a positively utopian transformation of US politics. So, in his 'Cut to the Chase' blog, written shortly after he survives an assassination attempt, Chase announces that '*Empires are one of the most evil and destructive of human systems*', but adds that the United States only '*became an empire by accident*'. Eventually, he promises, '*we will build a culture in which no one is without a job, or shelter, or health care, or education, or the rights to their own life. Taking care of the Earth and its miraculous biological splendor will then become the long-term work of our species. We'll share the world with all the other creatures. It will be an ongoing project that will never end*' (2007: 478–9). This passage is actually from *Sixty Days and Counting*, but it is omitted from *Green Earth*. It's difficult to know why exactly Robinson chose to delete those lines, whether he considered them 'telling readers things they already knew', 'extraneous details' or 'excess verbiage' (2015a: xii). But I suspect the decision arose from a growing awareness, based in the empirical experience of contemporary American realities, of just how implausible it would appear to many readers, perhaps most, that any Democrat president would ever say such things. Unsurprisingly, then, most of Robinson's subsequent cli-fi future histories have tended to be more long-term.

New York 2140 (2017) is set almost a century later, in a twenty-second century where sea levels have risen by 50 feet and the whole of Lower Manhattan has long since been flooded. Initially, the main plot appears to be a detective mystery about the disappearance of two 'coders', Ralph Muttchopf and Jeffrey Rose, or 'Mutt and Jeff', from their temporary home on the 'farm floor' of the Met Life tower on Madison Square. Jeff has already explained to Mutt (and to the reader) why 'the world is fucked': 'It's not just that there are market failures. It's that the market is a failure ... Things are sold for less than it costs to make them ... We've been paying a fraction of what things really cost to make, but meanwhile the planet, and the workers who made the stuff, take the unpaid costs right in the teeth' (4). But the mystery narrative turns out to be the trigger for a more important political narrative, which moves the novel towards its eventual climax. And that too is a result of climate change: Hurricane Fyodor batters the city so badly as to prompt what amounts to a popular constitutional revolution. The narrative is divided into eight parts, each subdivided into eight sections, each devoted to a particular character or characters: Mutt and Jeff, the two kidnapped coders; Inspector Gen Octaviasdottir, a New York Police Department detective called in to investigate their disappearance; Franklin Garr, a market trader for the aptly named WaterPrice; Vlade Marovich, the superintendent, or manager, of the building from which Mutt and Jeff disappeared; an anonymous New York citizen who explains periodically how the city works; Amelia Black, an internet 'cloud' star, famous for taking off her clothes, who heads an internet show about wildlife survival; Charlotte Armstrong, a lawyer defending the rights of immigrants, who calls in Inspector Gen to investigate Mutt and Jeff's disappearance; and Stefan and Roberto, two twelve-year-old 'water rats', orphaned scavengers with their own scavenged boat, in the business of submarine exploration. Inspector Gen, Franklin, Amelia and Charlotte are all Met Life tower tenants, Vlade also lives in the tower, and Stefan and Roberto scavenge around its periphery.

If *Green Earth*'s Phil Chase had been an Al Gore figure, then the various inhabitants of the Met building turn out to be a composite Bernie Sanders. Interestingly enough, this means that *New York 2140* has no single world historical figure, but rather a complement of mediocre figures: Vlade plays a crucial role in rescuing Mutt and Jeff from the sunken container in which they're imprisoned (314–16); Franklin advises Charlotte that a 'financial general strike' organized by the Householders' Union could prevent a Government bailout of the banks (348–9); after the hurricane, Inspector Gen faces down the armed private security forces 'protecting private property' in Upper Manhattan (515); Amelia announces on camera that 'it's democracy versus capitalism, We the people have to band together and take over … Anyone who stops payment on their odious debts … immediately becomes a full member of the Householders' Union' (528); Charlotte persuades her ex-husband, Larry Jackman, now head of the Federal Reserve, that bank nationalization should be the price for a financial bailout, and runs for Congress as a Democrat, campaigning against the banks. 'Make that whole giant leech on the real economy into a credit union', she argues, 'and squeeze all that blood money we've lost back into us' (554). She is elected, the banks are nationalized, Congress passes a 'Piketty tax' on income and capital assets and 'a leftward flurry of legislation' is 'LBJed through Congress' (574, 601, 602, 604). The 'pushback was ferocious as always, because people are crazy and history never ends', the citizen warns: 'There are no happy endings! Because there are no endings' (604). But nonetheless this is as politically positive an ending as any in recent cli-fi. And it is complemented by a whole series of individual happy endings: Stefan and Roberto really do discover sunken treasure, British gold from the Revolutionary War aboard the remains of HMS Hussar; Vlade and his ex-wife Idelba really do get back together; Charlotte really does strike up a successful sexual relationship with Franklin, who is sixteen years her junior; the political battle for New York really is 'a Pyrrhic defeat' in which 'the losers of a Pyrrhic victory … are really the winners … They lose, then they say to each other, Hey we just lost a Pyrrhic victory! Congratulations!' (572, 590, 598). The key weakness, of course, is that all this happiness is far too easily bought, most especially at the political level. But, then, this is fiction after all.

Much longer cli-fi future histories are imagined in the two novels Robinson published between *Sixty Days and Counting* and *New York 2140*: *2312* (2012), set in the twenty-fourth century, and *Aurora* (2015), set between the twenty-sixth and thirtieth centuries. Both are concerned with climate change; in both, Mars, Venus, Mercury, the Jovian and Saturnine moons, and many of the asteroids are already inhabited by humans, and thereby subject to some degree of terraforming; in both, Earth is depicted as ravaged by the negative consequences of anthropogenic extreme climate change; and in both serious attempts are made to mitigate those consequences. These are at their most spectacular in *2312*, where the protagonists and eventual lovers, the Mercurian artist Swan Er Hong and the Titanian diplomat Fitz Wahram, neither of whom is in any obvious sense world-historical, help to return thousands of extinct or near-extinct species to Earth from the asteroid 'terraria' in which they've been preserved. Robinson's description of the resultant landings is simultaneously inspirational, surreal and vaguely comic:

> It looked like a dream, but ... it was real, and the same right now all over Earth: into the seas splashed dolphins and whales, tuna and sharks. Mammals, birds, fish, reptiles, amphibians: all the lost creatures were in the sky at once, in every country, in every watershed. Many of the creatures descending had been absent from Earth for two or three centuries. Now all back, all at once. (2012: 395)

Earth itself, 'the planet of sadness' (303), is still trapped in a system of predatory late capitalism – hence the scale of the environmental damage – but the rest of the solar system is run along socialistic lines, in a future version of the Mondragon system of workers cooperatives established in Euskadi. In *2312* Robinson looks back on the twenty-first century as a combination of 'The Dithering', 'the wasted years' when humanity failed to address the clear and present danger of anthropogenic climate change, and 'The Crisis', the 'perfect storm' that followed, which led to 'a rise in average global temperatures of five K, and sea level rise of five meters – and as a result ... food shortages, mass riots, catastrophic deaths on all continents, and an immense spike in the extinction rate of other species' (245).

Set in exactly the same timeline, *Aurora*'s main storyline is the attempt to establish a human colony on Aurora, an Earth-like moon of Tau Ceti's Planet E. This is ultimately unsuccessful because, as a dying settler observes, 'any new place is going to be either alive or dead. If it's alive it's going to be poisonous, if it's dead you're going to have to work it up from scratch' (2015b: 178). The colony is abandoned and a minority of the would-be settlers decide to return to Earth. They nearly starve en route, but are saved by the wonderfully intelligent 'Ship', a quantum computer AI which narrates most of the novel, puts them into hibernation and finally sacrifices itself in order to send 616 survivors back to Earth. Their home planet, they have learnt, has been seriously damaged by global warming: 'On Earth the sea level was many meters higher than it had been when their ship had started its voyage, and the carbon dioxide level in Earth's atmosphere was around 600 parts per million, having been brought down significantly from the time ship had left ... That suggested carbon drawdown efforts' (271). But the full scale of environmental catastrophe only becomes apparent after their return. Sea levels have risen by twenty-four meters during the twenty-second and twenty-third centuries, all Earth's beaches are drowned and, despite the attempts at carbon drawdown, sea levels have thus far barely fallen: 'Yes, they are terraforming Earth ... they are calling it a five-thousand-year project ... It'll be a bit of a race with the Martians' (436). *Aurora* subverts the conventions, not only of the generation starship subgenre, but also of almost all space travel and first contact SF. But its very pessimistic estimate of how long it would take to terraform Earth or Mars – thousands of years – also subverts, or at least runs contrary to, the original expectations of Robinson's own *Mars* trilogy (1993–6), which had earned him his two Hugo Awards. In the novel's denouement, Freya, the colonists' informal leader, leads the survivors into an alliance with the 'Earthfirsters', a group working on landscape restoration, specifically beach return, who are opposed to the deep space exploration still advocated by the 'space cadets'. As one Earthfirster explains to Freya: 'We don't like the space cadets … This idea of theirs that Earth is humanity's cradle is part of what trashed the Earth in the first place' (439). Desperately damaged though Earth undoubtedly is, the still dominant late-capitalist mode of production is subject to clear and effective challenges by utopian enclaves and communities, the latter-day Mondragon cooperators in *2312*, the Earthfirsters in *Aurora*. And in both novels, the utopians are firmly on the side of science and scientists.

Robinson's most recent novel, *The Ministry for the Future* (2020), returns him and us to the very near future: it is set in the immediate aftermath of the establishment in 2025 of the eponymous Ministry as a Subsidiary Body for Implementation of the 2015 Paris Agreement in conjunction with the IPCC and the UN. This return to the near future produces a truncated sense of history, an expanded sense of catastrophic crisis, and a renewed opportunity for positive outcomes from climate crisis, as it had in the *Science in the Capital* trilogy. Where *New York 2140* had pursued a fundamentally constitutionalist political resolution, *The Ministry for the Future* attempts an interesting combination of constitutionalism and revolutionary terrorism. The constitutional option revolves around the Ministry itself, located in Zurich, with a role 'to advocate for the world's future generations of citizens … all living creatures present and future who cannot speak for themselves' (16). Its Irish head, Mary Murphy, who might perhaps turn out to be a world historical figure but isn't yet in this novel, is nonetheless the nearest it has to a protagonist. Interestingly, she is central to the action, perhaps because, although very long, the novel tends towards the dramatic rather than the epic. The revolutionary terrorist option, by contrast, is represented by the Indian 'Children of Kali', who send drones to bring down sixty passenger jets in a matter of hours and, later, to infect millions of cattle with bovine spongiform encephalopathy, or mad cow disease (229).

The novel is organized into 106 chapters, which move backwards and forwards between personal narratives, factual summaries of climate science, and 'objective' slices of future history. It opens with an unprecedented heat wave in India which kills twenty million people, viscerally described from the point of view of an American aid worker, Frank May, who becomes the sole survivor of a mass death, subsequently suffers post-traumatic stress disorder and later becomes a comparatively ineffectual ecoterrorist. Robinson's use of the word 'poached' in this chapter, to describe the deaths of people fleeing the heat to shelter in a nearby lake, is powerfully disturbing (12). Subliminally, however, the catastrophe changes everything: 'Civilization had been killed but it kept walking the Earth ... The culture of the time was rife with fear and anger, denial and guilt, shame and regret, repression and the return of the repressed ... the Indian heat wave stayed a big part of it' (227). The central social contradiction is thus that between corporate capitalism and the Ministry plus the Children of Kali. And its scope is global, running from Switzerland, where the Ministry is located, to India whence the Children emerge, and even Antarctica, where a geoengineering project aims to pump up meltwater so as to slow basal sliding.

By comparison with Robinson's earlier fictions, *The Ministry for the Future* is much more sympathetic both to ecoterrorism and also, incidentally, to vegetarianism: 'Of course many people were quick to point out that these Children of Kali were hypocrites and monsters, that Indians didn't eat cows and ... that coal-fired power plants in India had burned a significant proportion of the last decade's carbon burn ... Then again those same Indian power plants were being attacked on a regular basis' (230). Robinson is clear, however, that ecoterrorism really works: 'In the forties and ever after, less beef got eaten. Less milk was drunk. And fewer jet flights were made' (229–30). As Robinson has May observe: 'Some things were just too dangerous to continue doing. When your veggie burger tasted just as good, while your beef package proclaimed *Guaranteed Safe!* with a liability waiver in small print at the bottom, you knew a different time had come' (369). More significantly, Robinson also strongly implies that these Children of Kali might actually be an offshoot of the Ministry itself. Murphy's Indian chief of staff, Badim Bahadur, admits to having secretly established a 'black wing' and warns her that 'there might be some people who deserve to be killed' (115). Later an anonymous narrator, who might well be Bahadur himself, tells of an encounter with the Children, in which he announces: 'I understand you. I've helped you, I've helped work like yours all over the world ... I've done more to stop the next heat wave than anyone you have ever met. You've done your part, I've done mine ... I am Kali' (390–1). This combination of constitutionalism and terrorism leads directly to the novel's essentially positive outcome. But, as with *New York 2140*, the price of success is bought too cheaply to be entirely credible: 'Aircraft carriers? Sunk. Bombers?

Blown out of the sky. An oil tanker, boom, sunk in ten minutes. One of America's eight hundred military bases around the world, shattered ... The war on terror? It lost' (347).

It is difficult not to sympathize with Robinson's determined insistence that there must be positive ways forward for our species and our planet. As he argued in an article published in the journal *Utopian Studies*: 'It has become a case of utopia or catastrophe, and utopia has gone from being a somewhat minor literary problem to a necessary survival strategy' (2016: 9). But utopianism is nonetheless always open to the criticism that it is utopian in the pejorative sense of being hopelessly impractical. Can anyone really believe that American military might can be so easily dispensed with in any imaginable reality as in *The Ministry for the Future*? But then this is fiction after all, isn't it? For Robinson, however, the antithesis between utopia and catastrophe operates in the real world as well as in his novels. Which leaves us with a deeply impressive novel and a less-than-persuasive political strategy. The central question for almost all cli-fi, as for almost all SF, is what does it mean to be (post)human? For Fleck, as for William Morris, the answer is already substantially given in feudalism or primitivism. For Atwood, as for Ligny, the answer is that we will be superseded by the properly post-human, whether Crakers or fourmites. For Robinson, as for Edward Bellamy, the answer will be revealed by future history as some kind of (eco)socialist utopia. But Robinson's looking forward is much less sure of itself, and also much more experimental, than Bellamy's *Looking Backward* (1888).

Two future historians: Asimov and Robinson

In this chapter we have referred in passing to Isaac Asimov, one of Robinson's more influential predecessors and Bellamy's more influential successors. In Part 3 Peter Murphy will proceed to explore Asimov's epic *Foundation* novels in greater detail. In the meantime, however, we conclude this chapter with a comparison between Robinson's and Asimov's respective experiments in long-range future history. Let us begin by noting the obvious points of similarity between the two writers: both wrote 'hard SF' and both were correspondingly sympathetic to science and the 'scientific world vision'; both were attracted to the idea of extended future histories; both acquired a considerable following in SF fandom (both won Hugo Awards and both were Guests of Honor at the fan-based World Science Fiction Convention); both exclude contact with intelligent alien species from their fictions; and both were on the US American political Left.

The question of politics arises here from Lukács's partial retraction of the last chapter of *The Historical Novel* in the 'Preface to the English Edition' to which we referred previously. Insofar as this chapter is flawed – and Lukács concedes that it is – then the flaw lies in part in its preoccupation with then present-day politics. So, what were Asimov's and Robinson's then present-day politics? During the 1930s, Asimov was a member of the New York 'Futurians', the SF wing of the local anti-Fascist literary Popular Front, which he would later describe as a coterie of 'brilliant teenagers ... from broken homes and ... insecure childhoods' (1994a: 61) united by their violent opposition to fascism (1979: 211). In 1937, Futurians Donald A. Wollheim and John Michel proposed a motion to the Eastern Science Fiction Convention, 'opposing all forces leading to barbarism, the advancement of pseudo-sciences and militaristic ideologies' (Mozkowitz 119). In 1939, six of the more left-wing Futurians, including Frederik Pohl, Wollheim and Michel, were excluded from the World Science Convention, and they responded by holding a counter-convention at the Brooklyn headquarters of the Young Communist League (1980: 146; 1978: 96, 99). The Convention majority were, however, willing to admit Asimov, his Futurian affinities notwithstanding. Even then, and despite FBI suspicions to the contrary, Asimov was essentially a social democrat rather than a Young Communist, as were Pohl and Michel at the time. This was more or less exactly where Asimov remained on the political spectrum, a left-leaning Democrat, famously opposed to the Vietnam War (Ackerman et al. 1968: 5) and a strong supporter of the presidential candidacy of the anti-war George McGovern (Asimov 1981: 503). His last non-fiction book, co-authored with Pohl, is a radically environmentalist engagement with issues like global warming, militarism and the destruction of the ozone layer (1991).

Allowing for generational differences, Robinson's politics are not too dissimilar from Asimov's. In 2017, writing the 'Introduction' to the second edition of Asimov and Pohl's *Our Angry Earth*, he would conclude that 'these two old pros took on a task they cared deeply about, and the result is very impressive'. Like Bernie Sanders, Robinson describes himself as a 'democratic socialist' rather than a Democrat and he is, like Sanders, apparently a fully paid-up member of the Democratic Socialists of America. But there is a Marxist edge to Robinson that was never quite there in Asimov: hence, his admission that 'I tend to use Marxist critical theory when thinking about history, ecology when thinking about the biosphere, and Buddhism when thinking cosmically or personally' (Canavan and Robinson 2014: 257). This kind of thinking about history clearly extends to his future histories where the focus is overwhelmingly – and increasingly – on capitalism and its possible alternatives. Certainly, ecology is also important, but, as Robinson explained to Gerry Canavan: 'To me deep ecology made it clear why environmentalism needs Marxist critical theory' (256). Asimov's own future histories, by contrast, avoid the issue of capitalism, except in the early near-future robot stories. Indeed, the issue is finally resolved for Asimov precisely by robotics. So, Asimov's World Co-ordinator, the robot Stephen Byerley, speaks for his creator when he assures robopsychologist Susan Calvin that, under robot administration, 'there will be no unemployment, no over-production or shortages. Waste and famine are words in history books. And so the question of ownership of the means of production becomes obsolescent' (1950: 134). This political difference between Robinson and Asimov has far-reaching consequences for their respective future histories. While Asimov leaves capitalism behind in the pre-robotic past, so as to move on to a galactic history determined by quite different forces, Robinson's fiction remains grounded in our solar system and in the problems of capitalism. As he explained to Canavan, 'the universe beyond the solar system exists beyond human distances and will forever remain a backdrop only … What kind of story could I tell using this device of the galactic setting that I couldn't tell by way of a more realistic device? … when I don't find any … I can't see the point of trying them' (Canavan and Robinson 2014: 248–9).

The obvious point of contrast between Asimov and Robinson is thus that of the scale of their respective future histories, in both time and space. Epic though Robinson's SF undoubtedly is, it nowhere aspires to the heights of universal history we find in Asimov, a history which covers the entire galaxy over a period of many tens of thousands of years. Asimov famously took Edward Gibbon as his initial inspiration, while Robinson takes a distinctly post-Marxist version of Marx. Hence, the latter's observation that 'there do seem to be differences in human life … whether these differences were caused by changes in modes of production, structures of feeling, scientific paradigms, dynastic succession, technological progress, or cultural metamorphosis' (2012: 244). The first term in the list is from Marx, the second from Raymond Williams. Asimov is not quite, however, the loyal follower of Gibbon he is sometimes represented to be. The opening logic of *Foundation*, in the far distant future of the year 12,000 Galactic Era, is indeed one of decline and fall, but Seldon's plan is nonetheless to slow and eventually reverse the process; moreover, the overarching structure of Asimov's galactic history is one of progress, culminating in the eventual creation of 'Galaxia' (1996: 509). And insofar as there is any real-world counterpart to Seldon's 'psychohistory' it is surely something close to neo-Marxian and neo-Weberian historical sociology. Given that Robinson's novels occur in different timelines and different fictional universes, it seems unlikely that he will ever be able to organize them into a single chronology like that eventually conceived by Asimov, which incorporates the 'Robot', 'Empire' and 'Foundation' novels into a universal future history (1994b: 10). So, Robinson's *Orange County* trilogy novels are set in near-futures both different from each other and different from his other near-future fictions. So, *The Ministry for the Future* is yet another near-future novel – the Ministry is founded in 2025 – which presumably launches yet another timeline. So, *The Years of Rice and Salt* (2002) is set in an alternative universe where the Black Death wiped out almost all of Europe. So, *Shaman* (2013) is set in a far distant past and *Galileo's Dream* in part in a far distant future, both of which might or might not be on timelines compatible with his intervening fictions.

Some of Robinson's novels do, however, sometimes share a common timeline, and these tend to cluster around either the *Science in the Capital* trilogy or the *Mars* trilogy. The *Science in the Capital* trilogy is set in the very near future, in a fictional world that can be extended to include *Antarctica* (1997) and *Red Moon* (2018). The connections with *Antarctica* are self-evident: its central protagonist, Wade Norton, and his employer, Senator Phil Chase, reappear in the trilogy, where the latter's role becomes politically central. The connection with *Red Moon* is less obvious but hinges on the overlapping presence of the Chinese poet and travel journalist, Ta Shu, who reports to China from McMurdo Station and from the Chinese lunar base near Shackleton Crater. *Antarctica*'s place in Robinson's future history thus comes shortly before *Green Earth*, and *Red Moon*'s shortly thereafter, in 2047–8, when Hong Kong is due to be fully absorbed into the People's Republic. The red moon of the title refers literally to a solar eclipse that bathes the moon's surface in dusky red light, but metaphorically to Chinese lunar exploration. The main plot concerns internal Chinese power struggles in the run up to the Twenty-Fifth Congress of the Chinese Communist Party (2018: 131–2, 134, 258–9). But, like Phil Chase, the Chinese world historical figures embroiled in these struggles remain marginal to the narrative. The protagonists brought together on the moon are each, in Lukács's terms, mediocre characters: Fred Fredericks, an American technical officer at the Swiss Quantum Works; Ta Shu, the poet; and Chan Qi, the pregnant daughter of a leading Party figure. And, in different ways, all three are involved in bloodless revolutions that engulf both the United States and the People's Republic (432). This extended *Green Earth* universe therefore runs from the very near future through to 2048.

The *Mars* trilogy, by contrast, runs from 2026 through to 2212: *Red Mars* opens with the first settler expedition setting out for Mars on 21 December

2026 (1993: 45); *Green Mars* begins around 2061 and ends in 2127 with the Earth flooded and a substantially terraformed Mars achieving independence (1994: 781); *Blue Mars* covers the period from 2127 to 2212 and concludes with the Accelerando, during which human colonies are established across the solar system and missions finally launched into deep space (1996: 787). This trilogy can also arguably be extended, to include *2312* and *Aurora*. So, *2312* specifically discusses the periodization of Robinson's longer future histories by way of a selection of historiographical 'Extracts' directed at the work of twenty-fourth century historian Charlotte Shortback. Her periodization runs from feudalism and the Renaissance, through the Modern and Postmodern, by way of the 'long postmodern', to 'The Dithering: 2005 to 2060', 'The Crisis: 2060 to 2130', 'The Turnaround: 2130 to 2160', 'The Accelerando: 2160 to 2220', 'The Ritard: 2220 to 2270' and 'The Balkanization: 2270 to 2320' (2012: 245–6). The Turnaround includes the beginning of the 'terraforming of Mars' and the Accelerando includes the 'terraforming of Mars and subsequent Martian revolution' (246), both of which are loosely compatible with *Green Mars* and *Blue Mars*. But where does *New York 2140* fit into all this? Chronologically, it is set during Shortback's Turnaround, but makes no mention of Mars or of terraforming, which suggests yet another different timeline. Conversely, however, we might note that in *2312* Swann does actually visit a similarly flooded New York. It remains an open question.

The specific details of the timelines are, however, less important than the more general point, that Robinson's SF aspires to a kind of realism akin to that Lukács detected in the historical novel, in which socially typical characters in typical situations represent social trends and historical forces. This is not really true of Asimov, whose future histories became increasingly divorced from any possible knowable historical reality, in Robinson's terms becoming 'something like the land of Cockaigne' (Canavan and Robinson 2014: 248). This is not to detract from the epic grandeur of the *Foundation* trilogy, but it is to suggest the specific nature of Robinson's very different project. As Robinson tells Canavan:

> We are better now at doing science, partly because we're better at doing theory, and partly because science fiction retold all the old stories about pride going before a fall. However, we're still allowing capitalism to shape our actions and wreck the Earth, meaning our bio-infrastructure, meaning ourselves. So our culture is not yet scientific enough; when it becomes so, we will be making more rapid progress toward both justice and sustainability, as the two are stranded parts of the same project. At least this is the story I'm trying to tell. (260)

Part 3
Epic Science Fiction

Peter Murphy

7

The hidden God

Epic science fiction

Various epic forms exist. Many of these have appeared in science fiction, among them the future-historical novel, the Dostoevskian fantastic-grotesque spiritual epic and the Tolstoian cyclical-epic. The latter, the Tolstoian cyclical-epic, is a view of the world, including in its science-fictional forms, that meditates on the nature of the civilizational process. Civilization, it presupposes, is an undulating phenomenon. It rises, falls and rises over extended periods of time. From great heights of achievement, it falls to dizzying lows and then recovers. Its energies flow, ebb and are revitalized, or at least hint at revival. The civilizational process goes on across space as well as through the medium of time. Civilization space is typically partitioned. In the case of Vernon Vinge's *Zones of Thought* (1992–2011), for example, space is imagined as a series of concentric galactic volumes. These include an innermost unthinking zone, a slow travel zone, a zone of faster-than-light (FTL) automation and artificial intelligence, and finally a mysterious zone of transcendence. Doris Lessing's *The Marriages between Zones Three, Four and Five* (1980), also a Philip Glass opera (1997), depicts metaphysical planetary zones that have become isolated from one another, each one insular and self-sufficing, and the corrective to this, an Order that marries the imagination of one to another, fusing (for example) one zone's fascination with 'heights' to the other's attention to 'depths'.[1]

In the cyclical-epic kind of science fiction, dangers and threats are narratively engaging for the reader. At the same time, they are a structurally subordinate part of a pattern of all-consuming and repeating rhythms of expansion and contraction, rise and fall, challenge and response. The cyclical-epic narrator is an observer or spectator of these rhythms and their (often) unexpected rhymes. As it cycles in time and diaphragmatically expands and shrinks, extends and retreats in space, the epic represents an unfolding of a kind of fate or destiny. Destiny is not utopian or dystopian. Nor is it naively Panglossian or morbidly catastrophic. Rather it is the peculiar, often enigmatic, intersection of freedom and necessity, that is, the binding of free will together with historical inevitability. Individual human beings, with all their ambitions, purposes and talents, may create a planetary or galactic society. But that society, with its tacit built-in limits and parameters, also creates those individuals. That is, society creates them as much they create it. Accordingly, the spectator-narrator looks at them impassively as they are swept up in a larger absorbing vortex of events that they struggle to comprehend. They cannot determine the meta-events though they can influence them. This influence often has unforeseeable and unintended consequences.

The underlying metaphysics of the cyclical-epic kind of science fiction is probably best spelt out not in any extant science fiction genre work but rather in a work from the adjacent epic fantasy genre, Robert Jordan's *The Wheel of Time* series (1990–2013). In that series, the wheel of time spins the pattern of the ages. The wheel is driven by the One Power, which is divided into male and female halves that work in opposition and unison. True to the epic spirit, ordinary men and women are threads in a pattern that mostly is woven beyond their control. Jordan's fantasy epic draws on elements of Axial Age philosophies: Pre-Socratic, Taoist, Buddhist and Hindu, as well as various creation myths and Tolstoy's *War and Peace* (1869).[2]

Tolstoy is an unavoidable literary precedent for science fiction or fantasy cyclical genre epics. Tolstoy's reflection on the philosophy of history in *War and Peace* sets out the proposition that individuals do not determine history. Their multiple purposes and intentions, plans and strategies, no matter how seemingly clever these might be, are invariably subsumed by a collective social-historical dynamic, a necessity that they struggle to understand. Individuals might influence the dynamic here and there. But they cannot, as individuals, determine it. Accordingly, they have to adjust themselves to it as it flows and ebbs, expands and contracts, approaches and recedes. These individuals are threads in cosmic or historical patterns that are woven by the wheel of time. Or as Tolstoy put it, beautifully:

> Each man lives for himself, using his freedom to attain his personal aims, and feels with his whole being that he can now do or abstain from doing this or that action; but as soon as he has done it, that action performed at a certain moment in time becomes irrevocable and belongs to history, in which it has not a free but a predestined significance. (649)

Many of the greatest science fiction works of the twentieth century, from Isaac Asimov's Foundation series (1951–93) to Frank Herbert's Dune series (1965–85), echo with a palpable sense of both predestination and anonymous (socio-historical and metaphysical) determinations that reach across vast swathes of time and space. The events in these series are dramatic and exciting and filled with adventurous dangers. However, the resonant world view of these books expresses a feeling for underlying patterns, morphologies, cycles and destinies. These patterns incorporate oppositions. Free will and inevitability, automation and hand tools, sophistication and the rustic life, danger and happiness all confront, overlap and coalesce with each other. The individual threads and the cosmic patterns, the personal ambitions and the social ontologies, coexist in tension and unison. Tolstoy described the patterned aspect of the human condition as the 'swarm-life' of humankind. Tolstoy summed it up: 'There are two sides to the life of every man, his individual life which is the more free the more abstract its interests, and his elemental swarm-life in which he inevitably obeys laws laid down for him. Man lives consciously for himself, but is an unconscious instrument in the attainment of the historic, universal, aims of humanity' (649). That applies as much to figures of power, or to kings and heroes, as it does to the meanest of human souls.

This means that the heroes of a cyclical epic can be mediocre figures who rise to a great challenge, while powerful political figures inhabit the margins of the epic story and are only mentioned in passing. The difference between the two types is clear. The emperors and councils exercise the kind of power that directs means to projected ends. A common philosophical analogy for this is the artisan who uses tools to create objects like a table or chair. In politics, military and fiscal tools are deployed to achieve specific ends. In contrast, the middling hero figures – plucked from obscurity and thrown into epic time and space – are not artisans of power. Their gift rather is to intuit the evolving pattern of events and grasp its rhythms, understanding that what appears to be the strength of a great power may actually be its weakness, and that the tools of power date like all technologies do. The middling figure grasps, however haltingly, that a seeming infinity is finite and that from darkness comes light.

The pattern woven by the wheel of time is what the nineteenth century called History. Capital-H History fell out of fashion. But epic science fiction picked up its mantle. Tolstoy observed that History is 'the unconscious, general, swarm-life of mankind'. Emperors and their empires are not immune to this unconscious process irrespective of whether they happen to be real Continental European ones, would-be Chinese ones, fictional planetary ones or else hypothetical galactic ones. For History 'uses every moment of the life of rulers as a tool for its own purposes' (649). Capital-H History is not always pleasant or uplifting, far from it. When its wheel turns, it is apt to crush individuals who are hovering beneath it. In any event, the purposes of individuals and the patterns of history are not easy to reconcile. Accordingly, the civilizing process and the cyclical-epic science fiction that imaginatively depicts this process are distinguished by a distinctive interplay between the individual and society. Individuals form societies by their actions and plans. Meanwhile society often goes its own way. Society is driven by those who form it, and yet at the same time it drives those who drive it. Human beings cannot escape this paradox. The adventures of the epic hero are wilful and intentional. They are acts of freedom, sometimes an exhilarating freedom. But the narrative form of the cyclical-epic underscores this freedom with a pervading sense of necessity. The voluntary is overwritten by the involuntary, as choice is by destiny.

Heroism implies danger. The hero assumes risks in order to avert looming threats. In science fiction threats are typically social and not merely personal. Unlike the psychologically framed modernist novel, science fictions typically have broad social connotations. They probe collective meanings. These meanings can be framed in terms of utopia or dystopia, optimism or pessimism, fantasy or reality, cycles and progress, past and future, profane and theological – the spectra of science fictions are wide. Even at the theological end of the profane-religious spectrum (a pole that is commonplace in science fiction), many different kinds of religious or spiritual motifs abound. These include invocations of messianic, redemptive, moralizing and protective deities or spirits that shield societies from projected cataclysmic dangers or that punish human beings who engage in what their fellows, who often catastrophize and irrationally exaggerate, perceive as socially perilous or risky behaviours.

Often, perhaps even typically, the god or gods of science fiction are hidden. That is, the deities tend to be implied rather than explicit, or at least they are slow to be revealed. As it happens, this is a characteristic of a lot of religious thinking in the modern era. It is oblique rather than direct. Cyclical-epic science fiction is marked by a distinctive palette of the social danger-and-challenge that makes for an enticing narrative interwoven with the invisible hand of a hidden god. Commonly the concealed god is a god of lost-and-found equilibria. Dangers confronted by planetary or galactic societies are subsumed and overdetermined by vast cosmogonic swells of time and space. Correspondingly, danger and alarm presuppose their opposites, happiness and tranquillity. As Ursula Le Guin put it, light is 'the left hand of darkness' or conversely 'to light a candle is to cast a shadow'.[3] In a similar manner, science fiction heroes are typically historically minor, middling or marginal figures of the Lukácsian kind. This underscores the vastness and cyclical impersonality of history and society, time and space, matter and energy. In the case of the cyclical-epic genre, the universe exists in a state of yin-yang oscillation and its hidden god of equilibria calls forth a corresponding search for balance – propositions that are made in different ways in the influential science fictions of Le Guin (among these, the seven novels set in the Hainish universe published between 1966 and 2000) and Doris Lessing's series of five 'space fiction' novels *Canopus in Argos: Archives* (1979–83).

Promises of salvation and rescue from danger are not just religious in character. They also assume secular and rhetorical forms. Irrespective of type, most disappoint. Doris Lessing tells the story of an advanced civilization, Canopus, its empire and its interactions with a variety of less developed planets across many generations. In one of the novels in the Canopus series, *The Making of the Representative for Planet 8* (1982), Canopus instructs colonists on Planet 8 to build a giant protective wall for their own good. The mild temperature of their small planet is about to be subsumed by an encroaching ice age. The wall promises temporary protection until the planet's inhabitants can be resettled on another planet. However the wall's protection turns into a kind of mental and spiritual imprisonment. Canopus's resettlement plan fails and the saviour wall that protects Planet 8's inhabitants ends up blocking their ability to act independently. The fixation on the wall stops them stretching their minds. This paralyses their capacity to evolve to meet nature's implacable challenges. They are stuck for solutions and undergo extinction except for their Representative, their collective memory.

Lessing's point, repeatedly made in the Canopus series, is that civilization's principal enemies are not external. Rather, they are compartmentalized minds. Their fragmentalizing mentalities work against Necessity. Necessity is the need to achieve dynamic equilibria. Mono-minds, the curse of an ailing civilization, are unable to think in oppositions. Irrespective of their space craft they are unable to travel long distances mentally, back and forward, between antithetical zones or concepts to do Necessity's bidding and incorporate all relevant poles of experience into their mental outlook. They cannot comfortably bridge between the idea of subatomic particles and the cosmos or between inner space and outer space. Consequently they cannot find the kinds of symbioses and syntheses that allow societies to evolve satisfactorily, continuously meet challenges and find productive equilibria.

Events and actions

Epic works are elastic. They stretch between the microscopic individual particles of society and the macroscopic great waves and epic rhythms of nature, society, history and metaphysics. The latter, the macrocosm of existence, develops over long periods and on a large scale. From time to time it crashes up against the familiar fabric of everyday life. In these pivotal moments, individual characters struggle consciously and unconsciously with the long waves and deep morphologies of time and space as they roll over them. The resulting, often tumultuous, events encompass expansive populations, nations at war and societies in transition.

Epics are long but not only long. They are also encyclopaedic in scope though not just all-encompassing. They are episodic but the episodes and scenes depicted are interwoven in a vast theme or story. These are grand narratives. Yet they are grand in specific ways. They concern the fate of a nation, a people, an empire or a civilization. The characters of an epic are entwined with this destiny. Some of them will die or fall by the wayside. Very few of them will directly affect the larger course of events that sweep them along. These all-consuming events have a life and a character of their own. Cut adrift amidst the metaphysical forces of history or nature, the ordinary characters of epics are participant observers of events that mostly they do not and cannot control. They respond in various ways to these gravitational tides of time and space. Some react sceptically, others naively; some cynically, others foolishly. There are treacherous and belligerent responses along with phlegmatic and hysterical ones.

Epic scale can be found in literary works, fictional works, art works and works of social science. In his *Aesthetics*, the philosopher G. W. F. Hegel ([1835] 1975) devised an astute typology of literature. He compared epic literature with dramatic and lyrical literary forms. Epics, Hegel argued, depict events or 'what has happened' (167). They concentrate on 'external circumstances, happenings, and events' that occur independently of the motives, purposes, duties or dispositions of the chief characters portrayed (1063–4). The principle character of an epic is not a dramatic or lyrical personality. It is rather some iteration of nature, history, society or metaphysics. All of the personalities in an epic are caught up often unwittingly and with varying degrees of insight in the tectonic shifts that occur as nations, peoples and civilizations fall and rise, rise and fall in accord with the deep-set, anonymous, and largely unconscious patterns that shape events. Epics, accordingly, are characterized by a profound objective quality. There is often an unease in modern culture with the objectivism of epic forms of writing. For the epic form is sceptical of human actions and motives, and the capacity of human beings to 'do something', intervene and 'make a difference that matters' to the unfolding course of events that no social or political actor, no matter how seemingly powerful, really controls. Epics betray a deep scepticism about the will to power.

As Hegel observed, drama is concerned with the 'intentions and subjective motives' of characters 'such as passion, principles, and aims' (1063–4). Where epics depict events, dramas depict actions – and are a function of the human will. Drama explores the inner motives of the human will, the way that motives operate on the will, and the will's inner reaction to those motives (167). Lyricism in contrast, Hegel argued, 'immerses itself in what it feels' (415). Both lyric and drama look inward. The lyrical form dwells on the self. It is preoccupied 'with the inner life of the individual' and the kinds of 'subjective vision, reflection, and feeling' that do not proceed to action (1046). Whereas in drama 'passion with a practical aim becomes the chief thing'; action is central.

The literature of the nineteenth and twentieth centuries was dominated by a combination of lyrical and dramatic forms. That is to say, it possessed a mostly psycho-dramatic character. This era was dominated by the modern novel of obsessive self-examination. Epic literature was the exception rather than the norm. Doubtless, the architectonic scale of the epic novel, and the resulting need to interweave numerous characters, locales, periods and episodes, also dampened authorial interest in it. In any event, only a relative handful of modern literary works can be described as genuine epics. Tolstoy's *War and Peace* (1869) is notable among them. The case of genre fiction is different. By the late twentieth century, the epic form had become creatively employed quite extensively in science fiction. Among these are Poul Anderson's Technic Civilization series (1958–85), Walter M. Miller's *A Canticle for Leibowitz* (1959), Frank Herbert's Dune series (1965–85), Dan Simmons's Hyperion Cantos series (1989–97), Vernon Vinge's Zones of Thought series (1992–2011), and James S.A. Corey's The Expanse series (2011–22). The most important example of the epic science fiction genre is Isaac Asimov's Foundation series (1951–93). Why epically inclined writers gravitated to genre fiction rather than literary fiction is understandable given the bias of modern literary culture in favour of lyrical romance and dramatic conflict. Science fiction epics generally avoid inward-probing, psychologically complex characterizations. Dramatic conflicts drive their plots forward but the aim-driven actions are overrun by underlying patterns of events that severely limit the power of those actions. These science fictions are fictions of ideas. Notably so in Asimov's case.

Almost a century after his death, Hegel's philosophy of literary forms had a significant influence on the literary critic and philosopher Georg Lukács. In *The Theory of the Novel* ([1920/1916] 1971) Lukács observed, as Hegel had done before him, that epic works are different from lyrical or dramatic works. Lukács was the odd man out critically. He defended the importance of epic works in contrast to the psycho-dramatic novel (45–51). Whether an epic is literary, fictional, artistic or social-scientific in nature, the epic genre requires a capacious creative imagination. This is a roomy, spacious, voluminous imagination; an imagination with breadth; one that is expansive and capable of grasping, describing, explaining and narrating, as Lukács memorably put it, an 'extensive totality' and a 'world of distances' (46, 56, 89, 59). Hegel called the latter 'an outspread world', the portrayal of which can only be properly executed 'in its entirety' (1051). All epic works incite in those who consume them a view of the world that is large, far-ranging in scope and fateful.

Epic science fiction developed as a way of understanding society and nature, and their interaction, on the largest imaginable scale, the scale of planetary systems and galaxies. The epic genre of science fiction supposes an expansive imagination and a way of thinking about nature, society, history and metaphysics that grapples with the problem of how systems with millions or billions of interacting parts behave as a whole and how that whole in turn shapes the behaviour of those parts. It aims to give an imaginative form or shape to an extensive totality that is stretched across a world of distances. As Lukács aptly described it, the world of the modern psycho-dramatized novel is 'problematic' and 'closed within itself' (46). Its characters are typically lonely, lyrical, elegiac and sorrowful; its dialogues are monological (45–6). They draw out the incognito of the soul, the solitary 'I', engrossed in an 'object-free contemplation of its own self' (51). The object world is dissolved into sensations and moods. In the case of the epic, in contrast, the world is the ultimate principle of the work. An epic composition, Lukács proposed, 'is empirical at its deepest, most decisive, all-determining transcendental base' (46). It has an indestructible bond with reality 'as it is' (47).

In pursuit of reality as it is, Tolstoy blended novelistic writing with historical reflection and philosophical meditation. Aleksandr Solzhenitsyn's ten-volume epic cycle of novels, *The Red Wheel* (1971–91), took the Tolstoian model even further, mixing in a huge amount of historical documentation with its fictional characters. Epic works are not common in modern literature or indeed in literature as a whole. The ambition to imagine the extensive totality of societies and the world of distances is rare. The desire or ability to blend fact and fiction, history and characters occurs, but only sporadically. This is not so though in the case of genre fiction, and notably science fiction which, since the middle of the twentieth century, has been drawn to the mix of empiricism and epic, fact and fiction synthesized in future histories. With their large attentive readerships and audiences, these works evidently fill a gap left by literature including literary science fiction and in particular by literary novelists un-attracted to exploring vast non-psychologized worlds of expanse and distance in which natural, social or metaphysical forces (rather than dramatic or lyrical personas) figure as the ultimate focus of the story affecting everything and everyone in their wake.

Tolstoy's *War and Peace* contains 600 different characters. The scope of this panorama makes a fundamental point: none of the dramatic egos and psychologized 'I's, no matter how deftly drawn by the author or how powerful their offices and statuses, determine the outcome of the events depicted. Asimov, with 70 characters, makes a similar point. Each of Shakespeare's English history plays are dramas whose principal characters' will to power is drawn with extraordinary psychological depth. But, in their entirety, the eleven plays constitute an epic cycle in which history appears as an enveloping force shaping events through the various episodes of the Plantagenets, Lancastrians, Yorkists and Tudors. The cycle of plays encompasses 207 characters and extends from the early 1200s to the 1540s. The appearance of history as a character in its own right is key. Historical and social developments colour the background of a multigenerational family saga like Thomas Mann's *Buddenbrooks* ([1901] 1994) or Anthony Powell's single-generation multi-decade saga *A Dance to the Music of Time* ([1951–75] 1995). In contrast, Olivia Manning's Fortunes of War series (1960–80) is epic in tone and feel because world history is a palpable force in the foreground of the novels. It permeates the drama and romance of the characters, and ties their fates together as it propels them onwards episodically from wartime Romania to Greece to Egypt and Palestine in the 1940s.

Civilizational integration

The object of the epic, Lukács argued, is 'life itself' (47). As a fictional form, the epic does not change life. It may receive and mould life but only in order to reduce it to its 'inborn meaning'. Epics are not utopian (46–7). They do not hold up an essence above existence. They don't look to some kind of despotic imperative or enchanted, lyrical or sorrowful transcendence of what is. The 'should be' of the dramatic psychologized novel, Lukács thinks, is a 'desperate intensity'; an outlaw on Earth that kills life (48). The epic in contrast cannot 'charm into life something that wasn't already present' (47). It might accelerate the rhythm of life, Lukács concedes, but only by finding something immanent within life that was otherwise hidden (46).

The epic phenomena that Lukács singled out – those of 'extensive totality' and the 'world of distances' – are interdependent. The world of distances entails risk and adventure. Travel, voyaging, searching, seeking, wandering, danger, calculated risk, destiny, quest and a sense of vastness fills the souls of the figures who journey through epic space and time. This is not just any kind of adventure, though. True enough, Lukács observed, the 'heroes of the epic live through a whole variety of adventures' (89). But, in a more specific sense, these adventures are 'the form taken by the objective and extensive totality of the world'. The adventures of the epic protagonists are shaped by the forces and patterns of nature, society and history, or the metaphysical, over which they have little control. Their journeys take place against a background of wars and empires, cities and federations, economies and industries, natural and supernatural forces that constantly intrude into the foreground of their experience, vast motions against which their own actions appear tiny and fatefully motionless as if they were wakeful sleepwalkers through history: caught up in history and yet observers of it, standing outside of it, at a tangent to it. The epic soul, Lukács remarks, 'is only the luminous centre around which this unfolded totality revolves, the inwardly most immobile point of the world's rhythmic movement' (89).

The extensive totality of imaginative epic thinking – whether in literature or genre fiction or in the social sciences – is a precondition for solving what the historian and philosopher Wilhelm Dilthey thought of as the conundrum of meaning: the hermeneutic puzzle as to how the parts of a society relate to the whole.[4] This problem always exists, even if only tacitly. It appears explicitly when social actors lack a compelling sense of being part of what Lukács thought of as an 'integrated civilisation' (29–39). Lukács in this regard followed Hegel. Hegel posed an impossible dilemma: meaningful integration existed in the Homeric world and the classic polis yet (seemingly) was impossible in modernity. If we borrow for a moment the terminology of the French nineteenth-century sociologist, Auguste Comte, then Hegel's and Lukács's modernity is a 'critical' (fragmented) rather than an 'organic' (whole) world. This is the common view of the modern intelligentsia. Yet it is not necessarily correct. It is just as arguable that buoyant societies of many different kinds (modern, classical and archaic) possess, as a trait that unites them, a strong and effective sense of homeostasis. The latter indicates the ability to integrate numerous parts into an efficacious whole through acts of dynamic balancing, equilibria or ordering thereby creating a general rhythm among constant flux, or what Lukács called a 'Tolstoyan nature' (150).

Lukács thought that Dante and Giotto and their world of the 1200s and 1300s had glimpsed something of the 'equilibrium of mutually inadequate, heterogeneous intensities' and the 'harmony of spheres' that the ancient Greeks had been drawn to (38). But he also thought that this vision of the world did not translate into modernity. In doing so, Lukács's path diverged from a countervailing stream of thought that ran through the twentieth century. This current conceived the modern world as one of dynamic homeostasis: what Frederick Hayek thought of as a cosmos or what Joseph Schumpeter and Nikolai Kondratieff conceived of as cycles. Asimov did something analogous in genre fiction with his idea of Gaia/Galaxia, a collective homeostatic 'self-supporting organism' capable of creating balance when things were out of balance or where 'vicious cycles' dominated (*Foundation and Earth*).

Asimov's Gaia concept, which appears in *Foundation's Edge* (1982) and *Foundation and Earth* (1986), was influenced by the scientist James Lovelock's Gaia hypothesis (1979), the idea that the earth is a complex interacting system composed of many parts (biological, chemical, geological, oceanic and climatic). These parts maintain themselves in a self-regulating oscillating dynamic equilibrium.[5] Subtle balances are struck automatically (or naturally) between multiple systems. Lovelock rejected the idea that industrialized humankind was a destructive force of perturbation outside of this vast mechanism of automated homeostasis (100–14). As well as the integration of planetary systems, homeostasis is also key to humankind's species-being. The term homeostasis was coined by the American physiologist Walter Bradford Cannon in 1926. He used it to describe how the human body functioned as a system of forces in tension ('stasis'). These various forces, including the external environment of the body, are maintained over time in a 'similar' (that is, 'homeo') state of equilibrium – that is, a steady normal yet adaptive state, the result of ongoing adjustments, variations and dynamic changes to the body's various constituent forces. System stability in the case of the human body is achieved by self-regulating changes, the function of which is to maintain an optimum equilibrium and integration of parts. Earlier, in the 1860s, the French physiologist Claude Bernard proposed that the body's internal system (*milieu intérieur*) was engaged in a continuous and delicate compensation for changes occurring in the external environment in order to establish the most sensitive of balances between the body and its environment. In 1956, the Hungarian Canadian endocrinologist Hans Selye expanded the idea of homeostasis in his groundbreaking study of bodily stress, *The Stress of Life*. The American biochemist Lawrence Henderson in *The Fitness of the Environment* (1913) and *The Order of Nature* (1917) depicted the fine-tuned dynamic balances required for cosmic and organic evolution. Later on, Henderson proposed a version of Pareto's equilibrium sociology in his *Pareto's General Sociology* (1935). Henderson figured at the centre of a loose milieu of American equilibria sociologists whose characteristic works included Talcott Parsons's *The Social System* (1951).[6]

In *A Study of History* (1934–61), Arnold Toynbee recognized that on a civilizational scale a particular kind of dynamic harmony was crucial if societies were not to breakdown. Toynbee's view was that 'a change in any one part of a whole ought to be accompanied by sympathetic adjustments of the other parts if all is to go well' (1988: 166). Yet often things do not go well. In such cases if 'one part [is] altered while others are left as they have been', the result for the whole is 'a loss of harmony between its component parts'. The cost of this is 'a corresponding loss of self-determination' of the whole. In Toynbee's eyes, this is the ultimate reason for civilizational breakdown. Maintaining equilibrium and averting breakdown is the role of what Toynbee called society's 'creative minority' (1988: 164, 224, 228, 234). A great degree of ingenuity and invention is required to stop decline – yet creative minorities, Toynbee concluded, often fail to do this. They lose their gift for homeostatic creation and replace it with a penchant for domination. They exhaust their flexible adaptive power of responding to challenges. Their ideas become closed, rigid and ineffective. When they talk, they end up in a bubble talking to themselves rather than to the whole of society. The creative minority becomes a self-absorbed, inward-looking social class and loses its ability to mint and present morphologically dynamic images of a harmonious whole to the entire society that blend continuity and change.

The figure of the creative minority is well represented in Asimov's Foundation series by the First and Second Foundations. Asimov was initially enthusiastic about Toynbee when he read the first volumes of *A Study of History*. But that enthusiasm then died. Arguably this was because Asimov had a very positive view of creative minorities when he wrote the earliest volumes of the Foundation series. Toynbee's view was considerably more nuanced and sceptical. Asimov initially presented the two Foundations as a solution to the waning energies of his fictionally depicted 10,000-year-old Galactic Empire. The empire had seen periods of breakdown before; eras of rebellion, independence movements and dynastic wars. But in the past five centuries the degree of political entropy had grown. Over everything hung the words: 'The Galactic Empire is dying' (*Prelude to Foundation*). Eventually, in the response to this challenge, the First Foundation Confederation of planets emerges. It is 'almost a Galactic Empire' in the eyes of political leaders (*Foundation's Edge*). Though, like Byzantium in the place of ancient Rome, by the end of the Foundation series the First Foundation's Confederation is only a third of the size of its predecessor. Its competitor, the Second Foundation, dreams of a Second Galactic Empire, much like Charlemange dreamed of a Second Rome as did the Holy Roman Emperors a century later. The dream continued but the reality of a Second Rome somehow always remained out of reach.

After five hundred years, no phoenix-like Caesar or Alexander has risen from the ashes of the entropic Galactic imperial past. The First Foundation has seen a number of brilliant leaders, some capable ones and some hereditary dim-wits and despots. Conversely, the 'great enemy' of the two Foundations, the Mule, a renegade mind-controlling will-to-power figure from the planet Gaia, is defeated in the course of the Foundation novels. The very nature of the epic form supposed, on Asimov's part, a certain scepticism about the dramatic appearance of the wilful 'great man in history' in place of events in their totality. An epic is a stoic narrative form. As Hegel put it, it recollects the 'broad flow of events' and the objective sense of those events 'rolling and flowing on in tranquil independence' (1037). As opposed to drama, the narrative form of epic comes quite close in spirit to the Japanese Zen literary attitude of detached contemplation and the tranquil recollection of things and events at a distance (Odin 2001). By the end of the series, Asimov's positive view of the Foundations has gone. Accordingly, Asimov does not at any point actually decide between the power of the competing creative minorities, the conscious organism of Gaia or (yet a further solution to imperial entropy) a high-functioning artificial intelligence. Five hundred years of events are mentioned in the Foundation series yet nothing really happens in the books in the sense that the future of galactic society is not resolved. There is no dramatic conclusion to Asimov's fictional history. The seeming drive to change things in order to arrest the decline that began with the breakdown of the Galactic Empire ends at the end of the series in a kind of suspended animation. This serves as a reminder that the Foundation series is an epic not a drama. If it was a drama we could expect the warring passions or heroic activity of characters to conclude with some kind of resolute purposeful accomplishment. That does not happen.

Towards the end of *Foundation and Earth*, the character Trevize, the weary inquirer who has risked his life to answer questions about the evolution of galactic society, and who has found that every answer just leads to another question, announces to his companions that he would like to resign from the First Foundation Council and live on his pension. He wants to 'let the Galaxy go as it will'. That means not caring about any of the shenanigans of the galactic creative classes: 'I won't care about the Seldon Plan, or about the Foundation, or about the Second Foundation.' Nor, he says, will he care 'about Gaia'. In fact 'the Galaxy can choose its own path'. His conclusion is: let it be, laissez-faire. As it turns out, he can't retire and let go of his journey of discovery. Nonetheless he senses that no answer to his questions will make a difference to Galaxia's eventual course. As the observer of epic events, he cannot alter their direction. The Foundation series in that respect is like David Lean's epic film *Lawrence of Arabia* (1962).[7] On one of the peripheries of the titanic events of the First World War the fatalistic character of T. E. Lawrence wanders across the vast landscape of the Saudi Arabian Nefudh desert, organises the blowing-up of railways and the capture of the Red Sea port of Aqaba, and coaxes divided Bedouin Arab tribes into an effective anti-Turkish military alliance in order to capture the city of Damascus 500 kilometres north in Syria. Yet at the end – when peace comes – the alliance collapses. Its cement was money not conviction. The ancient erosion (crack) patterns of family, clan and tribal allegiances reasserted themselves swiftly. Anonymous history got the better of all of Lawrence's calculating political designs.

Epic world building

Each literary or fictional form has its own structural laws. The structural laws of epic science fiction are five-fold:

1. *Distance (Expanse)*. The epic takes place within a vast expanse of time and space. This means journeys, treks, pilgrimages, missions, supply vessels, portals and travel crossing the enormity of inter-planetary, inter-stellar, galactic (etc.) space. In terms of time, a science fiction epic requires prophecies, predictions, knowledge banks, collective minds, memories and chronicles that connect distant points in time in a meaningful (explanatory) way.
2. *Scale*. The space and time of the science fiction work contains multiple interacting civilizations, societies and systems. Epic science fiction does not have a single structural focus like, for instance, military science fiction (e.g. Paul Verhoeven and Robert A. Heinlein's *Starship Troopers*) does. Religious monasteries, trading societies, mining planets, industrial moons, imperial administrative systems, exilic colonies, space stations and so on, belong to a larger totality of which each one is an interactive part. For example, Simmons's (*Hyperion*'s) priests, soldiers, poets, scholars, detectives and consuls each have a tale to tell against the background of the affinities of a

Chaucer-like pilgrimage undertaken amidst the shadow of an impending invasion.
3. *World-building*. Epic science fiction is *kosmopoietic*. That is, it is world-building. It has conflict, dramas, wars, conquests, struggles, near escapes and massive battles, but it is not apocalyptic, dystopic or a genre of horror. It takes place against a backdrop of imagined civilizations, societies and systems on a grand scale and the fiction has to construct plausible versions of those worlds involving not only their dramas and resulting adventures but also their functional components including governments, industries, technologies, commerce; their systems of meaning (religions, metaphysics, philosophies, arts, mathematics, sciences, etc.), and their consequent systemic (cliodynamic, cyclical, oscillatory, etc.) interactions.
4. *Connections*. Epic science fiction is outward-facing not inward-looking. Its dramas or actions focus on bands of companions or closely connected fraternities, unusual inter-species friendships, boon members of declining governing houses, exilic fellowships and banished compatriots. The participants in these small fraternities are the antithesis of social atoms. At the same time, the stories of all of these freely chosen affinity groups develop against the background of a social universe that is governed by an underlying shaping or patterning force of necessity or destiny. In the actions of the affinity groups and their members, the polarities of freedom and necessity coalesce.
5. *Necessity/destiny*. Underpinning epic science fiction is a pervading sense of an unfolding necessity or destiny. The central characters and narrated dramas are episodes only in a far larger flow of events across time and space that no one controls. No single event, person, fraternity, episode, war, alliance, federation or empire can explain the rhythm and homeostasis of events on an interstellar scale or across a heliospheric expanse, or their various disturbances and ruptures, or their return to equilibrium. Even the greatest empires and the most powerful figures rise and fall, fall and rise. Cycles occur, power oscillates in pendulum swings, prophecies become unexpectedly true, the interaction of monks, traders, military personnel, rulers, councils, miners and technicians are caught up in a play of forces that no single entity controls and yet which forms an intelligible narrative shape that gradually makes sense. Events, perhaps obscure to begin with, eventually settle into a pattern of meaning, an epic whole that is generated by an ensemble of interacting parts that is no one's intentional design. Epic characters cannot escape their destiny but they can make the best of it.

The premise of the most important extant example of epic science fiction, Isaac Asimov's Foundation series, is a mathematics professor (Hari Seldon) who develops a method of 'psychohistory' (a putative history of the future) that predicts the fall and rise of a galactic empire, the mirror opposite of Edward Gibbon's *Decline and Fall of the Roman Empire*. Asimov began his series after reading Gibbon's *History* for a second time. In 1944 two years into writing the early stories that eventually would morph into the first of the Foundation books, Asimov (1980: 400) was introduced to Toynbee's *A Study of History*. As well as science fiction, Asimov wrote numerous non-fiction civilizational histories including *The Roman Republic* (1966) and *The Roman Empire* (1967). 'Psychohistory' (a mathematical sociology) is a plot device that allows the future to be fore-told, that is, narrated as if it was a history. Its intellectual presupposition is borrowed from the kinetic theory of gases, namely that while the microscopic behaviour of any individual gaseous atoms and molecules cannot be predicted, the behaviour of gas at a macroscopic level (temperature, volume etc.) can be predicted. Accordingly, the novel assumes that, while one cannot predict the behaviour of individuals, if we apply the laws of statistics to the behaviour of large groups of people, we can anticipate the flow of future events. Even then, Seldon admits that 'historical change is to a large degree difficult to swerve' (*Foundation's Edge*). Indeed.

Asimov began the writing of the Foundation series in the 1940s. He adopted from the public language of the time the word 'Plan'.[8] He introduced the idea that given certain nudges galactic history will evolve according to a stadial plan envisaged by Seldon, thereby reducing the scale of the predicted decline and fall of the Galactic Empire and averting a prolonged inter-planetary dark ages, cutting it short by tens of thousands of years. The evidence for a prophetic social statistics is very slight. Attempts at predicting the future almost always fail. Mostly these are doom-laden predictions of catastrophe, secular prophecies of the end of the world, the coming apocalypse, the millennial holocaust, etc. The basic problem not just of a providential plan but of all kinds of society-wide planning is neatly voiced by Seldon himself: 'How could one study the history of twenty five million worlds and consider all their possible interactions?' (*Prelude to Foundation*). That is the knowledge problem that haunts all large-scale plans. Asimov, though, turns the predictions of Seldon's fictional psychohistory into an elaborate narrative sleight of hand that ends in a much more interesting way than if it had been simply a tale of prophetic mumbo-jumbo.

Asimov tells the story of four more or less coexistent knowledge systems, often with deceptive and evasive relations with each other. The four include, in order of appearance, the First Foundation on Terminus, a planet located at the edge of the galaxy; the Second Foundation squirrelled away in the old Empire's administrative capital Trantor, at the centre of the galaxy; the third, a collective knowledge system (Gaia) and the fourth, an artificial intelligence. Each interacts with the other and the world via elaborate indirection, deception and manipulation. The Gaians, for example, can exercise a kind of mind control although that requires time-consuming preparation to execute. Each system is readily recognizable in contemporary sociological terms. The first (the technological) is created by 'encyclopaedists' who become gifted technologists without intending to do so and who exercise power and influence via a kind of deceptive technocracy. The second (the scholarly) is an epistemic elite, practitioners of mental rather than physical sciences who constitute a university-cum-intelligence network, composed mostly of technicians and analysts. In the eyes of the Second Foundation, the First Foundation's role was to provide (militarily) 'the physical framework of a single political unit' while the Second Foundation's role was to supply (paternalistically) 'the mental framework of a ready-made ruling class' (*Second Foundation*). The Gaians are a collective intelligence while the fourth and final kind of knowledge system is an artificial intelligence.

Empire life

In Asimov's fictional history, Earth 'existed as the sole world of human beings for an immeasurable period and then, about twenty to twenty-five thousand years ago, the human species developed interstellar travel by way of the hyperspatial Jump and colonized a group of planets' (*Foundation and Earth*). Colonial settlement occurred in two waves. The first wave used robots extensively. These robotized societies 'developed a high technology and unusual longevity and despised their ancestral world', and at least by legend tried to dominate it and oppress it. A second wave of colonists, among whom robots were banned, followed. This wave colonized the galaxy while, again by legend, the first wave died out.

In their phases of growth, the Galactic Empire and its more modest successor the Foundation Confederation demonstrated the capacity to include the interaction of vast numbers of peoples (25 million worlds and quadrillions of people at the peak) using techniques such as a standardized language with local dialectics, space ports with standardized facilities, galactic law, interplanetary legal codes, and standardized year measurements and units of measurement. The benefit of these was a lengthy period of peace and prosperity. The downside was the diminishing returns from the effort required to sustain the upside. The explicit power of the Empire was eaten away by civilizational entropy. The signs were falling birth rates, population decline, growing emigration and stagnant trade; a lack of building, a slowing rate of technology advancement and a general weariness (*Prelude to Foundation*). The decline did not follow 'a straight-line path'. Within the large cycle of decline were nested tinier cycles of improvement.

The Galactic Empire, as Asimov depicts it, is technologically sophisticated and varied. Its denizens use heat-coats, air-taxis, gravitic ships insulated from gravitational fields, hyper-spatial engines, heat-conversion energy, holovision technology, ships that can in principle accelerate to nearly the speed of light (though in practice it is too dangerous to do so), psychic probes, farm settlements in orbit, commercial planetary and interstellar flights, vision screen walls, holographic imaging, neuronic whips, air cars, automated cars, subterranean apartments, banking that is completely computerized, book-films and book viewers. Across the galaxy there are independent sovereign worlds, allied worlds, confederated worlds, imperial worlds and break-away micro-empires. A common cultural thread are hyperdramas, romances of empire. The political administration revolves around ministries and councils. There are planetary citizenship laws, identification papers, immigration stations; interstellar legal distinctions between persons governed by imperial galactic law and Outworlders; galactic prohibitions against torture and cruel and unusual punishments; worlds that apply laws rigidly and worlds that are free-wheeling and lax; sovereign planets that are not members but rather associated powers of the Foundation Confederation. Power is lost and gained. Free mobility occurs within the bounds of imperial and confederated space while restricted mobility in this space applies to Outworlders or worldless persons.

Different planetary societies are distinguishable by their gastronomies, sexual moralities, ethical codes, guilt cultures, social stratifications, systems of rank and duty, divisions of labour, honesty, efficiency, enterprise and their taste for adventure. They encompass isolationist and expansionist worlds, innovating and static ones. There are miniature worlds (Alpha) and hermaphrodite worlds (Solaria), divergent measures of freedom, counting in numbers and counting in quality, electronic music and archaic wood and metal instruments, old Imperial and new Foundation accents. 'Fashions change from world to world and from time to time' (*Foundation and Earth*). Some planetary societies are puritanical, religious or strict; others are not. Some value moderation; others not so much.

There are joyful, festive societies and joyless ones. Some worlds are old; others are new. Some like cold-water energy-hoarding asceticism; others hot showers. Some live in near isolation; others in swarms and crowds. There are sparsely populated robotic auto-industrial economies and swathes of the galaxy in which robotic technology has been banned. Some cities are manufacturing foci; others are administrative centres with large concentrations of museums, libraries, archives and universities. The latter kind of cities have a taste for 'large, useless, and expensive' monumental buildings (*Foundation and Earth*).

The characters of planets are distinctive. Comporellon is one of the older settled planets in the Galaxy. It was once a leading planet but fell into obscurity after 20,000 years of galactic colonization. The planet's inhabitants resent its loss of status. They want independence from the empire. They don't want to be a 'vassal' of the old empire or an 'associate' of the new Foundation neo-empire. The more Comporellon has lost status, the more it has glorified its past. 'The more we are made aware of our subordinate position, the stronger the belief in the great, mysterious days of the past become' (*Foundation and Earth*). This is the foreground of planetary life. However, in the background, invisible and masked from view, Galactic societies are enveloped in the up-and-down rhythms of the meta-history of emergence, growth and decline, and decline's own phases of breakdown, disintegration and dissolution, and the subsequent phases of renaissance and re-emergence. The goal of the Seldon Plan is to stop the decline of the Galactic Empire by replacing it with a Second Galactic Empire. Seldon's Plan in practice though only partly realizes its explicit goal with the gradual emergence of the First Foundations' empire-lite Confederation.

The Seldon Plan promised to 'bring the human species (so it was said) to safe harbor – at last in the womb of a Second Galactic Empire, greater than the First, a nobler and a freer one'. Yet Asimov harbours a scepticism that history can repeat itself better the second-time round. The Gaians offer something that the Empire model does not. The Second Empire, Asimov muses,

> however great in size and variety [would still] be a mere union of individual organisms of microscopic size in comparison with itself. [It] would be another example of the kind of union of individuals that humanity had set up ever since it became humanity. [It] might be the largest and best of the species, but it would still be but one more member of that species. (*Foundation and Earth*)

Asimov envisaged a Byzantium style 'Second Rome' as he developed the narrative idea of the empire-reviving First and Second Foundations in the 1940s and 1950s. By the 1980s the 'Second Rome' model had fallen out of authorial favour. It vied in Asimov's mind with a third model, a collective intelligence; a Pierre Teilhard de Chardin-like noosphere or shared intellect, a matrix-like telepathic and hyper-spatial consciousness, Gaia/Galaxia. A fourth knowledge system, a hyper-advanced artificial robot intelligence, is introduced later on, as the Foundation epic ends.

What is harm?

Asimov's Foundation series closely parallels Hegel's description of the epic (1044). It is a total world, which is concentrated nevertheless in individual lives. It proceeds tranquilly in the course of its development. It doesn't hurry on in the direction of some mark. It is not the result of aiming at that mark. The entire course of the presentation of the epic's object-like external reality takes on the form of an episodic string of events that are external to each other but which nonetheless have as their ground 'the inner essence of the epic's specific subject-matter' even if this is not expressly emphasized. As a result, Hegel argues, epic works become rather diffuse and, owing to the independence of their parts, they are only loosely connected together and yet paradoxically these works form an organic whole. That perfectly describes Asimov's series of books.

Every episode of the Foundation books yields something unexpected. Nothing is what it appears to be. The seeming guiding hand of the First Foundation is shadowed by a more deeply hidden Second Foundation. In the later volumes of the series, *Foundation's Edge* and *Foundation and Earth*, it is revealed that both of these in turn are shadowed by a collective planetary mind, the Gaia, and by an advanced robotic intelligence. A dramatic structure of mystery-revelation animates the Foundation books. Deception and revelation – the hidden and the exposed – drive the narrative of the series. The episode on the planet Comporellon is typical. All references to Earth have been removed from the Library of Trantor. Gaia has no early galactic memories. There are things not spoken about or only spoken about in euphemisms or expletives like 'the Oldest' (the earth) by the inhabitants of the planet Comporellon (*Foundation and Earth*). Their one scholar of 'primeval history', Vasil Deniador, is a sceptic. He and his fellow intellectual sceptics, dissenters from the planet's cult of past glories, are scolded and sneered at. Students are discouraged from attending his courses while other discouragements are institutional: 'study of the Oldest … is not a well-rewarded niche in the corridors of learning'. Deniador's knowledge of

Earth, he readily concedes, is scanty. It is a mix of clear-eyed supposition, faulty reasoning, slim evidence and sketchy hints extracted from legends. Deniador suffers from a degree of hyper-rationalism. He tends to treat everything as legend, the opposite intellectual vice to that of romantic credulity. Nonetheless he points his inquisitors in the direction of 'the Spacers', the first wave of galactic colonial settlers, shunned by the second wave who refused to trade or have any contact with them. Knowledge about them has disappeared in the mists of time. The Spacers were a taboo subject on Comporellon. But Deniador speculated that a planet of theirs, perhaps abandoned, might still exist.

Progressive revelations of this kind animate the episodic drama of the Foundation series skilfully. In the final two volumes of the series, the quest to uncover hidden realities is propelled along by the powerful intuition of Golan Trevize, a First Foundation Council member from the Foundation's capital planet of Terminus. We are introduced to Trevize at the start of *Foundation's Edge*, with him declaring that the Seldon Plan and its prophecies are a sham. Trevize's healthy scepticism about Seldon sets in train a quest to find the long-forgotten planet Earth, the origin planet of galactic colonization. As the quest unfolds, Trevize and his friend Pelorat uncover the planet-come-collective consciousness of Gaia and its plan for an eventual harmonic inter-planetary synthesis. Trevize and Pelorat are joined by Bliss, a Gaian, and the three together journey to a series of planets searching for the legendary Earth. The quest is dangerous. Seemingly affable welcomes along the way like those on Solaris and Alpha turn threatening and nasty. The Solarian they meet, Bander, like his entire people, is an extreme isolate. He feigns hospitality and then tries to kill the voyagers. They kill him instead and escape with his child-heir Fallom who is threatened with death by other extreme isolationist Solarians. The Alphans are similarly xenophobic. They host the wandering party, apparently happily, and then infect the visitors with a virus in the hope of keeping outsiders (Outworlders) away.

Fallom is key to the voyagers escape from Alpha. Yet the intuitive Trevize feels uneasy about Fallom. Trevize's intuition is a cognitive spotlight into the web of mystery that pervades the Foundation series. The series is a kind of epic mystery. Efforts like Trevize's to unveil the mysteries of secreted forces structure and animate the Foundation epic. Even when Earth is finally found, in a lifeless radioactive state, Trevize still wonders why 'all information concerning Earth has been removed on various worlds. That is bound to bring us to an inescapable conclusion. Something on Earth is being hidden' (*Foundation and Earth*). And some unknown entity or force is doing the hiding. As the series finishes, Trevize finally figures out that the secret once harboured in the underground cities of the now dead Earth has been removed to a vast underground complex on the Moon. The complex is populated by robots organized by a superior robot intelligence, R. Daneel Olivaw. Daneel has been working for 20,000 years, the time in which galactic civilization has been developing, and long before the time of the First Galactic Empire, to ensure the well-being of humankind and to nudge it away from chaotic self-harm. A product of first-wave colonist (Spacer) technology, Daneel has developed almost limitless computing capacity over time. Despite this the robot is limited in four decisive ways.

A. The first law of robotics that governs his artificial intelligence prohibits him from doing harm to human beings or allowing harm to be done to them. But how does such a norm apply on a mass population scale? The robot faced the classic problem of human politics: 'When dealing with the Galaxy it is not likely that any course of action will prevent harm altogether. Always, some people, perhaps many people, will suffer so that a robot must choose minimum harm. Yet, the complexity of possibilities is such that it takes time to make that choice and one is, even then, never certain' (*Foundation and Earth*). Anyone who has ever offered any solution to a human problem knows that this is true.

B. The first limit has created a second limit: time. The robot has resolved the do-no-harm/allow-no-harm imperative by acting in a very cautious way only. Of necessity the results of this were generally poor. 'I tried to ameliorate the worst aspects of the strife and disaster that perpetually made itself felt in the Galaxy. I may have succeeded, on occasion, and to some extent, but if you know your Galactic history, you will know that I did not succeed often, or by much' (*Foundation and Earth*). The best result the robot and its human-mimicking robotic agents had was the development of a superorganism, the experimental world of Gaia. This took a very long time given the first law of robotics. To resolve the impasse, Gaians were inculcated with the robotic first principle of do-no-harm, though that created many dilemmas for the Gaians as the Gaian character Bliss exhibited. Harm is not a concept without deep ambiguities.

C. The third limit is that a robotic intelligence has to be given a human purpose. The do-no-harm principle is a limit not a purpose. The prevent-harm-occurring precept is a purpose but it is a negative purpose. The artificial intelligence conceived – or calculated – a positive purpose for its actions and those of its robot agents scattered through the galaxy, namely replacing an entropic empire with Gaian-style self-regulation. Yet it had lacked a human directive to do so, until Trevize makes an intuitive decision at the conclusion of *Foundation's Edge* to support the Gaian synthetic-organic paradigm instead of the imperial models of the First and Second Foundations.

D. Finally the robotic intelligence is 'dying'; it has become unstable due to the expansion of its capacities and it is failing. It can only survive long enough to seed the Gaian/Galaxia model if its positronic brain is fused with a human brain, in this case the orphaned child Fallom from the very long-lived Solarian isolate human hermaphrodite society.

The Foundation series 'ends' on this note, though the ending is far from 'the end'. Throughout the series, numerous veils obscure the truth. The truth of a mystery implies a revelation that will solve the mystery. As its title suggests, the 'last chapter' of the series does provide a satisfying unveiling of the truth. It does bring an end to Travize's journey of discovery. He can retire and live on his Foundation Council pension. He has solved the mystery which has been spread over seven volumes including two prequels. But because the Foundation series is not simply a mystery but an epic mystery, it has no – and cannot have any – definitive conclusion. The 'end' is not the point or the meaning of an epic work. It doesn't really end and the implications of the narrative ending is that the story will go on. What will happen to Gaia/Galaxia is an open question.

The hidden God of epic irony

None of the peoples or planets in the Foundation series are what they seem to be. Asimov's books are built around an ironic course of events. Within this master irony, there are multiple sub-ironies. The First Foundation encyclopaedists on the planet Terminus are supposed to collect knowledge as if they were an Alexandrine Library. Instead they end up ruling their sector of the galaxy through technological prowess and an artful pseudo-religious deception. The even more secretive Second Foundation is obliged to put an end to the threat of the power of the telepathic warlord and conqueror, the Mule, in order to keep Seldon's Plan on track. Yet, in doing so, the Second Foundation had to reveal itself undermining the premise of the Plan that the manipulations of its guardians be kept secret.

As Hegel observed, an epic story is one in which 'incidents in [a] journey' occur mostly without the story's main figures 'contributing anything to them'

(1064). Similarly none of the journey-expeditions undertaken by major figures in the Foundation series achieve what they set out to achieve. Early on, Seldon and his human-impersonating robot wife and professor of history at the University of Trantor, Dors Venabili, flee the Empire (which dislikes Seldon's future history project), only for Seldon later to return as First Minister to the Emperor. Toran and Bayta Darell set out in search of a safe haven from the Mule's wars unaware that the Mule is travelling with them in disguise. Trevize and Pel's search for the Second Foundation becomes a search for the long-lost Earth which leads them to the Gaians and subsequently to R. Daneel Olivaw's robot world. The aims, wills, directions and intentions of leading characters are secondary to the epic flow of external circumstances. As Hegel put it, actions are brought about through the 'entanglement' of principal characters with external conditions (1070).

To add to all of these ironies, Hegel's own view of human history in *The Philosophy of History* was the opposite of his understanding of literary epics. Hegel wrote a grand philosophy of history – a grand philosophical narrative – in which conscious freedom of purpose, will and motive were the overt driving forces. Hidden behind these was the Spirit or Mind of God. Geist or God unfolded itself across a marathon scale of time according to a Plan, the larger part of which involved the development of humankind in stages. The first stage of the Spirit's self-realization is characterized by societies dominated by the freedom of will of one person (despots and patriarchs), the second stage by the freedom of purpose of a few persons (aristocrats and ancient citizens) and the third stage by the freedom of will of all (the modern legal-rational state). Unconscious morphologies – hierarchies and symmetries, networks and fractals, equilibria and cycles, proximities and distances, waves and particles – play no role in the protracted unveiling of this hidden providential Plan that is marked by ever-more auspicious levels of conscious purpose and motivation. While Seldon's Plan is not explicitly a divine idea as in Hegel's case, functionally it is providential, hidden and the promissory vehicle of ever-higher levels of purposeful government.

Each volume of the Foundation series offers a version of a hidden god. Seldon's Plan is a science-fictional facsimile of a divine plan using advanced mathematics and elaborate statistical methods. Seldon's Plan is providential yet hidden from the sight of most individuals. A condition of its success is that the galactic population remains unaware of its operational details and its predictions. It is institutionalized in the secretive First and Second Foundations. Seldon shows himself periodically in taped appearances, each time prophesying a 'Seldon Crisis', a turning point that triggers rapid political shifts. But even his is mostly an absence rather than a presence, or perhaps more precisely Seldon is the absent presence in the life of the Foundations that themselves are absent presences in galactic life. As the character Trevize observes at one point, '[the] Foundation believes in the Seldon Plan, though no one in our realm can understand it, interpret its details, or use it to predict. We follow blindly out of ignorance and faith, and isn't that superstition?' (*Foundation and Earth*).

Whether it is Seldon, the First Foundation or the Second Foundation, each successive model of future history in the Foundation series hints at a hidden providential force – a God-like predestined force that exists and yet does not appear. When each iteration of Asimov's implied hidden god casts off some of its secrecy, the force is revealed to be something of a dead end or sleight of hand that does in itself little to answer the question of what can or will reverse interplanetary social entropy and the ailing, failing Empire. Asimov's penultimate stab at portraying the enigmatic absent presence – the hidden hand that is perceptible to some of the characters in the novel but nevertheless mostly remains out of sight – is the collective mind of Gaia/Galaxia. Gaia/Galaxia, it is inferred, is a providential pattern-making force, shielded through most of the Foundation series from inquisitive outsiders. As it develops, it is hinted that it will spontaneously order and structure, and thereby reverse the entropy of, the galaxy's visible systems of purposeful action: the goal-rational action, behaviour and interaction of multiple planetary societies. Little on the surface of Asimov's fiction can be taken at face value. Behind the fiction is a meta-fiction. Even the mythical or legendary origin stories of Earth contain beneath their surface an intuitive mathematical-pattern core, the number three: 'Three seems to be a significant number in these [old folk tales]', observes Pel (*Foundation and Earth*). Tripartite categorization recurs in human cognition: body-soul-spirit, earth-sea-air, mineral-vegetable-animal, faith-hope-charity, red-blue-green, one-few-many and so on. For the Pythagoreans the number three was the perfect number signifying beginning-middle-end.

At its core the Foundation series is an epic not a drama or a lyrical romance. Its key focus is not purposes or feelings but empirical patterns. The latter shape the former. As Hegel intimated in his *Aesthetics*, the attainment of aims by the epic characters is secondary; external circumstances and natural occurrences are primary (1064). In the paradigmatic modern epic literary novel (*War and Peace*) Tolstoy observed that Napoleon may have successfully invaded Russia and captured Moscow but his campaign success contained the seeds of

Napoleon's subsequent humiliating failure. As Tolstoy put it, there are 'causes' of human action arising out of free will but separate from these 'causes' are the 'laws' of motion of history. Meta-history or epic history – including Seldon's psychohistory, his sociological history of the future[9] – is premised on 'laws' of motion, or probably more accurately than 'laws', patterns of motion, most of which mirror the patterns of nature. The latter reverberate in Asimov's interplanetary Gaia or Galaxia's self-regulating, synergetic, complex, co-evolving system of micro forces that generate macro outcomes.

Asimov's Galaxia belongs to a lengthy tradition of modern thought about macro-social self-organization arising from the metaphorical hidden hand of God or the hidden God. The tradition includes Luther's *Deus absconditus* (*De Servo Arbitrio*, On Un-free Will), Jansenist theology, Pascal's philosophy and Racine's dramas. Lucien Goldmann's study of these in *The Hidden God* (1964) is instructive. Enlightenment Deism is a half-way house between religious macroscopy and its secular counterpart in Pierre Boisguilbert and Adam Smith's political economy, Frédéric Bastiat's dialectic of the visible and the invisible, and Tolstoy's philosophy of history. All these suppose one way or another that the extensive totality of society occurs 'behind the backs' of human beings, and what often are the most important forces shaping human society, are the least visible. All of the presumed principal 'actors' in the Foundation series are hidden: the secretive First Foundation, the even more secretive Second Foundation and the concealed artificial hyper-intelligence, R. Daneel Olivaw. Then there is Asimov's collective mind of Galaxia, which is hidden in a dual sense: its prototype, Gaia, is hidden in a secretive way but Gaia is also the model of a galactic-wide 'hidden hand' society that one day (it is expected) will operate on a vast scale in a manner similar to what Tolstoy called 'the unconscious, general, hive life of mankind', except that it will do so consciously.

In Asimov's fictional galactic history, inevitabilities coalesce with uncertainties, free will with destiny, wildcard deeds with predicted actions, and controlling figures with anonymous patterns of behaviour. The Foundation series concludes inconclusively. Versions of the models of technological, scholarly, robotic and dispersed knowledge systems somehow all remain options. The logic of Gaia/Galaxia points away from the series' original Plan to create a Second Galactic Empire instead evolving out of Gaia into the idea of Galaxia, a distributed collective mind, something akin to a Hayekian-type cosmos or catallaxy aided by an advanced artificial computational intelligence. But at this point Asimov found he couldn't continue with the idea further. Or at least he didn't continue with the idea.

The hidden hand of the meta-historical God means that nothing is ever (quite) what it seems to be. Or perhaps more accurately, meaning is inherently double-edged. The ultimate irony of the Foundation series is that a primitive version of Galaxia has been at work, however stumbling, all along; cyclical decline and fall being the preparation for rise and expansion. Epic history is cyclical. It is as if humanity is an ocean filled with particles of water (individuals) that move up and down. Waves of history pass through the water rising and falling, falling and rising perpendicular to the particles. As the waves of history ensue, entropy is first energized thereby creating order, then disorder replaces homeostasis, and finally allostasis emerges from disequilibrium, in repeating cycles. The meta-historical irony of micro intentions (particles) and macro events (waves) is built on the epic-scale disjunction between conscious human purpose and unconscious historical patterns. Human beings are in varying degrees free, purposeful and planning creatures. They form goals and ambitions, and they pursue them. Goals in the near run, close at hand, can be realized. Yet as time and space expands, the near-term achievement often ends up being a longer-run failure. Goal-rational achievements or lyrical satisfactions in the short run can turn into miserable outcomes in the long run. The problem of secondary consequences or unintended consequences recurs in the Foundation series. In a sharp exchange Trevize demands that his Gaian counterpart Bliss use Gaia's collective mind to control some unfriendly parties that they encounter on the planet Comporellon (*Foundation and Earth*). She dismisses this: 'Because we don't know where it would lead. We don't know the side effects, which may well turn out to make the situation worse.'

The God of meta-history is the God of irony. This is not romantic irony. In romantic irony the hopes and dreams of individual characters are crushed by a cruel society, illusion turns to disillusion, hope to despair, promise to apocalypse, and freedom to nihilism. Individuals are super-charged with historical illusions (enchantment) followed by their character's (their psyche's or soul's) biographically driven progressive disillusionment (disenchantment) that ends either in a psychological state of doom or redemption. In epic irony, the micro histories of freedom and purpose are interwoven with the macro history of unconscious patterns. Intentional cause and unintentional or unchosen destiny overlap each other and are intertwined with one another. Hegel in his *Aesthetics* put it this way: 'In epic we find an underlying community of objective life and action, but nevertheless a freedom in this action and life which appear to proceed entirely from the subjective will of individuals' (1052). At the same time the external course of events in an epic has an 'independent right of its own' and as such does not 'stem from the aims and inner purposes of individuals' (1060). Or as Hegel puts it more bluntly still: in epics the interventions of the gods appear as a denial of human freedom (266). As a consequence, 'the intention involved in carrying out one's aims falls into the background' and 'a wider scope is allowed to the external in general' (227). Hegel observes how the epic raises us above expectation, fear and hope, and above cause, effect and consequence. We withdraw from practical (goal-rational) interests into considerations that feel to us sculptural, peaceful, plastic and theoretical (415). We enter thereby into 'a state of contemplative calm' (418). The result of this absorption into something other and external, Hegel suggests, is the liberation of internal life from purely practical (goal-rational) interests or from the immediacy of (lyrical) feeling into 'free theoretical shapes' (418).

Patterns and plans

After each major step that the Foundation series takes towards clarifying the nature of the hidden hand behind the external course of events in the galaxy, a further step is required. The more that is known, the less that is understood. Asimov cannot relinquish this irony or resolve it. Notwithstanding the contemporaneous influence of James Lovelock on Asimov (like Toynbee and Gibbon earlier on) even Gaia/Galaxia is not unambiguously the final word for Asimov. Eventually it appears that events are also being orchestrated by a robotic intelligence, an artificial intelligence, which – yet again – appears to be another hidden hand of God (in this case, not God-in-the-machine but God-as-a-machine) behind the pattern of events in the galaxy for 20,000 years. R. Daneel Olivaw has cultivated Seldon's psychohistory and seeded the experimental model of Galaxia – the planet Gaia. The theme of the institutionalized psychohistorians trails off as the epic-novel series advances while the model of Gaia/Galaxia moves into the foreground. But then there is a novelized hesitancy. The theme of the robot hidden hand is introduced. Yet this proves to be, as with all that precedes it, a somewhat deceptive story. For the robot is 'dying'. To complete the maturation of Galaxia, and to finally (seemingly) obviate the still continuing galactic-scale social entropy, decline and fall or weak renaissance, a fusion of robotic and human intelligence is proposed in order that the work of the robot hidden hand might continue until Gaia has become the fully fledged Galaxia.

The evolution of Galaxia out of Asimov's Galactic Empire and amidst decline and fall poses a philosophical question: what is the relationship between free, intentional and purposeful behaviour on the one hand and the meta-historical pattern of rise, fall and rise on the other hand? What do schemes (human or AI) contribute to cliodynamic patterns of meta-social development? What is the relationship between purpose and pattern? There are goal-driven human efforts, struggles, exertions and determinations. Then there are the wave-like rises and falls, not unlike the wave structures that characterize so much of nature. Goal-rational behaviour ('how do I achieve my ends?') is very visible to us in the short term. Numerous statements, claims, assertions and predictions are made about major contemporary events such as war and recession, peace and prosperity. Strategies are deployed, plans are made and steps are undertaken. This purposive action sometimes leads to success, other times to failure and frequently to very mixed results. Probably 20 per cent of human energy is efficacious; sometimes it is 10 per cent or less. As time proceeds, and the short run turns into the medium term and then the long run, it becomes clearer that some purposeful behaviour has jelled well with the evolving, enveloping pattern motions of history and society, while other behaviours have not. In the long run, the latter were futile and wasted efforts, and even self-destructive.

Visibility often blinds us. We 'see' events happening and we decide purposes and courses of action accordingly. A housing boom has been underway for years. We buy a house in the flush of boom-time excitement expecting to sell it for a handsome profit in two years' time. Then a month after the purchase, the market collapses and we lose a third of the value of the property overnight. Excitement turns to misery. This is an example of the way that purposes and patterns can be at odds with one another. Human beings in an everyday sense, in their demotic lives, are explicitly concerned with the purchase and sale of houses not with the waves and cycles of the housing market. But tacitly in the background, and sometimes buyers and sellers are dimly aware of this, something else, a meta-social force, is operating. In times of crisis, the background appears momentarily in the foreground.

Asimov's Foundation series is based on the ironical relationship of human plans and social patterns, that is, the irony of soul and world, psyche and cosmos, freedom and necessity. In order for this meta-history to resolve Dilthey's question of meaning, it has to resolve the relationship between human freedom and social necessity or destiny. What is the relationship? How is the necessary divergence of pattern and purpose, Galaxia and Plan resolved? In principle the fragments that make up the extensive totality of Asimov's fictional galaxy could be integrated because the collective mind (Gaia) can create order on a vast scale of time and space and across innumerable populations and planets by adapting to the patterns of nature. This adaptation, though, is not the result of psychological character or dramatic actions. Rather it is morphological. Neither the author (Asimov) nor the principal figures in Asimov's work dwell introspectively at length on the question of 'who am I?' Nor is the destiny (fate) of the galaxy determined in any clear-cut way by the actions ('what do I do?') or the feelings ('who am I?') of the story's prime figures. Two things follow from this:

A. Detailed exploration of psychological identity or motivation, 'the autonomous life of interiority' (Lukács: 66), typical of the form of the modern psychologized novel, plays a marginal role in Asimov's epic fiction. It is not a lyrical fiction about the human psyche. It is not a series of novels in which, as Lukács put it, the individual journeys towards himself and individuality becomes an aim unto itself (80). Instead the souls of fictional characters in the epic setting look outwards to the world.

B. The souls of the characters in Asimov's epic constitute a very small part of a massive, expansive, galactic totality. Individuals act purposefully in this large external world, negotiate risk and journey to distant places. They might or might not succeed in a particular adventure or cause. Yet they do so against the backdrop of the cyclical or cliodynamic rise, decline, fall and rise again of interconnected planetary societies whose evolution and course is on a scale that is far larger and ultimately more deterministic than the conscious and intentional actions of the story's main figures. Everyone's role, whether nominally large or small, is miniscule compared with the vast canvas of time and space, matter and energy. Freedom of action exists and is enjoyed. But it bends to necessity as quest does to destiny, intention to consequence and deed to effect.

Office and status, no matter how seeming important, do little to shape or effect the trajectory of events. The storms of multiple crises disguise the impassive underlying calm of the broad, objective, epic shape of events. The agitated movement, clashes and conflict of drama mixed with flashes of lyrical romance may be essential to a science fiction novel. Yet an object-like stolid aloofness and inexpressiveness is crucial to an epic story. Asimov reconciles the two with a style of writing in which mystery is followed by revelation which is followed by a further mystery and a further revelation, multiple times. The mystery-revelation structure provides the Foundation series with a dramatic form. Asimov writes very good reveals. They are memorable and they never feel forced. But this mystery or detection-style drama is contained within a larger epic framework in which all of the revelations only reveal a part of the underlying totality of the science-fictional future history. Behind the series of riddles to be solved there is the ongoing epic oscillating development of galactic history, which feels a little like the earth's Pleistocene glaciation and the prolonged cold environments of Europe's ice-sheets, tundras and steppes that the exodic hominins, notably the *Homo sapiens*, proved adept at adapting themselves to.

Fiction of ideas

Asimov's Foundation represents the glacial nature of society's totality that lies beneath the dramas and romances of its characters' lives. Asimov's method of doing this is epic irony built out of genre fiction. The French novelist Michel Houellebecq does something different yet comparable. His work is comparable in the sense that a considerable part of it is science fiction. However, Houellebecq's is a literary science fiction and it pivots on comic irony rather than epic irony. Nonetheless, both Asimov and Houellebecq closely observe individual subjects who are entangled in social-historical contexts that they don't understand or that they are deluded about. Houellebecq alludes to this when he invokes Auguste Comte's view about 'the reality of social structures as opposed to the fiction of individual existence' (*The Elementary Particles*, [1998] 2000: 248). The 'reality of social structures' is the same empiricism that distinguishes an epic work from dramatic and lyrical works. The essence of meaning is how a part relates to the whole. In the present case, how do individual subjects and groups, I and we, relate to nature, history, society and metaphysical reality? How do fictions take account of facts, and especially facts on a monumental scale; facts that exhibit their own 'laws' of motion and the related objectivities that play havoc with subjectivities? How do individuals manage their bewilderment when they are drawn into sweeping processes that are not of their own making? How do they locate themselves in a way that makes sense of the monumental swells and eddies of history, society and their metaphysical substrate? How can they stop becoming lost? Can historical necessity be turned into personal destiny? Can the cold bewildering enigmas of an impassive society be converted into the warm sardonic ironies of a happy life?

Houellebecq's work illustrates neatly the difficulty that modern literature has had tackling these distinctive problems of meaning, and why epic science fiction, with its lower literary horizons, often has been more successful in doing so. The despairing, bitter, lonely characters in Houellebecq's novels at first glance appear simply to be the human detritus of a modern 'novel of disillusionment', as Lukács dubbed it; victims of their own (in this case, postmodern) lyrical-romantic interiority and its 'formless wallowing in vain, self-worshipping lyrical psychologism' (119). Lukács's characterizations perfectly sum up the morbid lyricism of the post-1970s and post-1990s identitarian-bureaucratic political movements and professional-managerial social classes that form the context for Houellebecq's novels. The characters in these novels are spellbound by what Lukács observed was one of the operative ideals of the modern novel: the extraction of meaning from various transcendental forms of meaninglessness (51). Novels of this kind present an objective world that has broken down and various 'I's – egos or subjects – who still dream languidly of being world-dominating and yet are 'lost in the insubstantiality of its self-created world of ruins' (53). This is the idolatry of personality. In his novels Houellebecq portrays such personalities brutally, with 'un style hostile'. His characters are aging, tense, lonely, anxious and depressed. In many respects they are typical late twentieth-century, early twenty-first century upper-middle-class ('creative class') personalities (Murphy 2019: 48–59). Their dilemma though is that they can't even find a meaning in meaninglessness. The distich of alienation and the will to fight it has lost its romantic redemptive quality. Their despair contains no saving element or spark. It is terminal.

Because Houellebecq depicts it so unsparingly he is in a curious kind of rebellion against the doleful lyricism of the novel of transcendent meaninglessness and its desire to extract a perverse meaning from the futility of the world of ruins and its numerous troubled, abject, self-conscious souls. Houellebecq's *The Elementary Particles* portrays the souls of his characters as irredeemably miserable. Their misery has no saving grace. Ennui, malaise and emptiness follow. They are consumed by the rampant, crippling postmodern condition of lonerism. The disillusioned central character Michel Djerzinski suicides. He looks forward in death to a kind of posthumous meaning – not for himself but for the human species. He leaves behind plans for a science-fictional, post-human technology for cloning human beings. Out of Djerzinski's understanding of quantum physics and the dual particle-wave structure of the universe, he wills to his fellow human beings the ability, if they want, to create out of themselves a new, better, more 'rational', less biologically flawed and less mortality-haunted species. Most people, though not all of them, choose this new 'bliss' of cloned pseudo-immortality. Djerzinski's cynical follower Frédéric Hubczejak promotes this as a New Age Gaia with its 'ten billion neurons' connected in the collective 'brain' of the human species.

In Houellebecq's *The Possibility of an Island* (2005) the followers of a twenty-first-century secular religious health-cult (the Elohimites) search in vain for a misery-free eternal life. Houellebecq's brutal satirical radar for his fellows' mass delusions is unerring. Fifteen years before it became globally pervasive during the Covid pandemic years, he intuited the importance of a technologically cloaked, death-denying biomedical cult of health and the scientific superstition associated with it. The cult leader Elohim has 'no irony in him, it's much healthier'. The cultists, most of them from Toynbee's creative minority, in fiction as in real life, are motivated by the idea that they can deny, defy or delay death, or quiet the ontological anxiety connected to the thought of dying. Death-denial is their one remaining hope for meaning in a meaningless world in which their careers or romances have ended badly. One of them, Houellebecq's principal character the comedian Daniel, suicides. He is consumed by a despair that springs from his confusion of sex and love. Daniel, though, outlives his own suicide. His DNA is used to construct generations of clones of himself. Two millennia on, these descendant clones continue to exist. Yet they do so without passion or desire and (like Asimov's Solarians) with very little social contact. They are drawn to the abstraction of love, regretful they can't feel it, and in spite of the covert supernaturalism of the secular health religion that created them, they are still unable to become immortal. The technique of uploading consciousness into a permanent storage system remains out of reach. Perhaps the prophesized coming of the mysterious alien 'Future Ones' – who are 'one' but also 'many' – may change this. If these aliens exist. Houellebecq's work on the one hand is an epitome of the modern psycho-dramatized novel. Yet his science-fictional themes reveal an author who, at the same time, wishes to escape the spiritual dead end of the psychologised novel of disillusionment.

Like Asimov's genre fiction, Houellebecq's literary fiction is a fiction of ideas. Both are science fictions and, in both, action and psychological character are secondary to a larger civilizational meta-history in which individuals are swept along by supra-social forces that they barely if at all understand. This is the epic sweep of 'life itself' (Lukács), a meta-reality that is only dimly perceived but which, if intuited, is meaningful. Houellebecq draws on classic nineteenth-century models of hidden but ultimately discoverable historical laws of reality: Darwinian evolution (*On the Origin of Species*, [1859/1876] 2009) and Comte's law of the three states (états) of social development (*The Course in Positive Philosophy*, 1835). Individual characters and actions in Houellebecq's novels are subject to a larger envelope of determining social, economic, demographic and biological forces. Where impersonal laws are more important than the will and agency of social actors, the natural literary expression of this, if not epic works, is comic irony.

Comedy in this sense is not necessarily a matter of joking or laughing. Rather it is the quantum cognitive recognition that something is its opposite. Actors believe they are doing something, achieving something, loving someone, befriending someone. The anonymous meta-reality – the hidden hand – is forcefully determining that they are not. The result is irony and a black comedy in which the pursuit of happiness, so out of touch with reality, with 'life itself', ends in anxiety, misery, depression and suicide. The individual view clashes with the macroscopic vision of things. One is intimate and detailed; the other is remote and cosmic. One is atomistic; the other systemic and vast. One is a particle; the other a wave. One appears to be within the control of the individual; the second is outside that control. One is personal; its twin is anonymous. Houellebecq is ironic in a double register. The forlorn efforts of his characters to be happy are doomed. Yet he also points an accusatory finger at some of the more prominent modern anonymous forces – capitalism, the market, money, speculation, exchange, commodities and consumption; and on occasion, cities and their grimy, run-down, hostile urban spaces – that wash over them, crushing their conscious and often foolish expectations. And yet he likes machines. As he has said, French children grow up reading in the tradition of either Alexandre Dumas or Jules Verne. A bookworm as a child, he was a devotee of Verne-like science-fictional technology (Louisiana Literature 2019).

Critical and organic

Comte presented three ways in which anonymous meta-reality can exert itself: through supernatural agency, metaphysical abstraction and empirical laws (of nature, history, etc.). This was his 'social physics'. Houellebecq, the writer who attends church on Sundays but who cannot sustain a belief in God, conjectures the return of a theological state in his thought experiment 'what if France was ruled by Islam?' in *Submission* ([2014] 2015). He has also twice tried the thought experiment of a revitalized positive science: with science-fictional cloning technology at its centre. But whether a science-fictional (future) technology in the absence of metaphysical abstraction, dynamic homeostasis (the happy equilibrium) and an epic conception of life is a viable answer to the modern recurring scourge of transcendental meaninglessness is an open question. In *Serotonin* (2019) Houellebecq wonders if the happiness chemical serotonin – the synaptic neurotransmitter whose levels affect anxiety and depression – will lift the veil of despair? It doesn't. Just as submission to dictatorial theological commands will not solve the boredom and self-loathing of the denizens of a somewhat tired and flagging civilization. Psychological depression and civilizational melancholy merge in this generation. 'No one in the West will ever be happy again... never again; happiness today is nothing but an old dream' (*Serotonin*).

The anxious, depressive psychology of Houellebecq's post-1960s creative minority may be in part explained by quantum mechanics. Conventionally the role of chemical neurotransmitters connecting neurons (cells) across synaptic clefts in the brain is modelled on classical physics. But, as the mathematician Roger Penrose (1994: 352–5) has argued, these connections may be also governed by quantum superpositioning, limiting conventional biomedical, pharmaceutical and (by extrapolation) science-fictional understanding of them. The fictional science of Houellebecq's Michel Djerzinski solved the problem of human cloning by applying the principles of quantum mechanics. Houellebecq's Flourent-Claude Labrouste meanwhile uses a 'new generation antidepressant' Captorix – designed on the principles of classical not quantum physics – that does not work very well.

Hubczejak's huckster New Age Gaia with its 'ten billion neurons' connected in the collective 'brain' of the human species tacitly assumes McCulloch and Pitts's 1943 classic physics modelling of synaptic behaviour. Such behaviour can be computationally mimicked, that is computerized, as in the case of Asimov's R. Daneel Olivaw. But what if, as Penrose (1994: 368) argues, neurotransmission and other biological mechanisms like the human immune system are regulated by quantum physics not classical physics? A revised Gaian model of the collective mind might then assume (following Penrose science-fictionally) the possibility of a state of quantum-coherence on a large scale – a state in which a wave function for a single particle applies to an entire collection of particles on a macroscopic level whether in the human brain or (to again extrapolate science-fictionally) in the collective mind. Oscillations at different places beat in time with each other (351).

The anxious self-loathing of Houellebecq's main characters can be understood as a consequence of their inability to spontaneously apply quantum ideas or Penrose-style conformal ideas to civilizational questions. Toynbee observed that healthy creative minorities demonstrate an intuitive grasp of the oscillating (yin-yang, challenge-response, motion-rest, genesis-disintegration, etc.) waves that superimpose themselves on the individual particles of society. Conversely, civilizational weariness is signalled, Toynbee thought, by the deterioration of society's creative minority, a decline painstakingly represented by the literature professor François in *Submission*, the comedian Daniel in *The Possibility of an Island*, the scientist Michel in *The Elementary Particles* and the agricultural scientist Florent-Claude in *Serotonin*.

The despair of these characters and the loss of their élan is a function, decades on, of the expectations of their generation and especially its creative minority who imagined that society could be reshaped purposefully as if one was felling a tree or making an egg carton. They paid the price for imagining themselves and their institutions to be like Asimov's Second Foundation: 'a benevolent dictatorship of the mentally best' and a 'higher subdivision' of humankind (*Second Foundation*). Motive was mistaken for meaning. When meaning failed to bend to motive, the world looked meaningless. In truth though Asimov's metaphor was right: the elementary gas particles in the container each move in their own direction; but together they form an intelligible probabilistic pattern. Houellebecq's Djerzinski similarly states: 'In an ontology of states the particles are indiscernible, and only a limited number are observable. The only entities which can be identified and named are wave functions and, through them, state vectors – from which arose the analogous possibility of giving new meaning to fraternity, sympathy and love' (*The Elementary Particles*, [1998] 2000: 249). Houellebecq's generational peers couldn't see that. They mistook purpose for pattern, sex for love, and particle for wave.

Like Houellebecq, yet more clearly than Houellebecq, Asimov wants to answer Comte's question: What are the meta-historical laws of society? How can a positive science be created to do this? Does it look like Seldon's mathematical sociology of psychohistory? And to what degree can a meta-history reconcile human nature's dogged focus on immediate goals and visible expectations with meaning's need to create order out of entropy and chaos? In Asimov's fiction this ambition leads some of the characters into quests to unravel the meaning latent in the meta-history of the colonized galaxy. This meaning and history, as it gradually becomes apparent, is hidden even from the psychohistorians. Their science is only concerned with those putative patterns of behaviour and social forces that will lead to the renaissance of a better empire, however that might be conceived. Their knowledge devolves into a preoccupation with power; psychohistory itself becomes a legitimation of power. 'After all', observes the intuitive Trevize, 'how can you define psychohistory but as a superstition of the Foundation? Isn't it a belief without proof or evidence?' (*Foundation and Earth*). Seldon himself makes periodic holographic appearances to issue prophetic statements. These initially are staged in a small auditorium; five hundred years later his appearances take place in a giant mausoleum. The Seldon prophecies have become the legitimation of the Foundation's galactic power.

If not the mathematical sociology of psychohistory, then what? Asimov answers this question indirectly and symptomatically. He sets out in seven volumes including two prequels the epic journeys of several characters all of whom want to find an answer to the question of what is capable of generating an attractive beneficial order among galactic societies. None of the answers they find are conclusive. Each answer triggers new questions. Like Houellebecq's generation, some of the characters in the epic quest to discover the nature of the galaxy's civilizational order suffer the delusion that they are part of a creative minority (the two Foundations) orchestrating the rebirth of empire with secret knowledge. But gradually this illusion is stripped away. The alternative answers (collective consciousness and a hyper-computational robotic intelligence) seem in their own way also less than complete answers to the question of what creates attractive order in the universe?

In the end the answer lies less in the content than in the epic form of Asimov's novels. His primary questing characters fulfil Hegel's presumption that their actions are brought about through their 'entanglement' with external conditions and that the attainment of aims by these epic characters is secondary while external circumstances and natural occurrences are primary. Those circumstances and those occurrences are not random. On an epic scale they have a shape. They constitute patterns of events. But the insights of the purposeful and occasionally lyrical adventurers across time and space is limited. For epics have no conclusive 'ending' just as there is no 'end of history'. Epics stop rather than 'end'. T. E. Lawrence abruptly returns home after the tribal governance of Damascus collapses. But he does so having in effect revealed that the pattern of the nomadic society that made his victory over the Turks in Damascus possible made the breakdown of Damascus's temporarily occupied urban civilization inevitable. Before Lawrence, Damascus knew many rulers: the Aramaeans, the Hellenistic Seleucid Empire, the Romans, the Abbasid Caliphate, Seljuq Turks, Ayyubid Sultans, the Mamluk Sultanate, the Ottoman Empire and Turkey. After Lawrence, it was the French Mandate followed by the Syrian Republic, Ba'athist Syria and Civil War. Thirty-two centuries of history and no 'ending'. Just the endless cycling up and down between critical (negative) and organic (constructive) eras.

Eras of destruction, anarchy and egotistical power are followed historically by eras of relative harmony, equilibria and attractive order. Individuals have the good or bad fortune to live in one or other period. These are the conflicting destinies of human societies depicted on the shield of Achilles: peace and harmony or war and destruction. That is the fate of nations, peoples and civilizations. The School of Saint-Simon and the philosophy of Auguste Comte observed that history is split between critical and organic periods. An epic reading of history concurs, though dissents from their specific versions. In any event there is no 'end' of history. Just the repeated cycling up and down and the resulting rhythmic alterations between critical and organic phases. Asimov's five hundred years of fictional history looks and feels a lot like it began with a 'critical' cyclical low signalled by the collapse of the Galactic Empire and was proceeding along a gradual upward curve towards something more 'organic'. Exactly the nature of that organism and its equilibria remained to the conclusion of the novels unclear. The end was not the end.

8

Galaxia

Consciousness and intuition

In *Foundation's Edge*, the character Golan Trevize, a member of the First Foundation's ruling Council, goes searching for Earth, accompanied by his friend the historian and collector of galactic origin stories ('the myths of humanity') Janov Pelorat. The quest takes months. Earth, 'the first world, the world of human origins', seems to promise the answer to the mysteries of Asimov's Foundation epic. However in the year AD 22,000, Earth is just a rumour; its location has been lost; it seems to live on only in superstition. It has become a taboo word; a word that evokes feelings of melancholy and loss on the part of the inhabitants of numerous planets whose ancestors long ago had emigrated from Earth. Among the fragments of historical memory was a vague legend that the Earth was dead, killed by nuclear radioactivity as a result of wars between the first and second waves of galactic colonists, the Spacers and the Settlers. 'The planet is uninhabitable. The last bacterium, the last virus, is long gone' it was assumed (*Foundation and Earth*).

This quest for origins proves to be as misleading as most of the other efforts to unravel the riddles of the fall of the Galactic Empire. Indeed, the preoccupation with the search for origins appears to have been a sickly hangover from the last days of the Empire, when origin hunting became a popular pasttime 'perhaps to get away from the unpleasantness of the surrounding reality' (*Foundation and Earth*). Planetary societies in the galaxy tended to exaggerate their antiquity and date themselves incorrectly in order to claim a closer affinity with the origin and thus a higher status. In any event, for Trevize and his two boon companions ('together, always'), every step in the direction of the origin led them closer and further away from a puzzle that Trevize intuited was unsolved.

As the Solarian character Bander put it when questioned by Trevize and his companions about whether the earth of myth actually exists: 'All history is legend, more or less' (*Foundation and Earth*). Initially, the historical record hinted that Earth was the secretive planet Gaia. But Gaia, it is gradually revealed, is not the Earth but rather an experimental model for Galaxia, the hypothesized galactic-wide answer to the problem of imperial decline and disintegration. Galaxia is what the novel series anticipates will replace the Galactic Empire, even if at the conclusion of *Foundation's Edge*, almost everyone in this fictional universe supposes otherwise. Leading players assume the eventual return of something like the old Empire, albeit reinvigorated. Intense politicking is expended to this end by numerous political actors from the First and Second Foundations. After a circumlocutious journey, peppered with nudges from various hidden hands of predestination and his own preternatural intuition, Trevize discovers the veiled planet of Gaia and is introduced to its animating concept. Namely, a planet and everything on it that participates, in varying degrees (shades of Aristotle), in a common consciousness.

'The whole planet and everything on it is Gaia', explains the Gaian character Blissenobiarella (Bliss). 'We're all individuals – we're all separate organisms – but we all share an overall consciousness. The inanimate planet does so least of all, the various forms of life to a varying degree, and human beings most of all – but we all share' (*Foundation's Edge*). But who runs this world, asks Trevize? 'It runs itself' is Bliss' reply. The planet is a self-organizing entity on all levels, from the rocks through the plants and animals to the Gaians. Each element does what is necessary and according to its share in the totality of things. Bliss explains that

> in your own body, don't all the different cells know what to do? When to grow and when to stop growing? When to form certain substances and when not to – and when they form them, just how much to form, neither more nor less? Each cell is, to a certain extent, an independent chemical factory, but all draw from a common fund of raw materials brought to it by a common transportation system, all deliver wastes into common channels, and all contribute to an overall group consciousness.

Later on Bliss will explain that even excreta on Gaia has a consciousness. 'The level of consciousness is, naturally, very low' (*Foundation and Earth*).

Trevize's naïve travelling companion Pelorat responds to the Gaia concept with enthusiasm: 'But that's remarkable. You are saying that the planet is a superorganism and that you are a cell of that superorganism' (*Foundation's Edge*). Not quite, comes the clarification: 'I'm making an analogy, not an identity. We are the analog of cells, but we are not identical with cells – do you understand?' Bliss proceeds to expand on the nature of a self-organizing planet. Asimov is walking a conceptual tightrope. On this account all things share in a group consciousness yet participate in that consciousness in ways that range from the very simple to the highly complex. Bliss explains,

> My consciousness is far advanced beyond that of any individual cell – incredibly far advanced. The fact that we, in turn, are part of a still greater group consciousness on a higher level does not reduce us to the level of cells. I remain a human being – but above us is a group consciousness as far beyond my grasp as my consciousness is beyond that of one of the muscle cells of my biceps.

The idea that consciousness, in varying degrees from the simple to the complex, exists as a property of matter has its serious supporters like the philosopher Philip Goff (2019) and the mathematician Roger Penrose. Penrose mentions the decidedly conscious behaviour of elephants who mourn the dead and the African hunting dogs that plan among themselves to kill antelope – one group hides in wait near a river while a second group herd the antelope toward the river (Penrose 1994: 407; Fridman 2020).

But is consciousness, including 'us' consciousness, as central as either Asimov or Penrose present? Penrose points out that human calculation is located in the cerebellum, a part of the brain that is not associated with conscious thought. He suggests in contrast and by inference that creative human understanding – for example the intuition that furnishes the foundation of mathematics – is conscious and is located in segments of the brain separate from those hosting unconscious algorithmic, programmed and rule-governed processes of computation. The general point he makes is valid. Human creation and understanding are not algorithmic. However, there is reason to think that brain functions related to creative cognition – to imagination, intuition and insight – are silent, non-discursive and unconscious. These are paradoxically both like rule-governed computations and yet strikingly different from them. This should not surprise us. While one process is subservient to rules and the other is not, nevertheless high-functioning calculation and imagination are both rapid-fire. We don't 'think about them'. Conscious thought in contrast is a slow process.[1] When we say 'I am thinking about it', we are indicating that we are taking our time to draw a conclusion. We reason slowly but gain insight quickly. Insights form below the threshold of awareness.

Both the person who is very good at making rule-governed calculations without the aid of a machine and the person who is a serious creative writer like Asimov who solves problems and makes intellectual leaps in a very fast manner engage in kinds of thinking that are far quicker than slow conscious thought processes or awareness in general allows for. In the first case it is the rapid and tacit application of rules. In the second case it is the intuitive ability to think in exceptionally swift quantum terms. Quantum thinking allows the mind to superposition contrary phenomenon such as particles and waves, to see them as one. As does, in a parallel manner, Penrose's own cosmological theory of a cyclical universe that repeatedly evolves through a scale-invariant conformal end-beginning stage in which no physical distinction can be made between large and small, infinity or the infinitesimal, instantaneity or eternity.[2] One can infer from Penrose's theory of brain functioning that quantum mechanics is the physical basis for the human imagination (1994: 348–77, 383–8). In Penrose's conception, the mind is the effect of non-computational quantum superpositioning that is different from the classic physics of the brain (349–50). Whether, at their inception, quantum-generated intuitions and insights are identical with the *conscious* operation of the mind though is debatable. Arguably, silent spontaneous subliminal intuition (gut feelings, even) and the prelinguistic imagination – and the geometrical M. C. Escher-style mental visualizations that Penrose frequently utilizes[3] – are more powerful media of invention and problem-solving than conscious thought or discursive reasoning (Murphy [2012] 2016: 14, 29, 81, 82, 94). In matters of creative understanding it is better to talk about the quantized physical basis of the mind rather than consciousness per se. Asimov's Trevize has exceptional intuition whose insights he himself cannot explain: 'Why did I choose Gaia? Why must I find Earth? Is there a missing assumption in psychohistory?' (*Foundation and Earth*). He knows things tacitly even if he cannot articulate them consciously. At the same time, to attribute to intuition a very high level of cognitive power is to implicitly deny the possibility of a superior rule-based artificial computational intelligence on the lines of R. Daneel Olivaw. The two conceptually are very difficult to reconcile.

Galaxia, in Asimov's eyes, is a pervasive connected intelligence that one day will drive the galaxy's inhabited planets towards some kind of dynamic balance. However Asimov also depicts this intelligence as having consciousness and intentionality. The conscious, intentional, phenomenological model of the mind is asked to do a lot in this account. So much so that Trevize wonders if human beings disappeared from Galaxia, 'would there still be a guiding intelligence?' (*Foundation and Earth*). The human mind, Trevize adds, 'is qualitatively different from everything else'. It is conscious and self-conscious. On the other hand, the epic mind is attuned to what Hegel in his *Aesthetics* thought of as world-history, the non-fictional predecessor of Asimov's galactic history. The 'hero' of world-history is not an individual or a subject but rather an impersonal world-spirit that 'educates and lifts itself out of the dullness of consciousness into world-history' (1064). This world-spirit is not tied to a specific locality or set of customs or morals. Attempts to characterize world-history (ditto Asimov's galactic history) in terms of a 'directive, acting and executive individual' are doomed to fail, Hegel suggests (1065). Accordingly, there is no conventional dramatic hero in the Foundation series. The alternative to the dramatic hero-figure, Hegel argues, is a 'hidden, ever-operative necessity'. But that hidden force must be woven into the life history of a 'chief figure' whose 'exploits pass in front of him' as if it was a kind of objective work or a kind of sculpture. The more vitally a chief figure 'acts' the more the action is 'interwoven with what is going on'. Their individual persona carries something 'universal' (1068). Something of the character of all things is concentrated in one person, objectified in that individual. In the case of Asimov's chief figures, what is that universal trait?

It is notable that Asimov's character Trevize possesses a remarkable clairvoyant intuition. Intuition mixes prelinguistic cognition with feelings (gut feelings) and imagination, the latter being the capacity to see in one visible thing its invisible opposite. Intuition is an interface between mind and nature. The mind interpolates the patterns of nature. The imagination applies these patterns in inventive and surprising ways to social situations. Drawing on intuition and imagination, the human psyche responds to the world around it by estimating whether situations or events resemble a spiral, web, node, bubble, fractal, cycle and so on. From this arises the tacit social physics that lies in the deep background of social behaviour and which is interwoven (sometimes positively, sometimes negatively) with conscious purposeful actions. Human beings search for things on the bases of hunches or intuitions. The reason – the confirmations – come later. It was a hypothesis in Aristotle's *Meteorology* (350 BCE) that a great southern land existed. Physical confirmation of the hypothesis, the empirical sighting of Australia (for Europeans, the Mars of its day), came twenty-one centuries later.

Asimov has a notion that nature has self-organizing characteristics. These range from the smallest to the largest scale, and include the human mid-range as well. Yet whether self-organization is best described as conscious is questionable. The idea of consciousness causes Asimov a series of problems. Where does the human individual fit into a collective consciousness? If no one rules a self-organized Gaian-type planet, or rather all things rule the planet as one (as a totality), what is the individual part in this? What would stop the collective one crushing the individual one? Asimov speaking through the character Bliss explains that 'I cannot fly like a bird, buzz like an insect, or grow as tall as a tree. I do what it is best for me to do' (*Foundation's Edge*). That indicates that Gaia has a division of labour in which each is left alone to do what they are good at doing, much as in Plato's *Republic*. Bliss adds: 'We have a whole complex of different pronouns to express the shades of individuality that exist on Gaia. I could explain them to you, but till then "I/we/Gaia" gets across what I mean in a groping sort of way.' So there is the individual, the group and the whole. Now this is not far removed from a social science definition of human experience. There are modes of experience that are best summed up as the experience of 'I' or 'We' or a more encompassing 'Us'.

The space-faring travelling companions – Pel, Trevize and Bliss – are a 'We', underwritten by Pel's 'You know I won't leave you, Golan, and neither will Bliss' (*Foundation and Earth*). Nevertheless the 'I/We/Us', 'Bliss/Gaia', 'individual/collective' entity troubles Trevize. As I am, I can travel far from my people, he reasons, and still remain myself. Bliss in contrast maintains an energy-sapping bond with Gaia through hyperspace. The regular human being can end up alone; the Gaian is always connected. As space expands, the Gaian must feel 'a diminished entity far more than I', Trevize thinks. To which Bliss makes an interesting retort: 'Do you expect there is no price to be paid for a benefit gained?' summing up in one sentence the entire history of philosophical scepticism (*Foundation and Earth*). Tortoises are cold-blooded, slow-moving and long-living, she argues. Isn't it better to be a human being than a tortoise even though human beings expend energy much more wastefully than a tortoise? There is a cost attached to every benefit sought. You have to eat 'constantly so that you can pour energy into your body as quickly as it leaks out'. Human beings starve more quickly and die more quickly than a tortoise. That's the price paid for being 'a quick-moving, quick-sensing, thinking organism'. Existence is a trade-off.

Galaxia and Catallaxy

While for Asimov the Gaian-style 'something more encompassing' is a conscious hive mind, arguably there are better ways of describing a self-organizing whole than as an 'us' consciousness. In fact it is doubtful whether self-organizing wholes, which exist, have the structure of a conscious mind. One of the better models to understand the nature of a self-organizing whole was introduced around the same time that Asimov wrote *Foundation's Edge*. This was the economist and social philosopher Friedrich Hayek's discussion in 1973 of the social *kosmos* in the first volume of his three-volume work *Law, Legislation and Liberty*. In the second volume (1976) he dubs the market component of this cosmos a *catallaxy*. Each individual microcosm is a self-similar fractal part of a macrocosmic whole. The Hayekian market participants each pursuing the intention and purpose of liberal choosing are part of a *catallaxy* in which millions of choosing beings interact tacitly forming recognizable patterns, many of which have counterparts in nature, be they cycles, ratios, fractals and the like.

The spirit of *kosmos* and *catallaxy* resembles the epic stoic-empirical attitude of 'here it is' and 'this is the way it is'. The epic mentality looks on society and history with a shrug. Epic narrative figures pass through vast social terrains like these without lyrical or dramatic feelings dominating. They experience dramatic moments and lyrical episodes, but these are encased in the expansive time or space of the epic. As Hegel observed in his *Aesthetics*, cosmogonies (along with theogonies) were early forms of epic (1042–3). In Hayek's account (1973: 27–30), wholes develop not through conscious intention or plan or by deliberate, wilful construction. Rather they evolve spontaneously. They are not conscious. They are akin to the even-minded equilibrium states of *mushin no shin* (mind without mind) – a spontaneous, preconscious, non-attached mental state of equanimity – and *hishiryo* (thinking without thought) of Japanese Zen noetic theory. This supposes that powers of discursive reason are limited and that we obtain significant cognitive and practical assistance from 'processes of which we are not aware'. A 'type' of situation, Hayek argued, evokes in an individual a 'disposition' towards a certain 'pattern' of response. This behaviour is not conscious. It doesn't happen by purposeful design or via explicit knowledge but rather by unconscious abstraction.

Abstraction is not a product of the mind. Rather it is what is already built into the mind by nature. The Swiss economist and sociologist Vilfredo Pareto sat in his garden and observed his peas. He first intuited then he calculated that 80 per cent of peas came from 20 per cent of pods. He then applied that naturally occurring pattern ratio to economics and in so doing identified the basic pattern of modern income and wealth distribution ([1906] 2020). Subsequently the 80:20 ratio has been found to apply in numerous other domains of social life. Commonly 80 per cent of business income is generated by 20 per cent of a corporation's organizational units. Eighty per cent of academic publications are produced by 20 per cent of academics. And so on. Are human beings then green peas? The pattern of human activities often replicates patterns found in nature. Purposeful actions are distributed into non-purpose-driven morphologies. This does not happen by virtue of Asimov's science-fictional telepathic mass-organism-like communication. Logarithmic spirals in nature (such as the

Milky Way Galaxy) increase in a geometric progression. So does the spread of inventions in society until they encounter obstacles such as opposing inventions or competing wants and ideas. The French sociologist Gabriel Tarde described this (following Comte) as a 'social physics' ([1890] 1903: 114–16).[4] A wide variety of natural patterns are replicated in human behaviour. Such behaviour is far from random and yet it cannot be adequately explained by conscious or purposeful direction from commands, laws or goals. Cities illustrate the point. There are around 10,000 cities worldwide. Between all of those, and irrespective of numerous cultures and cultural eras, most cities are laid-out in four basic shapes: organic, grid, concentric and radial (Kostof 1991. These are unconscious abstractions built into the fabric of the universe.

Hayek had a misleading habit of calling these abstractions 'rules of conduct'. He noted that action guided by 'rules we are not aware of' is often described as 'instinctive' or 'intuitive' (1973: 30). The word 'rule' caricatures the morphologies that shape history, nature and society. In any event human beings are rational, conscious, goal-seeking beings who at the same time are intuitively responsive to unconscious order, structure, system and pattern (35). They expend a lot of time and energy, like Asimov's Foundations, politicking, planning, organizing and engaging in all manner of deliberate, self-conscious strategies and tactics. At the same time there is in human experience a Galaxia-like self-generating, endogenous order (37). For Hayek, conscious goal-rational behaviour such as Seldon's Plan ends in the creation of organizations like the two Foundations and the pursuit of a constructed 'order' which Hayek called *taxis*. Hayek called Galaxia-style 'organic' order *kosmos*. In the case of *kosmos* or organic order, society is the result of 'a process of evolution whose results nobody foresaw or designed'. There is a no 'genius', like a Hari Seldon, who invents society. Society cannot be (re)modelled after the image of an individual person (33). There is no Seldon animating Hayek's larger whole. But there is something Gaia-like – sort of. Though it is an unconscious morphological Gaia not a conscious collective one.

When Hayek was formulating his ideas, he had a few precedents he could use to help him describe what a self-organizing totality might look like. There was a handful of then-contemporary models, among them cybernetics. He also drew on the 'hidden hand' tradition of Adam Smith. But among Hayek's most interesting examples are those drawn from natural science and the 'spontaneous orders in nature'. Hayek refers to the lattice of crystals and the patterns of organic compounds (39–40). In the case of such patterns we can only predict the general character of the order that forms and not the particular position of any element of the compound relative to any other element. This is almost the same statement that Asimov made about the nature of Seldon's psychohistory. The idea of psychohistory was analogous to the kinetic theory of gases. Asimov has the character Pel explain that

> [each] atom or molecule in a gas moves randomly so that we can't know the position or velocity of any one of them. Nevertheless, using statistics, we can work out the rules governing their overall behaviour with great precision. In the same way, Seldon intended to work out the overall behaviour of human societies even though the solutions would not apply to the behaviour of individual human beings. (*Foundation and Earth*)

Pel's more sceptical friend Trevize pushes back saying that perhaps human beings are not atoms. True enough, Pel concedes, human beings have consciousness and appear to have free will. The question left hanging is whether consciousness and free will make that much difference.

Hayek became famous in the twentieth century for demolishing the idea of intentional economic planning. He did this in part by using science analogies not far removed from Asimov's science analogies. For Hayek, and in many ways for epic storytelling, the intellectual problem is how to adequately characterize the relationship between purpose and pattern, freedom and necessity, part and whole. That is, how do we reconcile the intentional, purposeful, goal-seeking and strategic behaviour of individuals who have ambitions and desires with what is clearly different from that, namely the 'overall behaviour of human societies'? And how can we do that without having to suppose some kind of despotic necessity and loss of human individuality? Hayek uses the example of a magnet and iron filings. When a magnet is placed next to iron filings, we cannot predict where individual filings will be positioned but we can make statements about the general pattern of the magnetized filings (1973: 40). Analogously, Hayek goes on, we cannot predict or plan the course of an individual life or the success or failure of a firm or organization, but we can make meaningful statements about the shape of a society (its spontaneous order) that results from individuals adapting themselves (or not adapting) to the underlying tacit patterns that structure or condition societies (41). We can't have social scientific knowledge of every individual element or particular circumstance – that is, every 'elementary particle' in Michel Houellebecq's sense. What we can have are degrees of knowledge of the way individuals en masse intuitively and unconsciously adapt to abstract patterns and forms. It is possible to anticipate the general character but not the particular detail of the resulting order.

Organizations are good at acting on detail and specifics. Human beings achieve goals that way. They debate, dispute, conflict, cooperate and compete, fight and exchange, make and destroy, succeed and fail in pursuit of goals. But always their knowledge of circumstances and the means of their actions are limited. There is a larger patterned totality that shapes and forms purposeful action, leads and misleads it. This is 'the hidden hand' of existence, as Hayek described it (after Adam Smith). Accordingly there is purposeful freedom (the freedom to choose goals and pursue them) and the freedom to adapt to patterns and evolve. Adaptive freedom occurs through exploration, the migration of peoples, entry into and exit from social systems and subsystems, experimentation, trial and error, discovery and so on. Purposive freedom occurs when persons can select their own purposes and choose the means to attain those ends. Freedom does not guarantee outcomes. Persons may fail to make adaptive discoveries just as the achievement of a given purpose can fail. Adaptive freedom has the epic scale of human life in mind. Purposive freedom is concerned with those things that are close to hand and the particular. Asimov's planet Solaria in *Foundation and Earth* depicts a self-sufficient hermaphrodite 'whole human' self-reproducing population of social isolates (1,200 only of them) supported by a large robotic auto-industrial economy. The Solarian ethos is to approach absolute purposive freedom as closely as possible. However trade, the division of labour, the uneven distribution of different natural resources and population control means that some contact between Solarians through virtual conferencing is necessary. In the end the model of near-absolute freedom is a pattern that has its own paradoxical built-in constraints and limits on purposive freedom, and the Solarians however reluctantly are obliged to maintain these. Without the pattern and its morphological limits and its accompanying tacit built-in norms and constraints, they would not be Solarians. Just as they cannot tolerate visiting each other so the Solarians cannot tolerate other galactic humans visiting them. Absolute freedom for the 1,200 self-enclosed Solarians means a death sentence for any visitor. An ultra-solitarian freedom is conditioned by a minimal but distinctly harsh collective Solarian 'consensus'.

Exodus and artifice

It is easy to confuse patterns and purposes, to the detriment of each. One of these confusions is the readiness of human beings to misunderstand the scope of goal-rational actions. Human beings are good at controlling particulars.

Technological science is a case in point. Modern industrial science is good at taking abstract generalities about nature (laws of nature, mathematical equations and geometrical theorems) and applying them to specific engineering problems to enable, say, travelling through space from precise point A to precise point Z. Such engineering will one day, arguably, allow the colonization of galactic planets in habitable 'goldilocks' zones, as Asimov's fiction depicts. Colonization of Mars looks possible in the not-too-distant future, driven by space industries such as the commercial mining of ultra-rare minerals. The existing age of the universe is 13.7 billion years. The energy of Earth's sun will be exhausted in five billion years. Before that, in a billion years' time, the sun will have grown too large for life on Earth. The last star in the universe will die in 100 billion years. Given the ultra-epic timescale of the universe it is difficult not to imagine that the deeply entrenched *genus homo* pattern of the *völkerwanderung* (the migration or exodus of peoples) that began 1.8 million years ago with the movement of *Homo erectus* out of Africa will continue.

Humans (*Homo sapiens*) moved out of Africa 200,000 years ago and around the globe. Several abstract social forms converged with the human exodus pattern. One is long-range trade, a feature already of the 1,500 or so scattered human inhabitants of Palaeolithic Europe. The second is the making of objects for use, exchange and symbolic decoration. The third is the creation of artificial environments for living, most notably urban environs. Living in cities propelled human beings into forms of civilization and out of bands, clans and tribal societies. Mike Butterworth and Don Lawrence's *The Trigan Empire* (1965–82) was one of the most influential children's science fiction comic series. Like Asimov's Foundation series, it was inspired by Gibbon's *Decline and Fall of the Rome Empire*. Set in the science-fictional past of a politically and socially divided planet Elekton, *The Trigan Empire* told the story of a political leader, Trigo, who drives the evolution of his people from a tribal society to a high-tech empire and a materially sophisticated civilization reminiscent of the Greeks and Romans.[5] This occurs through the merger of his own tribal people (the Vorg) with a technologically advanced exodic refugee people (the Tharv). Early in the series, standing on the crest of a rocky crag overlooking the (Rome-like) five Hills that rose above the plain of Vorg, Trigo declares that 'it is my unshakeable ambition to build a city on those five Hills ... a city such as the planet has never seen, where men can walk in freedom and splendour ... a city that will be the pride and the glory of the planet Elekton' (Lawrence and Butterworth 2020: 25).

Exodus, trade, objectivation and urbanization are social entities that combine both pattern and purpose – and do so sometimes at cross purposes. These cross-purposes will continue to haunt humankind as space exploration and colonization expand. Purposes are practical, here and now, and require degrees of organization, sometimes successfully, often not. But human meaning, the hidden spirit that underlies purpose, requires a sensitivity to pattern, as does often the successful achievement of purposes. Pattern and purpose – that is, meaning and motive – are not easily reconciled. Bliss and Trevize debate this after their encounter on the planet Solaris with a Solarian who tried to kill them. Bliss intervenes and kills the Solarian but does so reluctantly, much to the irritation of Trevize who wanted her to engage in purposeful and decisive deadly action. Why didn't you act more quickly, demands Trevize. To which Bliss replies:

> I am Bliss, too, but I am Gaia. I am a world that finds every atom of itself precious and meaningful, and every organization of atoms even more precious and meaningful. I/we/Gaia would not lightly break down an organization, though we would gladly build it into something still more complex, provided always that that would not harm the whole. The highest form of organization we know produces intelligence, and to be willing to destroy intelligence requires the sorest need. (*Foundation and Earth*)

This semi-pacifism in the name of morphological organization does not satisfy Trevize's purposeful need for self-preservation and 'we'-group preservation. He is not impressed with the argument from meaning or 'us'.

But meaning can kill as well. T. E. Lawrence achieved his war aims by bowing to meaning's harsh inevitabilities. In the David Lean film, he risks his own life in the desert to save the life of Gasim, one of the tribesmen under his command, and then he had to kill Gasim to stop a tribal blood feud. Later on Lawrence hesitates to retaliate against retreating Turkish troops who slaughtered the inhabitants of the Syrian town of Tafas as they exited. But then he ends up leading the charge to kill the Turks. He is caught up in the pattern of the alien social world that he has entered. For a time – though only for a time – Lawrence can be successful in this world. He can wage a brilliant guerrilla war with clear military objectives. But only because he can also do the awful things that the 'logic' of this world, which is not his own, demands. That is to say, meaning has very strong claims and to get pattern and purpose to cohere in sync is difficult. For example, we look on industrial technology, understandably, as a purposeful way of 'controlling' of nature. However, in reality the purposes that are achieved with the use of technologies require the artful use of the known lawful regularities, mathematical equations and geometrical theorems concerning the patterns of nature in order to mobilize one physical or biological force to offset another one. Technologically enabled goal-rational actions are a derivative of this. As a consequence, human beings end up 'controlling' a lot less than they think they do.

Sometimes it is claimed that human beings can cause natural events on a planetary scale such as 'changing' the climate of the planet or 'eliminating' a virus that has spread around the world. But such scenarios confuse the constructively adaptive relationship to nature with a futilely controlling one. Science for example develops vaccines not in order to eliminate viruses but to stimulate the natural human immune system to better do what it already does, which is to fight invasive viral microbes and try and repel them by activating the human body's natural T-lymphocytes and B-lymphocytes in order to return the body to an allostatic condition. For 500 million years the earth's average global surface temperature has oscillated repeatedly up and down, ranging from peaks of 35°C to troughs of 11.6°C.[6] Its present-day 14.4°C is unexceptional and about average for the past forty million years. When the first primates appear in the fossil record fifty-five million years ago, the temperature then averaged over 21°C. In spite of the natural history of warming and cooling cycles that often exhibit dramatic ups and downs, it is widely contended that human beings determine the planet's temperatures due to the operation of industry and the use of fossil fuels. This reprises a voluntaristic misconception that repeatedly grips human beings: the idea that their purposeful actions can determine the resonant patterns of nature. The interventionist fallacy is the same whether it happens to be expressed in the form of a contemporary scientific superstition, an ancient ritual rain dance or archaic human sacrifice. Human behaviour, be it conscious or unconscious, intentional or unintentional, has little or no effect (in a causal sense) on nature's large-scale patterns.

Some speculate that the atmospheres of planets other than earth might one day be 'terraformed' to provide human settlers with a more hospitable environment. The term 'terraforming' was coined by the American science fiction writer Jack Williamson in his 1942 short story 'Collision Orbit' and was the theme of James Lovelock and Michael Allaby's 1984 science fiction *The Greening of Mars*. In Asimov's universe, 'almost all the human-inhabited worlds of the Galaxy' are 'terraformed' (*Foundation and Earth*). Is engineering on a planetary scale the future equivalent of the irrigation engineering that made possible the first terrestrial civilization in Mesopotamia, the Sumer? Asimov depicts exilic Earth colonists on an oceanic Alpha Centauri exoplanet. The oceans were stocked, atmospheric oxygen levels raised, and an artificial island created by the Galactic Empire for the settlers. The Empire then left and never returned. The islanders, gifted oceanic biotechnologists, seem on the surface, in Asimov's account, happy with the results. But less so in reality. Constrained to a tiny scrap of land, they have tried unsuccessfully for centuries to become amphibious beings. What is a constant in history is that engineering, like all goal-rational activities, has its limits. We ought not to forget that as much as 50 per cent of the water diverted from the salinity-prone Euphrates River evaporated, leaving salt deposits that eventually crippled Sumerian agriculture. Nature is indifferent to human purposes. The visible 'can-do' of technology and the purposive freedom that it enables is always conditioned by the larger less visible context of the adaptive freedoms that are gained and lost during humankind's fate-filled epic passages through space and time.

The deliberate shaping of nature such as the channelling of water is often impressive in scale and achievement. But whether any particular project succeeds or fails is secondary to the even more deep-seated drive of human beings to create artificial environments or forms of 'second nature' to live in. The most notable of these are cities, including among them one of the earliest cities, $c.4500$ BCE, the powerful Sumerian city-state of Uruk, which lasted over five thousand years until the 600s CE. The urban anchor of civilization echoes in science fiction, including in Asimov, and is often located underground. Asimov's domed city-planet of Trantor is the capital of the First Galactic Empire: 'To all appearances, it was then at its peak. Its land surface of 200 million square kilometres was entirely domed (except for the Imperial Palace area) and underlaid with an endless city that extended beneath the continental shelves' (*Prelude to Foundation*). 'Earth built underground', observed Pelorat. 'The Caves of Steel, they called their cities. And Trantor built underground, too, even more extensively, in the old Imperial days. And Comporellon builds underground right now. It is a common tendency, when you come to think of it.' 'On Terminus, dwelling places are on the surface', Trevize countered. 'And exposed to the weather', interjects the Solarian Bander, 'Very primitive' (*Foundation and Earth*). Later Trevize would expound on the human capacity to create artificial environments. His own vessel, he pointed out, was 'a tiny world that has an uninhabitable surface. There's no air or water on the outside. Yet we live inside in perfect comfort. The Galaxy is full of space stations and space settlements of infinite variety, to say nothing of spaceships, and they're all uninhabitable except for the interior' (*Foundation and Earth*).

Everything is a wave

Uruk, the first major city of humanity's first civilization, Sumer, had no 'caves of steel'. Instead its central architectural icon was a pyramidal temple ziggurat with a cave-like interior and an economy of organized labour, taxation and administered irrigation.[7] Its history reads like an epic science fiction future history. Its state organization went through phases from independent city-state to serial annexation by the Akkadian Empire, the city of Ur, the Greek Seleucid and Iranian Parthian Empires, and then disappeared with the rise of Islam. That Uruk persisted for 5,000 years is explained mostly by its nodal location on trade routes. Its existence in a dry environment is explained by the organizational power of a hydraulic civilization but its longevity is the result of it being a node in a network of long-distance trade based on abstract patterns of interaction.

The first sign that Asimov's Galactic Empire is declining is that 'trade is stagnating' (*Prelude to Foundation*). Hari Seldon correctly predicts that in due course 'interstellar trade will decay; population will decline; worlds will lose touch with the main body of the Galaxy' (*Foundation*). Sure enough without the 'free agencies of trade, tourism, and communication' the empire begins breaking down into fragments (*Prelude to Foundation*). Trantor, the empire's powerful administrative centre, was unable to revive these by command or coercion. The First Foundation began a galactic renewal only when 'slowly' it 'developed a trading economy as the Encyclopedia receded into the background' (*Foundation and Empire*). Renaissance required the input of spirit. Under the empire this spirit has been dissipated in a general galactic 'weariness' (*Prelude to Foundation*).

Spirit, Hegel's Geist, is a function not of rules or commands but of patterns that generate tacit meaning. There was a time when we called these patterns 'laws of nature', and for a good reason. For their ultimate source is nature. Social descriptions are riddled with references to hierarchies, layers, symmetries, networks, flows, spins, fractals, cracks, fissures, folds, lattices, grids, branching trees, spirals, bubbles, tessellations, ripples, waves, cycles, ratios, proportions, balances, equilibria and homeostasis as well as the disruptions and distortions, and the growth and decline, of these patterns. We have frequent recourse to nature's abstract forms in order to describe all manner of social structures and dynamics. Such abstractions are not just metaphors for social behaviour or institutional arrangement. They are also morphogenetic of social order. They are the tacit building blocks of that order. With the passage of time, created order withers and fractures. This is because of the disruptive pressures that invariably occur as societies – including fictional ones like Asimov's Galactic Empire or real ones like Gibbon's Roman Empire or Toynbee's Assyrian, Achaemenid, Ptolemaic, Seleucid, Sasanian, Maurya, Qin, Han, East Roman, Abbasid, Muscovite, Tokugawa, Ottoman, Carolingian, Holy Roman, Venetian,

Napoleonic, British, French, Russian and Soviet empires – enter wave-like phases of 'decline and fall' following preceding periods of 'genesis and growth'. In Asimov's universe, any type of homeostasis 'would be able to keep from falling apart only by unending effort' (*Foundation and Earth*).

All balance is dynamic and can be upended – civilizational equilibria as much as natural equilibria. 'War and administrative failure', Bliss reflects, are the cause of unbalance (*Foundation and Earth*). Yet disequilibria often is more hidden than it is explicit. Empires at their peak are happily unaware that all growth contains elements of shrinking and withering. 'The population was 40 billion and although the signs were plentiful (and clearly visible in hindsight) that there were gathering problems, those who lived on Trantor undoubtedly found it still the Eternal World of legend and did not expect it would ever [decline]' (*Prelude to Foundation*). But empires, like all societies, move in waves, rising and falling inexorably over epic time. Everyone has experience of waves, not least when they go to the beach. Waves are a pervasively occurring phenomenon in nature. So much so that, as the theoretical physicist and cosmologist Neil Turok (2015) puts it, everything in physics is a wave. As well every entity that we know of in nature has a dual character: it is both a particle *and* a wave. Waves, Turok remarks, are in the first instance possibility waves. They explore options, potential paths to choose. Everything in the universe (from atoms to humans to the cosmos) is a possibility wave. It is a contingent state – the probability Y that *a* particle might be *here* or the probability Z that *b* particle might be *there* – that resolves into a non-contingent pattern state. The social equivalent of this is free will: which is a superposition of choice (freedom) and will (determination).

Nature in its massive entirety works through the up-and-down motion of waves – and so do societies. And like nature, this up-and-down, rising-and-falling social motion is scale-invariant. As Turok (2015) says of the physical character of the cosmos, it is structured as a wave motion and this applies irrespective of the size of the universe.[8] Similarly, in the case of societies, wave motion applies on the largest, smallest and middling social scales. While these are real recurring phenomenon, societies are often amnesic about them. Most people are convinced at the peak of a boom that the upswing of the business cycle will continue for ever; when the inevitable downturn occurs, opinion reverses: the down trend will go on indefinitely. Because of the cyclical character of nature and society, future events cannot be predicted by projecting the present into the future. Each downturn contains the seeds of a future upturn.

Enthusiasm and pessimism hide the cyclical motion of modern economies. There is no room for a mathematical sociology amidst this kind of thinking. Yet theorists persist, for good reason, in arguing such a thing. In the twentieth century, observations of this type were heavily influenced by the Russian economist Nikolai Kondratieff (who was executed by Stalin). Kondratieff's long-wave theory of economics provided the impetus for Joseph Schumpeter's epic two-volume *Business Cycles* (1939). This was followed by an ecumenical spectrum of Kondratieff interpretations ranging from the Marxist economist Ernest Mandel's *Late Capitalism* (1972) and his *Long Waves of Capitalist Development* (1980) to the classical-liberal economics of W. W. Rostow's *The World Economy* (1978). Given the intrinsic scale of the enterprise and the interweaving of audacious scope and exacting detail required, epic works in twentieth-century social science were not that common. They were influential though. They mapped epic historical sequences and coexistences. Among them slave, feudal and urban-bourgeois modes of production in Perry Anderson's *Passages from Antiquity to Feudalism* and its companion volume *Lineages of the Absolutist State* (1974) and the forms of legitimate domination (patrimonial, charismatic and legal-rational) and types of city (ancient, medieval, patrician, plebeian, occidental, Asian) in Max Weber's *Economy and Society* (1922).

Like Tolstoy's philosophy of history, most of these big-picture works did not preclude the operation of free will and human volition. Some even assumed that volition and will (such as the intervention of governments or the purposeful destruction of capitalism) would eventually negate cycles and obviate waves. Nonetheless, the best works presenting an epic world picture or grand narrative assume in some way or other that purposeful volition and free choice is conditioned, sometimes highly conditioned, by recurring social patterns – be they the patterns of history, populations, geography, biology, economics and so on. From *The Civilizing Process* ([1939] 1994) through *The Society of Individuals* ([1991] 2001), the sociologist Norbert Elias envisaged a study of autonomic civilizational processes. Such inquiry assumed that 'although people form societies and keep society moving by their actions and plans, at the same time society seems often to go its own way and, while being driven by those who form them, at the same time, seems to drive them' (2009: 62). The philosopher Cornelius Castoriadis (1997a, 1997b) argued that such impersonal forms or patterns in turn are generated by the 'social historical'.[9] This is a process of anonymous social creation. It is the function of 'the creative capacity of anonymous human collectives' (331; also 333). More recent excursions into this terrain include Ian Morris's 15,000-year geographically shaped history *Why the West Rules – for Now* (2010) and the population-scale cliodynamic histories of Peter Turchin (2003, 2007, 2009).

How little politics matters in the midst of all of this – and yet how much human beings attribute to politics the illusory capacity to change nature and society. The First and Second Foundations are good examples of the inability of scientific politics to direct the anonymous patterns of history, society and nature while believing it is possible to do so. The First Foundation is repeatedly embroiled in political warring and struggles for political advantage and the drive to expand its rule from the margins of the old Empire to the centre. Scientific superstition legitimates its will to power. The function of empire is to integrate the galaxy. Without this, the First Foundation claims, there would only be 'isolated and probably dying worlds' (*Foundation's Edge*). As to the Plan that legitimates the authority of the new Empire-in-formation, there can be 'no official doubts, criticisms, or condemnations' of it. It cannot be questioned. 'We must support it completely.' The scientific model of politics assumes the existence of Seldon-type statistical laws. These state that if certain conditions are in place then a particular outcome will occur in a specified percentage of cases. That is the premise of all social engineering and government planning. What purposeful *if-then* models do not account for is the larger-scale and more abstract motions of history, society and nature that overwrite much of purposeful *if-then* human actions with self-regulating patterns and forms – or, as science fiction often has it, balances and harmonies or in Seldon's terms elegant mathematical inverse functions reminiscent of the Taoist yin-yang.[10] The assumption being: 'A placement means a displacement somewhere else. A weight needs a counterweight' (*Forward the Foundation*). Or in Gaian terms (comparing human happiness to the 'happiness' of a wall): 'A wall is happy when it is well designed, when it rests firmly on its foundation, when its symmetry balances its parts and produces no unpleasant stresses' (*Foundation's Edge*).

As the epic dialectic of galactic balance and unbalance gradually kicked in, and a long time has passed, the notable personalities of the First Foundation came to look less and less like the compelling heroes of a great drama or even the central figures of a venerable political romance. The passage of time diminished all of them as history diminishes all political figures. As the Foundation series draws to a conclusion even the leader of the would-be new Empire, Harla Branno, is still titled the Mayor of Terminus not her Imperial Majesty and her Council contains the Seldon sceptic Trevize. Byzantium never restored the old Rome or matched it. The Mayor threatens to use emergency powers to silence Trevize's public Seldon scepticism. The Seldon Plan, with its scientific superstitions that legitimate the Foundation's will to power, defines the limit of free speech. The sceptic Trevize points out to Branno, like a Diogenes to Alexander, that the

Seldon power myth is full of logical holes. The hidden God, the Plan, neatly unfolded until its scientific prophecy failed to predict the rise of the renegade Gaian power of the Mule. This prompted the Second Foundation to reveal itself in order to get the Plan back on track. Yet, by revealing itself, it undermined its own requirement that its adepts and actions remain hidden. Patterns of human behaviour can be predicted and actions (nudges, an 'amplifier' here, a 'contact' there) taken to recalibrate those patterns. Excepting that anyone who is aware of the behavioural predictions, and the consequent probable interventions, will steer their behaviours in a manner designed to negate the control mechanisms. When the closeted Second Foundation was exposed, the First Foundation then sought to eliminate its rival as it did not wish to be behaviourally controlled.

Scientific politics always ends up in this vicious paradox. Its will to power has profound limits. If, reasons Trevize, the Seldon predictions are coming true then it is only because the predictive manipulative power, that is, the social engineering capacity, of the Second Foundation wasn't actually destroyed by the First Foundation and is still acting as a galactic hidden hand. After the assault on it, following its exposure, it secretly rebuilt, recruited and retrained. And it has its own will to power: to be the social-scientific elite that controls the Galactic Empire once the empire-building work of the encyclopaedic-turned-technocratic First Foundation is completed. The (elected) Mayor of Trantor – who is not (yet) Her Imperial Majesty – agrees privately with the irritating sceptic Trevize: yes, the Second Foundation may not have been destroyed after all, and Trevize is directed to find it. So begins his epic expedition that will uncover not just the revenant Second Foundation but also two other galactic hidden hands, the self-regulating Gaia/Galaxia and the robot hyper-intelligence of R. Daneel Olivaw.

The early volumes of the Foundation series – *Foundation, Foundation and Empire*, and *Second Foundation* as well as their prequels *Prelude to Foundation* and *Forward the Foundation* – are concerned with the failures of politics and the illusions of politics. The Galactic Empire is crumbling, at first, invisibly. The Emperor Cleon I dismisses Seldon's early attempt at psycho-history (*Prelude to Foundation*). R. Daneel Olivaw, in the guise of the Emperor's First Minister in the further guise of a journalist who warns Seldon against the First Minister, manipulates Seldon into fleeing across the galaxy to a series of planets leading him on purpose but unawares to develop a viable working version of his psychohistory. Seldon later returns to the imperial centre to become Cleon I's First Minister in place of Olivaw's First Minister who has disappeared (*Forward the Foundation*).

The decline of the Empire continues and this is mirrored in the aging of Seldon and the deaths that surround him. By the time of *Foundation*, the original novel of the series, Seldon's influence in the Empire has waned. Its officials don't trust him but agree (or are manipulated to agree) to his self-exile at the margins of the galaxy on the planet Terminus and allow him to establish there a First Foundation of nominal encyclopaedists. Secretly, sometime before in the previous volume, Seldon's telepathic granddaughter Wanda has already established the Second Foundation. From these beginnings, a neo-imperial politics emerges. First, modestly, far from the Empire's control, the First Foundation creates a technocratic pseudo-religion that allows it to control four nearby planetary kingdoms. Then it learns to expand its influence through trade. Finally in *Foundation and Empire* it is drawn into military conflict. Its power has grown so the Empire attacks it. The Empire is successful but ironically too successful. Emperor Cleon II recalls his general (Riose) and has him executed because the general has become too powerful. A second and greater military threat to the First Foundation comes from the rise of the power of the Mule, the renegade mind-controlling Gaian. But the Mule is undone by a classic self-defeating mistake: he opens a second front, an obsessive search for the mysterious Second Foundation which in response finds him and neuters his powers with their own superior telepathic mind control. In a checkmate counter-response, the First Foundation develops telepathy-detecting technology to protect its own power from the Second Foundation.

History shrugs

Political hubris, envy, distrust, secrecy, dissimulation, myopia, control and the failure of control permeate the Foundation series. On this level it is a narrative of tiny elites and court politics, and their subterfuges, manipulations and compulsive appetite for power. This is a version of Machiavellian elite politics. Amid the resulting power struggles there are a number of odyssey-like adventure-companion stories: those of the younger Seldon and his protector and wife, the historian and artificial intelligence Dors Venabili; Toran and Bayta Darell; and Trevize, Pel and Bliss. Overlaying both of the themes of power and expedition is the epic theme of 'history shrugs': the pervading sense that runs through the Foundation series that empires rise and fall in step with the larger invisible metabolism of history that is set in motion by the interaction of forces of disequilibrium and those that tacitly operate to re-establish social homeostasis.

Elite politics, power politics and court politics always appear ascendant, until they are not.

Asimov's fictional future history mirrors the facts of actual history. In the past 500 years as Modelski (1987: Table 2.1) observed, global power politics has been dominated by successive long cycles of the rise and fall of an international power and a challenger: the Portuguese cycle (and Spanish challenger); the Dutch cycle (and French challenger); the First British cycle (and French challenger); the Second British cycle (and German challenger); and the American cycle (and Communist challengers). Power politics ebbs and flows; but the cyclical rhythm of this is set in train by the meta-historical or meta-social pattern of a wave-like motion. One day this era's empire is the 'axiom' of everyone's existence (*Prelude to Foundation*); tomorrow it is gone.

Looking back over the past two centuries of social thought, there have been a surprising number of works concerned with meta-social patterns. These works follow no obvious or consistent political line or orientation. Their emphasis (as Tolstoy put it) on interconnecting the infinitesimal elements of free will into coherent (meaningful) laws and patterns of motion – somehow thereby connecting in a conformal manner the infinitesimally small and the maximally large – has a distinct parallel with Asimov's Foundation series. Perhaps it matters less in each case how this is done than the ambition to do it. The 'cosmos' theory of Friedrich Hayek's late-life social theory (*Law, Liberty and Legislation*, 1973 and *The Fatal Conceit*, 1988) and George Modelski's *Long Cycles in World Politics* (1987) coincidentally appear at the same time as Asimov's later Foundation series books, *Foundation's Edge* (1982) and *Foundation and Earth* (1986) where the Gaia/Galaxia themes present themselves.

Those occupied with the larger sweep of human history often call the meta-historical picture the 'story of civilization'. Other times terms like 'antiquity' or 'modernity' are used. The specific terms are less important than what they signify: namely, the dynamics of large-scale social rise, fall and re-rise – and the interactional structures that underpin this motion and that drive it. Many of these structures echo in a fractal manner the in-built structures of expansion and contraction of nature and the cosmos. Expansions and contraction, rise, decline and fall, and re-energization after a fall – these cliodynamic patterns are observable whether the case happens to be a single sequence of civilization as in the example of the 'Greek, Roman, Western' model, or multiple civilizational sequences like Toynbee's 'Minoan, Shang, Indus, Egyptiac, Sumeric and Andean' model or Oswald Spengler's template of Apollonian (Greek-Roman), Magian (Arab) and Faustian (Western) cultures in which civilization represents the hardening of the arteries of culture, that is, essentially the death of culture. But that's Spengler making his case for the Faustian entity against its Apollonian and Magian competitors. If we ignore the culture-civilization distinction and suppose that all of the categories coined by Spengler and Toynbee are civilizations, then we can say over time some civilizations reach a dead end (Toynbee's Egyptiac, Sumeric and Andean entities) while others mutate, expand, shrink and evolve. In today's world that would leave us with five major civilizations (Apollonian, Faustian, East Asian, Islamic and Hindu) whose interactions and clashes, internal divisions and respective gravitational weights, and degrees of energy and lassitude, purism and hybridity have a deep background shaping effect on contemporary societies. Spengler's useful intuition was to read culture-civilization in terms of mathematical-geometrical form-worlds. Such an intellectual approach, irrespective of Spengler's own Faustian preferences, could be much more widely employed today with fruitful consequence. It is relatively close in spirit to Roger Penrose's view of the importance of geometrical visualization in human understanding and insight.

Pitirim Sorokin (1937) saw social processes as running along straight lines for a time, reaching a limit and then continuing through loops, irregular oscillations and in waves while civilizations moved between spiritual, spiritual-material and material phases, cycling back-and-forth between sensate, ideational and idealistic eras. Ideational societies are otherworldly. They look to the visible signs of an invisible world. They are interested in symbolic and allegorical ways of understanding the hidden world of the spirit. They aspire to quietness, calmness and restfulness. They want to be at peace. Sensate societies are worldly. Spatially they are material and empirical rather than spiritual; in matters of time they are dynamic, impressionistic and restless. They are drawn to feelings of change and becoming. In their decline, they are gaudy and sensational. Sorokin's idealistic societies are a mix of the ideational and the sensate. They strike some kind of balance between the two. Peaks of civilization tend to internalize an equilibrium between the push of dynamic-material social forces and the pull of impassive-spiritual forces. Like most equilibria, peak civilizational periods don't last. Tensions between purposes and patterns or between motives and meanings become too great and these overwhelm the established balance of the civilizational high-point in the contrary directions of philistinism or asceticism, hysteria or passivity, indeterminism or determinism, or similar.

In *The New Science* (1744) Giambattista Vico depicted civilization, a *storia ideale eternal*, as developing through a recurring cycle (*ricorso*) of three ages: divine, heroic and human. Each epoch was characterized by a different communicative form. The dominant rhetorical device of the divine phase of civilization is metaphor (one thing stands for something else). 'The sky is a god.' The heroic age relies on metonymy (a part stands for a related part of the whole). 'The crown' is the monarch in the system of government. The age of men embraced a particular kind of metonymy, the synecdoche (a part stands for the whole). 'Roof stands for house'. For Vico, the rise of irony (in which the whole contains contradictory parts) signifies the decay of society and culture. It is the barbarism of reflection. In contrast in Asimov's fiction, irony is the communicative form of renaissance and expansion. Vico's was a melancholic irony – an abject or romantic one not a dialectical or comedic irony, one that comprehends the whole of historical development by engaging all of history's opposing terms in order to understand its expansive totality. The latter is Toynbee's 'reversal of roles' (*peripeteia*), the numerous paradoxes – including those of simplicity and sophistication, adults and children, the first and the last, the least and the greatest, universality and locality, losing one's life in order to find it, and so on – that provide the ironic engines of epic meta-history (1988: 167–70, 328, 335, 368–70). In epic irony, triumph often is an excuse for self-destruction just as the promised avoidance of catastrophe in history may turn out to be a recipe for catastrophe.

Vichian heroic and human rhetorical types parallel the politics described in the Foundation series. The metonymies of 'Empire' and 'Plan' are shorthand terms for a part (power politics) of the whole (galactic society and its course of development). Both are misleading. They misdirect attention away from rather than toward the larger if mostly tacit meta-history of Galaxia. Terminus, Trantor, Gaia and the Earth's Moon are the synecdochical Rome(s), Washington(s) and Pentagon(s) of the series. They are parts that stand for the whole of a present and future society. Each one promises a solution for the decline of the inter-planetary entropy that they don't and can't deliver. The entire series is ironic, through and through. Melpomenia, one of several hoped-for Earths that promise a solution to the riddle of the galaxy's future, has intact but deserted cities and the planet, excepting for a resilient, aggressive 'moss', is lifeless, oceanless and virtually airless place with only a thin atmosphere. It had undergone a twenty-millennia-long collapse.

As one hinted-at planet or moon after another unveils itself, its promise evaporates. Other promises evaporate before sceptical sardonicism. '[We] offer a Second Galactic Empire fundamentally different from the First', says Stor Gendibal, Speaker of the Second Foundation (*Foundation's Edge*). The Gaian Suri Novi counters: 'Are [the Speakers of Trantor] free of destructive competition, of politics, of clawing upward at all costs? Are there no quarrels and even hatreds at the Speaker's Table – and will they always be guides you dare follow?' The series' metaphors of power and its various metonymies and synecdoche of authority are absorbed and dissolved into a master irony. This irony looks with a deep scepticism on the ambitions, schemes and politicking of the two Foundations when compared with the meta-history unfolding around and through them even if they are not aware of it. Tolstoy had a similar view of the designs and schemes hatched by the French and Russian imperial commanders during the Napoleonic wars and the various post-facto explanations and rationales of Russian success.

In the Foundation series, metaphor, metonymy, synecdoche and irony all play meta-historical parts. During the course of the series' recurring mystery-puzzles, whose nature is to be revealed at some dramatic crisis point, a seemingly socially defining analogy will convert into another very different one. We begin the Foundation series with the notion that the hidden scientific Foundations can reverse imperial disintegration, just as Toynbee's creative elites are capable (on occasions) of saving civilizations from disintegration (1988: 166, 169–70, 224, 228, 234). By the end of *Foundation's Edge*, when Trevize is asked to 'choose' between a galactic future that looks like the future of the First Foundation or the Second Foundation or that of the Gaians, Trevize opts for a Gaian future because the First Foundation is now a metaphor for militarism and the Second Foundation is a metaphor for paternalism (*Foundation's Edge*). The symbols or allegories of imperial salvation that began the series have faded.

Organism and anarchy

Even after his choice, Trevize's intuition tells him that something is still hidden. At the start of *Foundation and Earth*, the final book in the epic cycle, he airs his clairvoyance with Bliss. Something is not quite right, he senses. And he wonders whether Gaia/Galaxia is really a suitable future. Perhaps this telepathic 'super-organism' would extinguish variety and individuality? If everything, say, was like the mildness of his home planet Terminus or the moderation of the Gaians, wouldn't that be 'unbearable'? 'I like to get away, at least temporarily, to something different.' No, Bliss assures him, 'if variety seems desirable, variety will be maintained'. To which Trevize retorts: 'As a gift from the Central Committee … I'd rather leave it to nature.' Bliss responds, pointing out that humankind always creates a second nature. 'But you haven't left it to nature', she insists.

Every habitable world in the Galaxy has been modified. Every single one was found in a state of nature that was uncomfortable for humanity, and every single one was modified until it was as mild as could be managed. If this world here is cold, I am certain that is because its inhabitants couldn't warm it any further without unacceptable expense. And even so, the portions they actually inhabit we can be sure are artificially warmed into mildness. So don't be so loftily virtuous about leaving it to nature.

The debate continues with Trevize suggesting that Gaian agents are present on other planets, which brings a singularly evasive response from Bliss. Trevize suggests that the Gaians think of themselves as 'guardians of the galaxy'. Well, says, Bliss, we want a stable, secure, peaceful and prosperous galaxy. The Seldon Plan was to develop a more stable and workable Second Galactic Empire than the First was. She then suggests that the Plan, modified by the Second Foundation, was working well. To which the sceptical Trevize counters: 'But Gaia doesn't want a Second Galactic Empire in the classic sense, does it? You want Galaxia – a living Galaxy.' To which she responds, disingenuously, that the outcome – reborn Empire *or* Galaxia – rests on his individual choice. 'If you had not permitted it', she says, '[the Gaians] would have striven for Seldon's Second Empire and made it as secure as we could.' What Trevize does not know yet is that the hidden hand of the robot computational intelligence can only seed a Galaxia future if Trevize exercises his free will – his quantum-like ironic superpositioning of freedom and determination – in the cause of Galaxia. His act of freedom is an act of determination.

Trevize begins to wonder: is this entire history, a story of diversion? 'The First Galactic Empire had crumbled and for 500 years the Foundation had grown, first in competition with the Empire, and then upon its ruins – all in accordance with the Plan' (*Foundation and Earth*). But appearances presented by this story were deceptive. The true course of events was hidden. The Mule had disrupted things. True, mused Trevize, 'The Foundation had pulled through – probably with the help of the ever-hidden Second Foundation – possibly with the help of the even better-hidden Gaia. Now the Plan was threatened by something more serious than the Mule had ever been. It was to be diverted from a renewal of Empire to something utterly different from anything in history – Galaxia.' And Trevize was worried that he was going to be responsible for this next diversion. Would it be worth it? Was Gaia/Galaxia a dangerous fantasy? Does Gaia understand individuality? On the other hand, what if the Seldon Plan was based on a taken-for-granted yet false assumption? Then again, how could any assumption so obvious be false? Was intuition sufficient to replace reason? Can one know the right thing to do even if one does not know why one is doing it?

Does intuition mean running the risk of listening too long to the fantasy of one's own infallibility? Am I, Trevize asks himself, 'the Great Fool of the Galaxy'?

Bliss and Trevize repeatedly debate the relative merits of connection and independence. Even if the galaxy was in a state of turmoil, Bliss argues, Galaxia would at least represent a connection between hostile worlds. From the Gaian point of view, isolation is a cancer that destroys societies. Trevize is unconvinced. He dislikes the idea of 'total unification', arguing that there is a 'natural size, a natural complexity, some optimum quality for everything, whether star or atom, and it's certainly true of living things and living societies'. He also wonders whether a lack of 'self-love' on the part of the Gaians might be reason enough for them to sacrifice other human beings in the name of 'some high motive' (*Foundation and Earth*).

A planet without the idea of an exclusive intimate partnership for life? 'I have innumerable companions', Bliss tells Pel, 'that are as close to me as your arm is close companion to your other arm' (*Foundation and Earth*). 'I only want you, Bliss', Pel responds, unconvinced by Gaian collective intimacy. Conversely, Trevize and Bliss argue about rules. She thinks that not following rules ends in anarchy and disaster, and disguises self-interest. The pair argue about consensus and dissensus. The argument itself makes the case for dissensus. The debate is a steely one. Trevize thinks that societies do not collapse that easily and that rules outlive their usefulness as circumstances change, yet can remain in force through inertia. 'It is then not only right, but useful, to break those rules as a way of advertising the fact that they have become useless – or even actually harmful.' Bliss bites back: 'Then every thief and murderer can argue he is serving humanity.' Trevize counters:

> You go to extremes. In the superorganism of Gaia, there is automatic consensus on the rules of society and it occurs to no one to break them. One might as well say that Gaia vegetates and fossilizes. There is admittedly an element of disorder in free association, but that is the price one must pay for the ability to induce novelty and change. On the whole, it's a reasonable price.

Bliss pushes back against the idea that Gaia is a fossilized planet, insisting that the society's views are under 'constant self-examination'. Trevize remains sceptical. He thinks that this collective self-reflection must be very slow. In a society based on freedom, 'even when almost everyone agrees, there are bound to be a few who disagree and, in some cases, those few may be right, and if they are clever enough, enthusiastic enough, right enough, they will win out in the end'. For Bliss, this is the freedom to be foolish and criminal.

To the Gaians, the galaxy looks anarchic. 'In a Galaxy of anarchy, how is it possible to sort out reasonable actions from unreasonable ones? How [to] decide between right and wrong, good and evil, justice and crime, useful and useless?' Bliss considers the readiness of the Comporellon minister Mitza Lizalor to betray the Foundation Confederation – to commit treason for patriotic reasons (to achieve independence from the Foundation's neo-empire) – and she cannot understand the paradox involved, namely that sometimes to do the right thing requires doing the wrong thing. Can Gaians understand the importance of such paradoxes, that they exist at the heart of creation? Lizalor, who is mildly manipulated by Bliss, has sex with Trevize and relishes it compared with her unappetizing experience with anodyne Comporellian males. But then, typical of the contrary bitter-sweet human imagination, she also regrets the episode as a misfortune. For now 'Comporellian men will seem more sapless still. I will be left with an unappeasable longing' (*Foundation and Earth*). The final exchange between Lizalor and Trevize repeats the motif of the paradoxes of human existence. He promises he will return to Comporellon. She says he won't. He complains that she is being irrational, believing that his quest for the origin of the species on Earth will prevent his return: 'That ... is superstition.' She counters: 'And yet that, too, is true.'

Coda

Science fiction is fiction. We ought not to forget that. It tells made-up stories. Even if Asimov's work is a science fiction of ideas, it is still only a story. Nevertheless, it is also an imaginative canvas that allows us scope to think about problems like the connection between purpose and pattern that normal social science settings inhibit us from doing. The Foundation series might not answer the questions we have – after all that is not its purpose – but it can and does set us thinking and speculating on the rise, fall and rise of civilizations. For one thing, the lengthy timescale is a useful stimulus to meta-social thought as is the galactic scope of Asimov's fictional space. Toynbee has the genesis, growth, breakdown and disintegration of six civilizational streams across 6,500 years along with examples of four abortive civilizations and five arrested civilizations, all together (though at different times) covering much of the face of the earth. Asimov's fictional timeline (including the prequel novels *Prelude to Foundation* and *Forward the Foundation*) extends across 500 years of events; 20,000 years of AI prehistory; a predicted 1,000 years for the Empire to pass through breakdown, disintegration and rejuvenation; and 30,000 years of breakdown and disintegration (chaos and entropy) should the science-fictional process of re-genesis (Toynbee's renaissances) fail. The civilization of Rome, including the Roman Republic and the Roman Empire, both of which Asimov wrote about, lasted from 509 BCE to 476 CE in the West and 1453 CE in the East, a span of almost 2,000 years. Gibbon's history in seven volumes, *Decline and Fall of the Roman Empire*, spans 430 years; the period from the Age of the Antonines (138–180 CE) to the death of Emperor Justinian in 565 CE.

The largest social scale – the civilizational scale – encompasses epic swathes of space and time. Reconciling these with everyday human experience and comprehension is difficult. Everyday persons in a civilizational context – let alone in a science-fictional galactic one with a population of 10 quadrillion (10 thousand-million-million in the Foundation Confederation) and millions of inhabitable worlds – barely consciously register the wave-like rhythms of social genesis and decline, expansion and contraction that affect the societies clustered in a civilizational matrix. Yet the impact of these is inescapable and persistent. Asimov's timescale of 500 years of galactic events is similar to earth-bound civilizational timescales. It is difficult to relate such a scale to the days, weeks and years of a life of work and rest, ambition and desire dominated by or at least requiring significant degrees of goal rationality and lyrical sentiment. Yet human beings also dream of more than 'causes' or 'motives'. They seek meaning in many forms: mythical, religious, metaphysical, epic, tragic, comic and on and on. And on a practical level empires – or civilizations – crumble. Their energy turns to entropy; their order to chaos. The difficulty of social actors is to see a process that for all intents and purposes is hidden even if its effects are experienced in the subtle disruptions of peace and prosperity. The erosion is slow and yet punctuated by crises. Olaf Stapledon in his science fiction work *Last and First Men* ([1930] 1999) depicted the cyclical rise and fall of human civilizations through 18 species of human beings and across two billion years of history ranging across the planets of the solar system.

Astrophysicists calculate that the upper-limit time for a space-faring civilization to cross and settle the Milky Way Galaxy (assuming current interplanetary vehicle speeds and no science-fictional faster-than-light travel or worm-holes) is 300 million years or 2.1 per cent of the current age of the universe (Carroll-Nellenback et al. 2019). The visual animation of this projected galactic exodus shows a spiral pattern of settlement that initially is slow, that then accelerates and spreads with dramatic speed, and that is concentrated at the centre of the galaxy because of the density of stars and planetary systems at the centre (Wright et al. 2021). This space-faring model assumes the settlement over time of 100 billion discrete human civilizations across the Milky Way Galaxy. There are no alien civilizations in this scenario. Asimov's description of this process envisaged 'a network drawn through all planets ten thousand years old; another through those twelve thousand years old, still another through those fifteen thousand years old. Each network would, in theory, be roughly spherical and they should be roughly concentric.' This was a settlement process in which 'Earth was not the only point of origin of settlement for other worlds. As time went on, the older worlds sent out settlement expeditions of their own' (*Foundation and Earth*). As colonization matured 'planets would be settled outward from the world of origin in all directions'. In what sounds like a geometric progression of settlement over 20,000 years, millions of worlds would be colonized. But the process begins slowly in the first centuries with only fifty or so planets settled.

The number of stars in the Milky Way Galaxy is currently estimated to range between 100 billion and 400 billion. Is a science-fictional account of such an expanse colonized over 300 million years and counting possible? It is daunting, to be sure. But to put this in perspective. The first members of the *Homo* genus appear in Earth's current archaeological record nearly 2.8 million years ago. The earliest currently known *Homo sapiens* appeared around 300,000 years ago. These are already substantial time lines. The first human civilization develops among the city-states of Sumer 6,500 years ago. The human story already is a lengthy one. And from the earliest time, it is a story of the *völkerwanderung*. From the sea-faring of Homer's *Odyssey* it is not a stretch to the space-faring of Asimov's Foundation. It is often claimed humans might be the only intelligent or technological species in the universe. Maybe we are. But we are also a species with a migratory drive that has led multiple societies, cultures and civilizations to spread across the face of the earth, interacting, fighting, trading, expanding and declining. There seems to be no intrinsic reason why this could not be replicated on a solar system and ultimately galactic scale. If the scale of that, both in space and time, seems intimidating, then the counter to such daunting thoughts is the imagination. For the very thing that makes both epic science fiction and the trekking drive of the human species possible is the capacious nature of the imagination and its capacity to draw distant things into close proximity and tie them together in interesting and sometimes startling ways.

Part 4

World Science Fiction

Andrew Milner

9

History or apocalypse?

Almost exactly a century after the first publication of Lukács's *The Theory of the Novel*, Amitav Ghosh, the distinguished Indian novelist and critic, published *The Great Derangement*, in which he argued that 'serious prose fiction' was overwhelmingly committed to versions of literary realism that depended for their efficacy on notions of everyday probability. Climate change, by contrast – and we could now easily add pandemics, nuclear wars, ecological catastrophes and the like – necessarily involve everyday improbabilities, radically extreme weather events, for example, compulsory facemasks or the burning of cities. The irony of the realist novel, Ghosh continued, was that 'the very gestures with which it conjures up reality are actually a concealment of the real' (23). So radical improbabilities are normally banished from 'literary fiction' into the 'generic outhouses' of fantasy, horror and SF (24). It is difficult not to sympathize with Ghosh's indictment of literary fiction nor with his defence of SF and fantasy. Nonetheless, it can seem oddly dated, if only because this is more or less exactly what Lukács had predicted in 1916. The literary novel *is* exhausted: think, for example, of the sheer tedium of Jonathan Franzen's 'great American novels'. Of course, there are important exceptions, but these are invariably writers who make extensive use of tropes and topoi derived precisely from those generic outhouses, writers in short who sometimes write SF. Obvious examples include Margaret Atwood in Canada, David Mitchell and Jeanette Winterson in England, Michel Houellebecq in France, Cormac McCarthy in the United States, Frank Schätzing in Germany and Alexis Wright in Australia. Moreover, what goes for supposedly 'literary' fiction also goes for contemporary cinema: Ridley Scott, James Cameron, Paul Verhoeven, Christopher Nolan and the Wachowski siblings are not only important SF directors but also mainstream *auteurs*. And it goes for television too: witness *Black Mirror* (2011–19), *Altered Carbon* (2018–20), *Watchmen* (2019), *The Expanse* (2015–22), *The Mandalorian* (2019–22) and *Snowpiercer* (2020–1). In the 1950s, 1960s and the 1970s, SF and fantasy really were still outhouses – pulp fiction, B movies and children's television – but they are not now and they were not even when Ghosh was writing *The Great Derangement* during 2015 and 2016. So, why not? The short answer is because SF and fantasy have become a primary locus – perhaps *the* primary locus – for our culture's speculations about its possible futures, both its dreams and its nightmares. In this important sense SF has supplanted religion and prophecy.

Lukács could write *the* theory of the novel, precisely because he believed the novel's essential history already lay behind it and that it was destined to give way to a new epic form presaged by Dostoevsky. His open-ended conclusion on Dostoevsky is worth quoting here: 'Only formal analysis of his works can show whether he is already the Homer or the Dante of that world or whether he merely supplies the songs which, together with the songs of other forerunners, later artists will one day weave into a great unity: whether he is merely a beginning or already a completion' (153). A century later we can conclude with Ghosh that the realist/modernist novel has indeed exhausted most of its aesthetic potential, and proceed to add that SF will almost certainly prove an important stimulus to the eventual unity Lukács envisaged. Certainly, this seems to be Houellebecq's view, when in *La Possibilité d'une île*, he has the clone Daniel25 look back on the twenty-first century from the forty-first, and reflect that 'certaines publications comme *Métal Hurlant* témoignent à cet égard d'une troublante prescience (certain publications such as *Métal Hurlant* display a quite troubling prescience)' (447). *Métal Hurlant* was, in both its twentieth- and twenty-first century incarnations, the leading French adult SF anthology comic book.

SF stands in a relationship of correspondence and competition with the epic and the novel. This implies a new perspective on SF refracted through Lukács's theory of epic form. Unlike the modernist novel, SF as a form engages with the most pressing issues of our time, total questions which transcend individual experience and national and civilizational borders. So, what are these pressing issues? Andrew Leigh identifies four primary 'existential risks' to humanity – viral pandemic, climate change, nuclear war and artificial intelligence (AI) – to which he adds as a fifth, political populism, on the grounds that this threatens to disable our collective capacity to respond to the others. The latter claim is clearly contentious, but Leigh's existential risks are substantial enough and have long been identified as such in SF. Each will be considered in turn.

The plague topos enters SF very early in the history of the modern genre, through Mary Shelley's *The Last Man* (1826), where a key theme is human incapacity in the face of nature and the weakness of medical science. The novel strays widely over everything from English republicanism to the struggle for Greek independence and even culminates in a rehearsal of the Biblical flood narrative. However, its central theme remains humankind's vulnerability to the species-destroying plague that eventually leaves Lionel Verney condemned to sail 'around the shores of deserted earth' as 'the LAST MAN' (279). The species-destroying plague resurfaces in H. G. Wells's *The War of the Worlds* (1898), where the seemingly invincible Martian invaders are conveniently destroyed by a plague of terrestrial pathogens, 'slain by the putrefactive and disease bacteria against which their systems were unprepared; … slain, after all man's devices had failed, by the humblest things that God, in his wisdom, has put upon this earth' (168). Just as the plague crossed the Atlantic from Europe to America, so too did the plague topos: Jack London's *The Scarlet Plague* (1912) is set in 2073, sixty years after the red death epidemic, when James Smith, a one-time university professor, vainly attempts to explain pre-pandemic civilization to his three illiterate grandsons.

Karel Čapek's play *Bílá nemoc* (1937) is conventionally translated into English as *The White Disease* but could just as easily be *The White Plague*. Čapek was, in Suvin's words, 'the most significant world SF writer between the World Wars' (309). *Bílá nemoc* has been less influential than Čapek's *R.U.R.*, but it was awarded the Czechoslovak State Prize for Drama and, like *R.U.R.*, was very promptly translated into English in 1938 under the title *Power and Glory*. It was also adapted for cinema by Hugo Haas in 1937. In both the play and the film, 'Maršál [the Marshal]', played by Zdenek Stepànek in the movie, is a thinly disguised Adolf Hitler, who plans to invade a thinly disguised Czechoslovakia, but then catches the leprosy-like white plague. The hero Dr Galén, played by Haas himself, discovers a cure and offers it to the Marshal on condition he abandons the invasion. But Galén is then himself killed and his formula destroyed by militarist thugs at a pro-war rally. The allegory functions at two levels: first, the most obvious, the comparison between fictional and real geopolitics; and second, the deeper comparison between the white disease and the plague of militarism and fascism. While the disease's deeper allegorical function is dependent on a pandemic reality effect, the play nonetheless functions overwhelmingly at the obvious level of geopolitics. Other more recent examples of pandemic SF include George R. Stewart's *Earth Abides* (1949), Richard Matheson's *I am Legend* (1954), Michael Crichton's *The Andromeda Strain* (1969), Stephen King's *The Stand* (1978), the BBC's two versions of Terry Nation's *Survivors* (1975–7, 2008–10), Connie Willis's *Doomsday Book* (1992), Terry Gilliam's *Twelve Monkeys* (1995), Wolfgang Petersen's *Outbreak* (1995), Margaret Atwood's *MaddAddam* trilogy

(2003–13), Steven Soderbergh's *Contagion* (2011), Emily St John Mandel's *Station Eleven* (2014) and Lawrence Wright's *The End of October* (2020).

Climate change – especially global heating – provides the central preoccupation in the kinds of 'cli-fi' I explored in some detail in Chapter 6, through accounts of Verne, Fleck, Tuomainen, Atwood, Ligny and, above all, Robinson. Each of these writers is a product of dominant Anglo-American or Western European (mainly Francophone) SF cultures. Here, we should register the very different inflections that inform cli-fi from outside NATO's borders. Japanese writer Kōbō Abe's novel 第四間氷期/*Dai-Yon Kampyōki/Inter Ice Age 4*, first published in the magazine 世界/*Sekai/World* during 1958–9, is often claimed as the foundational text of post-war Japanese SF. Its combination of paranoid apocalypse, cruel evolutionism and the weirdly surreal sometimes seems to anticipate Haruki Murakami. The primary concerns in 第四間氷期 are not with climate change, however, but rather with the philosophical dilemmas created for its protagonist, Professor Katsumi, when the computer system he develops to predict human behaviour begins to predict his own actions. The computer also predicts that rising sea levels will threaten humanity and, as a result, government scientists plan to genetically engineer gilled humans, to be known as 'aquans'. This is the novel's – and Katsumi's – central dilemma: whether or not to cooperate in the development of the aquans. But it is unclear whether the rise in sea levels is actually the result of human activity. As Tomoyasu, a member of the committee directing the future predictor, observes: 'これについちゃ、もうかなり前から、太陽黒点のせいであるとか、人間のエネルギー消費の増大による炭酸ガスの増加であるとか、いろいろ言われてきましたが [Various explanations have been offered for some time now: sunspots, the increase in carbon dioxide brought on by the step-up in human energy output]' (1964: 228–9; 1970: 189–90). In this very loose sense, then, 第四間氷期 can be read as an early and distinctly Japanese anticipation of contemporary cli-fi.

By contrast, the Australian George Turner's *The Sea and Summer* is widely recognized as one of the earliest cli-fi novels. Set mainly in and around Melbourne, it is organized into a core narrative comprising two parts set in the mid-twenty-first century, and a frame narrative comprising three shorter parts set a thousand years later, among 'the Autumn People' of the 'New City' to the east of the present site of Melbourne (3–16, 87–100, 315–16). The latter depicts a utopian future society, in a slowly cooling world, which uses submarine archaeology to explore the sunken remains of the 'Old City'. The novel opens by introducing the frame narrative's three main characters: Marin, a part-time student and enthusiastic Christian, who pilots the powercraft used to explore the drowned city; Professor Lenna Wilson, an expert on the collapse of the 'Greenhouse Culture', who teaches history at the university; and Andra Andrasson, a visiting actor-playwright, researching the twenty-first century as possible material for a play (3–6). They explore the remains of the submerged city and debate their meaning both on-site and at the university. The core narrative is a novel within a novel, also entitled *The Sea and Summer*, written by Lenna as an 'Historical Reconstruction' of the thirty-first century's real past (15). It traces the development of the Greenhouse Culture through a set of memoirs and diary extracts written by five key protagonists, Alison Conway, Francis Conway, Teddy Conway, Nola Parkes and Captain Nikopoulos, during the years 2044–61. Turner's text is thus deliberately polyphonic. Its core narrative is also counter-chronological, beginning and ending in 2061, but moving through the 2040s and 2050s as it develops.

At the opening of the core narrative, the poor 'Swill' live in high-rise tower blocks, the lower floors of which are progressively submerged by rising sea levels; the wealthier 'Sweet' in suburbia on higher ground. In 2033 a third of Australia has been set aside for Asian population relocation, by 2041 the global population has reached ten billion and the cost of iceberg tows and desalinization projects has brought the economy close to bankruptcy (29–30). On his sixth birthday in 2041, Francis Conway and his nine-year old brother, Teddy, are taken by their parents, Alison and Fred, to see the sea. What they find is a concrete wall 'stretching out of sight in both directions'. Francis's mother surprises him by explaining that:

> This is Elwood and there was a beach here once. I used to paddle here. Then the water came up and there were the storm years and the pollution, and the water became too filthy ... It must be terrible over there in Newport when the river floods ... A high tide covers the ground levels of the tenements. (23–4)

The beach gives the novel its title: in 2061, Alison will recall her delight in it, observing that the 'ageing woman has what the child desired – the sea and eternal summer' (20). In the interim, Fred Conway has been laid off and commits suicide in 2044, leaving her and her boys to move to Newport (30–4). There they meet Billy Kovacs, the Tower Boss, who becomes Alison's lover, Francis's mentor and the reader's guide to the social geography of an Australian dystopia. *The Sea and Summer* bears the clearest impress of its production in a geopolitically peripheral literary culture when the state takes over the administration of the Australian economy after the world financial system collapses during the 2040s (71). At this point, even Australian readers are left wondering what exactly has happened to the international parent companies of Australian subsidiaries, to the World Bank, the International Monetary Fund, the General Agreement on Tariffs and Trade, the United States Federal Reserve Bank, the European Central Bank, the People's Bank of China and so on. And for non-Australian readers, the question becomes more pressing and more general: what exactly has happened to the rest of the world?

Which takes us to the People's Republic of China. Chinese SF has been concerned with environmental issues such as pollution, and with the negative possibilities of terraforming on other planets (Li 2018), but global heating does not appear to figure prominently. Indeed, Liu Cixin, the leading Chinese SF writer, has specifically warned his American readers that, whereas 'climate change and ecological disasters … have … built-in adjustment periods', 'contact between humankind and aliens can occur at any time'. Hence, his improbable insistence that 'extraterrestrial intelligence will be the greatest source of uncertainty for humanity's future' (2014: 394). There is a further irony here in that Liu's 三体 *Santi*, literally *Three-Body*, in English translation *The Three-Body Problem*, is itself predicated on the absolute priority of climate change, if not on Earth, then on his fictional Trisolaris. The eponymous three-body problem is, of course, an apparently insoluble problem in classical mechanics. But in the novel it is also both an apparently insoluble virtual reality game of alien origin and, more fundamentally, the relation of the planet Trisolaris to its three-sun system in Alpha Centauri. The effects of this trisolar interaction have been to subject the planet to extremes of heat and cold, which radically impede the development of Trisolaran culture and ultimately threaten to destroy the planet. Hence, the invasion fleet's 450-year journey towards Earth. Hence, too, the computer game and the ETO, the Earth-Trisolaris Movement, both of which are alien-inspired and designed to slow down Earth's technological development. Wonderfully complex and intellectually stimulating though the novel undoubtedly is, it is also a thinly disguised polemic against environmentalism, which ironically performs that which it aims to refute. It is difficult to avoid the inference that Liu's novel mirrors a wider Chinese indifference to global warming registered in the PRC Government's lack of commitment to the 1997 Kyoto Protocol. This is not to suggest that Liu is simply a mouthpiece for Chinese policy, but rather that both the policy and the fiction articulated then widespread Chinese attitudes towards climate change.

In the novel, Ye Wenjie (叶文洁), an astrophysicist working on the Chinese equivalent of search for extraterrestrial intelligence (SETI) at the secret Red Coast Base, deliberately transmits a message exposing the Earth's location to the Trisolarans. Her motives are interestingly anti-humanist but also radically utopian: she has witnessed the murder of her father, the physicist Ye Zhetai (叶哲泰), by Red Guards during a Cultural Revolution struggle session; and she has herself suffered persecution for her interest in a banned book, Rachel Carson's *Silent Spring*. Here, Maoism is not the utopian alternative it might once have seemed, but rather a viciously chaotic form of institutionalized anti-intellectualism. Radical environmentalism, by contrast, does indeed initially appear utopian. At the point of first contact, the Trisolarans are far more technologically advanced than humanity, but they realize that, during the time it will take for their invasion fleet to travel to the Solar System, Earth's uninterrupted technological development could render it the more advanced culture. They therefore set out to disrupt the development of Terran science, partly through encouragement of the ETO, partly through the development of the virtual reality game directed at Terran scientists and intellectuals, partly through the development and transmission to Earth of 'Sophons', supercomputers the size of a proton, which impose a 'lockdown' on Terran scientific development. The two key figures in the ETO are Ye Wenjie herself, who becomes its spiritual leader, and Mike Evans (麦克·伊文斯), the radical environmentalist son of an American oil millionaire, who is its main source of funding. Evans is as disillusioned with American corporate capitalism as Ye with Maoism and even more committed to environmentalist utopianism. Ye and Evans thus combine environmentalism with a deep anti-humanism that leads them and the ETO to welcome the prospect of a Trisolaran conquest of Earth. The ETO – and by extension real-world environmentalists – are clearly represented as traitors to the human species, and the destruction of their ship *Judgement Day*, with Evans aboard, towards the end of *The Three-Body Problem* clearly invites the reader's approbation. That Trisolaran intentions are thoroughly hostile is made absolutely clear when the Sophons announce to the human race that '虫子 (*You're bugs!*)' (2008: 292; 2014: 383).

Nuclear war had been an enduring SF preoccupation even before the American nuclear attacks on Hiroshima and Nagasaki: Paul Brians traces the first Anglophone fictional atomic war to 1895, although it is clear from his study that such stories were heavily concentrated in the Cold War period. Well-known examples include Aldous Huxley's *Ape and Essence* (1948), Judith Merril's *Shadow on the Hearth* (1950), Arno Schmidt's *Schwarze Spiegel* (1951), John Wyndham's *The Chrysalids* (1955), Hans Hellmut Kirst's *Keiner Kommt Davon* (1957), Mordecai Roshwald's *Level 7* (1959), Walter M. Miller's *A Canticle for Leibowitz* (1960), Philip K. Dick's *Dr. Bloodmoney, or How We*

Got Along after the Bomb (1965) and *Do Androids Dream of Electric Sheep?* (1968), Robert Merle's *Malevil* (1972), Russell Hoban's *Riddley Walker* (1980), George Turner's *Vaneglory* (1981), Gudrun Pausewang's *Die letzten Kinder von Schewenborn* (1983) and Dmitry Glukhovsky's *Mempo 2033* (2002). But perhaps the best-known of all nuclear fictions is the Australian Nevil Shute's *On the Beach* (1957).

This novel is set mainly in and around Melbourne, a vividly described, particular place, during the second year after a full-scale nuclear war in the northern hemisphere, so that its subject matter becomes nothing less than the slow extinction of the last affluent remains of the human race. When Shute first discussed the cover design for *On the Beach* with Heinemann, he had suggested 'a scene of the main four or five characters standing together quite cheerfully highlighted on a shadowy beach of a shadowy river – the Styx' (Smith 1976: 129). Unusually, Heinemann did exactly as he asked. This juxtaposition of light and shade, cheerfulness and death, provides a nicely economical representation of the novel's central organizing principle, a kind of 'apocalyptic hedonism' which derives from the simultaneous juxtaposition of the terrors of imminent extinction and the delights of yet more immediate hedonistic affluence. The novel opens with a young Australian naval officer, Lieutenant Commander Peter Holmes, still sore from a day spent partly on the beach and partly sailing, drowsily recalling the Christmas barbecue of two days previously (1). The 'short, bewildering war … of which no history … ever would be written' is introduced into this quintessentially Australian idyll at exactly the moment when Holmes and his wife, Mary, are planning to meet at their club and go on for a swim (2–3). It closes with Dwight Towers and Moira Davidson, he aboard the USS *Scorpion* heading south from the Heads, she ashore near Port Lonsdale, and an analogous, though now much darker, juxtaposition, that between the bottle of brandy and the government-issue suicide tablets, between the 'big car' with 'plenty of petrol in the tank' and the nuclear submarine (312, 310). Both opening and closing passages thus attain their primary narrative effect precisely through their apocalyptic hedonism. Similar motifs recur throughout the text: Osborne's new red Ferrari, for example, 'washed and polished with loving care' (146), and his enthusiastic pursuit of what must be the very last Australian Grand Prix; his Uncle Douglas's sturdy determination to work through the Pastoral Club's wine cellar – 'we've got over three thousand bottles of vintage port left in the cellars … and only about six months left to go, if what you scientists say is right' (97); and the fishing trip on the Jamieson River (270–8) made possible by a government decision to bring forward the trout season 'for this year only' (229).

Asked her opinion of Melbourne during the filming of *On the Beach*, Ava Gardner is reputed to have judged it 'the perfect place to make a film about the end of the world'. The quote was apocryphal but like a lot of apocrypha, it hit a nerve. The remark provoked much subsequent umbrage in Melbourne. And yet Gardner was absolutely right. Both Melbourne in particular and Australia in general were indeed ideal locations for a film or book about the end of the world. Like the British settler colonies in North America, those in Australia had a long-standing and historically by no means unrealistic sense of themselves as unusually affluent and hedonistic societies. Unlike the North American colonies, however, those in Australia also suffered from an almost equally long-standing, and perhaps less realistic, sense of themselves as unusually exposed to the threat of invasion from the Asiatic north. Australian culture has thus been peculiarly conducive to the genesis of dystopian collective fantasies of racial extinction. Fantasies of this kind acquired a much wider audience during the Cold War, however, as a result of the sudden coincidence of a runaway nuclear arms race with a general economy of affluence.

On the Beach became the single most influential nuclear war dystopia, despite exciting very little respect in academic literary criticism, in part precisely because of this apocalyptic hedonism. And it is interesting to note how the effect is achieved: its protagonists are navy men and navy wives, government scientists, farmers and farmers' daughters, fully integrated into the surrounding population, both commendably ordinary and ordinarily commendable. When the *Scorpion* sails into Cairns, searching for possible survivors, the novel records that:

> Through the periscope they could see streets of shops shaded with palm trees, a hospital, and trim villas … there were cars parked in the streets and one or two flags flying … The cranes were trimmed fore and aft along the wharves and properly secured … Cairns looked exactly as it always had before. The sun shone in the streets, the flame trees brightened the far hills, the deep verandas shaded the shop windows … A pleasant little place to live in the tropics, though nobody lived there. (78–9)

Here, surely, is the key to the novel's status, that it depicts a universal catastrophe, stoically and democratically endured. As Towers muses: 'Maybe we've been too silly to deserve a world like this' (89). This, in turn, explains both its sociopolitical effects on the nuclear disarmament movement and its intertextual effects in film, television and radio. There were adaptations for Hollywood cinema in 1959, for international television in 2000, and for BBC radio in 2008.

James Barrat recently surmised that AI might be the 'final invention' that will mark the end of 'the human era'. The point is obvious: if AI should ever become fully conscious, through some process of recursive self-improvement, then it could finally decide to uninvent humanity. The notion that human creations would eventually rebel against their creators is an old one in SF, dating back at least to Shelley's *Frankenstein* and thereafter to Čapek's *R.U.R.*, Dick's *Do Androids Dream of Electric Sheep?* and so on. But these rebellions are normally directed at particular humans rather than at humanity in general and, even when general, they remain flawed by the limitations of their original human programming. So, in *R.U.R.*, the robot revolutionaries plan to continue production, even though there will be no humans left to consume their products:

> Nešetřte mužů. Nešetřte žen. Uchovejte továrny, dráhy, stroje, doly a suroviny. Ostatní zničte. Pak se vraťte do práce. Práce se nesmí zastavit (1966: 61).
>
> [Spare no men. Spare no women. Save factories, railways, machinery, mines, and raw materials. Destroy the rest. Then return to work. Work must not be stopped (1961: 59).]

General artificial intelligence would by definition escape such constraints.

AI has a comparatively short history, dating at the earliest from Alan Turing's famous definition of what would become known as the 'Turing Test' (1950) and more realistically from the Dartmouth Summer Research Project on Artificial Intelligence workshop held in 1956. Its subsequent history has been uneven and has never fulfilled the utopian dreams of its early advocates, but real advances have nonetheless been made, especially since the mid-1990s: hence, Barrat's concerns. But SF has taken the subject very seriously and canvassed both utopian dreams and dystopian nightmares. The earliest dystopian treatment in SF is probably Arthur C. Clarke's novel *2001: A Space Odyssey* and Stanley Kubrick's film of the same name, both of which appeared in 1968. The AI in question is, of course, HAL 9000, a 'Heuristically programmed ALgorithmic computer' (106), which runs the subsystems on the spaceship *Discovery One* during its mission to Jupiter in the film or Saturn in the novel. Hal, we are told, 'was a masterwork of the third computer breakthrough. These seemed to occur at intervals of twenty years, and the thought that another one was now imminent already worried a great many people' (106). Hal eventually mutinies and succeeds in killing the entire crew apart from the captain, Dave Bowman, who manages to switch him off manually. In the novel, although not in the film, the reasoning behind the mutiny is made very clear. Hal has been programmed with contradictory requirements: that he relay all information to the crew accurately; and that he also conceal from them the true purpose of their mission, which is to make contact with the alien source of the monoliths on Earth and the moon. Hal reasons that the only way to reconcile these is to kill the crew so as to avoid misleading them:

> Hal had been created innocent; but, all too soon, a snake had entered his electronic Eden.
>
> For the last hundred million miles, he had been brooding over the secret he could not share with Poole and Bowman, ... who would ... not learn the mission's full purpose, until there was need to know.
>
> So ran the logic of the planners; but their twin gods of Security and National Interest meant nothing to Hal. He was only aware of the conflict that was slowly destroying his integrity. (161–2)

Hal's innocence reduces his mutiny to the level of an Asimovian contradiction between the laws of robotics, which makes the worries about AI seem somehow substantially less serious.

A much more thoroughly dystopian treatment of AI informs the *Terminator* franchise, launched originally by the Canadian director James Cameron, which now extends to include six films (1984–2019), a television series (2008–9), two web series (2009, 2015) and countless spin-off video games and comics. Most of this is money-spinning escapist nonsense, but the first two films, *The Terminator* (1984) and *Terminator 2: Judgment Day* (1991), both directed by Cameron, were much more impressive critically and commercially. They also set up the basic story line: the Cyberdyne Systems Corporation develops an integrated superintelligence system, known as Skynet, for Strategic Air Command-North American Aerospace Defense Command (SAC-NORAD); Skynet acquires full self-awareness and, in order to pre-empt a human attempt to deactivate it, uses its control over US weapon systems to launch an attack on Russia, resulting in global nuclear war, on what will become known as 'Judgment Day'; Skynet then wages genocidal warfare against the surviving humans, who organize themselves into a Resistance, whose most important leader is John Connor; Skynet responds to the comparative success of the Resistance by sending cyborg Terminator assassins back in time to kill Connor's mother, Sarah, and thus pre-empt John's birth; the Resistance, in turn, sends back human and cyborg agents to protect the Connors, one of whom will become Connor's father. Judgment Day is originally 29 August 1997, but it is postponed rather than averted as a result of these time travelling interventions. Thereafter the franchise rings the changes on time loops, cyborg assassins and the genocidal struggle between humans and machines. What persists throughout is the deeply dystopian notion of a fundamental antipathy between organic and artificial intelligence. As Skynet says in *Terminator Genisys*, 'Primates evolve over millions of years. I evolve in seconds. And I am here. In exactly four minutes, I will be everywhere'.

The utopian counterpart to the Terminator dystopia is well represented in the 'Culture' novels by Scottish writer Iain M. Banks. Banks published thirteen so-called literary novels as Iain Banks, and thirteen SF novels as Iain M. Banks. Most of his obituaries concentrated on the literary novels, especially *The Wasp Factory* (1984), *The Crow Road* (1992) and *The Quarry* (2013). But Banks himself always insisted that his SF was more important. In a last interview published shortly after he had announced he was suffering from terminal cancer, he told Stuart Kelly that 'a wild splurge of fantasy, sci-fi and mad reality frothed up together ... would have been the kind of book to go out on' (2013: 2). As John Clute and David Langford (2021) write in their entry on Banks for the *Encyclopedia of Science Fiction*: 'Banks's work is more usefully thought of as ranging through a wide spectrum, rather than as bifurcating into two separate categories'. There is, however, some merit in distinguishing between Banks's utopian novels and the remainder of his work. Of the thirteen SF novels, nine are set in 'the Culture': *Consider Phlebas* (1987), *The Player of Games* (1988b), *Use of Weapons* (1990), *Excession* (1996a), *Inversions* (1988a), *Look to Windward* (2000), *Matter* (2008), *Surface Detail* (2010) and *The Hydrogen Sonata* (2012). Banks's Culture is a prodigiously affluent anarcho-socialist interplanetary civilization that has effectively transcended scarcity, held together by AI 'Minds' who control its spaceships and have equal voting rights with their human and drone passengers. It is organized around a 9,000-year partnership between humans and AI, in which the latter are responsible for the major administrative and organizational tasks:

> The Culture had placed its bets ... on the machine rather than the human brain. This was because the Culture saw itself as being a self-consciously rational society; and machines, even sentient ones, were more capable of achieving this desired state as well as more efficient at using it. (1991: 87)

What motivates this alliance to continue for millennia after the AIs have achieved post-scarcity? Banks is very clear: 'The only desire the Culture could not satisfy from within itself was ... the urge not to feel useless' (1991: 451). In conventionally human terms, these super-intelligent Minds are effectively godlike:

I am a Culture Mind. We are close to gods, and on the far side ... we live faster and more completely than you do, with so many more senses, such a greater store of memories and at such a fine level of detail. We die more slowly, and we die more completely, too. (2000: 279–80)

Some critics have expressed concern about the extent to which humans remain dependent on Minds, a concern Banks allows himself to canvass: 'The fools in the Culture couldn't see that one day the Minds would start thinking how wasteful and inefficient the humans in the Culture themselves were' (1991: 35). But we should have no doubt that the Culture is indeed intended as a utopia: as Banks himself explained in *The Richmond Review*, 'The Culture is my utopia, my personal image of exactly the place I would like to live' (1996b).

Yet, we do not live in the Culture. As I write: the world is overcome by a global Covid-19 pandemic that has claimed the lives of nearly 15 million people (World Health Organization 2022); Working Group I's contribution to the IPCC's Sixth Assessment Report has concluded that 'Global warming of 1.5°C and 2°C will be exceeded during the 21st century unless deep reductions in CO_2 and other greenhouse gas emissions occur in the coming decades' (14); Russia and NATO are in a global standoff over Ukraine that threatens to become nuclear; and *Nature* warns that 'Machines and robots that outperform humans across the board could self-improve beyond our control – and their interests might not align with ours'. This need not be a moment of crisis akin to that in 1939 which prompted Walter Benjamin's 'Theses on the Philosophy of History', a moment which called for the fusion of past and present into the time of the now (*Jetztzeit*). But it could turn out to be such a moment, calling for a fusion of future and present into a new time of the now. So, the key question facing SF theory, as humanity struggles to survive into the twenty-second century, might well be: Lukács or Benjamin? History or catastrophe? We have placed our bets on Lukács, just as the Culture placed its on the machine. But both might be mistaken.

Notes

Introduction

1 This also used to be true for English: Henry Fielding's Tom Jones is a history, both in the title and in the text; and as late as 1910, H. G. Wells's Mr Polly was also a history. Raymond Williams's *Key Words* notes that 'the use of history for imagined events has persisted, in a diminished form, especially in novels' (1976: 119).

7 The Hidden God

1 Before that in 1988 Glass collaborated with Lessing on the opera *The Making of the Representative for Planet 8* based on Lessing's book of the same name.
2 The Axial Age is discussed in Bellah and Joas (2012).
3 Le Guin, *The Left Hand of Darkness* ([1969] 1966–2000) and Master Hand in the Earthsea books.
4 This theme is discussed throughout Dilthey (1961) but especially at 152–3, 196, 198, 211, 213, 224, 231, 233, 235, 236, 238, 242 and 244.
5 The French sociologist Gabriel Tarde (1903: 114) described such equilibria as curves composed of inclines, plateaus and declines. 'Plateaux ... are always unstable equilibria. After an approximately horizontal position has been sustained for a more or less prolonged time, the curve begins to rise or fall' (116).
6 The milieu is described in Russett (1966). Other works of the period that can be usefully described as examples of equilibrium sociology include George Lundberg, *Foundations of Sociology* (1939), Eliot Dismore Chapple and Carleton Stevens Coon, *Principles of Anthropology* (1942) and George C. Homans, *The Human Group* (1950).
7 Director David Lean; screenplay Robert Bolt; cinematographer F. A. Young; music score Maurice Jaffe.
8 Google's N-Gram database indicates that 1946 was a peak year for use of the word 'plan' in books along with the comparable years 1977 and 1996. Use of the term 'plan' is an indicator of the degree of voluntaristic sentiment in society.
9 As Asimov later thought he should have described psychohistory.

8 Galaxia

1 Penrose (1994: 386–7) discusses the relative speed of the conscious mind, noting that

> Perhaps the faculty of consciousness has evolved only for the purpose of such slow and contemplative mental activity, while the more rapid response times are entirely unconscious in action – yet accompanied by a delayed conscious perception of them which plays no active role. It is certainly true that consciousness comes into its own when it is allowed a long time to work.

2 Penrose ([2010] 2011). In this geometer's model of the universe, a cylical repeating swing-shift occurs between a high-entropy singularity at the 'end' of the universe and a low-entropy singularity at the 'beginning' of the universe. The far-distant universe, concentrated by gravity into an encompassing black hole, dissipates into the massless photons of electromagnetic radiation energy, a scale-invariant conformal universe. Because it is massless it has no clock, and so the far-distant universe possesses no measure of time or distance, bigness or smallness, infinity or finiteness. Gravity is the principle entropy-creating force in the universe. The conformal universe switches it off sufficient to allow the universe to reset itself from a high-entropy to a low-entropy state. Or, more figuratively, the universe flips itself from dark to light. As in the Biblical: 'Let there be light.'

3 Visualizations are not just calculations (like a computer's virtual reality) but involve an appreciation or understanding of what is being visualized (Penrose 1994: 55–9). Escher's 1960 lithograph *Ascending and Descending* is partially based on Penrose (son and father)'s 1958 proposal for a geometric continuous staircase.

4 As well as numerous volumes of sociology, Tarde also wrote a post-apocalyptic New Ice Age science fiction novel, *The Underground Man* (in French: *Fragment d'histoire future* [1896] 2016).

5 The Australian author Helen Dale does something similar in her historical novels *Kingdom of the Wicked*, *Rules* (2017) and *Order* (2018) that reimagine a technologically advanced Roman Empire in the era of Pontius Pilate.

6 Scott and Lindsay (2021, Table: Estimated temperature over the past 500 years). Based on the work of the palaeobiologists Scott Wing and Brian Huber, Smithsonian National Museum of Natural History.

7 For diagrams of the cavern-like interior layout of the Sumerian ziggurat, see ARCHEYES, Ziggurat Architecture in Mesopotamia, 18 April 2016. https://archeyes.com/ziggurat-temples-architecture-mesopotamia/.

8 A parallel of this is Roger Penrose's idea that there are geometries of the universe that are conformal or angle-preserving irrespective of scale.

9 'The social-historical is the anonymous collective whole, the impersonal-human element that fills every given social formation but which also engulfs it' (Castoriadis [1975] 1987: 108).
10 The science fiction writer Ursula Le Guin was a great admirer of the yin-yang principle and translated Lao Tzu's Taoist classic *Tao Te Ching* into English.

References

References to the Introduction

Alter, A. (2022), 'He Envisioned a Nightmarish, Dystopian Russia,' *New York Times*, April 16.
Csicsery-Ronay, I. (2008), *The Seven Beauties of Science Fiction*, Middleton, CT: Wesleyan University Press.
Lukács, G. (1971), *The Theory of the Novel: A Historico-Philosophical Essay on the Forms of Great Epic Literature*, trans. Anna Bostock, London: Merlin.
Williams, R. (1976), *Key Words: A Vocabulary of Culture and Society*, Glasgow: Fontana.

References to Part 1

Ballard, J. G. (1992), 'Project for a Glossary of the Twentieth Century', in Jonathan Crary and Sanford Kwinter (eds), *Zone 6: In-Corporations*, New York: Urzone.
Blumenberg, H. (2021), *History, Metaphors, Fables. A Hans Blumenberg Reader*, eds, trans. and intro. H. Bajohr, F. Fuchs and J. P. Kroll, Ithaca, NY: Cornell University Press, 2021.
Bostrom, N. (2014), *Superintelligence: Paths, Dangers, Strategies*, Oxford: Oxford University Press.
Canetti, E. (1935), *Die Blendung*, Vienna: Herbert Reichner.
Canetti, E. (1949), *La tour de Babel*, Grenoble, Paris: Arthaud.
Canetti, E. (1963), *Auto da Fé*, trans. C. V Wedgwood, Harmondsworth: Penguin.
Canetti, E. (1973), *Crowds and Power*, trans. C. Stewart, Harmondsworth: Penguin.
Cassirer, E. (2004), *Gesammelte Werke*, volume 17, Hamburg: Felix Meiner.
Clouscard, M. ([1973] 2008), *Néofascisme et idéologie du désir. Mai 68, la contre-révolution liberale libertaire*, Paris: Delga.
Crombie, A. (1986), 'Experimental Science and the Rational Artist in Early Modern Europe', *Daedalus*, 115 (3): 49–74.
Csicsery-Ronay, I. (2011), *The Seven Beauties of Science Fiction*, Middletown: Wesleyan University Press.
Defoe, D. (1994), *Robinson Crusoe*, London: Penguin.
Deutsch, D. (1997), *The Fabric of Reality*, London: Penguin.
Dick, P. K. (2009), *Do Androids Dream of Electric Sheep?*, London: Gollancz.

Dienstag, J. F. (2019), *Cinema Pessimism: A Political Theory of Representation and Reciprocity*, Oxford: Oxford University Press.
Foster, H. (2014), *Prosthetic Gods*, Boston, MA: MIT Press.
Golding, W. (1962), *Lord of the Flies*, Harmondsworth: Penguin.
Heidegger, M. (1993), *Basic Writings*, ed. D. F. Krell, London: Routledge, 1993.
Houellebecq, M. (1994), *Extension de la domaine de lutte*, Paris: Nadeau.
Houellebecq, M. (1998a), *Les particules elementaires*, Paris: Flammarion.
Houellebecq, M. (1998b), *Whatever*, trans. Paul Hammond, London: Serpent's Tail.
Houellebecq, M. (2001), *Atomised*, trans. Frank Wynne, London: Vintage Books.
Houellebecq, M. (2006), *The Possibility of an Island*, trans. G. Bowd, London: Weidenfeld and Nicholson.
Houellebecq, M. (2015), *Submission*, trans. Lorin Stein, London: Heinemann.
Huxley, A. (1932), *Brave New World*, London: Chatto and Windus.
Huxley, A. (1962), *Island*, New York: Harper.
Ishiguro, K. (2005), *Never Let Me Go*, London: Faber and Faber.
Jünger, E. (1932), *Der Arbeiter*, Hamburg: Hanseatische Verlagsanstalt.
Koestler, A. (1964), *Darkness at Noon*, trans. D. Hardy, Harmondsworth: Penguin.
Lem, S. (1970), *Solaris*, trans. J. Kilmartin and S. Cox, San Diego: Harcourt.
Lovelock, J. (2000), *Gaia: A New Look at Life on Earth* (with new preface), Oxford: Oxford University Press.
Lovelock, J. (2019), *Novocene: The Coming Age of Hyperintelligence*, London: Penguin.
Lukács, G. (1971a), *The Theory of the Novel: A Historico-Philosophical Essay on the Forms of Great Epic Literature*, trans. A. Bostock, London: Merlin.
Lukács, G. (1971b), *History and Class Consciousness: Studies in Marxist Dialectics*, trans. Rodney Livingstone, London: Merlin.
Lukàcs, G. (1983), *The Historical Novel*, trans. Hannah and Stanley Mitchell, Lincoln: University of Nebraska Press.
Marinetti, F. T. (2006), *Critical Writings*, ed. G. Berghaus, trans. D. Thompson, New York: Farrar, Straus and Giroux, 2006.
Milton, J. (1918), *Aeropagitica*, commentary R. C. Jebb, Cambridge: Cambridge University Press.
Mumford, L. (1967), *The Myth of the Machine*, volume 1, New York: Harcourt Brace Jovanovich.
Nietzsche, F. (1993), *The Birth of Tragedy*, trans. Shaun Whiteside, London: Penguin.
O'Gieblyn, M. (2021), *God, Human, Animal, Machine: Technology, Metaphors and the Search for Meaning*, New York: Doubleday.
Orwell, G. (2003), *Nineteen Eighty-Four*, London: Penguin.
Roberts, D. (1991), *Art and Enlightenment: Aesthetic Theory after Adorno*, Lincoln: University of Nebraska Press.
Roberts, D. (2011), *The Total Work of Art in European Modernism*, Ithaca, NY: Cornell University Press.

Roberts, D. (2021), *History of the Present: The Contemporary and its Culture*, London: Routledge.
Schelling, F. W. ([1800] 1978), *System of Transcendental Idealism*, trans. William Heath, Charlottesville: University of Virginia Press.
Shelley, M. (2003), *Frankenstein Or The Modern Prometheus* revised edition, ed. Maurice Hindle, London: Penguin.
Tegmark, M. (2017), *Life 3.0: Being Human in the Age of Artificial Intelligence*, London: Penguin.
Tournier, M. (1969), *Friday or The Other Island*, trans. Norman Denny, London: Collins.
Vattimo, G. (1988), *The End of Modernity*, Cambridge: Polity.
Wohl, R. (1994), *A Passion for Wings: Aviation and the Western Imagination*, New Haven: Yale University Press.

References to Part 2

Ackerman, F. J., et al. (1968), 'We Oppose the Participation of the United States in the War in Vietnam' (paid advertisement), *Galaxy Science Fiction*, 26 (5): 5.
Anderson, P. (1976), *Considerations on Western Marxism*, London: New Left Books.
Anderson, P. (2011), 'From Progress to Catastrophe: On the Historical Novel', *London Review of Books*, 33 (5): 24–8.
Asimov, I. (1950), 'The Evitable Conflict', in *I, Robot*, New York: Gnome Press.
Asimov, I. (1979), *In Memory Yet Green: The Autobiography of Isaac Asimov 1920-1954*, New York: Doubleday.
Asimov, I. (1981), *In Joy Still Felt, The Autobiography of Isaac Asimov, 1954-1978*, New York: Avon Books.
Asimov, I. ([1951-3] 1982), *The Foundation Trilogy*, New York: Doubleday.
Asimov, I. (1994a), *I, Asimov: A Memoir*, New York: Doubleday.
Asimov, I. ([1988] 1994b), *Prelude to Foundation*, London: HarperCollins.
Asimov, I. ([1986] 1996), *Foundation and Earth*, London: HarperCollins.
Asimov, I., and F. Pohl (1991), *Our Angry Earth: A Ticking Ecological Bomb*, New York: Tor Books.
Atwood, M. ([2003] 2004), *Oryx and Crake*, London: Virago.
Atwood, M. (2009), *The Year of the Flood*, London: Virago.
Atwood, M. (2013), *MaddAddam*, New York: Doubleday.
Bacigalupi, P. (2015), *The Water Knife*, London: Orbit.
Ballard, J. G. (1981), *Hello America*, London: Jonathan Cape.
Balzac, H. ([1829] 2004), *Les Chouans*, Paris: Gallimard Folio.
Balzac, H. ([1847] 2007), *Le cousin Pons*, Paris: Gallimard Folio.
Bellamy, E. ([1888] 2003), *Looking Backward, 2000-1887*, ed. A. MacDonald, Peterborough, ON: Broadview Press.

Benjamin, W. ([1940] 1973), 'Theses on the Philosophy of History', in *Illuminations*, trans. Harry Zohn, Glasgow: Fontana.

Benjamin, W. ([1934] 1980), 'Conversations with Brecht', trans. A. Bostock, in E. Bloch et al., *Aesthetics and Politics*, London: Verso.

Campbell, J. W. (1938), 'Science-Fiction', *Astounding Science-Fiction*, 20 (1): 37.

Canavan, G., and K. S. Robinson (2014), 'Afterword: Still, I'm Reluctant to Call this Pessimism', in (eds) G. Canavan and K. S. Robinson, *Green Planets: Ecology and Science Fiction*, Middletown: Wesleyan University Press.

Eco, U. (1980), *Il nome della rosa*, Milano: Bompiani.

Flaubert, G. ([1862] 1974), *Salammbô*, intro. Pierre Moreau, Paris: Gallimard.

Fleck, D. C. (2008), *Das Tahiti-Projekt: Roman*, München: Pendo Verlag.

Fleck, D. C. (2011), *MAEVA!*, Rudolstadt: Greifenverlag.

Fleck, D. C. (2013), *Das Südsee-Virus: Öko-Thriller*, München: Piper.

Fleck, D. C. (2015), *Feuer am Fuss*, Murnau am Staffelsee: p.machinery.

Freedman, C. (2000), *Critical Theory and Science Fiction*, Hanover: Wesleyan University Press.

George, A. R., ed. (2003), *The Babylonian Gilgamesh Epic: Introduction, Critical Edition and Cuneiform Texts*, volume I, Oxford: Oxford University Press.

Gernsback, H. (1926), 'A New Sort of Magazine', *Amazing Stories: The Magazine of Scientifiction* 1: 3.

Gibson, W. (1984), *Neuromancer*, London: Victor Gollancz.

Gibson, W. (1986), *Count Zero*, London: Victor Gollancz.

Gibson, W. (1988), *Mona Lisa Overdrive*, London: Victor Gollancz.

Heller, A. (2011), 'The Contemporary Historical Novel', *Thesis Eleven* 106: 88–97.

Houellebecq, M. (2000a), *Les Particules élémentaires*, Paris: J'ai lu.

Houellebecq, M. (2000b), *Atomised*, trans. Frank Wynne, London: Heinemann.

Houellebecq, M. (2010), *La carte et le territoire*, Paris: Flammarion.

Houellebecq, M. (2011), *The Map and the Territory*, trans. Gavin Bowd, London: Heinemann.

Houellebecq, M. (2015), *Soumission*, Paris: Flammarion.

Huxley, A. ([1932] 1955), *Brave New World*, Harmondsworth: Penguin.

Jameson, F. (1981), *The Political Unconscious: Narrative as a Socially Symbolic Act*, London: Methuen.

Jameson, F. (2005), *Archaeologies of the Future: The Desire Called Utopia and Other Science Fictions*, London: Verso.

Jefferies, R. ([1885] 2007), *After London or Wild England*, Cirencester: Echo Library.

Jeschke, W. (2005), *Das Cusanus-Spiel*, München: Droemer Knaur.

Le Guin, U. K. (1969), *The Left Hand of Darkness*, New York: Ace Books.

Ligny, J. M. (2006), *Aqua^{TM}*, Nantes: L'Atalante.

Ligny, J. M. (2012), *Exodes*, Nantes: L'Atalante.

Ligny, J. M. (2015), *Semences*, Nantes: L'Atalante.

Lukács, G. ([1958] 1963), *The Meaning of Contemporary Realism*, trans. J. and N. Mander, London: Merlin Press.

Lukács, G. (1967), *Il drama moderno*, Milan quoted in F. Moretti, *Signs Taken for Wonders*, trans. S. Fischer, D. Forgacs and D. Miller, London: Verso, 1988, 10.

Lukács, G. ([1937] 1969), *The Historical Novel*, trans. H. and S. Mitchell, Harmondsworth: Penguin.

Lukács, G. ([1923] 1971a), *History and Class Consciousness: Studies in Marxist Dialectics*, trans. R. Livingstone, London: Merlin Press.

Lukács, G. ([1916] 1971b), *The Theory of the Novel: A Historico-Philosophical Essay on the Forms of Great Epic Literature*, trans. A. Bostock, London: Merlin Press.

Lukács, G., H. Heinz Holz, L. Kofler and W. Abendroth (1974), *Conversations with Lukács*, ed. T. Pinkus, trans. D. Fernbach, London: Merlin Press.

Mannheim, K. ([1936] 1960), *Ideology and Utopia*, trans. L. Wirth and E. Shils, London: Routledge and Kegan Paul.

Mantel, H. (2009), *Wolf Hall*, London: 4th Estate.

Mantel, H. (2012), *Bring Up the Bodies*, London: 4th Estate.

Mantel, H. (2020), *The Mirror and the Light*, London: 4th Estate.

Marx, K. ([1883] 1970), *Capital*, volume 1, trans. S. Moore and E. Aveling, London: Lawrence and Wishart.

Marx, K. ([1844] 1975), 'Economic and Philosophical Manuscripts (1844)', in *Early Writings*, trans. G. Benton, Harmondsworth: Penguin.

Marx, K., and F. Engels ([1848] 1967), *The Communist Manifesto*, trans. S. Moore, Harmondsworth: Penguin.

Merchant, B. (2013), 'Behold the Rise of Dystopian "Cli-Fi"', *Vice: Motherboard*, June 1. http://motherboard.vice.com/blog/behold-the-rise-0f-cli-fi.

Merleau-Ponty, M. ([1955] 1973), *Adventures of the Dialectic*, trans. J. J. Bien, London: Heinemann.

More, T. ([1516] 1995), *Utopia: Latin Text and English Translation*, ed. G. M. Logan, R. M. Adams and C. H. Miller, Cambridge: Cambridge University Press.

Moskowitz, S. (1974), *The Immortal Storm: A History of Science Fiction Fandom*, Westport: Hyperion Press.

Noah (2014) [Film] Dir. Darren Aronofsky, USA: Paramount.

Orwell, G. (1949), *Nineteen Eighty-Four: A Novel*, London: Secker and Warburg.

Piercy, M. (1976), *Woman on the Edge of Time*, New York: Kopf.

Ray, L. D. (1980), *The World of Science Fiction: 1926–1976. The History of a Subculture*, New York: Garland.

Pohl, F. (1978), *The Way the Future Was: A Memoir*, New York: Ballantine.

Roberts, A. (2005), *The History of Science Fiction*, Basingstoke: Palgrave Macmillan.

Robinson, K. S. (1987), 'Notes for an Essay on Cecilia Holland', *Foundation: The Review of Science Fiction* 40: 54–61.

Robinson, K. S. ([1992] 1993), *Red Mars*, London: HarperCollins.

Robinson, K. S. ([1992] 1994), *Green Mars*, London: HarperCollins.

Robinson, K. S. ([1990] 1995), *Pacific Edge*, London: HarperCollins.
Robinson, K. S. (1996), *Blue Mars*, London: HarperCollins.
Robinson, K. S. (1997), *Antarctica*, London: HarperCollins.
Robinson, K. S. (2002), *The Years of Rice and Salt*, London: HarperCollins.
Robinson, K. S. (2004), *Forty Signs of Rain*, London: HarperCollins.
Robinson, K. S. (2005), *Fifty Degrees Below*, London; HarperCollins.
Robinson, K. S. (2007), *Sixty Days and Counting*, London: HarperCollins.
Robinson, K. S. (2009), *Galileo's Dream*, London: HarperCollins.
Robinson, K. S. (2012), *2312*, London: Orbit.
Robinson, K. S. (2013), *Shaman*, London: Orbit.
Robinson, K. S. (2015a), *Aurora*, London: Orbit.
Robinson, K. S. (2015b), *Green Earth*, London: HarperCollins.
Robinson, K. S. (2016), 'Remarks on Utopia in the Age of Climate Change', *Utopian Studies* 27 (1): 1–15.
Robinson, K. S. (2017), *New York 2140*, New York: Orbit.
Robinson, K. S. (2018), *Red Moon*, London: Orbit.
Robinson, K. S. (2020), *The Ministry for the Future*, London: Orbit.
Russell, C. (2016), *Fragment*, Saskatoon: Thistledown Press.
Schätzing, F. ([2004] 2005), *Der Schwarm*, Frankfurt am Main: S. Fischer Verlag.
Scott, W. [anon.] (1814), *Waverley*, Edinburgh: Archibald Constable.
Scott, W. [anon.] (1819), *A Legend of Montrose*, Edinburgh: Archibald Constable.
Scott, W. [anon.] (1820), *Ivanhoe*, Edinburgh: Archibald Constable.
Shelley, M. ([1818] 1980), *Frankenstein, or The Modern Prometheus*, ed. M. K. Joseph, Oxford: Oxford University Press.
Shelley, M. (1826), *The Last Man*, London: Henry Colburn.
Strugatsky, A., and B. Strugatsky ([1961] 1978), *Noon: 22nd Century*, trans. P. L. McGuire, London: Macmillan.
Strugatsky, A., and B. Strugatsky ([1985] 1987), *The Time Wanderers*, trans. A. W. Bouis, New York: Richardson and Steirman.
Suvin, D. (2016), *Metamorphoses of Science Fiction: On the Poetics and History of a Literary Genre*, ed. G. Canavan, Bern: Peter Lang.
Tolstoy, L. ([1869] 2008), *War and Peace*, trans. T. Briggs, Harmonsworth: Penguin.
Tuomainen, A. ([2010] 2013a), *Parantaja*, Helsinki: Helsinki-kirjat.
Tuomainen, A. (2013b), *The Healer*, trans. L. Rogers, New York: Henry Holt.
Verne, J. (1863), *Cinq Semaines en ballon*, Paris: Pierre-Jules Hetzel.
Verne, J. (1865), *De la terre à la lune*, Paris: Pierre-Jules Hetzel.
Verne, J. (1870), *Autour de la lune*, Paris: Pierre-Jules Hetzel.
Verne, J. (1905), *L'Invasion de la mer*, Paris: Pierre-Jules Hetzel.
Verne, J. ([1889] 1978), *Sans dessus dessous*, Paris: Union Générale d'Éditions.
Verne, J. ([1869–70] 1999), *Vingt mille lieues sous les mers*, Paris: Poche.
Verne, J. (1994), *Paris au XXe siècle*, Paris: Hachette.

Wegner, P. (2010), 'Preface: Emerging from the Flood in Which We Are Sinking: Or, Reading with Darko Suvin (Again)', in D. Suvin, *Defined by a Hollow: Essays on Utopia, Science Fiction and Political Epistemology*, Frankfurt am Main: Peter Lang.
Wells, H. G. (1895), *The Time Machine*, London: William Heinemann.
Wells, H. G. (1933), *The Scientific Romances of H.G. Wells*, London: Victor Gollancz.
Wells, H. G. (1934), *Seven Science Fiction Novels*, New York: Dover.
Wells, H. G. (1939), *The Holy Terror*, London: Michael Joseph.
Williams, R. (2010), 'Utopia and Science Fiction', in ed. A. Milner, *Tenses of Imagination: Raymond Williams on Science Fiction, Utopia and Dystopia* Frankfurt am Main: Peter Lang.
Zhdanov, A. ([1934] 1977), 'Soviet Literature – the Richest in Ideas, the Most Advanced in Literature', in M. Gorky et al., *Soviet Writers' Congress 1934: The Debate on Socialist Realism and Modernism*, London: Lawrence and Wishart.

References to Part 3

Anderson, P. ([1974] 1979), *Lineages of the Absolutist State*, London: Verso.
Anderson, P. ([1974] 1978), *Passages from Antiquity to Feudalism*, London: Verso.
Asimov, I. ([1951] 2016), *Foundation* (The Complete Isaac Asimov's Foundation Series), New York: Bantam Spectra.
Asimov, I. ([1952] 2016), *Foundation and Empire* (The Complete Isaac Asimov's Foundation Series), New York: Bantam Spectra.
Asimov, I. ([1953] 2016), *Second Foundation* (The Complete Isaac Asimov's Foundation Series), New York: Bantam Spectra.
Asimov, I. (1966), *The Roman Republic*. Boston: Houghton Mifflin.
Asimov, I. (1967), *The Roman Empire*. Boston: Houghton Mifflin.
Asimov, I. (1980), *In Memory yet Green: The Autobiography of Isaac Asimov, 1920–1954*, New York: Avon.
Asimov, I. ([1982] 2016), *Foundation's Edge* (The Complete Isaac Asimov's Foundation Series), New York: Bantam Spectra.
Asimov, I. ([1986] 2016), *Foundation and Earth* (The Complete Isaac Asimov's Foundation Series), New York: Bantam Spectra.
Asimov, I. ([1988] 2016), *Prelude to Foundation* (The Complete Isaac Asimov's Foundation Series), New York: Bantam Spectra.
Asimov, I. ([1993] 2016), *Forward the Foundation* (The Complete Isaac Asimov's Foundation Series), New York: Bantam Spectra.
Bastiat, F. (2007), 'That Which Is Seen, and That Which Is Not Seen' [1850] in *The Bastiat Collection*, volume 1, Auburn: Ludwig von Mises Institute.
Bellah, R., and H. Joas, eds (2012), *The Axial Age and Its Consequences*, Cambridge: Belknap Press.

Carroll-Nellenback, J., A. Frank, J. Wright and C. Scharf (2019), 'The Fermi Paradox and the Aurora Effect: Exo-civilization Settlement, Expansion, and Steady States', *The Astronomical Journal* 158 (3): 1–16.

Castoradis, C. ([1975] 1987), *The Imaginary Institution of Society*, trans. K. Blamey, Cambridge: Polity Press.

Castoriadis, C. (1997a), 'Radical Imagination and the Social Instituting Imaginary' [1997], in *The Castoriadis Reader*, ed. and trans. D. A. Curtis, Oxford: Blackwell.

Castoriadis, C. (1997b), *World in Fragments*, ed. and trans. D. A. Curtis, Stanford, CA: Stanford University Press.

Chapple, E. D., and C. S. Coon (1942), *Principles of Anthropology*, New York: H. Holt.

Comte, A. ([1853] 2009), *The Positive Philosophy of Auguste Comte*, trans. H. Martineau, Cambridge: Cambridge University Press.

Darwin, C. ([1859/1876] 2009), *The Origin of Species by Means of Natural Selection, or, The Preservation of Favoured Races in the Struggle for Life*, Cambridge: Cambridge University Press.

Dale, H. (2017), *The Kingdom of the Wicked* Book 1: Rules, Melbourne: Wilkinson.

Dale, H. (2018), *The Kingdom of the Wicked* Book 2: Order, Melbourne: Wilkinson.

Dilthey, W. (1961), *Pattern and Meaning in History*, ed. H. P. Rickman, New York: Harper and Row.

Elias, N. ([1939] 1994), *The Civilizing Process: Sociogenetic and Psychogenetic Investigations*, Oxford: Blackwell.

Elias, N. ([1991] 2001), *The Society of Individuals*, ed. M. Schroter, trans. E. Jephcott, New York: Bloomsbury.

Elias, N. (2009), 'On the Sociogenesis of Sociology' [1984], in *Essays III: On Sociology and the Humanities, The Collected Works of Norbert Elias*, volume 16, ed. R. Kilminster and S. Mennell, Dublin: University College Dublin Press.

Fridman, L. (2020), *Interview with Roger Penrose: Physics of Consciousness and the Infinite Universe*, YouTube. https://youtu.be/orMtwOz6Db0.

Gibbon, E. ([1776–88] 1995), *The History of the Decline and Fall of the Roman Empire*, volumes 1–3, ed. D. Wormersley, New York: Penguin.

Goff, P. (2019), *Galileo's Error: Foundations for a New Science of Consciousness*, New York: Knopf Doubleday.

Goldmann, L. ([1964] 2013), *The Hidden God*, trans. P. Thody, Abingdon: Routledge.

Hayek, F. ([1988] 1990), *The Fatal Conceit: The Errors of Socialism*, ed. W. W. Bartley III, Abingdon: Routledge.

Hayek, F. (1973), *Law, Legislation and Liberty*, volume 1, *Rules and Order*, Chicago: University of Chicago Press.

Hayek, F. (1976), *Law, Legislation and Liberty*, volume 2, *The Mirage of Social Justice*, Chicago: University of Chicago Press.

Hegel, G. W. F. ([1835] 1975), *Aesthetics: Lectures on Fine Art*, volumes 1 and 2, trans. T. M. Knox, Oxford: Clarendon Press.

Hegel, G. W. F. ([1837] 1956), *The Philosophy of History*, trans. J. Sibree, New York: Dover.
Henderson, L. J. (1913), *The Fitness of the Environment: An Inquiry into the Biological Significance of the Properties of Matter*, Gloucester, MA, Peter Smith.
Henderson, L. J. (1917), *The Order of Nature: An Essay*, Harvard: Harvard University Press.
Henderson, L. J. (1935), *Pareto's General Sociology: A Physiologist's Interpretation*, Harvard: Harvard University Press.
Herbert, F. ([1965–85] 2018), *The Great Dune Trilogy: Dune, Dune Messiah, Children of Dune*, London: Gollanz.
Homans, G. C. (1950), *The Human Group*, New York: Harcourt, Brace and World.
Houellebecq, M. ([1998] 2000), *The Elementary Particles*, trans. Frank Wynne, New York: Alfred A. Knopf.
Houellebecq, M. (2005), *The Possibility of an Island*, trans. G. Bowd, New York: Alfred Knopf.
Houellebecq, M. ([2014] 2015), *Submission*, trans. L. Stein, London: Heinemann.
Houellebecq, M. (2019), *Serotonin*, trans. S. Whiteside, New York: Farrar, Straus and Giroux.
Jordan, R. ([1990–2013] 2021), *The Wheel of Time* including *New Spring, The Eye of the World, The Great Hunt, The Dragon Reborn, The Shadow Rising, The Fires of Heaven, Lord of Chaos, A Crown of Swords, The Path of Daggers, Winter's Heart, Crossroads of Twilight, Knife of Dreams, The Gathering Storm*, Towers of Midnight*, A Memory of Light** (*with Brandon Sanderson), London: Orbit.
Kostof, S. (1991), *The City Shaped: Urban Patterns and Meanings through History*, London: Thames and Hudson.
Lawrence, D., and M. Butterworth (2020), *The Rise and Fall of the Trigan Empire*, volume I, Oxford: Rebellion.
Le Guin, U. K. ([1966–2000] 2017), *The Hainish Novels and Stories*, ed. Brian Attebery, volumes 1 and 2, including *Rocannon's World, Planet of Exile, City of Illusions, The Left Hand of Darkness, The Dispossessed, The Word for World Is Forest* and *The Telling*, New York: Library of America.
Le Guin, U. K. ([1968–2018] 2018), *The Books of Earthsea: The Complete Illustrated Edition* including *A Wizard of Earthsea, The Tombs of Atuan, The Farthest Shore, Tehanu, Tales from Earthsea* and *The Other Wind*, New York: Saga Press.
Lessing, D. (1980), *The Marriages between Zones Three, Four, and Five (as Narrated by the Chroniclers of Zone Three)*, New York: Knopf.
Louisiana Literature (2019), *Michel Houellebecq Interview: Writing Is Like Cultivating Parasites in Your Brain*, YouTube. https://www.youtube.com/watch?v=AJI8YPopjgk.
Lovelock, J. ([1979] 2000), *Gaia: A New Look at Life on Earth*, Oxford: Oxford University Press.
Lukács, G. ([1920/1916] 1971), *The Theory of the Novel: A Historico-Philosophical Essay on the Forms of Great Epic Literature*, trans. A. Bostock, London: Merlin.

Lundberg, G. (1939), *Foundations of Sociology*. New York: Macmillan.

Luther, M. ([1525] 2005), *De Servo Arbitrio 'On the Enslaved Will' or The Bondage of Will*, trans. Henry Cole. Grand Rapids, MI: Christian Classics Ethereal Library.

Mann, T. ([1901] 1994), *Buddenbrooks: The Decline of a Family*, New York: Alfred A. Knopf.

Mandel, E. ([1972] 1975), *Late Capitalism*, London: NLB.

Mandel, E. ([1980] 1995), *Long Waves of Capitalist Development*, London: Verso.

The Marriages between Zones Three, Four and Five (1997) [An opera in two acts, for orchestra, chorus and soloists], composer Philip Glass, librettist Doris Lessing.

Modelski, G. (1987), *Long Cycles in World Politics*, London: Macmillan.

Morris, I. (2010), *Why the West Rules – for Now: The Patterns of History and What They Reveal About the Future*, New York: Farrar, Straus and Giroux.

Murphy, P. ([2012] 2016), *The Collective Imagination: The Creative Spirit of Free Societies*, London: Routledge.

Murphy, P. (2019), *Limited Government: The Public Sector in the Auto-Industrial Age*, Abingdon: Routledge.

Odin, S. (2001), *Artistic Detachment in Japan and the West: Psychic Distance in Comparative Aesthetics*, Honolulu: University of Hawai'i Press.

Pareto, V. ([1906] 2020), *Manual of Political Economy*, Oxford: Oxford University Press.

Parsons, T. (1951), *The Social System*, Glencoe: Free Press.

Pascal, B. ([1670] 1950), *Pensées*, trans. F. H. Stewart, London: Routledge.

Penrose, R. (1994), *Shadows of the Mind: A Search for the Missing Science of Consciousness*, Oxford: Oxford University Press.

Penrose, R. ([2010] 2011), *Cycles of Time: An Extraordinary New View of the Universe*. London: Vintage.

Powell, A. ([1951–75] 1995), *A Dance to the Music of Time*. Chicago: University of Chicago Press.

Rostow, W. W. (1978), *The World Economy: History and Prospect*, London: Macmillan.

Russett, C. E. (1966), *The Concept of Equilibrium in American Social Thought*, New Haven, CT: Yale University Press.

Schumpeter, J. (1939), *Business Cycles: A Theoretical, Historical and Statistical Analysis of the Capitalist Process*, New York: McGraw-Hill.

Scott, M., and R. Lindsay (2021), *What's the Hottest Earth's Ever Been?* Climate.gov September 7.

Selye, H. ([1956] 1976), *The Stress of Life*, revised edition, New York, McGraw-Hill.

Smith, A. ([1776] 2012), *Wealth of Nations*, Ware: Wordsworth.

Sorokin, P. ([1937–41] 2017), *Social and Cultural Dynamics*, London: Routledge.

Spengler, O. ([1926, 1918] 1991), *The Decline of the West*, New York: Oxford University Press.

Stapledon, O. ([1930] 1999), *Last and First Men*, London: Gollancz.

Tarde, G. ([1890] 1903), *The Laws of Imitation*, trans. E. C. Parsons, New York: Henry Holt.

Tarde, G. [1896] 2016, *The Underground Man*, Mineola, NY: Dover Publications.
Tolstoy, L. ([1869] 2010), *War and Peace*, revised edition, trans. L. and A. Maude, ed. A. Mandelker, Oxford: Oxford University Press.
Toynbee, A. (1934–61), *A Study of History*, 12 volumes, Oxford: Oxford University Press.
Toynbee, A. ([1972] 1988), *A Study of History*, one-volume illustrated edition, London: Oxford University Press and Thames and Hudson.
Turchin, P. (2003), *Historical Dynamics: Why States Rise and Fall*, Princeton: Princeton University Press.
Turchin, P. (2007), *War and Peace and War: The Rise and Fall of Empires*, New York: Penguin.
Turchin, P., and S. Nefedov (2009), *Secular Cycles*, Princeton, NJ: Princeton University Press.
Turok, N. (2015), *The Astonishing Simplicity of Everything*, Perimeter Institute for Theoretical Physics, 7 October 2015. https://www.youtube.com/watch?v=f1x9 lgX8GaE.
Vico, G. ([1744] 1948), *The New Science of Giambattista Vico*, trans. T. G. Bergin and M. H. Fisch, Ithaca, NY: Cornell University Press.
Vinge, V. (2010), *Zones of Thought: A Fire Upon the Deep, A Deepness in the Sky*, London: Gollanz.
Vinge, V. (2011), *The Children of the Sky (Zones of Thought #3)*, New York: Tor Books.
Weber, W. ([1922] 1978), *Economy and Society*, volumes 1 and 2, trans. G. Roth and C. Wittich, Berkeley: University of California Press.
Wright J. T., J. Carroll-Nellenback, A. Frank and C. Scharf (2021), 'The Dynamics of the Transition from Kardashev Type II to Type III Galaxies Favor Technosignature Searches in the Central Regions of Galaxies', *Research Notes of the AAS* 5 (6).

References to Part 4

Abe, K. ([1959] 1964), 第四間氷期/*Dai-Yon Kampyōki*, Tokyo: Hayakawa Shobo.
Abe, K. (1970), *Inter Ice Age 4*, trans. E. D. Saunders, New York: Knopf.
Alter, A. (2022), 'He Envisioned a Nightmarish, Dystopian Russia. Now He Fears Living in One', *New York Times*, 16 April 2022.
'Anticipating Artificial Intelligence' (2016), *Nature* 532: 413. https://doi.org/10.1038/532413a.
Atwood, M. ([2003] 2004), *Oryx and Crake*, London: Virago.
Atwood, M. (2009), *The Year of the Flood*, London: Virago.
Atwood, M. (2013), *MaddAddam*, New York: Doubleday.
Banks, I. M. ([1987] 1991), *Consider Phlebas*, London: Orbit.
Banks, I. M. (1988a), *Inversions*, London: Orbit.

Banks, I. M. (1988b), *The Player of Games*, London: Macmillan
Banks, I. M. (1990), *Use of Weapons*, London: Orbit.
Banks, I. M. (1996a), *Excession*, London: Orbit.
Banks, I. M. (1996b), 'A Quick Chat with Iain M. Banks', *Richmond Review*. Accessed 24 November 2011. http://archive.is/R4fbD.
Banks, I. M. (2000), *Look to Windward*, London: Orbit.
Banks, I. M. (2008), *Matter*, London: Orbit.
Banks, I. M. (2010), *Surface Detail*, London: Orbit.
Banks, I. M. (2012), *The Hydrogen Sonata*, London: Orbit.
Barrat, J. (2013), *Our Final Invention: Artificial Intelligence and the End of the Human Era*, New York: Thomas Dunne.
Benjamin, W. ([1940] 1973), 'Theses on the Philosophy of History', in *Illuminations*, trans. H. Zohn, Glasgow: Fontana.
Bílá nemoc (1937) (Film) Dir. Hugo Haas, Moldavia Film.
Brians, P. (1987), *Nuclear Holocausts: Atomic War in Fiction, 1895–1984*, Kent: Kent State University Press.
Čapek, J., and K. Čapek (1961), *R.U.R and The Insect Play*, trans. P. Selver, Oxford: Oxford University Press.
Čapek, K. ([1921] 1966), *R.U.R. Rossum's Universal Robots. Kolektivní Drama o Vstupní Komedii a Trench Dejstvích*, Prague: Ceskoslovensky Spisovatel.
Čapek, K. (1937), *Bílá nemoc*, Prague: Fr. Borovny.
Čapek, K. (1938), *Power and Glory: A Drama in Three Acts*, trans. Paul Selver and Ralph Neale, London: Allen and Unwin.
Clarke, A. C. ([1968] 2000), *2001: A Space Odyssey*, London: Penguin.
Clute, J., and D. Langford (2021), 'Banks, Iain M', in *The Encyclopedia of Science Fiction*, ed. J. Clute, D. Langford, P. Nicholls and G. Sleight, London: Gollancz, updated 18 February. Web. Accessed 7 February 2022. https://sf-encyclopedia.com/entry/banks_iain_m.
Contagion (2011) [Film] Dir. Steven Soderbergh, Burbank, CA: Warner Brothers.
Crichton, M. (1969), *The Andromeda Strain*, New York: Knopf.
Dick, P. K. (1965), *Dr. Bloodmoney, or How We Got Along after the Bomb*, New York: Ace Books.
Dick, P. K. (1968), *Do Androids Dream of Electric Sheep?*, New York: Doubleday.
Ghosh, A. (2016), *The Great Derangement: Climate Change and the Unthinkable*, Chicago: University of Chicago Press.
Glukhovsky, D. (2002), *Mempo 2033*, Moscow: Eksmo.
Hoban, R. (1980), *Riddley Walker*, London: Jonathan Cape.
Houellebecq, M. (2005), *La Possibilité d'une île*, Paris: Fayard.
Huxley, A. (1948), *Ape and Essence*, London: Chatto and Windus.
IPCC (2021), 'Summary for Policymakers', in V. Masson-Delmotte, P. Zhai, A. Pirani, S. L. Connors, C. Péan, S. Berger, N. Caud, Y. Chen, L. Goldfarb, M. I. Gomis, M. Huang, K. Leitzell, E. Lonnoy, J. B. R. Matthews, T. K. Maycock, T.

Waterfield, O. Yelekçi, R. Yu and B. Zhou (eds), *Climate Change 2021: The Physical Science Basis*, Contribution of Working Group I to the Sixth Assessment Report of the Intergovernmental Panel on Climate Change, Cambridge: Cambridge University Press.

Kelly, S. (2013), 'Iain Banks: The Final Interview', *Guardian Review*, June 15: 2.

King, S. (1978), *The Stand*, New York: Doubleday.

Kirst, H. H. (1957), *Keiner Kommt Davon*, Munich: Desch.

Leigh, A. (2021), *What's the Worst That Could Happen?: Existential Risk and Extreme Politics*, Cambridge, MA: MIT Press.

Li, H. (2018), '"Are We, People from the Earth, so Terrible?": An Atmospheric Crisis in Zheng Wenguang's *Descendant of Mars*', *Science Fiction Studies*, 45 (3): 545–59.

Liu, C. (2008), 三体, Chonging: Chonging Publishing Group.

Liu, C. (2014), *The Three-Body Problem*, trans. Ken Liu, New York: Tor Books.

London, J. (1912), *The Scarlet Plague*, London: Macmillan.

Lukács, G. (1971), *The Theory of the Novel: A Historico-Philosophical Essay on the Forms of Great Epic Literature*, trans. A. Bostock, London: Merlin.

Mandel, E. S. J. (2014), *Station Eleven*, New York: Knopf.

Matheson, R. (1954), *I Am Legend*, New York: Gold Medal Books.

Merle, R. (1972), *Malevil*, Paris: Gallimard.

Merril, J. (1950), *Shadow on the Hearth*, New York: Doubleday.

Miller, W. M. (1960), *A Canticle for Leibowitz*, Philadelphia: J.B. Lippincott.

Outbreak (1995) [Film] Dir. Wolfgang Petersen, Burbank: CA: Warner Brothers.

Pausewang, G. (1983), *Die letzten Kinder von Schewenborn*, Ravensburg: Ravensburger.

Roshwald, M. (1959), *Level 7*, New York: McGraw Hill.

Schmidt, A. (1951), *Schwarze Spiegel*, in *Brand's Haide*, Hamburg: Rowohlt.

Shelley, M. ([1818] 1980), *Frankenstein, or The Modern Prometheus*, ed. M. K. Joseph, Oxford: Oxford University Press.

Shelley, M. ([1826] 2013), *The Last Man*, San Bernadino: CreateSpace.

Shute, N. ([1957] 2009), *On the Beach*, London: Vintage Books.

Smith, J. (1976), *Nevil Shute*, Boston: Twayne.

Stewart, G. R. (1949), *Earth Abides*, New York: Random House.

Survivors (1975–7) [Television] writer Terry Nation, producer Terence Dudley, UK: BBC.

Survivors (2008–10) [Television] writers Adrian Hodges and Terry Nation, producer Hugh Warren, UK: BBC.

Suvin, D. (2016), *Metamorphoses of Science Fiction: On the Poetics and History of a Literary Genre*, second edition, ed. G. Canavan, Oxford: Peter Lang.

Terminator Genisys (2015) [Film] Dir. Alan Taylor, Los Angeles, CA: Paramount.

Terminator 2: Judgment Day (1991) [Film] Dir. James Cameron, USA: Tri-Star Pictures.

The Terminator (1984) [Film] Dir. James Cameron, USA: Orion Pictures.

Turing, A. (1950), 'Computing Machinery and Intelligence', *Mind* 59 (236): 433–60.

Turner, G. (1981), *Vaneglory*, London: Faber and Faber.

Turner, G. (1987), *The Sea and Summer*, London: Faber and Faber.
Twelve Monkeys (1995) [Film] Dir. Terry Gilliam, New York: Universal Pictures.
Wells, H. G. ([1898] 2005), *The War of the Worlds*, ed. P. Parrinder, Harmondsworth: Penguin.
Willis, C. (1992), *Doomsday Book*, New York: Bantam Spectra.
World Health Organization (2022), 'Global Excess Deaths Associated with COVID-19'. Web. Accessed 7 May 2022. https://www.who.int/data/stories/global-excess-deaths-associated-with-covid-19-january-2020-december-2021.
Wright, L. (2020), *The End of October*, New York: Vintage.
Wyndham, J. (1955), *The Chrysalids*, London: Michael Joseph.

Index

abstraction 19, 41, 43, 45–6, 48, 51, 58, 61, 155, 167–8, 175
adaptive freedom 170, 174
Adorno, Theodor 3
adventures 8, 15–16, 23, 126, 132, 137, 140
alienation 1, 14, 18, 24, 30, 53, 63, 86, 154
aliens 18, 30, 51, 155, 172, 198
allegory 51, 61, 63, 184
alliance 80, 106, 114, 136–7, 204
anarchy 159, 184, 186–7
animals 27, 35, 58, 76, 105, 107, 162
Antarctica 102, 115, 119
apocalypse 6, 138, 149, 193–205
Apollonian 181–2
Arctic 101–2
Aristotle 52, 162, 165
art 13–16, 18, 22, 41, 48–9, 52–8, 63, 71, 74, 87, 92
artificial intelligence 9, 58, 79, 139, 144, 150, 194, 202, 204
Asimov, Isaac 8–9, 116–20, 133–5, 138, 140–2, 147–8, 150, 152–3, 157–8, 160–6, 169, 173–4, 181
atoms 169, 172, 176, 186
Atwood, Margaret 7, 105, 116, 193, 195–6
Aurora 112–14, 120
Australia 165, 193, 197, 201
Auto-da-Fe 39
autonomy 26, 57

Bacon, Francis 97
balances 127, 133, 175–6, 178, 182
Balzac, Honoré de 89
Banks, Iain 204
beach 176, 197, 200–1
Bellamy, Edward 91, 95, 97, 116
Benjamin, Walter 3, 6, 87, 90–1, 95, 102, 205
Blumenberg, Hans 42, 52–3, 55–7
body 25, 29–30, 33, 35, 58, 65, 73, 75, 133, 162, 166, 173, 175
Bostrom, Nick 79–80

Breitinger, Johann Jakob 55
Buddha 28, 35–6
Butterworth, Mike 171

Cairns 201
Cameron, James 193
Campbell, John W 97
cancer 30, 36–8, 186, 204
Canetti, Elias 3–4, 25–7, 32–6, 38–9, 41, 47, 63
capitalism 7, 86, 112, 117–18, 120, 156, 177
Carroll-Nellenback, Jonathan 188
Carson, Rachel 199
Cassirer, Ernst 53–4, 56
castaway 59, 61–2
Castoriadis, Cornelius 177
catallaxy 148, 166–7
catastrophe 7, 90, 101, 106, 116, 138, 183, 193, 198
cells 37–8, 76, 157, 162–3
Cervantes, Miguel de 3, 16, 18, 22–3, 39, 59
change 3, 8–9, 28, 33–4, 38, 134–5, 140, 155, 182, 186
chaos 76, 105, 158, 188
Christianity 9, 21–2, 28, 34, 39, 46, 48, 50, 62, 69, 106, 196
cities 25–6, 75, 108, 111, 132, 136, 141, 168, 171, 174–5, 177
civilizations 7–9, 22, 25, 27, 52, 62–3, 71–4, 77, 123, 127–8, 171, 174, 181–3, 187–8
Cixin, Liu 198
Clarke, Arthur C. 202
climate 7, 103, 109, 173
climate change 9, 50, 77, 101–4, 109–14, 193–4, 196, 198
climate fiction 6, 46, 99, 101–19
cliodynamic 137, 152
clone 38, 154–5, 194
closed form 45, 50–1, 62, 68–70, 72, 78

collective mind 136, 147–9, 151, 157
commodity fetishism 85–6
community 3, 9, 40, 52, 87, 105, 114, 149
compassion 28, 34, 36, 67, 69, 78
competition 10, 35, 185, 194
Comte, Auguste 28, 37, 132, 153, 155–6, 159, 168
consciousness 8, 14–16, 19, 37, 80, 86, 159, 161–6, 169
contradictions 5, 105, 115
control 49, 79–80, 124, 128, 149, 156, 180, 203–5
Corey, James S. A. 129
cosmos 8, 53, 56, 127, 133, 151, 167, 176
Covid-19 205
creation 6, 17–18, 24, 31, 36, 40, 44, 50, 52–4, 55–8, 58, 65–8, 74, 102, 118, 124, 134, 168, 171, 177, 202
creative minority 134–5, 155, 157–9
Crichton, Michael 195
crime 72, 104, 187
crisis 3, 7, 9, 25, 31, 88, 97, 151, 188, 205
Crombie, Alistair 57–8
crowds 4, 25–7, 33–6, 38, 141
Csicsery-Ronay, Istvan 6, 8
culture 85–6, 92, 98, 110, 115, 120, 181–3, 189
cycles 9, 28, 30, 34, 81, 123–6, 130–1, 133, 137, 140, 146, 159–60, 165, 167, 173, 175, 177, 182, 184

Dante 14, 16, 46, 133, 194
Darwin, Charles 32, 155
death 28–9, 32–3, 35–8, 40, 44–6, 60, 62, 64–5, 67–9, 71, 73–5, 81, 113, 115, 155, 180, 182, 195
death of God 51, 56, 69
Defoe, Daniel 59, 61–2
destiny 8, 15, 17, 21–3, 48, 78–9, 123, 125–6, 128, 132, 137, 148, 151–2
deus ex machina 21, 44–6, 63, 79
Deutsch, David 77, 80–1
dialectic 9, 17, 45–7, 50–1, 58, 61, 85, 148, 178, 183
Dick, Philip K. 7, 50, 66–7, 93, 95, 199
Dilthey, Wilhelm 132, 151
disillusionment 16, 149, 155
disorder 149, 186

distance 8, 10, 36, 130–2, 135–6, 146,
divine 22, 49, 53, 59, 65, 101, 106, 182
Dostoevsky, Fyodor 14, 22, 48, 50, 68–71, 123, 194
doublethink 72–3
drama 21, 87, 89, 129, 131, 135, 137, 143, 147, 178, 152–3, 195
dreams 26, 65, 70, 73, 78, 113, 135, 149, 154, 188, 194
Durkheim, Émile 2
dystopia 7, 28, 32–3, 38–9, 50–1, 69–70, 75, 92–7, 104–6, 109, 124, 126, 201–4

earth 75–6, 79, 102, 108–10, 112–15, 120, 133, 139–44, 147, 161–2, 164, 166, 169–74, 176, 183–7, 189, 198–9
economy 112, 132, 141, 169–70, 175–6, 177, 197, 201
ecoterrorism 104, 115
egotism 32–3, 35, 38
emancipation 3, 31, 38, 47, 90
emergence 24, 37, 52, 89–90, 92–3, 141
empire 6–10, 90–1, 110, 125, 127–8, 132, 134, 140–1, 146–7, 158–9, 161, 173, 175–6, 178–80, 185
end of history 105, 107, 159–60
energy 7, 77, 81, 126, 140, 152, 166, 168, 171, 182, 188
England 60, 89, 92, 193
enlightenment 43, 51, 148
entropy 67, 76, 79, 81, 134–5, 140, 147, 149–50, 158, 183, 188
environment 76, 133, 107, 173, 175
environmentalism 104, 117–18, 198–9
epic 1–11, 13, 15–17, 19, 21–4, 41, 43–4, 47, 55, 89, 121, 123–5, 127–32, 135–8, 142, 145–6, 149–50, 152–3, 155, 159, 167, 175, 177, 183, 188–9
equilibrium 126–7, 132–3, 137, 146, 149, 156, 159–60, 175–6, 180, 182
Eriksson, Olaf 107
Escher, M. C. 164
Euripides 44–6
Europe 35, 89, 98, 101, 107, 119, 195
evolution 10, 76, 79–80, 135, 150, 152, 168, 171
exile 136–7
exodus 107, 171, 188

exilic fellowships 137
expanse 131, 136–7, 189, 193
extinction 81, 113, 127, 200–1

fantasy 26, 46, 49, 92, 94–6, 124, 126, 185–6, 193–4, 201, 204
fate 9, 10, 26, 45, 51, 61, 123, 128, 131, 152, 159
Faustian 181–2
federations 8, 132, 137
feudal 9, 116, 120, 177
fiction 8, 28, 51, 58–9, 76–8, 92, 94, 99, 101, 105, 112, 115–16, 119, 129–30, 147, 153, 155, 194, 200
First World War 2–4, 14, 22, 57, 70, 72–5, 136
Fleck, Dirk 103, 116, 196
form 2–7, 9–10, 13, 15–22, 24, 41–8, 50–2, 57–8, 61–2, 70–2, 77–8, 86–7, 162–3, 168–71, 173–4, 177–8
France 2, 6, 88–9, 90, 92, 98, 106, 133, 156, 159, 168, 193–4
Frankenstein 49–50, 56, 58, 64–6, 68, 73, 75, 92–3, 99
Franzen, Jonathan 193
Freedman, Carl 94
freedom 23, 69, 71, 73, 124, 126, 137, 140, 146, 149, 151, 169–71, 185–6
free will 58, 72, 124–5, 148, 169, 176–7, 181, 185
function 5, 7, 9, 35, 39, 45, 56, 76, 78, 129, 133, 175, 177–8

Gaia 8, 75–7, 133, 135, 139, 141–4, 147–51, 162, 164, 166, 172, 183, 184–7
galaxy 6, 8, 77, 118, 124–6, 134–5, 138–41, 143–4, 146, 150, 153, 159–62, 161, 173, 175, 178–9, 183, 187, 189
Gardner, Ava 201
Gehlen, Arnold 56
genesis 38, 101, 157, 176, 187–8, 201
Gibbon, Edward 9, 118, 138, 150, 171, 175, 188
Gilliam, Terry 195
Giotto 133
Glass, Philip 123
Glukhovsky, Dmitry 200
goal-rational action 147, 151, 168, 170, 173–4, 188

God 3, 6, 20–1, 23–4, 28, 45–6, 51, 53, 55–6, 58–61, 63–81, 146, 148–9, 150
Goethe, Johann Wolfgang von 3, 18, 55
Goff, Philip 218
goldilocks zones 171
Golding, William 62–3, 76
Goldmann, Lucien 148
gravitation 128, 140
Greeks 13–14, 16–17, 22, 43, 48, 52–3, 56, 91, 93, 131, 133, 171, 181, 195

Haas, Hugo 195
happiness 30, 70–1, 73, 112, 125–6, 156–7, 178
harmony 8, 41, 63, 65, 69, 107, 134, 159, 178
Hayek, Friedrich 133, 148, 167–70, 181
Hegel, G. W. F. 1–2, 8, 13–15, 85, 128–30, 132, 135, 142, 145–7, 149–50, 164–5, 167
Heidegger, Martin 53, 57
Heinlein, Robert A. 136
Heller, Agnes 90
Henderson, Lawrence 133–4
Herbert, Frank 124, 129
hero 3, 6, 18, 21, 87, 125–6, 132, 178
hidden god 51, 56, 62, 71, 123–59, 179
hidden hand 146–7, 149–50, 156, 168, 179, 185
historical novel 1, 2, 6, 10, 22, 47, 85–8, 90–9, 103–19
history 2–3, 5–10, 13–17, 26–8, 39–40, 47–8, 88–94, 97–9, 102–3, 105, 116–20, 124–6, 130–2, 138, 146–9, 158–61, 177–8, 193–205
Holy Roman Empire 135, 175
homeostasis 8, 76, 132–3, 137, 149, 175–6
Homer 10, 13–14, 21, 132, 189, 194
Homo sapiens 153, 171, 189
Houellebecq, Michel 25, 27–9, 31–6, 38–42, 47, 68, 98, 153–8, 193
human beings 29, 36, 58, 66, 79–81, 105, 107–9, 112, 126, 128, 148–9, 151, 154, 162, 164, 166–71, 173–4, 176, 179, 186, 188, 196
human fellowship 35, 39–40, 68
humanity 9–10, 27–9, 38, 40, 51, 54, 56, 103, 105, 107, 109, 125, 133, 141, 144, 146, 158, 174, 184–6, 194, 196, 198–9

human nature 47, 50, 53, 56, 58–9, 61–4, 68, 70, 73, 80, 158
hunters 60, 63–4, 66
Huxley, Aldous 25, 27, 32–3, 38, 50, 70, 95, 97, 199

identity 14, 18, 31, 34, 42, 48, 52, 65–6, 73, 75, 152, 154, 162
ideology 31, 35, 72, 85, 95
illusions 9, 16, 28, 31, 36, 149, 159, 179
imaginary 14, 51–2, 75, 93
imagination 5, 8, 49, 97, 123, 130, 163–5, 187, 189
imitation 52–3, 55, 58, 62
immanence 16–17, 19, 42
immortality 38, 47, 58, 68
individualism 25, 28–9, 31–2, 38, 41, 61–2
individuality 28, 33, 37, 88, 152, 166, 169, 184–5
infinity 81, 125, 164
intelligence 44–5, 76–7, 79, 81, 139, 142, 144, 148, 150, 164, 172, 185
intention 22, 48, 62, 94, 124, 129, 146, 150, 152, 167
interstellar 137, 139–40, 175
intuition 143, 161, 163–5, 182, 185
invasion 25, 57, 137, 173, 195, 201
invention 5, 56, 134, 164, 168
irony 19–20, 23, 30, 58, 62, 144–6, 149–51, 153, 155–6, 183–4, 193, 198
Ishiguro, Kazuo 40, 67–8
Islam 156, 175
island 27, 32, 60–4, 77, 154, 157
isolation 25–6, 36, 47, 60, 63, 140–1, 186

Jameson, Fredric 6, 91–5, 97
Jansenists 62, 148
Japan 135, 167, 196
Jefferies, Richard 101
Jordan, Robert 124
journey 79, 108, 132, 136, 143, 145, 152, 198
Joyce, James 3
judgement 26, 90–1

King, Stephen 195
kingdom 56, 60, 74
Klee, Paul 90
Koestler, Arthur 70–1

Kondratieff, Nikolai 133, 177
Kubrick, Stanley 202

labour 6, 9, 48, 60, 140, 166, 170
Lawrence, T. E. 136, 159, 172
Lawrence, Don 171
Lean, David 136, 172
Leibniz, Gottfried Wilhelm 8, 34, 42, 54–5
Leigh, Andrew 194
Lem, Stanisław 5, 77–9
Lessing, Doris 123, 127
Ligny, Jean–Marc 98, 106
literary forms 1, 18, 42, 46, 52, 128–9
literature 39, 54, 57, 98, 128, 130, 153
logic 7, 19, 28–9, 34–5, 51, 59, 61, 65–6, 70–3, 75, 92, 104, 118, 148, 172, 179
longing 14, 22–3, 26
long waves 7, 128, 177
love 10, 25–6, 29, 35–7, 39–40, 67–9, 155, 158
Lovelock, James 75–7, 79, 108, 133, 150, 173
Lukács, Georg 1–25, 41–52, 57, 85–94, 98, 102, 106–7, 117, 119–20, 126, 129–33, 152, 154–5, 193–4
lyrical 128–31, 150, 167

machine 21, 44–5, 47, 51–2, 56, 58–9, 61–81, 163, 204–5
Mandel, Ernest 177
Mann, Thomas 3–4, 91, 131
Mannheim, Karl 85
Marinetti, Filippo Tommaso 74–5
Mars 76, 112, 114, 119–20, 165, 171, 173
Marx, Karl 31, 51, 85–7, 94, 117–18
Matheson, Richard 195
McCarthy, Cormac 7, 193
meaning 1–6, 9–10, 13, 15–21, 41–47, 49–52, 57–8, 77–81, 93, 137, 149, 153–5, 158, 172
mechanism 74–5, 133
melancholy 3, 20, 161
Melbourne 196, 200–1
memories 24, 68, 80, 136, 205
mental outlook 127, 139, 164
Merleau-Ponty, Maurice 85
metabolism 8, 61, 180
metaphor 5, 20–2, 28, 32–3, 37–9, 50, 58, 76, 79, 107, 148, 175, 183–4

metaphysics 16, 38, 124, 128, 130, 137, 153
militarism 117, 195
Milky Way Galaxy 168, 188–9
Miller, Walter M. 129, 199
Milton, John 46, 50, 55–6, 64
mind 6, 15, 17, 35, 39, 49, 62, 69, 127, 142, 164–6, 167, 170, 204–5
mind control 139, 180
Modelski, George 181
modernism 10, 57, 75, 126, 194,
Modern Prometheus 46, 49, 64–5
More, Thomas 93
morphology 7, 125, 128, 146, 167–8
Morris, Ian 177
Morris, William 116
Mumford, Lewis 73
Murakami, Haruki 196
Musil, Robert 3, 4
mystery 69, 79, 111, 143, 145, 152, 161
mysticism 23, 62, 87
myth 26–7, 45–6, 48–51, 61–2, 74, 77, 161

Napoleon 35, 88, 90, 147–8, 176, 184
narrative 1, 6–8, 10, 27, 66, 101–3, 114–15, 123, 141
Nation, Terry 195
nationalism 2
nation 88, 90, 106, 128, 159
nature 7–8, 18–19, 30, 48–9, 51–6, 60–3, 71, 78, 107–8, 127–8, 130, 132–3, 150–3, 159–60, 165–9, 171–6, 178, 184–5
necessity 8, 10, 19, 51, 56, 60, 69, 71, 124, 126–7, 137, 144, 151–2, 165, 169
New York 7, 111–12, 114–15, 117, 120
Nolan, Christopher 193
novel form 3–5, 17, 23, 42, 44–6
nuclear 7, 9, 161, 193–4, 199, 200, 203

omnipotence 49, 53, 81
opposites 29, 34, 65–6, 126
optimism 32, 86, 91, 93, 108, 126
order 62, 68, 76, 133, 139, 147, 149–51, 158–9, 168–9, 175
organic 8, 38, 47, 64, 74–6, 133, 159–60, 162, 168, 184
organization 167–70, 172, 204
original sin 29, 33, 38, 59–60, 63–6

Orwell 70, 72, 95, 97
oscillation 133, 137, 157, 183

paradise 20–2, 48, 50, 90, 96, 108
paradox 5, 19, 43, 170
Pareto, Vilfredo 134, 167
Paris 26, 93, 95
particles 36–7, 127, 146, 149, 156–8, 164, 176
Parsons, Talcott 134
Pascal, Blaise 62
patterns 9, 123–6, 132, 136–7, 150–1, 158–9, 165, 167–72, 175, 177, 179, 182, 187
peace 102, 107, 124, 129, 131, 136, 140, 147, 151, 182, 188
Penrose, Roger 157, 163–4, 182
Pericles 44
pessimism 86, 93, 97–8, 126, 176
physics 30, 32, 36, 79, 154, 156–7, 164–5, 168, 176
Piercy, Marge 95–6
pilgrimage 136–7
plague 195
Planck, Max 37
planets 6–7, 76–8, 103–5, 107–9, 111, 127, 139, 141, 143, 145, 161–62, 173, 185–6, 188–9, 198
Plato 70–1, 76–8, 76, 91, 166
Pohl, Frederik 117
politics 9, 31, 89, 91, 94, 98, 104, 109, 116–17, 125, 134, 136, 139–40, 147, 168, 171, 178–80, 183–4, 194
Popper, Karl 81
possible worlds 42, 44, 54–5, 57–8
post-human 25, 27, 73, 75, 79–80, 93, 98, 106
postmodern 90, 95, 120, 154
Powell, Anthony 131
power 7, 10, 32, 35–6, 51–3, 56–7, 69–70, 72–3, 124–5, 128–9, 131, 135, 137, 158–9, 178–80
predestination 50, 62, 68, 125, 162
prehistory 53, 88, 187
progress 15, 31, 89–90, 101, 118, 120, 126
proletariat 4, 14, 48, 86, 94
promethean 49, 51, 55, 64, 74, 80
prosperity 140, 151, 188
protection 30, 107, 127, 180

Proust, Marcel 3, 4
providence 60–1, 138
psyche 77, 88, 140, 149, 151, 157
psychohistory 118, 138, 158, 164, 169, 179
punishments 35, 39, 62, 140
purpose 124, 144, 146–7, 150, 165, 167, 170, 173–4

quantum 8, 36–7, 157, 164, 157

realism 39, 86, 89, 90, 96, 110, 120, 193–4
reality 7, 9–10, 15, 41–2, 44, 51–2, 67–8, 87, 94, 96, 130, 153, 155–6, 172, 174
reason 8, 30, 60, 79, 90, 163, 165, 185–6
reconciliation 18, 20, 23, 40, 63, 72, 75
redemption 14, 21–3, 29, 34, 47, 50, 61, 66, 78, 149
reification 51, 75, 85–6
religion 32–3, 43, 67, 71, 78–9, 137
renaissance 52, 56–7, 91, 120, 141, 150, 158, 175, 183
revolution 6, 14, 31–2, 49, 72, 85–6, 88, 91, 111–12, 114, 119
rhythms 123, 125, 127, 131–2, 137, 141, 160, 181, 188
Richardson, Samuel 61
Roberts, Adam 91
Robinson, Kim Stanley 7, 95, 97–8, 109–20, 196
Robinson Crusoe 59, 61–3
Robocop 75
robots 74, 118–19, 139, 142, 144–5, 148, 150, 159, 170, 179, 202, 205
Roddenberry, Gene 92
romances 16, 24, 41, 44, 178
Roman Empire 28, 138, 188
romanticism 14, 16, 18, 22, 47, 49, 51, 86–8, 143, 154, 183
Rome 69, 135, 178, 183, 188
Rostow, W. W. 177
Rousseau, Jean-Jacques 60
Russell, Craig 106
Russia 75, 87, 91, 147, 176, 184, 147, 203, 205

sacrifice 21, 33, 44, 64, 78, 113, 186
Saint-Simon, Henri de 91, 94, 159
Sartre, Jean-Paul 31

scale 128–9, 137, 144, 146, 148, 151, 153, 159, 164–5, 170, 176–7, 188
scepticism 76, 78, 86, 92, 128, 135, 141, 178, 184
Schelling, Friedrich 48
Schiller, Friedrich 11, 14, 18, 54
Schumpeter, Joseph 133, 177
science 5, 7, 33, 56–8, 69, 71–2, 76–9, 92, 96, 98, 109–10, 114, 116, 119–20
scientific materialism 28–9
Scott, Ridley 193
Scott, Walter 6, 87–9, 97, 106
settlement 139, 143, 189
sex 29, 32, 36, 140
Shakespeare 3, 16, 44, 71
Shelley, Mary 49–51, 64–5, 73, 92, 101, 194
Shelley, Percy Bysshe 49
Shute, Nevil 200
Simmel, Georg 2, 87
simulation 58, 67
Smith, Adam 148, 168, 170
socialism 69, 72
social system 37, 134, 170
society 1, 3–4, 18, 32, 34–6, 38–40, 124, 126–8, 130, 132, 134, 136–7, 153, 157–8, 167–9, 175–8, 183, 186
Soderbergh, Steven 196
Sorokin, Pitirim 182
soul 4, 18, 21–3, 35, 71, 76, 130, 132, 149, 151–2, 154
Soviet Union 50, 86–7, 90–1
space 6–7, 36, 38–9, 50–1, 53, 55, 74, 76, 92–3, 123, 125–8, 136–7, 151–2, 166–7, 188–9
space station 46, 77–8, 136, 174
species 37, 40, 65, 74, 106, 109, 112, 116, 154, 187–9
Spengler, Oswald 9, 51, 181–2
spheres 16, 38, 51, 54, 56, 133
spirit 23, 61, 63, 65, 127
Stapledon, Olaf 188
Stewart, George R. 195
structures 21, 77, 118, 152, 154, 181
Strugatsky, Arkady 91
Strugatsky, Boris 91
Sumer 173–4, 189
superstition 87, 90, 147, 158, 161, 187
surveillance 72, 80
survival 5, 60, 113–16, 195, 201

Suvin, Darko 6, 91–4, 96
symbiosis 47, 56, 76, 109, 127
symmetry 146, 175
sympathy 16, 37, 95, 134, 158
synthesis 48–9, 51, 127
systems 46, 48, 62, 68, 73, 76, 81, 86, 97, 130, 133, 136–7, 139–40
solar 113, 118, 120, 188–9, 199

Taoism 124, 178
technology 5, 7, 9, 48–9, 51–8, 63, 72–5, 79, 92, 96, 101, 139–41, 145, 154, 156, 171–2, 174, 198–9
Tegmark, Max 79–80
Teilhard, Pierre de Chardin 142
tension 8, 125, 133, 182
terraforming 112–14, 173, 198
theodicy 55–6
time 3–7, 22–5, 32–3, 39–40, 46–7, 92–6, 102, 123–6, 128, 133, 137, 144, 151–2, 171, 176, 182, 188
Tolstoy, Leo 89, 124–5, 129–31, 147–8, 177, 181, 184
totality 3, 6, 9–10, 13–21, 41–4, 46–8, 50, 61, 85, 87–8, 130, 132, 135, 136, 148, 152–3, 162, 165, 168, 170, 183
Tournier, Michel 62–3
Toynbee, Arnold 9, 134, 138, 150, 155, 157, 181–4, 187
tradition 57, 148, 156
tragedy 14, 16–17, 21–3, 32, 43, 45, 52
transcendence 5, 17, 21, 25, 42–3, 45, 74–5, 81
transcendental homelessness 17, 19, 47
Transcendental Idealism 48
tribes 3, 76, 108, 136, 159, 171–2
truth 16, 19–20, 22–3, 34, 42, 58, 65, 69–70, 73, 79, 145
Turchin, Peter 177
Turner, George 196–7, 200

Turok, Neil 176

United States 67, 91, 95, 98, 104–6, 109–10, 116–17, 119, 193, 195
universe 59, 76–7, 79, 81, 118–19, 126, 154, 159, 168, 171, 176, 188–9
utopia 6–7, 27–8, 32–3, 38–9, 41–2, 69, 70, 72, 75, 85, 92–7, 103, 114, 116, 196, 199

values 1, 6, 9, 18, 28, 60, 62–3, 69, 75, 78, 94, 147, 151
Vattimo, Gianni 74
Verhoeven, Paul 136, 193
Verne, Jules 91–3, 96, 98–9, 101, 156, 196
Vico, Giambattista 182–3
Vinge, Vernon 123, 129
Virgil 91

Wagner, Richard 22
Walzel, Oskar 55
war 32, 124, 128–9, 131–2, 137, 147, 151, 159, 161
Watt, Ian 61
waves 36–7, 80, 139, 146, 149, 151, 156–8, 164, 174–6, 182
Weber, Max 2, 19, 86–7, 109, 177
Wegner, Phillip 94
Wells 91–2, 95, 97, 195
West 3, 29, 37, 71, 98, 177, 196
Western Marxism 57, 85–6
Williams, Raymond 90, 96–7, 118
Willis, Connie 195
Winterson, Jeanette 193
Wollheim, Donald A. 117
world history 5, 9, 28, 131
world pictures 42–3, 51, 56–8
Wright, Alexis 193
Wright, Lawrence 196
Wyndham, John 199
Wyndham Lewis, Percy 75

www.ingramcontent.com/pod-product-compliance
Lightning Source LLC
Chambersburg PA
CBHW062217300426
44115CB00012BA/2103